HEIRS OF ETERNITY

ALSO BY E.M. WILLETT

GODS OF LEGEND, BOOK 1, DEAD BLOOD VOLUME I

LORDS OF RUIN, BOOK 2, DEAD BLOOD VOLUME I

HEIRS

OF

ETERNITY

Book 3
Dead Blood Volume I

E.M. Willett

www.pinetreepress.com
Printed in USA

DEDICATION

*For those who see the dark for what it is
and love it anyway.*

CONTENTS

E.M. Willett

ACKNOWLEDGMENTS

To my younger self, for pursuing a dream. To my family, for their unwavering support. To you, dear reader, for entering the Kingdom of Vanguards.

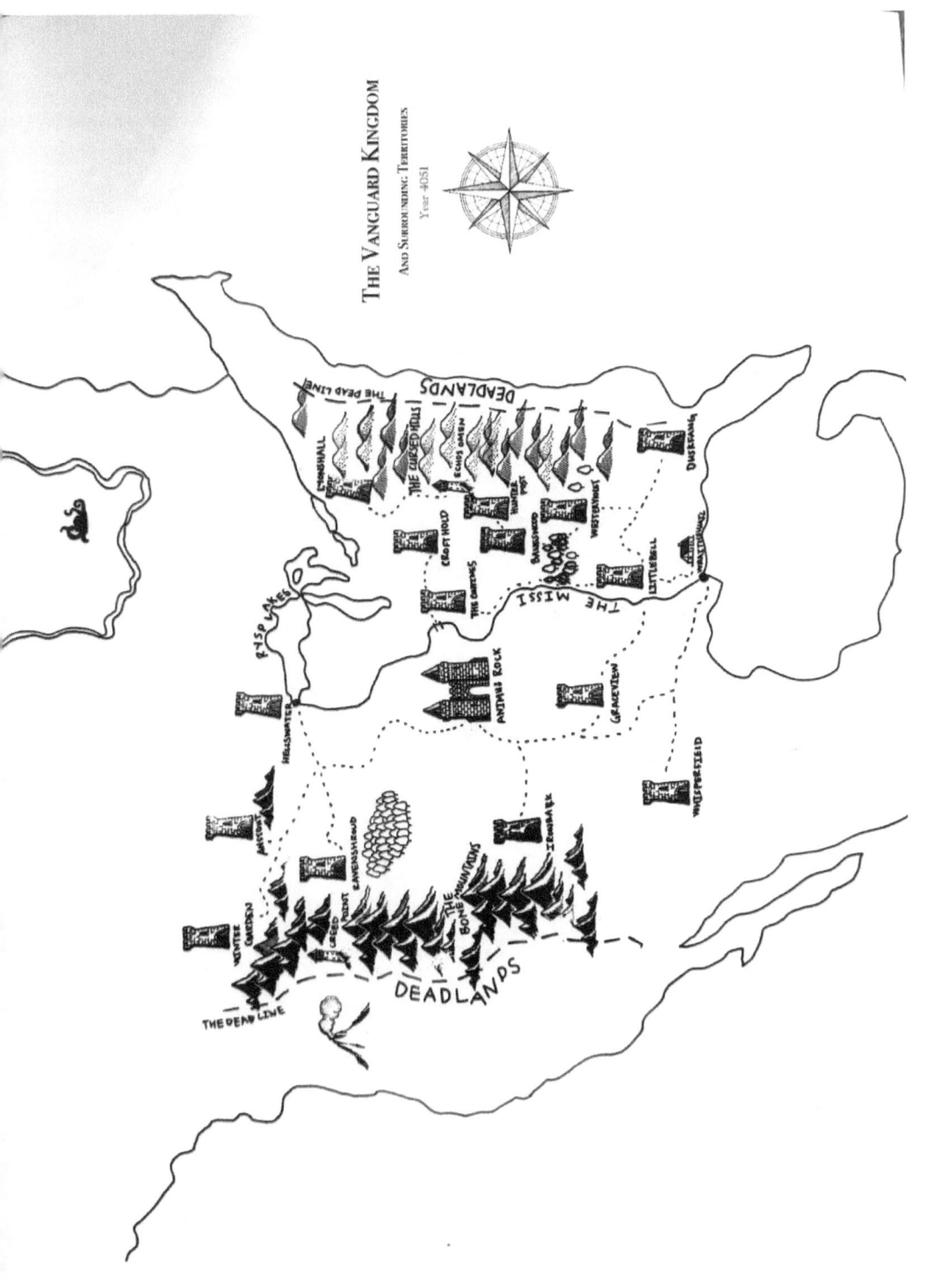

THE VANGUARD KINGDOM

AND SURROUNDING TERRITORIES

Year 4051

TIMELINE

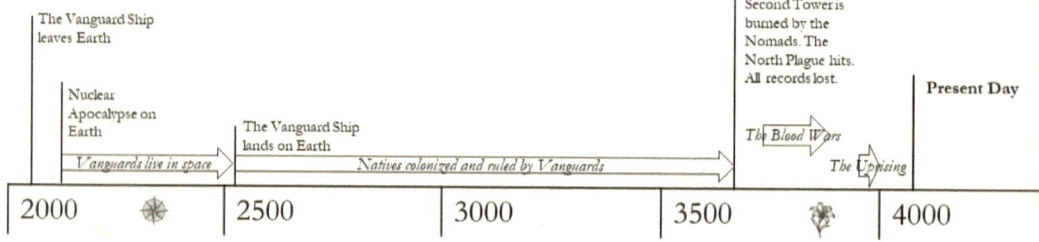

The Vanguard Ship
leaves Earth

Nuclear
Apocalypse on
Earth

The Vanguard Ship
lands on Earth

Second Tower is
burned by the
Nomads. The
North Plague hits.
All records lost.

Present Day

Vanguards live in space

Natives colonized and ruled by Vanguards

The Blood Wars

The Uprising

2000   2500   3000   3500   4000

BOOK 3

RAVENSHROUD CASTLE

About 100 years ago...

Lilli had grown accustomed to Ravenshroud's castle life, albeit it was a drastic change from her Littlebell upbringing. She took Bin as her husband almost immediately upon leaving with him and went on to give birth to a black-eyed baby girl not long later. The child, Lasha, was Bin's pride and joy, despite not having the blue-eye charm, and he fought ruthlessly with his kin to retain his elderclaim so it could be passed on to the girl. Alas, Elder Gauthier deigned Ruben, Bin's next brother in line, as Norland elderclaim upon his deathbed. Bin was scorned and shamed by his own disobedience as well as his affection for the Minney woman, however he was blood, so Ruben Norland permitted him to live. Since the Minney girl was of an interesting bloodline, despite not birthing a blue-eye initially, it was agreed that she be permitted to live as well.

"She may be of use yet," Ruben had said.

Now, the small family lived in the most southern facing wing of the castle, long ago abandoned from underuse after the deaths from the plague. These quarters initially were quite dusty and outdated with canopied beds and no tapestries, but Lilli made them quickly feel like home all the same. Because of the taboo against that part of the castle, Lilli and Bin had the whole South Wing to themselves.

Lilli did her best to make Ravenshroud's South Wing their home. She adored that no one could tell her what to do within those walls. She finally had freedom. She loved even more that she was the Lady of the whole wing, to decorate it as she pleased. Bin did everything he could to fulfil every one of Lilli's expensive whims and, within a few moons, the South Wing had been transformed. A young, transplanted grove of Tulip Poplar trees taken from the edge of Baneswood stood now out front of the wing, so Lilli could look down on them and sing to them, just like she did her own trees back home. The walls of the South Wing were soon covered in lively tapestries brought directly from Jojinoir. Every heavy curtain was removed and light, floral patterned ones were put in their places. Soon, the dreary feared South Wing came alive. Lilli was Ravenshroud castle's light.

All things considered, Lilli was happy. She had a man who adored her and did everything she asked of him and more, as well as a beautiful and healthy daughter. Only in her most private moments, nursing Lasha in the dark of night, did she miss her mother and brother, wishing silently to return to them someday, hoping they'd received the message she'd intended for them that she was well at Ravenshroud.

She wondered when her elderclaim ceremony would be.

Lilli preferred to be alone with her thoughts and her ballads, so, she didn't get lonely. Not at first, at least. There were long days when Bin was away that she wished she could travel with him, but he said the Dead Line was no place for a woman, and she figured he was probably right. She spent her time first exploring the ancient castle's south wing, trying on old gowns and crowns she discovered in dusty wardrobes, studying worn paintings and fading scrolls she dug out of hidden desk drawers. Then, once with child, she took most of her time daydreaming about what it would be like to be a mother. Preparing the babe's quarters. Making clothes. Writing ballads for the babe.

Once Lasha was born, everything became about her. Despite not having the blue-eyed charm, Bin was completely in love with his daughter just as Lilli was. He'd never imagined he'd feel this way about a living being, that he'd do anything to protect her, he'd die before she came to harm. This unselfishness was foreign to Bin yet he embraced it wholeheartedly.

Often though, Bin's meanness would show through in spite

of himself. He'd curse at Lilli without thinking. Once he even slapped her with the back of his hand during an argument, on instinct, because that was how he'd been taught to deal with dames. But the look on Lilli's face after those minor betrayals was enough to put him to shame. Soon he began actively trying to change his ways with the help of Lilli's kind and sharp understanding beside him. She brought out the softness within him. He never wanted to go back to the way he was before.

The two were an unlikely pair. Rumors swirled about Ravenshroud's realm of the affair. Most assumed she was a prize taken from Littlebell, in line with Lucien's tale, that she was being held against her will. The skirmishes with Morfit troops sent to retrieve her reinforced this story. The stories got stranger when witnesses noted how happy Lilli seemed, hand in hand sometimes with Bin. But, it was unbelievable that the Norland actually loved her.

Bin had been gone for nearly a moon and Lasha was getting new teeth, so, tonight Lilli was at her wits end. She couldn't sleep even when Lasha finally would rest, mostly because Bin wasn't home. She'd gotten used to his intense stare, doting ways and simple mind. This night though, she was standing at wide windows in the bed chamber watching the Warmen's night training poses in the center courtyard, thinking about Bin. Lasha lay in a bassinet nearby. The girl's faint fluttery breaths were comforting amidst the clashes and loud shouts from the training men below.

Without warning, a cloaked figure stepped out of the shadows.

"Lilli Minney," the cool voice hissed as light from the nearly full moon outside illuminated the intruder.

Lucien Graves had found his way into her bed chamber along with five elite Guardsmen, glistening green glass daggers at the ready, and small crossbows loaded at each hip. The Guardsmen wore expertly crafted armor and dark emerald green cloaked hoods that appeared black in the dark. They hovered like shadows behind their elder. Behind them, a twenty years man in a matching cloak to Lucien's, with equally matching features, hung back a bit, observing the scene with twinkling hazel eyes, as if he was enjoying himself greatly. Beside him, Florian Busk stood with a startled look and clammy hands, not sure if he was more terrified of Lucien Graves or the fate that would befall him if any Norlands discovered a Busk had broken into Ravenshroud.

Lilli's heart dropped to her stomach and she instantly darted towards the basinet, but alas, she wasn't quick enough. Lucien's only son, Guy Brochet, had already snatched up her daughter. As he smiled, Guy tucked the wailing baby under his cloak and turned away, exiting the chamber without so much as a word.

"NO!" Lilli wailed with heart-piercing intensity, harmonic voice piercing enough to shatter glass. She leapt forward towards her precious Lasha, but one of the Guardsman, who smelled strongly of tobacco, caught her and held her tight.

How did that man move so quickly? Lilli wondered briefly in the avalanche of thoughts that pummelled her. *Where were they taking Lasha? How did these men break in? Where is Bin?*

"Please," she wailed at Lucien, trying to appeal to his seemingly refined sensibilities. "You can't do this to me. I am Vanguard, like you are," she added, nodding to be convincing. "I can help you," she said. "My mother has much coin. I'm sure if you…"

"Quiet," Lucien hissed at the blue-eye. "This is about more than coin." The insinuation he was in this for coin alone insulted him. "This is about honor." Lucien gestured over his shoulder. "My son knows something about honor," he added with a hint of pride in his voice. "Unlike your husband."

"My baby," Lilli wailed, voice cracking, picturing the girl's honey brown complexion, mousy hair and questioning black eyes. She squinted at Lucien. "Where is he taking her?"

"It's no matter to you."

"But Bin," she exhaled, barely able to breathe from shock, listening to the clashes and shouts of the training men just outside, "he will never let you get away with this."

At that Lucien threw back his head in his typical good-natured laugh, eliciting several coy smiles and smirks from his surrounding men. Seeing such legendary and fearsome troops giggle like Academy maids was disconcerting, yet that was the pull Lucien had over all around him. Emotions fluttered at his command.

When he finally composed himself, his Guardsmen did the same, mirroring his stalwart face. "Bin Norland is a dead man," he said, a slow smile creeping up his cheeks. The moonlight from outside cast varying shadows across his handsome face, filtered through tall growing leaves. "He sealed his fate moons ago," Lucien added, "when he betrayed me. He was meant to bring you to me, by order of your own brother Amos."

"No," Lilli said under her breath. What the Brochet said couldn't possibly be true. Bin wouldn't have lied to her! And Amos was her beloved brother. He would have never betrayed her so.

"Yes," Lucien smiled. He took a step towards her, feeling her building insecurity, expertly flipping his green glass dagger around in his hand as if by magic. He didn't even glance at the blade and it spun around in his palm. "It's a bit of a pity that you are so fair," he added with a whimsical pause, "yet, your fate was set long ago."

Lilli pulled her shoulders, shaking her tobacco-smelling captor, trying to get free, but the man held a vice grip. "No one determines my fate but me," she shouted.

He held a finger to his mouth. "Quiet girl," he hushed, lowering his eyebrows low over warmly crinkled eyes. "Another scream and Haaris will silence you by force." He paused and the tobacco-smelling man nodded curtly. "We do not want that, do we sweet Lilli?" Lucien asked with a mocking inflection. He took another step towards her. "Not before a message is sent."

Lilli felt defeated. What little resolve she had left she clung to, for Lasha. She needed to have the girl returned safely to her arms. "Where are you taking her, Brochet?" she asked Lucien with a scathing whisper. Bin had told her much about the man but even the warnings were no preparation for what he was

7

like in the flesh.

Lucien was unnerving, terrifying even. She felt she couldn't be safe from him anywhere, even in her own mind. "Brochet!" she urged again in a squeak, cut short by the Guardsman Haaris's cool green glass blade pressing up against her neck.

ANIMUS ROCK, EDEN

Present Day

"My heart broke to hear," Sybil said in a breath. "Aftea told me everything. A pity, Faye. Truly."

"You are so kind," the larger woman said, patting Sybil's hand as they walked arm in arm.

Rupert Morfit followed closely behind the pair in this part of Eden's arid climate. Despite the late season, the air around them prickled hot and dry. Faye's rounded cheeks flushed red and pink. Sybil's hairline dampened with sweat. A bead ran down her forehead and caught on her eyebrow.

Another afternoon wasted clucking like hens, Rupert thought, listening to the women squawk. He noticed sweat pooling at his fine tunic's pits and at the crease of his chest and removed his gold and black embellished coat. He tucked it under his arm. He rolled up his sleeves to expose his hard forearms and wiped his brow with one of them.

"We were just shocked." Faye half-cocked her head over her shoulder. "Shocked and heartbroken, weren't we?"

"Yes," Rupert said flatly.

Faye smiled and nodded. She leaned in towards Sybil but spoke just as loudly. "Poor Rupert. He took it so hard, but you wouldn't know to look at him."

"Is that so?" Sybil enjoyed her old friend's discomfort, glancing back at Rupert's pained expression, then forward again. She patted the flighty Faye's arm as they strolled slowly. Such an annoying, yet useful companion.

"Oh yes. After," she lowered her voice and whispered, "*the incident...*" referencing her in-laws' recent deaths, "he locked himself in for days. Wouldn't speak to a soul. Wouldn't eat a thing. Tore him apart, isn't that right?"

Faye didn't glance backwards. If she had, she would have seen her husband's furious glare.

Sybil bit her lip, trying not to smile. She turned to look at Rupert. "I am sorry for your loss," she said.

He blinked at her and began to speak but was interrupted by a screech.

"Faye! Oh, is that you?" a woman with pitch-black skin fluttered to the group. She had sunken cheekbones and expressive red eyes. "Oh, Sybil, darling! Hi!" the woman waved a stubby fingered hand.

Sybil smiled politely and Rupert rolled his eyes. It was Aftea, Gachan Regnard's wife and his sister-in-law. He couldn't bear to be in the same chamber as that doltish woman for more than a moment. Gachan had met her while on patrol to Lily Valley and just like her native kin there, she was notorious gossip. She fit right in with Rupert's wife, Faye. The sight of her alone insulted his refined sensibilities, but as usual, he kept his true feelings close to his chest.

"Aftea!" Faye cried. She dropped Sybil's arm and scurried to her. The women fell into quick confidence, disappearing around a hedged bend.

Rupert was left standing next to a three-prong cactus and Sybil Brochet. He sighed loudly and rubbed his temple.

"Trouble in Eden?"

"What makes you say that?"

"I've known you forever Rupert," Sybil said warmly. "Longer than forever. You do that when you're," she paused. "Displeased."

He half smiled and lines creased at the corners of his eyes. "There's a benefit, Sybil, as there is to every covenant." *True, Faye isn't an ideal wife, embarrassing even, yet she has her purpose,* Rupert thought. And, although he would never admit it, even to himself, he valued her old blood. He was proud his children bore it as well.

Sybil glanced ahead while walking at his side down the sandy path. They turned left at a fork.

"Your cause?"

"What cause?"

"Don't be coy, Rupert. Only a fool would forget that Faye, your wife, is Ogo's daughter. Lachlan's granddaughter."

He chuckled. "You have met the woman?" he asked rhetorically. "You know she has no sway over her father. Or anyone."

"Still," Sybil replied. "It is why you broke tradition."

Sybil is as sharp as her father used to be, Rupert thought. *Maybe sharper.* "I've always been fond of you Sybil, but we are not children any longer."

"What's that supposed to mean?"

"It means the time for friendship has passed," Rupert said, remembering the games they would play after Lower particularly, flitting amongst the ever-present flowers at the center of Eden's garden maze. "We're from different worlds. You sit on Council now."

Sybil furrowed her brow, crossing her arms as they strode. "So?"

"I know you are smarter than that," Rupert said. "You are Brochet. I am Morfit. We'll never be allies. We cannot be friends. If the others even knew that..."

"You've not changed a bit," she interrupted. "As stubborn as ever," Sybil added, then sighed. She stopped walking.

They'd come to a cusp of the garden where scenery shifted from desert to arid valley. Wisps of grass poked through dry cracked soil beneath their feet. Rupert stopped too and faced her.

"I'm not saying we can't be cordial, Sybil," Rupert said with warm familiarity. "But the Kingdom is at stake, and I cannot trust you." She studied his eyes with hers, but apart from that, was expressionless. "Sybil, what? Don't look at me like that."

Sybil squinted at him. "I expected you to be different, but not..."

"Not what?"

Sybil pulled her crossed arms tighter. "I don't know." She looked him a bit longer, like she was reading through the parchments of his mind. He felt exposed. "What about the accord? Perhaps it's me who can't trust you."

"Why do you say that?" Rupert stepped closer, looming over her. Internally, his adrenaline spiked. She wasn't supposed to know about that. The accord between Morfit and Brochet was supposed to have died with Goodman.

She seemed to realize that she'd hit a nerve. "What else is obvious, begging to be revealed?"

"Sybil," he yelled in a whisper. "Sybil come back here." He hurriedly jogged after her and grabbed her upper arm, pulling her to a stop. She looked at him with burning indignation. He dropped it instantly, as if he'd stuck his hand into a kiln and grasped a molten piece of metal. Rupert said in a lower voice still, "You know as well as I do our fathers are foolish. Or," he thought of Goodman's last moments, the look in his eye as the rock crushed his skull, "were. The others would not have understood, on either side. I had to take control," he added. "You would have done the same."

Sybil was silent. She stood more than a head shorter than the swarthy man and looked up at him, knowing full well what he had done.

"What?" Rupert shifted his feet uncomfortably. "What is it?"

It was late in the day. The sun hung low, trapped beneath dark clouds that warned of rain. High above Eden's mystical garden's grounds, the air blew in chilling ripples and swirling waves.

Wisps of Sybil's hair fell to her face, tilted upwards at Rupert. "Why kill him?" she asked plainly.

Rupert took a step back. "Who?" he asked, gaze darting across hers, already understanding that she knew the truth.

"You know," Sybil told him, reading his face. "Must you make me say it?" she added flippantly. "Seems unlike you to murder your own father..."

"Enough!" Rupert shouted louder than she'd ever heard him shout, staring down at her with unrelenting intensity. Quite out of character for the typically even-tempered man. A small flock of tiny seed birds, hiding in the maze's hedge until now, flew away while squawking disapprovingly. Sybil didn't balk or retreat.

She unflinchingly held his gaze. "Am I wrong?"

"You are," Rupert said quickly, then lowered to a rumbling growl. He stepped closer to her and leaned to her ear. "If that ridiculous, *false* rumor were to spread, I would have no choice but to be rid the traitor who endangered my bloodline. It is the only honourable thing to do," he said. "Clear?"

"Yes, Lord Morfit," Sybil said, bowing her head to Rupert in mocking formality. Their days as friends had long passed. Only the faintest part of her cared.

"Ah, there you are! I see you! Wait for me!" Faye shouted shrilly from down a long stretch of path ahead. Rupert winced as she skipped towards them, chattering on. "Gachan called Aftea to introduce her to someone or other, but I'm so glad I ran into her! She said the baby is doing wonderfully and he is just beautiful. Just beautiful! I hear he has red eyes." She spoke with her hands as she approached. "Thank the Horned!"

"Ah, Faye. How good of you to re-join us," Sybil said as the fleshy woman clung to her arm again.

Rupert walked behind them in physical form, distant with glassy eyes.

Faye turned her head to Sybil, lowering her voice to a whisper. "Do you believe the reports?" Faye asked her.

They'd just left a Council session where Cronog Dale presented a worrying trend of disappearances within Baneswood's realm. He brought the problem to the King, hoping for aid. The vote had been delayed until the next Solstice.

Sybil was only half listening. "Of?" she asked.

"It's terrifying. Terrifying!" Faye shook her head, soft chin jiggling. "If anything happened to my children, I'd fling myself from the wall."

"Faye," Rupert groaned.

"I mean every word I said. Every word. I would do it in an instant," she retorted half over her shoulder to her husband. "Every single word. Why, I can't sleep at night not knowing where my boy is."

Faye's pause was loaded. Sybil gave in. "Why don't you know where Oscar is, Faye?"

"The boy is with..."

"Faye," Rupert growled from behind, but it was already clear what Faye meant. Oscar was with Ogo. Rupert was planning for war. "Enough," he warned.

"It is really so good to see you again," Faye changed the subject warmly, patting Sybil on the forearm. "How long has it been? What brings you to Animus? Has old Tomas found a suitable husband for you, finally?"

"Hm?" Sybil asked, distracted, processing what she'd just heard.

Galla was worked up, far beyond her usual hysterics. While the Old was typically bothersome, now, their behaviour was unforgivable. And past that, her own people were questioning her judgement. High natives that had always been her allies were withdrawing support. Most notably, the Costermongers Union had sent a representative threatening to ban trading within her entire realm if she did not change her ways. The high native had caught her ear just as she'd left the castle. She now needed someone to confide in, to vent to, and was grateful when she saw Monty unencumbered after the Council session ended. He was a good listener.

The pair paced side by side through snowy banks and dark evergreens.

"I couldn't take one more moment," Galla said in exasperated sigh, kicking a snowdrift with her foot, sending snow rabbits scurrying. "I wait moons and my energy is gone, already, not yet a fortnight in! They suck all the air out of the room. It's like I can't breathe. It's like I'm suffocating!"

"It is a lot," Monty said kindly.

"You know as well as I do the pressure," Galla went on.

"Why, the state of our realm rests in our hands. In my hands," she added in a mumble, mostly to herself. Galla felt enormous responsibility to save those less fortunate than herself. She felt it was all on her own shoulders. She knew she was the only one who truly cared for the natives. She refused to fail her Kingdom despite the difficult personalities she was forced to deal with.

"A lofty burden," Monty said, "to be sure."

"I know," Galla nodded adamantly. "I don't think they understand. I don't think they know how hard it is for me. They tease me on good days and hate me on bad ones. Even the high natives have begun to dissent. It is so hard. I'm fighting for them! They don't know. What it feels like, you know?"

"Tell me. What does what feel like?"

"I was born into this. Rupert to Magistrate, as father before, so I was to be on Council. I was groomed to sit in the Golden Chair. I," she paused and her voice cracked, "never had a choice."

"What about Glenn?"

"You know he's a dolt," she said dismissively, seeing her brother's perpetual confused expression clearly in her mind, "with that bare woman."

Monty smirked. That Norland was said to be striking, in an evil-looking kind of way, although most had never met her. They kept her confined to Croft Hold. "You never wanted to be the 'champion of the earthblood'? Not even a little bit?"

Galla was praised throughout the Morfit lands, and most of the Kingdom, by the low natives particularly, for all the laws she'd championed for the people. The women commonly fashioned their hair to mimic hers, cropped beneath her chin, in tribute to her good deeds. The fashion had taken root throughout Animus Rock as well. The men sang about her triumphs around their fires at night.

"Don't call me that," Galla said quickly. "I hate when they call me that," she adjusted her golden robes and smoothed her oiled hair, "but I see your point. I did. I've always wanted to help…" She trailed off, sliding mentally into a pool of self-pity. "I don't know."

"No, I understand it," Monty said. "You feel trapped."

She stopped walking along the icy, snow-dusted garden trail lined with clover and sparse grass. Monty stopped too.

"Exactly. That's exactly it," Galla said with wide brown eyes. "Prihim doesn't understand," she added sadly. She turned to walk again.

Monty fell into stride next to her. "How do you know he doesn't?"

"Why, by how he treats me!" she exclaimed, spinning, snow catching on her rounded cheek. "You are the only one who really listens to me, Monty." She considered him to be the brother Rupert never was to her.

"Happy to oblige," he replied with a tilt of his head and half a smile, obviously fond of Galla, mainly because he loathed her twin. Monty hated Rupert while attending Academy, although he was in Upper and Rupert was in Lower at the time. As a boy, Rupert was a bully. A smart one that never got caught. As adults, things were no different.

"Those pale-faced men make me crazy!" Galla snapped, unable to calm herself despite Monty's steadying presence. "They treat me like I'm from another world or have dead blood!" She looked with pleading eyes to him. "Cronog's right," she said, remembering the Dale's plea during the Council session earlier that day, "We must investigate these disappearances." Cronog had claimed Baneswood villages were missing men by the dozens. Whole hunting troops lost. No bodies recovered. "The Old laughs, but what if this is a new disease? Outbreak of Dread? Deadblood attacks? Something else entirely? We know not, unless we search for bodies, at the very least."

Light snow fell from an unknown, mystical source above, dusting the pair's shoulders as they left footprints in their wake. It was awesome; however, the Vanguards who frequented Eden took it for granted completely. Eden was how it had always been.

The path was lined on either side with needle-ridden fir trees. The air filled with spicy sap. A white squirrel barked at them from an overhead branch as they strolled by. "And, who does the fire-headed man think he is?" Galla went on like a pot over boil. "Each time the Kingdom needs Dale, he claims that the realms should keep to themselves. Yet when it is his own precious Baneswood threatened, Cronog the dog is the first to plead for aide!"

"Is there anything worse than hypocrisy?"

"I think not," Galla said adamantly. Her cowl neck cloak opened in front and billowed out behind her like gilded wings.

"What about the Omen?"

"The Omen?"

"Do you put it past Basil?" Monty clarified with sparkling verdant eyes.

Galla was quiet. "I don't put anything past Graves," she said, heavy pain deep in her throat.

"I didn't mean to..." Monty swallowed hard, realizing he'd hit a nerve. Galla had an unfortunate encounter with Basil Graves during her childhood. He didn't know the extent of it apart from she had been violated in some major way. Had her father Goodman not been so understanding, and politically savvy, it could have started another war. "I know how you..."

"Forget it." Galla didn't let herself think about what happened so many years ago. She had just been a girl then. She'd spent nearly her whole life trying to put it out of her mind but still often felt Basil's long, cold fingers reaching up her smock. It was largely what fuelled her quest to protect the unprotected in the Kingdom. "It's fine."

"Galla, I'm sorry," Monty stopped walking, turning to her. He grabbed one of her hands and took it into his. "I forgot. I forgot all about it. I shouldn't have mentioned..."

"It's fine," she pulled ahead, shaking his grip from her hand. Galla's tone steeled. "I said I'm fine." Her face tightened, like a drawbridge shut with a clank somewhere in her mind.

"Of course, Lady."

"Can you believe Edwarde?" she changed the subject.

Monty followed her lead and the shift in tone. "Nothing surprises me anymore."

"You have always been cynical."

"Realistic," he countered with a raised brow.

She shooed him with a flip of her wrist. "The audacity to hold another bloodline's castle…" She was a woman of the law and no matter Edwarde's potentially noble aims he had committed one of the highest crimes, if not the highest in the land. Treason.

"To be fair," Monty interrupted, playing defix's advocate, "he was raised there."

"You were raised here. I don't see you taking the Tourmaline Throne."

Monty grinned. "Perhaps I'm biding my time."

Galla looked at him and for the first time in their conversation, the lines of worry fell from her forehead. "I heard a rumor," she said eagerly.

"You did?" He leaned in. "You know how I like those."

Galla slowed down and took his arm into hers. "It's about the Arena," she whispered up at him.

Monty frowned. "Busk?"

"Yes," she nodded. "Talk is that one of Old Tomas's was amongst the crowd." Monty chuckled. Tomas Brochet would never attack another realm so crudely. It wasn't his style at all. "Why are you laughing?"

"Forgive me," Monty said and composed himself outwardly. "Tell me more."

"You think I'm just jealous of Sybil, don't you?" Galla spat. "That I'm making it up to spite her."

"Who said that?"

"I'm not, just so you know."

"Galla," Monty sighed, "what is it?"

"That's it, really."

"Well, now I'm intrigued," Money said. "You can't just tell me something like that and not explain, pet." It seemed the magical snowstorm had picked up pace above them in this section of Eden. Snow sprinkled his dark hair. "How would they know? That it was Tomas's doing, I mean. That place was a mad den."

Galla took a deep breath. "I don't know," she said to Monty's scepticism. "Something about the man's clothes. Or an emblem," she said defensively. "My sources say that he was an expert fighter and fended off all old Ralph's men before the place caught ablaze. Claimed he was of Westerviolet." A white owl hooted from an evergreen to their left and Galla jumped. She bumped into Monty. "Sorry," she said, smoothing her golden cape.

Monty gestured with his hand for her not to worry about it. "Why would Brochet fell the Confines?" he asked her. "Ralph Busk was a longstanding Brochet ally. He was more valuable to Lord Tomas alive than dead."

"I don't know." Galla narrowed her eyes. "I know you are close to them and fond of them. That is why I come to you first." She stopped walking. "Do you think there is merit? Should I pursue this claim?"

"Claim?"

"If it is truth, if Brochet toppled Busk into Edwarde's hands, I would have no choice but to demand the charming snake and his bitch daughter sent straight to the First," she said, brimming spite, "but, I'm too smart to accuse unless I'm sure I'm not wrong."

Monty stroked his shaven chin with long fingers, contemplating his answer before speaking.

Three Minney men sat in a row on the cold stone steps overlooking Eden's garden.

"He's no Minney. Not anymore. Unbelievable," Simon Minney said, then shook his head.

"I agree," Prihim nodded. "The Old only defends Edwarde because they see a play." He loved his kin as all Minney's did but was concerned about Simon's judgement. He understood how bitter the man was and knew how dangerous that could be. He wasn't thinking clearly. *If only I could reason with him*, Prihim thought, sitting with long thin legs bent and knees spread and an elbow on each.

Juste Minney sat between the older men with wavy black hair secured into a small, tight bun. A popular style amongst progressive young natives and Vanguards alike. The whipping wind pulled loose strands from it, sweeping them across his face, pinched tight as he listened to his elders. He swung his head back and forth as they volleyed conversationally. Juste stuck his legs out in front of himself, leaning backwards on his elbows, allowing his father and distant uncle to see each other as they spoke.

"I know that," Simon growled, slowly turning his head, narrowing his green eyes. "I am no fool."

"You will vote to unseat him, then?" Prihim said, imagining how horribly burned Edwarde must be after the Dark Arena fire. "Give the realm to Terje?" Simon's seat on Magistrate was priceless in this hour. Prihim needed to ensure he would vote New.

Simon scratched a pock on his cheek. "We aren't permitted to discuss that."

"Simon."

"What?"

"I need to know you won't allow our," Prihim paused, "issues to dictate your decision."

"It's an insult to suggest I would."

Yet Prihim knew Simon's attitude was because he would never hold Littlebell elderclaim, despite being the rightful heir. He was the eldest direct descendant of their shared ancestor and once elderclaim, the great Lord Amos. Although his father had not married a native, therefore lost elderclaim for their branch. The men fell into an uncomfortable silence. Black storm clouds churned above them where they sat. The wind blew faster.

"It looks like it might rain," Juste offered pleasantly.

Prihim ignored him. "You said it yourself, Simon. Edwarde is lost to us. He must not be permitted to keep the Confines."

"Hm," Simon grunted, glancing up. "The boy's right. It looks like rain."

Prihim sighed from the back of his throat, frustrated with his distant cousin's stubbornness. *It will be a disaster if Simon votes Old on this,* he thought to himself. "You know what Ralph was," he reasoned. "You know what Edwarde is. This is so much bigger than whatever disagreement our families share."

"Is that what *she* told you to say?"

"Simon," Prihim warned.

Juste turned to his father. "How's Essia?" he asked, clearly trying to change the subject.

The instant he heard the name, Simon's eyes widened, and his words caught in his throat. Prihim glanced to the side and caught his gaze. The men silently conferred, then Simon spoke. "Son, it may be," he swallowed hard, "too late."

"What do you mean too late?" Juste frowned. Had no one gone for her? Checked on her? Had she been sacrificed to Uncle Edwarde's political insanity? "She is Vanguard. She is… she is blood!"

"Juste," Prihim said softly, knowing the truth. The girl was likely dead.

"What!?" Juste shouted, indignant, normally pleasant face brimming scorn. His mood flipped so suddenly it fully caught the other men off guard. It was the traces of mad honey in his system. They left one volatile. "She's your blood! How could you not…"

Simon interrupted. "We've searched for her, son. Demanded Edwarde send her out to us. Threatened him if he put her in harm's way." He went on and on, trying to quell Juste's fury, but his son continued to boil. He finished with, "No one has seen her."

"Why didn't you tell me! I assumed…" Juste trailed off. He'd been distracted with the mad honey trade. His business with Leon and Monty was booming, so much so, he had little time for other thoughts. "I don't know," he lowered his shoulders, looking from his father to Prihim. "How could you not tell me?!" he shouted at them angrily. "We must do something!

Attack the Confines. Rescue her! Come on!" he screamed, even drawing the attention of passing high natives who frowned started to walk faster, but the older Minneys just looked at him. Juste was unravelling. "You are cowards! Edwessa and Karl are gone because of you, probably dead, and Essia needs us and you do nothing!" Tears welled in the young man's eyes.

"Son," Simon put his hand on Juste's shoulder. "You don't understand, it's…"

"No!" Juste shook off his hand "I can't do this," he stood up and stormed away.

Intermittent raindrops began to fall on Simon and Prihim. They put their cloak hoods up and stewed in silence, listening to the patter of rain for some time.

"He's changed," Prihim finally said, lowering his eyebrows into a worried line. "Something's different. I'm concerned about him."

"Don't be," Simon replied flatly. "He's my boy. Worry about yourself. Your own."

"What's that supposed to mean?"

"Nothing."

Silence blanketed the men once more until Prihim broke the lull.

"What do you make of Cronog's plea in Council today?" he asked, unnerved by the Dale's obvious concern. Dale men were traditionally stoic and to see Cronog tremble was unsettling, at best.

"In truth?" Simon turned to half face him with creases beside his green eyes. "Worrisome."

"Why?"

"Have you known Dale to ask for help?"

Prihim shook his head 'no'. He felt a knot in his stomach.

"Right. They don't," Simon said. "Ever. Why now?"

"Why do you think?"

"If I didn't know better," Simon scratched long curls at the top of his head, "I'd say it's a trap."

Prihim leaned a bit closer to Simon. "I can tell you something that wasn't discussed today at Council," he said. "A rumor," he added, brown eyes sparkling. Simon looked to his distant cousin in anticipation. Prihim continued, speaking with his hands. "Mimi heard something from a native at Apothecary. He came from a village on the outskirts, by the Baneswood border. The stories are," Prihim paused, narrowing his eyes, "odd."

"Odd? Like Cronog described?"

"Not exactly like he described."

"Why not?"

"You heard Cronog today," Prihim said. "Dozens of Baneswood men missing in the past moons. Not one body found."

"I heard him."

"Well," Prihim said, unblinking, eyes intense, "Mimi says a village on Littlebell realm's outskirts has bodies."

"In truth?"

Prihim nodded. "Windgrove." Simon made a pained face and Prihim understood why. They both had pleasant memories of the intimate fishing village down the river from Littlebell. Simon's father used to take them to holiday there when they were young, but things were much different now. *That was a different life*, Prihim thought to himself.

"The count?" he asked stoically.

"Several, I think."

"The state of them?"

"Where the oddities begin."

"Tell me," Simon said.

"Each is mangled differently," Prihim said. "Some stabbed, others cut into pieces, all with shattered bones. Some femurs snapped in two like tree branches. All in different levels of decay."

"How odd," Simon remarked, both confused and intrigued.

"I told you, but that isn't all."

"What more?"

Prihim glanced away and hesitated. Simon studied the man's conflicted expression as he loudly sighed. "It's why I didn't say anything to Council," Prihim finally said.

"Tell me," Simon demanded eagerly.

"The native brands aren't there."

"What!" Simon nearly shouted. That was unbelievable.

"Each is missing skin, as if it was intentionally carved away," Prihim said, voice lowered, "if that part can be found."

"It isn't beast or disease," Simon said quietly. "It is man." Prihim nodded solemnly. "Why not tell Cronog, or the others?"

"I sent Leon to investigate," Prihim explained, knowing his brother wanted to feel useful, hoping this caught two fish with one net. "There's a missive on the way to him with the instruction now," he added. "Let's wait for confirmation of truth first."

"Fair," Simon nodded. "Are we sure it's truth? Not a ploy by Cronog the dog? The whole occurrence seems incredible."

Prihim squinted his eyes, looking out over the dark and stormy afternoon. He said, "It does."

Hector Graves crossed a meadow within Eden filled with veilthorns of the Hunter Post realm with Cronog Dale at his side. Apart from humming insects and a cawing crow gliding overhead, they were alone.

"Your father," Hector said. "How is the Baneswood elder?"

Cronog grunted. "Alive."

"The extent of concern for the next in line?"

Cronog chuckled, low and deep, imagining the old man's wheezing breaths and pitiful shaking hands. "Aye."

They paced each other but stocky Cronog had to take double steps to keep up with the svelte, long-strided Graves. Hector walked like an ethereal spectre from pace to pace, so smoothly he appeared to glide. He wore a long black cape with draped hood that hung back behind his head loosely. His dark pointed beard made his already sharp-cheeked face particularly angular and it caught the light like a statue. He was more than a head taller than his stout companion. Cronog glanced up at him from time to time, outwardly composed but internally shaking. It was no small thing to confer with Graves, particularly Hector himself.

Hector kept his eyes unblinking, straight ahead. He did not look down at the flowers or to the side at Cronog as they walked. Not once.

"It is a pity about your brother," Hector offered politically, sans emotion, eyes locked on the path ahead. Cronog glanced up and grunted. "Your feelings for the young man aside, he was the best. Many mourn the coin lost."

"Was," Cronog said and chuckled again, reminiscing the fateful day his younger brother fell with glee. How the mighty, undefeated champion of Baneswood was taken out by such an unforeseen accident. Cronog couldn't be more pleased at Rhain's descent from his father's graces and the Kingdom's heart. "What is he now? Useless." He spat at the dirt.

Cronog's red and silver hair was swept into a tight and intricate knot at the top of his head, indicative of his rank, with a portion left out in a long braid at the nape of his neck that trailed down his back, disappearing beneath his enormous pelt coat, made from burnt orange, white, and grey furs. It billowed out slightly behind him in the wind as he walked, as Hector's black cape did.

"Is the mighty Cronog Dale jealous, perhaps?"

"Never," Cronog said quickly.

"Are there plans for him?"

"Hmph," Cronog grunted, irritated so much time speaking had been wasted already on Rhain, the useless boar. "To the dogs for I care."

"I thought so," Hector said, inwardly pleased, plans falling into place. "Send him to Basil, then."

"Never! Never would I send my own blood, a Dale, into the…"

Hector interrupted, "No, no. You misunderstand Lord Cronog," he added with irksome formality. "To join."

The idea stunned Cronog and he instantly fell into quiet contemplation. *Dale ally with the Omen? It was unthinkable, despite*

Rhain's blood, but how to turn Hector's command down, Cronog thought silently for many paces as the salt-scented air rushed by. Their footsteps fell without sound, absorbed into the dirt.

"What use do you have for him?" he finally asked, tilting his head up at the ghostly pale man. "His leg…"

"He walks," Hector countered. "Does he not?"

Cronog grumbled. *A technicality,* he thought. *The boy wears a brace. He hobbles everywhere he goes. Useless.* "Could he march with you?" he asked Hector rhetorically. "Never!"

"That is not my interest in him," Hector said cryptically. Cronog waited for elaboration, but none came.

"You can't have him," Cronog said with finality.

"So be it," Hector said, slightly bowing his head. "It is a pity, however…" he trailed off and turned to glance at Cronog, then looked forward again.

"What is?" Cronog asked warily. He didn't like feeling the way Hector made him feel. As if he was a lesser man. Like Hector couldn't even bother to take pity on him, he was that far below him. He was wary of Hector and did not trust him for an instant. But he had to know more.

"He was to be payment," Hector said casually, every word annunciated crisply. "Now, we must settle it otherwise." The veilthorn looked like grass and were crushed by the men's boots as easily. The petals were translucent, nearly clear, and only turned crimson red when someone nearby was lying.

Cronog frowned. He wasn't following. "What payment?" he asked in a bark.

"For not telling your father," Hector said, not skipping a beat. "For not exposing you and your treachery."

Cronog stopped abruptly. "Hector!" he bellowed, face glowing like the sun, eyes bulging, fists clenched.

Hector rubbed a temple. "No need to shout." At that his hawk appeared from above Eden's garden, circling. She let out an ear-screeching caw as if to echo his statement. Hector slightly smiled.

Cronog unsheathed a dagger from his thigh, took a bounding step to Hector and held the weapon to his body. Cronog was so much shorter he only barely reached Hector's chest. "I will gut you as a beast if you do not speak."

The veilthorns blushed.

Hector smiled. "Alright," he said, smoothing his hair with his long fingers, then crossed his arms at his chest. "I see that you are a simple man, so I will speak simply."

Cronog frowned but sheathed the dagger. He crossed his arms, unconsciously mirroring Hector, puffing his chest to appear taller than he was. The men faced each other.

Hector looked down. "I take it Baddon is not aware of your involvement with Ogo and Rupert."

Cronog's heart dropped into his stomach. His eyes ticked, but he did his best to appear calm. "How do you know I'm involved?" He'd been in secret contact with the men for moons, wary of his father's stubborn ways, wanting to get ahead of the shifting political tides. Old Baddon would die soon anyway. Cronog was attempting to be smart. To protect Baneswood, his birthright, as well as himself. At his heart, Cronog was a coward.

Hector saw right through his façade and continued pressing. "I also take it that he's not aware of your Council address today, either." Cronog looked like he was going to speak but frowned again instead. *The Graves is right*, he thought. "This is your opportunity, Dale," Hector added with a hint of distain. "Deny it now."

"I deny it," Cronog said quickly, but the veilthorns all around him burst with color.

Hector seemed to enjoy the exchange now, as much as he could enjoy anything. "You deny conspiring with Ogo, to back his claim to Lyonshall," he asked, "and the Kingdom, if it came to it?"

"No..." Cronog lied as he shook his head furiously, long braid bucking across his back, vividly remembering the pact he made with Ogo Regnard last moon, "I... no..."

"You deny you approached the Council to beg, no, *plead*, for help today?" Hector drew out his words as if each was a hateful insult. "You deny that you broke the way of Dale and the command of your own father, then lied of it to the King, himself?"

Cronog was fully panicked now, face pulsing hot, knowing he was caught. "No." He tried to think of an excuse. Baddon was a cautious, diluted old man but he was still Baneswood elder and for Cronog to disobey him was still technically treason. If Hector revealed Cronog's actions to Baddon, or anyone of note really, he would be sent to the First or hung. "No! I..." he frowned, eyes glancing around for any hint of something he could say, but all he saw were the walls of Eden's magical garden maze.

"Cronog?" But the fire-haired man fell quiet. "You know you have very few options," Hector added cruelly. Cronog hung his head, thinking it was the First for him, until Hector went on. "I can make this go away," he said, grey eyes studying the emerging bald spot in Cronog's greying red hair.

Cronog looked up. "How?"

"Tell me what you know," Hector said simply, "about them, the Rebellion, their plans."

"Betrayal?" Cronog said more hushed still, "They are friends. Some, blood. I... I couldn't..."

"Certainly, you could," Hector interrupted. "You've already done it, in fact. You have committed the highest treason, for there's nothing worse than betraying one's elder." Cronog stared ahead now, more through Hector than at him, in clear introspective hatred. Hector was right. "On top of it," Hector added, "to act against one's elder is to act against our laws. I should report you to Galla. I'm sure Baddon would be pleased, then Rhain would inherit Baneswood elderclaim and..."

"Enough!" Cronog shouted, throwing his hands up. "Enough!" he repeated, starting to pace furiously.

Hector watched the tantrum stoically until Cronog settled. He looked broken.

"You can make this go away?" Cronog asked quietly, eyes red-rimmed to match the veilthorns, face plastered with wisps of hair escaped from his long braid.

Hector Graves smugly nodded.

ANIMUS ROCK FAUBOURGS

Rhain Dale stalked the area of Animus Rock that lay outside the wall in the dim light of evening, as the sun had already fallen below the flat horizon in the west. The sky was painted a steely grey, streaked with clouds that burned a bright magenta as the sun dipped lower and lower. This area beyond the towering Animus wall was more sparsely populated, with thatched roof homes alongside tilled, empty fields in the mounting winter, or sleeping vineyards. Between some of the fields were dense cedar groves, so thick it was impossible to see into them, and most avoided them, for they were full of dread wolves. It was why most Animus farms outside of the wall, on the western side of the city, did not keep livestock and barred their doors as night, despite their ability to see in the dark. The dread wolves were large, fierce and hungry. They would not hesitate to attack anything that moved in the dark of night.

Rhain hid in one of these such cedar groves, unafraid of dread wolves. *Let them take me,* he thought, expecting an attack from the legendary beasts. He wasn't afraid of death. Past that, he welcomed it. Although he knew even those fearsome beasts would not be able to dispatch him.

He watched a round-faced Animus low native packing up his tools after a long day tilling his field. The donkey he worked beside looked tired, as did he. The native spoke to the donkey as if it was kin. Rhain could barely overhear, but the sentiment disgusted him regardless. He didn't even consider other Vanguards worthy of his words, much less beasts.

The sun sank lower and the clouds burned brighter, turning Regnard red and then a Bellamine burgundy. Rhain didn't notice. He was focused solely on his prey. He had told himself that he would not hunt while at Animus Rock, as it was risky, and he threatened being caught, but he could not stop himself. The red pulsing hallucinations in his vision were too great. His yearning for pain and blood was too strong. His head pounded angrily, threateningly, as if it was going to fall off if he did not hunt. He had no choice. There was no other way to stop the pain.

When the native finished loading up his donkey and turned his back, Rhain moved in. With swift, yet hobbling steps he trudged through the recently tilled field with the burning sky at his back, and the towering Animus castle in the near distance in front of him. The native didn't see him until it was too late.

Rhain grabbed the native by the neck forcefully, holding him high into the air, squeezing his throat so tightly the man couldn't scream. The donkey breyed in surprise, taking off, dropping several tools and a length of rope from the pack as he bucked before running.

Rhain dropped the native. The man gasped for air, red eyes wide, scooting backwards across the dark dirt beneath him. "Why?!" he choked. "Oh Horned, why?!"

Rhain smiled a crooked smile and shook his head. He had found in years of killing for sport that a man's last moments spoke to who they truly were. Most cried and begged. Pleaded with Rhain, trying to understand the attack. Some tried to fight back. Many uttered prayers. Only once did a man stoically take the beating, dying with honor. Rhain had left that man's brand.

The ones who prayed amused Rhain the most. "Do you think your goddess will save you?" he asked, low and deep. The native squinted his eyes, trying to see his attacker clearly in the low light of dusk. He nodded fearfully. "So be it. Pray," Rhain said, taking another hobbling step towards the cowering native, throat already bruising purple. "I will give you until the sky is black. Let's see if she can save you."

The native's eyes widened further and he attempted to jump up and flee, but Rhain lunged and caught him by the arm.

"Please, Lord," he said once noticing Rhain's white-grey eyes and pale skin up close, "I am but a low born farmer. I... I have done nothing. Please. I..."

Rhain interrupted. "Look, do you see?" He glanced behind himself. "The sky is fading. You are spending time praying to me. That will do nothing to save you."

The native nodded hurriedly. He shut his eyes tight. He began to mutter the customary prayers of the Faith of the Horned. Rhain listened with detachment. The sky dimmed further. When the man finished, he peeled open his eyes slowly, as if truly waiting for a goddess with horns on her head to appear. But he was alone in the dark field with Rhain still clinging to his arm. The sky was dim, with only a faint memory of light on the western horizon.

"Do you see anyone coming?" The native, eyes pouring tears silently, shook his head. "There is no goddess," Rhain said. "Do you understand?" The man nodded hurriedly.

"Please, Lord, let me live. Please. Please."

Rhain knelt, still holding the native's arm. He picked up the length of robe. *This will do*, he thought. "Stand still." The native froze as if made of ice. Rhain fashioned the rope into a noose. "Put this over your neck," Rhain said. The native, with shaking hands, obeyed. "To your goddess," he said, turning, pulling the rope over his shoulder, using his titanic height and size to hang the man from the ground as if from a tree. The native kicked and bucked wildly, realizing his fate as he pawed as his already bruised neck. He tried desperately to get away, but Rhain held strong.

Finally, the native stopped bucking. Rhain dropped the body into the freshly tilled dirt. The sky overhead twinkled with stars as torches lit in the distance along the Animus wall. The red pulsing in his vision dripped away like rain washing blood off a windowpane. The pounding in his head subsided. He felt a hollow calm.

That was when Rhain heard the growling. He turned his titanic shoulders slowly, already knowing what was behind him. The dread wolves had found him and his fresh kill. They were here to challenge him for it. Rhain watched their glowing yellow eyes approaching him with amusement. He had battled a rose bear before, but never a dread wolf. This, he thought, would be an interesting fight.

There were nearly a dozen wolves, all the size of horses, with foaming mouths and bared teeth. They quickly surrounded Rhain in the open field, closing in on him. One of the wolves was slightly larger, and greyer than the rest. The Alpha. Rhain turned as it did, meeting its yellow eyes. He growled back, slightly, lowering his brow in focus.

"You do not know who I am," he said to the Alpha evenly. "If you wish to live," he said slowly, "go. Attack me and die."

Offended by Rhain's words or inflection, or perhaps both, the Alpha pounced at Rhain, going for his neck. Rhain lunged at the same time, grabbing the large beast by the throat, throwing him to the ground. Rhain was stronger than a man. He had the power of the old gods in his veins.

The Alpha's yellow eyes flashed in anger mixed with fear, snapping with a frothing jaw at Rhain's neck as he slammed its body into the ground, harder and harder, pressing the dread wolf leader into the dark dirt. It was fully night now and the moon was rising higher above him in the cold sky.

The other dread wolves attacked Rhain in an attempt to free the Alpha, biting and swiping at him, but Rhain knocked them away with ease. One by one they came and one by one he fended them off with one hand as he still pounded the Alpha into the dirt with the other. Eventually, with a yelp, the Alpha expired.

The other dread wolves stopped their attack instantly. They circled around Rhain again, this time in respect. They all sat on their haunches and bowed low to him. Rhain stood, slowly, bleeding from his back and arms, and, still breathing hard, cold sweat running down his temples, he bowed slightly back.

THE VANGUARD SHIP, SPACE

About 2000 years ago…

Renyold's vision was of a castle high on a mountain, surrounded by mostly barren land. It was exceedingly brief, but he could feel the cold air in his lungs. It tasted like something that he couldn't place. Metallic, almost. Then, it began to snow. When the first flake should have landed on his hand, it materialized into ash like the leaf had. His vision left him. He was thrust back into the present with his wife Junia looking at him eagerly.

"It worked!" she cried, eyes tearing. Their goal of unlocking Reynold's visions had replaced the yearning for a child in her heart. This venture was now her baby. She hugged Reynold but he was stiff.

"More," he said. "It wasn't enough. I need more."

They worked for hours, days and weeks, then eventually years on Reynold's visions. Now that they knew that Junia's power was the key to unlocking his, they were able to replicate the scenario at will. At first, Reynold only saw glimpses. A butterfly flitting past his face, through a dense forest. A barge floating lazily down a wide, brown river. An angry animal with teeth growling at him. Then, his power grew stronger. He was able to stay in his visions for longer periods. He learned how to look around, then move about, but he was never able to touch anything. This rich, living world of his visions was just out of reach.

"It's still not enough," Reynold said one day in their shared laboratory. While they kept the content of their work a secret, the entire Vanguard team knew that Reynold and Junia were working on something furiously. The ship was perpetually awash with excitement, awaiting what new powers they planned to reveal.

"Not enough? You have been all over Earth, in this future time. We have mapped the entire United States, or the land where it used to be anyway. In this future you are tethered to, you have seen everything."

"I need more than to see it," Reynold said shakily. He was old, but his drive to reach the land of his visions never faded. It burned hot in his chest just as it had when first ignited nearly a century before.

Junia pursed her lips. Her life felt empty. While at first their aim of pursuing Reynold's visions was exciting, it had lost its lustre over time. It did not fill her the way she hoped it would. Even in her old age, hair turning silver and her skin drooping, she still yearned to carry life inside her. Hourly she mourned that she couldn't have a baby. It felt like a curse.

"There is new technology," she said finally, "from the Bellamine lab. You know how they like to tinker."

Reynold nodded. "I care not for the aims of other bloodlines," he said distantly.

"This you will care about."

He looked at her sharply. The artificial lights caught on his sharp features and glinted from his dark eyes.

Junia hoped that Reynold would tire of his obsession. She hoped that he would be satisfied with the visions alone, but he was not. She hoped she could convince him to reproduce medically, with the use of their scientific techniques, despite the taboo for competing bloodlines to do so, even utilizing a powerless surrogate, but he refused. He was too obsessed with his visions. She realized, sadly, that to keep him, she had to give him what he wanted.

"Bellamine is testing technology that will allow a person to travel to the future."

Reynold brightened. He hobbled to her. "Tell me more."

"Not in body," Junia said. "But in soul."

"In soul?"

"If a descendant can be identified with a matching blood signature, then theoretically, the technology would be able to transfer the soul of someone living now into a future body."

"What happens to the descendant's soul."

Junia shrugged. "Gone, I suppose."

ANIMUS ROCK GRAVESHOLD

Present Day

Herman Graves and Verity Bellamine hosted a dinner party for their close friends at their home. Graveshold was a brute of a structure with imposing stone blocks stacked four stories high. The stone was the same that made the Anstout castle herself. At the crest of the archway leading inside was a depiction of the Graves emblem, in much older, cruder etching than the Villa crests. This building was very ancient indeed. Older than the Animus Rock castle herself, many legends told.

No one really knew how old it was.

Graves had occupied the residence since long before the Plague. Over the years, the exterior remained cold and daunting, but inside greatly evolved. When Herman was given the opportunity to move in and Verity became the Lady of the home, she did all she could to eliminate every trace of evil that remained from before. The dungeon was dismantled. Haulfrun's glaring portrait was removed and stashed in the cellar, along with daggers still stained from the Blood Wars. She'd wanted to burn all of it, but Herman resisted, because, despite their dastardly ways, he had an affinity for his Bloodline and their traditions. Still, every inch was scrubbed, prayers were said and incense was burned. Verity filled the space with heavy, expensive wood furniture and lush pillows. Tapestries lined the walls.

"I adore your tapestries, darling," Faye cooed warmly, glancing up at the intricate embroidery. "Tell me, is it true? Are they really from the North?"

"It is truth," Verity confirmed humbly, shifting in her seat with a wide smile. Her extensive jewelled ornamentation jangled. "Herman had them made for me. He accompanied the old King, may he rest, when he journeyed to Jojinoir."

Nods, and "ah's" of understanding bubbled in the room. The guests studied the intricate, sought-after technique.

"To own the Nomad's work, most with coin can say," Galla said snidely.

"To have work commissioned in such intricate detail is most impressive," Rupert retorted.

"I adore them," Faye said lightly, gesturing to the six, floor-to-ceiling tapestries in blacks, burgundies and dark greens, sparkling with vertical silver lives. Each told a different legend of Vanguards past.

"Galla," Herman said. "Where is Henr this evening?" Verity squeezed his hand under the table. Galla's smug look melted to a scowl. She didn't respond.

"Your husband did come with you to Animus, didn't he?"

Galla frowned and slowly turned her head to meet Verity's statement. "He did not," she said tersely.

"Pity," Verity said blithely. "I can't even sleep when Herman's away. I don't know what to do with myself. I'm sure you miss your husband terribly."

"Ever so much," Galla replied through gritted teeth.

"What of your children, dear?" Faye asked kindly.

Galla relaxed slightly. "The twins are well. Rambunctious. Nothing less than you would expect from year ten."

"They are here, then?" Verity asked.

"No, but..."

"I remember mine young," Faye reminisced, kindly saving Galla from more torture. "Now Oscar is nearly a man. And Ola, nearly a woman."

"It must be so hard to see them grow up."

Faye leaned forward but spoke as loud as before. "Tell us, Verity. When is it your turn?"

"Turn?"

"Why, children, of course."

Verity chuckled lightly, grasping Herman's hand into hers. She placed her other hand on her stomach, ever so subtly.

"Wait," Faye's brown eyes opened wide. "Wait just one

moment!"

"Faye, what's gotten into you?"

She had the biggest grin of excitement on her face. "Are you?"

"Fine, alright. Yes, yes!"

"Praise the Horned!" Faye leapt from her seat and scurried over to Verity's side. "When does the babe arrive?" she asked, kneeling to Verity while she was still sitting.

"It's early yet," Verity said with a beaming smile. They had been trying for years, yet this was the first time seed had taken hold. She could barely wait. Herman was the same. He did have one child, from his first wife, but he did not raise the boy and now he was practically grown. He hardly considered Edgar his son – Herman barely knew him – although he did hold the Graves name. "Not until Spring."

"Congratulations, my friend." Rupert held up his pipe. "Your life will change."

Herman held an iron goblet up in cheers while still clutching Verity's hand with his other. "That's what I hear." He grinned and his grey eyes crinkled with smile lines.

"We are not planning to announce yet," Verity said in a hush. "You understand?"

"Of course," Faye returned to her seat, "of course." She adjusted her high neck blouse and draped gold skirt.

"Why did you wait so long? You are so old Verity. How reckless," Galla scoffed, but Herman, endlessly protective of his wife, interrupted her pointedly.

"Where is Prihim this evening?"

Galla's heart dropped into her stomach. "How should I know?"

"He's with Simon, perhaps," Faye offered.

"What could the Minneys be up to?" Rupert added with a snort.

"Who knows," Herman replied with a shake of his head. He had a complicated opinion of the Minney bloodline, at best. Their perpetual victimization bothered him to the core, particularly when the entire Kingdom was disrupted because of it. Prihim's inability to protect his own and his unhealthy relationship with Galla only further spoke to his instability. Deep down, Herman gave credit to Prihim's unaltered New blood.

Under her breath Galla said, "Prihim is more of a man than either of you."

Verity overheard and smirked.

"The only Minney with sense is the young one," Herman said loudly, knowing that sentiment would bother Galla to her core.

"Yes. But Prihim keeps him under tight watch," Rupert added. "As long as Giacomo lives it will stay that way."

"Has anyone seen him since the accident?" Herman asked.

"I think not," Rupert said, then took several puffs on his pipe, exhaling thick smoke through wide nostrils. "Old Laila has him well hidden. She is so proud." He added, "too proud."

"Are we sure he lives?"

Rupert shrugged and dragged his pipe again. "It is Minney business," he said through an exhale. "Prihim is essentially elderclaim. She will deign it eventually."

Herman tucked his hair behind both ears. "Simon won't be a problem for us, will he?" he asked. "There's no chance he'll vote Old? You know how bitter he is that Laila and Prihim hold Littlebell. He wants it for himself."

"He won't if he knows what is good for him," Rupert said.

"He won't be a problem," Galla replied. "Prihim is making sure."

"Ah, Prihim is, is he?" Rupert half smiled at his sister. Galla sunk a bit in her chair at his tone. "How is Prihim making sure?"

"I'm sure she means he is a strong councilman, isn't that right?" Faye offered innocently.

Rupert and Herman together, snickered.

"I won't tolerate you treating me this way."

Herman said offhandedly, "Lighten up, girl." He'd known Galla since she was in a smock and oftentimes treated her as a sister, since Rupert was like a brother to him.

"No!"

"Galla..." Rupert started to reason with her, knowing her tendency to overreact, but Galla pushed back her chair without warning.

"Thank you for having me," she said curtly to Verity, jaw set and face steeled, begging herself not to cry.

"Oh Galla," Faye leaned forward. "Wait. Oh, don't leave like this. They are teasing."

"They disrespect me," she said wearily, having reached her breaking point. "I won't stand for it. I'm worth more."

The men's expressions fell to shock and the women to surprise with a hint of awe as Galla walked with head high out of Herman and Verity's home.

The temperature dropped considerably from earlier in the evening. Galla wasn't wearing a thick enough gown for this.

She shivered as she paced the long Graveshold hallways alone, then descended shadow-filled switch-back stairs until she exited the ancient strong-hold. She walked along the adjacent street, feeling sorry for herself the whole time.

Why was everyone against her? She tried her hardest to do what was right, but time after time she was laughed at or berated. Why did she keep working so hard for people who didn't appreciate her? Who was she trying to save? She fell into a spiral of thought as she walked, barely noticing her surroundings as she passed by them.

This part of the city was noticeably older than in the east. Roadways were narrower and winding instead of grid-like. Buildings had no porches or stoops, rather, entryways led right out onto the road. They were constructed of mismatched stone, bricks, and cut mud blocks and varying heights and widths. The only similarity between most of the structures were long rectangular windows, around the height of a man and the width of a palm – a style of architecture long gone out of style. During the day, the panes reflected the sunlight like thousands of glinting scales embedded in the stone. At night, fire from within illuminated and exposed what lay behind in thin strips. There were enough windows that light was cast along the dark night street, although Galla didn't need it, as she'd been blessed with native eyes, unlike her brother. The neighbourhood was intimate and immodest. Not one windowpane was covered in cloth nor curtain.

The road she travelled back to the Villas was of old, weathered cobblestone pre-dating the rest of the city as well. It missed large pieces and had divots and cracks. There were few alleyways. Unlike elsewhere within the Animus Rock walls, these north-western alleys were uneven and so narrow at times that a man nearly had to turn sideways to pass through. Just like everywhere else in the city, however, these alleys were overrun with vermin. Several scurried across her path as she headed back to the Villas.

Galla kept to the pale, flickering firelight cast across the road. She pulled her thin gown around her tightly, although it did little to block the mounting wind. Gusts stung her cheeks and nipped her earlobes. She sniffled as her nose ran.

Lost in thought, Galla didn't notice the hooded figure approaching her, at first. It wasn't until he was a few paces away that she saw him. There was no one else around. Wary, Galla pulled her garments tighter and gravitated to one side of the walkway. She hugged it closely and watched the approaching stranger cautiously.

As she shifted to the side of the street, the figure did too. The hair on the back of her neck bristled as the figure removed his hood with both hands, not three paces from her. Even in the dim light it was clear who it was. Stars sparkled against the dark night behind him. She assessed his precisely trimmed beard, hollow cheeks, and unnerving grey eyes.

"Galla Morfit," Hector Graves said coolly. "The pleasure is mine." He bowed in outdated, unnecessary formality.

"Hector," Galla said tersely through a frown, arms prickling with goosebumps. "I must be going," she added quickly. She wanted to run but she reminded herself to be political. She had to work with him on Council, after all, but he made her so uneasy. She couldn't stand to be near him. She felt as if she'd happened upon a deadblood in the forest. As if she were prey.

But Hector didn't move out of her way. "What brings you out with no escort?"

She hated how he stared at people like that. "I could ask you the same," she said and crossed her arms at her chest.

Hector smirked. "To Herman's," he told her.

"You weren't invited."

"I need no invite," he said adjusting his black leather gloves at the wrist. "Graveshold is in my blood."

"Forget uninvited," Galla said. "You're unwanted."

Hector smiled. "Curious." He looked her up and down, as a white lion would assess a deer. "Why is it you are without an escort? Could it be you who is unwanted?"

Galla frowned. "No," she said quickly, but it was clear from her expression he was right. It was always safe to assume Galla left a party in a huff. She was known for it. "The hour is late. I leave because I am tired."

"Surely your brother should escort you as you stay together in your bloodline's Villa. Do you not?"

"We do," Galla replied quickly.

"Yet he remains at Herman's?"

She steeled her brow and ground her jaw. "None of your concern," Galla said tersely, Hector's icy eyes studying her. It made her anxious, feeling her thoughts naked beneath his gaze, and she took a step back, slowly.

"But that, there, is the issue." Hector stepped towards Galla, once, then twice.

"What is?" she asked nervously. "What..." she paused, noting his bounding movements, "what are you doing?" She took another step backwards, casted firelight half-illuminating her face.

Hector's eyes danced wildly. His bloodlust was palpable. "I am concerned," he said.

"Hector," Galla started, "I don't understand..." as Hector lurched forward.

Thoughts racing, Galla turned to flee but caught her foot on a cobblestone. She toppled with a painful thud. Hector stepped over her. As Galla scrambled to stand, Hector launched with superhuman speed, grabbing her with surprising strength of grip with long, cool fingers.

Galla screamed.

"Quiet," Hector commanded with bitter annoyance.

"Hector!" Galla choked through sobs, pleading him to release her. "Get... your... hands... off of m... m...me!" she cried, kicking indignantly, fabric of her black gown buckling and catching on her knees. Her golden cape dragged through dirt. She did all she could to free herself, yet Hector held an iron grip on the weak woman. "Hector!" Her scream cracked in higher, painful octaves as her thoughts tumbled on themselves, confusion battling fear. "Stop!" She flailed as he dragged her. Her knees painfully caught on cobblestones. One black boot fell off. "You can't!" she cried, mind racing, heart pounding, adrenaline spiked. "You can't do this!" Her eyes were wild with terror as his were focused and unfeeling. "I am Vanguard! You cannot!" *How can he do this to me*?! She thought in terror, clawing and grabbing at passing doorframes. She punched his thighs and legs from behind. She cried and mucus dripped from both nostrils down her chin. *Why is he doing this?* That's all she could think. *Why*?!

"Quiet," Hector growled again, then grabbed her by her hair.

"Please! H...h... help!" Galla screamed up at the chilly, grey-cloud night. It matched Hector's eyes. "Help me please!" she cried at the countless blank panes staring down at her, to her, the countless native lives she had saved in her long, tireless career. "No!" she shouted, trying to desperately spin her head backwards to look at Hector. What was happening? It was so sudden. She couldn't process it. How could he do this to her? She sat on Council! She was respected! She was Vanguard! "Why?!" she screamed, clinging to his wrist with both hands as he dragged her to the closest alleyway. She looked up at the panes above her. "Help me!"

Onlookers flocked to the long, rectangular windows as

Hector dragged Galla to the claustrophobic alley, seeking the source of the screams. Pair after pair of red eyes peered out. They listened to Galla's pleas and blood-curdling cries. They watched as Hector ripped the expensive garments from her body and tossed them aside like rags. They watched him beat her bloody and hold her face with both hands, staring into her eyes. They watched him draw out all the essence of Galla's soul until she was just a husk. They watched him rape her.

Once he snapped her neck, the onlookers silently scurried back into the depths of their homes and returned to their lives. Dozens of blank panes gawked at the naked corpse of Galla Morfit.

Then, Hector Graves manically laughed, eyes sparkling, so hard that he teared. Or was he crying?

Hours passed. Candles and fires burned low throughout Graveshold. "She takes everything so personally," Rupert said, sorry for how he treated his sister earlier. He sighed and rubbed his temple. "She just can't relax."

"Don't feel low," Faye replied. "You know Galla." Rupert took a drag of his pipe. He exhaled a large cloud of smoke. Faye went on kindly. "She'll be over it in the morn."

"You'd think she'd know to play nice by now," Verity said, face pinched like she smelled something awful. The way she usually looked.

Rupert shook his head. "That's not Galla," he said stoically. "She was born with a heart that bleeds for all suffering, not just her own. She feels it's on her shoulders to fix it," he added, "no matter the cost."

"Hmph," Verity looked to her husband. "Even so, we'd be more apt to listen to her if she wasn't so off-putting."

Herman chuckled and squeezed his wife's hand.

"I think she is just tired. You see how the Old treats her," Faye said sympathetically.

"Oh, please," Verity sighed. "She brings it upon herself. She is condescending, and rude, and snobbish. She plays the victim and wonders why no one likes her."

"She means well," Rupert said. He puffed again on his pipe.

Herman turned to him, unable to hold his tongue. "She refuses to end the nonsense with Prihim?"

"Yes," Rupert said. "Unfortunately," he added, exhaling smoke.

"You've spoken to her of it?"

"I have," Rupert slightly nodded. "Again, not a moon ago. As always, she denied the affair."

Herman shook his head in disappointment.

"Surely she denies it," Faye said, as no woman would outright admit to an affair so unmentionable. "It's against Vanguard law."

"But to me, her own brother?"

"The whole Kingdom knows of it," Verity told Rupert, visibly pleased. "Is she aware?"

"I'm not sure," Rupert said with a frown.

Verity looked to Herman. "She has to know, right?"

Herman shrugged. He knew better than to involve himself in women's speak. "It will betray her in the end," he said, then added wisely, "You catch more flies with honey than vinegar."

Faye smiled and nodded to Verity. "Nothing more true. Sybil always says that too." Verity slightly scowled. Before she could respond though, there was an interruption.

Double doors at the head of the hall burst open with a loud crack. Heads swung to investigate the unplanned disturbance. Hector Graves strolled casually into the room, presence alight as if he was brimming in white flames.

Herman stood immediately. Something was off about his brother and he could intimately feel it. His back bristled. The men were so close in age, they were nearly twins, and as boys they acted as such. Shared everything, including thoughts and feelings. Although, when Hector went cold, and Herman couldn't feel him anymore, he knew to be concerned. "Hector, what are you doing here?" he demanded angrily, tucking hair behind both ears in one movement.

Hector's heavy boots clacked on the floor as he approached the table without a word, then stood with his gloved hands on the back of the only empty chair. The chair where Galla had sat.

"To have company and not invite your own brother," Hector said without inflection, narrowing his icy grey eyes. "Curious."

"You are not welcome here," Rupert said in deep baritone. He retained his casual posture, leaning back slightly, smoking pipe in hand, but his eyes were stalwart and firm. Hector slowly swung his head to face the comment. He glared, unblinking, for an uncomfortable amount of time, then, without acknowledging Rupert at all, he turned back.

"You don't have to continue on this path," Hector addressed Herman, ignoring Rupert totally. "There is no honor in blind, stubborn ideology. Your time for this frivolity is through."

"Hector, leave." Herman was firm. "This is not the time." He glanced to Faye and Rupert and lowered his tone slightly. "We have guests."

Regardless, Hector spoke to his younger brother as if there was no one else in the room. "I have allowed your sympathetic preferences to continue and fester. I have ignored your problematic viewpoints and systematic degradation of our blood culture and values. I sat idly by as you fed the Kingdom's thirst for mistruth and insanity. It is time you quit this game, brother."

Herman frowned. "Hector, what are you talking about?" He was tired of his bloodline's single-minded ways. He had heard all the speeches. Nothing Hector could say would change his mind. "Why are you here?"

"I am a man of logic. I have reverence for blood, but…" Hector stared intently, "I will only allow you this choice once."

"Enough," Verity stood in a huff. "I will not allow you to ruin our evening."

Hector didn't even look at her. He continued to speak to Herman. "Come home."

Herman frowned deeper, lines cut into his jowls and forehead heavily wrinkled. "What do you mean?" he asked. "Home?"

He gestured around. "I am home."

"To Anstout," Hector said, as if it was obvious.

Verity grabbed Herman's hand and squeezed, fuming silently.

Herman didn't balk at Hector's suggestion. "This is my home now," he said firmly, squeezing Verity's hand back.

"Father nears death."

Herman caught Hector's meaning, that he was to ensure it himself. He'd expected as much would come to pass and had accepted it long ago, knowing his older brother well. He'd said goodbye to his father many, many years ago. He would not mourn. "What does that have to do with it?"

"What kind of son are you not to visit?" Hector's words fell on his younger brother like bricks. "You would prove his belief true," he said slowly, knowing the pain he caused with each word. "You are a coward."

"Leave, Hector," Rupert growled. Smoke billowed from his nostrils.

Finally, Hector acknowledged Rupert Morfit as one glances at a buzzing fly. "If my brother bids it, I go," he said. "I do not take orders from *earthblood*."

At that, Rupert jumped from his chair. He pointed emphatically to double doors at the end of the hall. "Out *deadblood*, OUT!"

"Hector, go right now," Herman in half anger, half concern.

"This is what you wish brother?" Hector looked down his angled beard. "You choose them?"

Herman clung to Verity's hand with white knuckles. He swallowed and set his jaw. "Yes," Herman said, blinking grey eyes once, understanding the rift he instantly caused within his bloodline with a single word. He braced himself for the ultimate outburst, expecting to settle it in a duel, just as they had as children and young men so many times before.

But oddly, Hector smirked and blinked, long and slow. "As you wish," he said gently, to Herman's surprise, then exited the hall like a shadow escaping the light.

As unexpectedly as Hector arrived, he was gone.

ANIMUS ROCK'S THIRD TOWER

The sky outside Animus Rock's steely stone fortress was pearly grey. There was no part in the swirling clouds from horizon to horizon as the churning haze shielded all light and warmth of the sun. It rained a pitiful mist that permeated clothing and chilled everyone to the bone. It had been raining for half a moon straight. This dreary weather brought down the general mood of the Kingdom. It visibly impacted the Vanguard children.

Today the young ones frowned, bickered, and squirmed in their seats.

Rotrude assessed the rambunctious lot with weary sigh as she adjusted her robe and smoothed her oiled hair once. She stood upright, took a deep breath, and addressed the room.

"Students!" Rotrude said in a shrill chirp. They settled as commanded. All faced forward, some with frowns. "I am sorry, that was a bit harsh," she added. "Good morning."

"Good morning Lessonmaster," the children said in sing-song harmony.

"Welcome all. It seems this weather impacts even me," she said kindly to a few smiles and a few heads swinging to look out the window at the drizzling sky. "Face forward." Rotrude added, "Please," tersely. "It's important that you pay attention. It's a large lesson." Today was to be a weighty lesson indeed, for it was the first introduction of the Lower Academy children to the intricacies of the Blood Wars. It was not a topic that Rotrude enjoyed, but it was a critical one to understanding present day Kingdom politics.

The children nodded respectfully. The grey mist outside was unrelenting and Rotrude glanced at it briefly. The cool rain reminded her of the chill of the mines. She shrugged the faint, distant memory off, then continued.

"I will jump right in. At the end of the North Plague of 3833," she said, then cleared her throat, starting to pace the front of the Lessonroom, "over two hundred years ago, only three Bellamines lived. Brothers Degory and Danil and their young sister Josslyn. Degory was the eldest and inherited the throne. This was expected, for he was born and groomed for the position. He was fit to rule with a sound mind and knack for military strategy, it is said. Although he was Old as the Bellamines all were back then, he was the first credited with leniency towards natives," she added to a few nods from newblood children. "He rebuilt the Kingdom in the wake of the Plague. Degory Bellamine was good man. A good king."

Avina raised her hand with a scrunched face.

"Yes?"

"What did he look like?"

"He was tall and handsome," Rotrude told the Minney girl, pausing pace to hover aside her seat. "Do you know the statue with the fountain? The one in the North?" She referred to a grand sculpture atop a fountain that was very popular in Animus Rock, said to grant fortunes if one offered it coin and curses if one dared to steal the coins within. The statue stood not far from the Vanguard Villas. The children nodded. "That is King Degory Bellamine," she told them. "The people loved him. When he died unexpectedly at the age of thirty years, they constructed that statue in mourning. The tradition of throwing him coins began as tribute to his legacy. When many found fortune after doing so, the superstition was born."

Darker clouds rolled atop the grey ones and shaded the light further outside. Shadows fell about the Lessonroom.

"How did he die?" Malla shouted.

"Hand, Malla," Rotrude reminded the girl. Today she wore choker with a lake green gem and her blonde hair was brilliantly fuzzy from the weather. "No one knows," Rotrude went on, eyeing the precious crystal the child wore enviously. She'd always dreamed of owning a throat stone but alas, did not bear the status and certainly didn't bear the coin. "One day he was healthy, and the next, dead. There were rumors of foul play." She paused, waiting for a reaction, noting the confused looks on the children's faces. She elaborated more simply, "That means, a lot of people thought he was murdered."

A few gasps.

"I know!" Rotrude spun her head, wide-eyed as she told the tale. She always felt invigorated by the children's innocence, almost like she was learning the information herself for the first time. "But, there was no way to prove it."

Rose raised her hand slowly. Rotrude glanced to the curiously quiet dark-eyed girl. She rarely socialized and always sat on the far side of the chamber, no matter the lesson, aside the windows. Rotrude felt a shadow of pity for her, assuming the girl had been horribly tortured at Westerviolet. She was a Brochet after all. Rotrude had heard the rumors of the horrors there. Who hadn't?

Rotrude nodded.

"Why kill a good king?"

Rotrude took a breath, taken aback by the insightful question.

"Because some men want power for themselves," she said wisely, thinking of so many she'd known in her past. "They don't care how it hurts the people. In this instance," she attempted to bring her statement back on lesson, "it's very likely that Gauthier Norland, Balthasar Graves, or Rufus Brochet had something to do with it."

"Why would they murder the King if he was Old like them?" Malla asked loudly.

"Malla, hand!" Rotrude scolded. The girl sunk in her seat to a goading smile from Evia Norland on the other side of the chamber. "Because," Rotrude said more calmly, "Degory was sympathetic to the natives. He stopped taking Old Council. King Degory even threatened to appoint Alden Morfit to Second, in place of Gauthier Norland. Most believe this prompted the King's murder and the Silent Siege of 3850, the two key catalysts the sixty year-long Blood Wars."

The children listened intently. Rotrude went on, pacing the

front of the lesson room in time with the rhythmic drone of chilly rain outside.

"I don't want to get ahead of myself," she told them, knowing how much there was to explain. "There were many factors that brought war. August Norland's kidnapping of Auina Beaumont. Or the assassination of Reggient Minney at Cassyon Beaumont and Anneia Minney's wedding in 3833, for example. The memory of the Old betrayal of the Beaumonts for their alliance with the Minneys was unforgivable."

The turmoil that struck the Vanguards in the wake of the North Plague fascinated Rotrude, despite its unpleasantness. She took a breath, pausing momentarily to consider how sharp the betrayals must have felt within each bloodline. She would give a lot to be able to travel back in time, to witness it all for herself.

"Besides that," she continued, "the Kingdom itself was in economic shambles after the Nomad conflict and the North Plague. Degory and Danil's grandfather and father, Aldus and Abner Bellamine respectively, bankrupted the crown and Bellamine name from excessive borrowing from various realms, mainly Thorne, to fund the fighting, and later, construction of the massive fortress wall. After thirty years went by, the Bellamine debts were not forgotten."

It was horrible what the Bellamines did to this Kingdom, Rotrude thought as she paced, watching the wide eyes of the Vanguard children as they absorbed her every word.

"Once Degory was dead too," she said, "Thorne, Graves, and Brochet used the outstanding Bellamine debts as weight over Degory's weaker and younger brother Danil. Therefore, the steady and climbing peace that King Degory cultivated in over a decade of rule dissipated twice as fast as it had blossomed under his younger brother's thoughtless rule. The leniency towards natives was brutally stripped away and harsh identification, weapons, travel, and breeding laws were fast enacted in the immediate days after Danil took power in 3850. This was almost exactly two hundred years ago, when Danil was not much older than all of you, only sixteen years."

A few hands shot into the air. Rotrude called on Lucette sitting on the far side of the chamber behind Rose, sulking into her seat as if she was trying to disappear into it.

Lucette's heart thumped in her frail chest as she felt all eyes on her, "Why was he so mean?" she asked quietly. She immediately wished she hadn't spoken.

Rotrude's heart tore for the sallow-eyed girl. Today she had evidence of faint bruising on her wrists and neck and tomorrow there would be more, Rotrude thought sadly. She's seen it before. It was the Busk way. "He was very young when he became King," she told Lucette gently. "He wasn't prepared. Imagine, being not much older than yourself and in charge of the whole land!"

Lucette's eyes widened. She could not imagine that at all. The idea terrified her. Although most things terrified her.

"You have to remember he was a child just like you," Rotrude explained, noting Lucette's expression. "Evil men corrupted Danil, however, the people at the time didn't see it that way. He quickly became the most hated Vanguard King in recorded history."

Rotrude nodded at Avina with hand raised. Her heavy blonde Littlebell braid rested on one shoulder, falling all the way down to her waist. "What was the Silent Siege?"

"I was getting to that Avina, thank you," Rotrude said to the brown-eyed girl. "Most Guildsmen point to the Silent Siege as the tipping point in Kingdom politics and beginning of the Blood Wars. Others argue that the Blood Wars didn't truly begin until the New Retaliation, but, one thing at a time."

Rainwater collected outside, racing in beads down the time-warped windowpanes.

"Gauthier Norland led the Silent Siege of Croft Hold," Rotrude explained. "Alden Morfit, hardened survivor of the Plague, brilliantly trained Guildsman and storied humanitarian was not there at his blood home for the attack. This was by design. Gauthier Norland waited until Alden Morfit travelled to the Capital for the Summer Solstice of 3850. Then, in the middle of a moonless night, he led the most fearsome Warmen he had on a raid of the man's blood castle."

Worry fell across the children's small brows.

"Gauthier Norland and his forces killed every man they found at Croft Hold and took the women and children as slaves. Worse, he murdered Alden's native wife and eldest heir Absalom. Absalom Morfit was just a small boy at the time. Obviously, Alden was outraged when he heard the news of what happened to his family and he demanded swift punishment for Norland, but the Boy King Danil stupidly defended the Siege." Distain was obvious in Rotrude's tone. "Alden then demanded that the Council overthrow the King for what had been done. King Danil, under advisement of the Old, declared all who follow Morfit to be traitors. Then, Alden Morfit claimed independence from the Old. He declared war on the King. This arguably marked the beginning of the Blood Wars."

Rotrude assessed wide eyes and distressed expressions. Third Tower robes flapping at her low-booted ankles, she went on.

"Vendalin Demos, sole Demos survivor of the plague and Croft Hold neighbour at Hellswater to the northwest supported Alden. The Minneys to the South did as well. Plague survivor Miles Minney died of a snake bite years before, leaving his son Jothan Minney, barely in his twentieth year, elder of Littlebell. Eric Warn, plague survivor and leader of the Ironbark mercenaries also backed the cause. That was the entirety of New at the start of the Blood Wars. The rest fought for the Old, even Baneswood at the start." She paused and took a deep breath. "Any questions?"

"Did the natives have any say?" Avina asked after Rotrude called on her.

"In Old realms, natives were akin to slaves," Rotrude explained, knowing that truth all too personally. She pushed the dark memories aside. "In the New, however, there was hope. Alden believed that the way of the future was harmony between all people, therefore, he declared all natives free."

"That's good, right?" Malla squawked, pale green gem sparking from her neck to match her eyes. Rotrude frowned at her and the girl retroactively shot her hand into the air. Rotrude nodded approvingly once, then shook her head "no" to answer the question.

"Unfortunately, the Old was ruthlessly patrolling borders and snatching any unlucky enough to live or wander too close," she said, "so they weren't fully free. This sparked skirmishes between natives and Old forces, including bloody battles amassing hundreds upon hundreds of casualties each time, particularly at the borders of the Confines, Lyonshall and Westerviolet particularly. Alden used this unrest to draw support for his cause, and with that, built an army. Unlike the armies of the Old realms where men had to fight or die, Alden gave his people a choice. Natives in Old realms heard about what he was doing and many attempted to flee their own realms to join too, but in most cases, this ended poorly. Early in the war, the Old realms locked all borders. It was nearly impossible to cross without threat of curse, capture or annihilation."

The children shuttered.

"It was a dark time," Rotrude said, in agreement with the mood in the chamber. "This went on for nearly five years as Alden, Vendalin, and the other New supporters built their army." Rotrude paced the room. "Interesting to note, around this time, the fashion became popular to line eyes with dark coal, in Croft Hold's realm especially. This was to mimic Alden Morfit's natural dark coloring around his own eyes. The tradition since took hold, and in today's Kingdom marks a visible difference between political alliances."

The children nodded.

Rose was glad to realize why so many in Animus black-lined their eyes. She'd never seen such a thing before as her mother never lined her eyes and Westerviolet natives, both high and low, were not permitted to use face colorings. The custom confused and intrigued her.

"Finally," Rotrude said, "in 3855, Alden and Vendalin led an attack on the impenetrable Ravenshroud."

Gracelia, middle of the three icy Thorne girls, raised a slender hand. "Yes?" Rotrude looked to her, noting the thin crystal crown atop her lifeless white-blond hair cut blunt at her chest, to match her sisters.

"What's impenetra… imped.."

"Impenetrable?" Rotrude finished her sentence. "It means no one can get in."

"If no one could get in," the eldest Thorne, Orosia, interjected hotly, "why would they attack it?"

"Because Alden was clever," Rotrude retorted, resting her hip against the stark desk in the front of the room. "He knew that his greatest weapon was perception, or rather, misperception. You see, children, he knew that the Old would underestimate him. He knew they wouldn't think he was a threat. Alden was a smart man and he was right." Rotrude always loved this story and it made her glad to tell it. "He marched straight up to the mighty Ravenshroud curtain wall," she explained, "with only a few hundred men in meagre armor with embarrassing weapons. Sticks, shards of glass, and stones were in the men's hands. The Norlands opened their drawbridge wide and walked out to greet them, laughing hysterically, thinking they had already won. Gauthier Norland thought that this was Alden's whole army. He was prepared to slaughter them all right there to end the war."

She paused, heavily lined red eyes scanning the children's faces.

"Alden Morfit had other plans," she finally said dramatically, with a smile.

The grey rain had slightly subsided outside, but the sky still hung heavy with dark clouds.

"When the mightiest Norland Warmen left the fortification of the wall, the real assault began," Rotrude explained, speaking with her hands, one sturdy leg crossed over the other from her leaning seat against the desk. "Alden gave the signal and nearly five thousand heavily armed and expertly trained soldiers rained down on the unsuspecting Warmen. It was a slaughter. Gauthier Norland only barely escaped to Anstout. There, he lived with his family the other survivors. He didn't take back his castle until 3858, after a three-year long siege with the help of Graves and Brochet. While this New Retaliation was a crushing blow to Norland, the ordeal decimated the best of Alden's forces too. It was ultimately a defeat for both the New and the Old."

"If it hurt his cause, why did he do it at all?" Tiphanie asked. Her flat white hair was pulled back with a length of string but it wasn't long enough to all stay, so large pieces fell out to frame her face in messy chunks. She had dried food on her cheek and smock, too. Even if she hadn't, she was the type of child that always looked messy.

Rotrude sneered at the Regnard. "I wouldn't say it hurt the cause."

"But, you said it decimated his forces," Tiphanie whined. "Doesn't that mean *destroy*?"

"Yes, it does, but even though he lost thousands of men over that span of three years, it proved something to the Old. For the first time the people came together against them. It was a victory for the spirit of the New cause. For the first time, the Old had something to fear."

Evia, silent up until now, raised a slim hand. "The Old doesn't fear the New," she said confidently.

Rotrude sighed loudly. "No blood teachings, Evia," she told the pale girl through gritted teeth. "What did I say?"

"That's not fair," Rose interjected. Her small, doll-like face scrunched in a frown.

Rotrude spun. What did you say?" She was shocked at the quiet girl's outburst.

"I said," Rose retorted boldly, "that's not fair." Her gaze was unnerving. Rotrude tried to shrug it off, unable to meet the girl's black eyes fully. She used a trick of Hidden Den, to stare at the nose instead of the eyes. This tactic was required for the most powerful of Vanguards.

"Why not?" she asked pointedly, subconsciously crossing her arms in front of her chest.

"You can't say those people felt one way just because it's how you feel now."

Rotrude was taken aback, as if slapped in the face. "What... what... no." Who had taught her to say such a thing? "No, Rose. It is the truth."

"That can't be if..." Rose started, but Rotrude angrily interrupted her.

"Rose!" Rotrude shouted making most of the other children jump. "Enough."

Rose stoically glared at Rotrude and sat back in her chair silently, realizing Rotrude was just as stupid and blind as Mathilda back home. She realized in that moment that adults were no smarter than children, in fact, probably more doltish because they never questioned what they'd been taught. Evia glanced at her and smiled proudly. The other children murmured amongst themselves, impressed and slightly in awe of the command she held over their Lessonmaster. Rotrude rubbed her temple and smoothed her hair once.

"Where was I?" she spoke mostly to herself, flustered, trying to re-center herself after the disruption. Rotrude was unnerved by the small girl's ability to rattle her, particularly after her extensive training at Hidden Den. She should know how to handle Vanguard children by now, she chided herself internally, even Brochets.

Luckily, the small girl had no idea what she was.

"Ah, of course," Rotrude's full cheeks pulled into a smile. "We're in the wake of Ravenshroud." She went on, seemingly unfazed, pacing the shadow-filled room once more. Her ornamented ears clanked loudly with each step. "After 3858, tensions amidst the Kingdom were high. A series of destructive conflicts ensued. I'll touch on the major ones. This will all be covered in more detail when you're older." She cleared her throat.

"The Old countered the New in 3863 by burning the mighty Vanguard bridge. You'll know it as Grim Pass, as it was later renamed," Rotrude said. "It was never the same again after that, as the fires scorched the alabaster stones used to fortify the base black. That was followed by the attack on Rysp Dam and Hellswater, when the Old sabotaged their dam, flooding dozens of fishing villages, and marched on the Hellswater Harbour in 3865. In this case, the Old underestimated the New again. Hellswater had built up her army." Rotrude noted Malla smile wide and proud. "There were nearly ten thousand Old troops but only one out of every five men came back alive. It was a disastrous defeat for the Old and win for the New."

Rotrude particularly loathed this next part of the story and swallowed hard before continuing.

"The New may have taken the war right then, had it not been for Regnard." She spit that particular blood name with antipathy. "Maxim Regnard made the error of leading an attack on Baneswood, near Glassy Stream, in parallel to the Hellswater battle," she explained. "This brought Dale into the war, who up until then had been more or less a neutral bystander in the conflict, although had favored the Old slightly."

"Why attack Baneswood?" Tiphanie asked with a frown. Everyone knew how tough Baneswood was.

"We don't know for sure," Rotrude told her. "Many think he received faulty information or possibly was just greedy or Lyonshall supplies were low. It's possible Dale offended the King and it was on Danil's command. Regardless of why, Maxim caused Dale to enter the war and a feud to erupt. Much blood was shed between them, particularly over Hunter Post's abandoned territory, for the remainder of the war."

As the children listened closely, Rotrude went on.

"Alden went on the offensive again after the momentum built at Hellswater. This time, he headed straight to Animus Rock to breach the fortress wall, kill the king, and take the throne. He attacked in summer of 3875 with nearly twenty thousand men and the latest siege technology. The Animus Assault went on for almost five years, until Alden's forces were whittled down to nearly nothing and he was forced to pull back. Meanwhile, Maxim Regnard had taken Croft Hold in Alden's absence. Because of that, in the early part of 3880, Alden retreated to Winter Garden under protection of the Beaumonts. The Beaumonts were markedly neutral throughout the war due to their involvement with bloodlines from each side, similar to Thorne and Dale. When they welcomed Alden into their walls after the failed Animus Assault, however, Beaumont unwittingly declared their support for the New. They were marked as traitors in the eyes of the King."

The children sat forward, enlivened by their harrowing Vanguard history. Rotrude continued to pace and went on.

"This ultimately led to the Beaumont bloodline's near-demise, then re-affirmed pledge to the Old," Rotrude said. "The King was unsatisfied after the Animus Assault and craved vengeance against the New for the attack, so, in 3880 he ordered a rebuttal, later called the Battle of Winter Garden. Eight thousand Warmen and Westerviolet Guardsmen marched on the tall, intricately stone worked castle in its rocky valley, sunken between snow-capped mountains. The beautiful Beaumont Winter Garden structure was unfortunately pitifully fortified with a thin wall and a narrow, light green moat. It didn't take long for the Old to overtake it." She paused. "It helped there was a betrayal from within."

The children still seemed to be listening closely. It was darker now outside.

"Bert and Lucia Beaumont, offspring of survivors of the plague as well as elders of the Beaumont bloodline, lived at Winter Garden with their married children Vanelt and Alla. Vanelt betrayed his family by conspiring with the Old to fell the castle. It's said he left a gate open and Warmen snuck in the middle of the night. He did it in exchange for passage to Animus Rock with Alla. Winter Garden fell and Bert and Lucia Beaumont were killed. When Vanelt and Alla reached Animus, they begged mercy from King Danil and their sister, Queen Aly Beaumont. Mercy was granted and all Beaumonts lived at Animus Rock moving forward. Winter Garden was destroyed, and the realm slowly fell to lawlessness and ruin, not unlike it stands today. Alden Morfit barely escaped to Hellswater, under protection of Vendalin Demos."

Rotrude took a breath, then went on.

"There, at Hellswater, the men plotted. In 3890 they led an attack against Croft Hold and finally in 3894 regained the castle for Morfit. This drove Regnard back to Lyonshall," she said, narrowing her eyes. That blood name sat like a wart on her tongue. "Finally, war came to a head when Alden led the New to attack Westerviolet in 3901. The Old had predicted the move and lay waiting. Alden brought over ten thousand men with him but was crushed by the Old's fifteen thousand. After, it's said Brochet stacked the bodies of the fallen along the road, so deep and high that the path was renamed Narrow Road in ominous ironic warning."

Rotrude studied the class. "What do you think happened next? What would you have done?" She called on the icy blonde with slim hand raised halfway.

"Yes, Orosia?"

"Compromise," the girl said, already full-well knowing the story. Her father taught her and her sisters the Kingdom's history long ago. Their academy attendance was merely a formality.

"Exactly!" Rotrude pointed at her excitedly. Orosia smiled smugly as her sisters gazed up at her approvingly. "Alas, King Danil, now in his sixties, had no room for compromise in his heart. His teenage son Ueli, on the other hand, was wise beyond his years. The young man conspired behind his father's back, and, amazingly, gained the ear of each elder. Unfortunately, Graves, Brochet and Norland refused to meet with the young Ueli, as he was not King. Eventually though, Ueli convinced Norland to fight for him, instead of his father, in exchange for a law stating Norland was to be Lord of Warman for all time. Gauthier Norland happily agreed. He gutted the old King Danil, his supposed ally, on the front steps of Animus."

The children looked horrified. Rotrude continued her momentum.

"After that, Council was held at the neutral Creed Point. All Bloodlines were represented, even the reluctant Graves and Brochet. Amazingly, Ueli listened to all the pleas and an accord was struck. The rulings that came out of that Council meeting, later named the Blood Council, are as follows:"

Outside, despite drizzling rain, the sun peeked through black clouds in a thin, bright beam that illuminated the side of Rotrude's rough face and glinted off of her white-oiled hair.

1.   "King Ueli declared that he and every Bellamine king so forth was to marry a native to promote unity, trust, and peace amongst the people and realms," Rotrude said. "Next,

2.   they agreed it was to be forbidden to harm a native from another realm. Then,

3.   Vanguards are to hold Vanguards first – any treachery is to be reported, lest you align with the traitor yourself. Then,

4.   it was agreed unanimously that areas with deadblood sightings or reported Dread Death cases are off limits and forbidden." She paused, smiling at the warm sunbeams on her face after so much rain. "Finally," Rotrude said, "

5.   no slavery. Natives must volunteer for any work, games, or fighting, and are free to believe what they choose to, so long as it does not incite violence."

She then flexed her jaw, knowing how far that last law was from behind upheld Kingdom wide, especially in Old realms. But, with the power the Old still held and the blind eye the natives of New realms turned to the strife, what could be done?

Rotrude assessed the drooping eyes and small bodies wiggling in seats. "Any questions?" she asked. "None? I must have done well explaining, then." The children chuckled. Rotrude smiled warmly. "I know you're tired. We are nearly through. And, finally to the best part."

"What?" one of the identical green-eyed boys asked. Rotrude frowned at him, then his twin shot his hand up into the air and shouted, "What part?"

Rotrude smiled. The Warn twins had heard this lesson before but must not have been paying attention. No wonder they were back for a second round. In her experience, Warns were notoriously distractable and not particularly bright. "The introduction to Echo's Omen."

The children collectively "oooh-ed" in excitement.

"See, I told you," Rotrude said warmly, then began.

"Josslyn Bellamine, sister to the King, went missing in 3864. It is assumed she ventured to Duskfang in search of mad honey. Although frowned upon, this was common for young people at the time. If the New were to intercept her, however, they would have had leverage over the King. This was a big problem and the Old could not let it happen, so King Danil went to his two best friends, Robert Brochet and Humfra Graves, sons of blood elders Rufus and Balthasar, respectively, for help. He sent them into the Cursed Hills to find his sister."

The children were enchanted by the story, mostly leaning forward on elbows with faces tilted up eagerly. Even Lucette was engaged. Only Rose stared wistfully out the window with the sun on her face. Rotrude couldn't tell, but she was still listening intently.

Rotrude went on. "The men searched for moons," she explained, "until they found her at an ancient, pre-Vanguard fortress buried in the Hills."

Avina raised her hand with a scrunched expression on her face. Rotrude called on her. "Is that Echo's Omen?"

"The beginnings of it, yes," Rotrude nodded. "Robert and Humfra found the princess in the capture of deadbloods that had taken up residence in the ruins. Shockingly, she was still alive."

Malla raised her hand aggressively, wiggling it high above her head, right in front of Rotrude's face.

Rotrude pressed a hand to her left temple and sighed. "Yes, Malla?"

"I thought deadbloods give you Dread Death and that kills you."

"It does. In very few people, however, there is a natural resistance to it. It's assumed that Josslyn was resistant. Although she was dying, for the moment, she was still alive."

The blonde girl nodded, wondering silently what living with

Dread was like, as Rotrude went on.

"Robert and Humfra wrote to Danil for guidance when they found Josslyn," she said. "For fear of Dread Death and another plague, King Danil ordered his sister to be killed." A few children gasped. "I know, I know," Rotrude said gently, "but you have to remember, Danil had lived through the Plague as a boy. He knew the horrors of the disease. In this instance, I believe he was making a smart decision, but Robert and Humfra didn't listen."

Loud raps against stone pavement interrupted as the sky opened up again and lazy, wide raindrops fell.

"The men lied to the King," Rotrude explained, rainstorm harmonizing in the background. "They reported to the King that his sister, the princess Josslyn, was dead, that they had killed her, but they had not. They told the King that they stayed at what was later named Echo's Omen to drive out the deadbloods, to build a base camp on this eastern front to mirror Creed Point in the west, however, most say they truly stayed to explore it. In the midst of war and its' chaos, King Danil lost focus on the pair. It was then, in the latter shadow of the Blood Wars, that the Echo's Omen's Brotherhood was born."

A few hands raised. Surprised that the Brochet showed an interest, Rotrude called on Rose.

"Why did they lie to the King?" Rose's dark brows pressed into flat lines and her forehead creased between her eyebrows. When she made that face, she looked like her infamous mother, Rotrude thought. "Why didn't they listen?"

"That is a great question," Rotrude said. "There is a lot of speculation as to why they didn't kill Josslyn or return from Echo's Omen. Neither bloodline, Graves nor Brochet, have confirmed nor denied any of the rumors as to why Robert and Humfra went against King Danil's orders. Many claim the men saw an opportunity for power and seized it, plain and simple. Others think it was their plan all along, and some go so far as to accuse them of kidnapping the princess just to give them an excuse to explore the Hills. The most popular theory, however, holds an explanation for the behaviour of Gravesblood in the generations to follow. I'll warn you; the tale is likely a mix of fantasy and reality, having been passed down by word alone. We have no way of knowing what really happened."

Rotrude looked from young face to face, each with varying features, skin tones, eye colors, and hair. All shared the same wonder filled, horrified expression. The same way she remembered feeling when she learned this part of the Kingdom's history.

"It's possible that Humfra Graves fell in love with Josslyn," she said after a baiting pause.

"No way!" Malla shouted. "Dead blood, can't love."

The classroom giggled at the popular ballad.

"Malla!" Rotrude chided.

Avina raised her hand. "Is that really why they didn't kill her? He loved her?"

The room hushed.

Rotrude nodded. "That's what's been said. Rumor has it, Humfra wouldn't allow Robert to follow the King's command. In exchange for his loyalty, Robert struck an alliance with Humfra and indebted Graves to Brochet. This was the spark that lit the flame of Echo's Omen. Together, after rescuing the princess and clearing the area of deadbloods, the men experimented. The assumption is that Robert held the key to curing Dread Death in his blood, as his father was the only man on record to ever overcome it. The men experimented on Josslyn in the hopes of curing her. This is thought to be the precursor to all of the Omen's experiments to come. Although no one but those in the Brotherhood itself truly know what goes on there."

Rotrude took a breath.

"But, as I mentioned before, Robert and Humfra were all but forgotten in the midst of the Blood Wars. This gave them the freedom to transform the ruins they discovered into the storied fortress that it is today. It also gave them time to develop an ideology and creed and create a bloodthirsty army. They operated in secret until 3907. That's nearly forty years from when the pair first went searching for Josslyn. By then, the men were old and weathered. Robert had distanced himself from the Omen while Humfra and his descendants were absorbed by it."

Lucette meekly lifted her slight hand to eye-level.

"Yes, Lucette?"

"Did they save the princess?" she asked in a small voice.

Rotrude made a pained face. "Not really," she said, to Lucette's forlorn expression. "By the time Graves and Brochet revealed what they had created at Echo's Omen to the other Vanguards, it was too large to be contained. The Kingdom had no choice but to accept their presence as a seventeenth realm. They had built their new realm by carving it from the Cursed Hills, along the edge of Lyonshall and Hunter Post territory." Rotrude took a breath. "Humfra returned to Animus Rock when his father died, after the Blood Wars had concluded, because he held elderclaim and was to become Graves elder. He and Robert were greeted by outrage, indignation, and naturally questions as to what really happened to Josslyn Bellamine so many years ago. At first, Humfra refused to share any information other than that she lived. Eventually, however, he did admit that they were unable to cure her. That fact is recorded from those long-ago council meetings."

"How did she live if they didn't cure her?" Lucette asked. It was more than Rotrude had heard her speak before. Josslyn Bellamine's story must resonate with the girl, she thought sadly.

"That didn't make sense to the Vanguards in 3907 either," Rotrude said. "They pressured both Humfra and Robert for more information, but the men were tight-lipped. All they would say is that they tried everything."

Rose raised her hand. Rotrude nodded to her.

"Then why do they say Graves was in love?"

"Humfra in love with Josslyn, you mean?"

"Yes," Rose said, not blinking, black eyes piercing.

"Because of whom was with him. The Vanguards and high natives alike noticed immediately."

"Who?!" Malla interjected, and Rotrude didn't scold her this time. She was pleased by the excitement. The other children leaned forward in anticipation.

"Humfra was in the company of a man of middle years with black Graves hair and a sharp nose. Oddly, the man was suspiciously Bellamine-looking too, with large ears and other distinctive features. Strangest of all, he had eyes and skin unlike anyone had seen. Both were a piercing pale grey, like a morning mist. Naturally, rumors of Humfra's union with Josslyn and her tainted dead blood swirled. Many believe that is why Graves mates with deadbloods and produces mixed offspring."

"Was that his son?" Malla asked.

"Yes," Rotrude nodded. "Humfra's half-dead son was named Harrye, the father of Haulfrun Graves."

THE MOON TRAIL

Ryd pointed. "What are those?"

It was the second such stone the pair passed in nearly three days on the winding dirt road; oblong and taller than it was wide, with green horizontal striations in lines on a backdrop of shiny black. The stone was foreign and conspicuous in the seeded grassland, placed along the side of the path. The polish reflected light and was visible from a great distance away, like the moon in the night sky.

"Guildsmen," Digory grunted while studying the sky ahead. He was trapped in a prison of his own making, riding aside the closest thing to a friend he'd ever had, and he'd killed the man's brother. Guilt filled his lungs with each breath. Grey clouds floated above blue horizon, splitting the sky in two, in opposition as oil and water, rolling out in front of the pair like a carpet. The air was biting.

Ryd patted Mable's flank. "The Guild put them there? What are they?"

"Creed markers."

"Ah," Ryd said. Digory was sure Ryd didn't understand but he fell into silence anyway. The men paced each other on Chester and Mable. Then, Ryd asked, "Why?"

Digory sighed. "What do you mean, why?"

"Why mark creeds?"

"Why do you care?"

Ryd slightly turned to study the stone behind them. "Look at it," he said as he glanced back at Digory. "Have you ever seen something like that? None of the other roads marked the creeds. I wonder what's special about this one."

"I thought you didn't care about Vanguards."

"The more I see, the harder it is not to ask." Ryd's mind shifted with every day away from Westerviolet as if he was fully coming alive. Now that the Oblivion sickness had subsided, he felt like he was seeing the world for the first time. Dreaming for the first time, too. He wanted to learn everything. He couldn't understand how he'd been so close-minded before.

"Alright," Digory adjusted his weight in his saddle. "I can tell you what I know from..."

"Sybil, right. Tell me," Ryd said, with the eagerness of a child.

"You know the Guild's year?"

Ryd shook his head.

"They don't use the sun. They use the moon."

"The moon? We do too."

"Well, sure, but only in the context of the sun."

"Tell me more."

"There are thirteen moons in a year."

Ryd nodded.

"Well, there are nearly 19 sun years for each moon year."

"Sun years?"

"It takes nearly 19 sun years for the moon to make one full cycle," Digory said, bouncing slightly atop his steed. "That's the Guild's year. It's why Vanguards are traditionally deigned elderclaim at that age. Sybil explained it once to me after she learned of it at Upper."

Ryd stared back blankly.

Digory's patience was thin. He'd spent the last several hours replaying the scene from Pinewood in his mind. It made him volatile. "What don't you understand?"

Ryd sighed. "I don't know what a cycle is. I..." he paused, feeling the dolt, as he did a lot of the time in Digory's presence. "I don't know what of any of it is."

Digory glanced at Ryd and softened. "It's confusing," he offered. Ryd nodded. "The Moon Trail was built by the Guild in ancient times."

"Why?"

Digory didn't really know why because no one really knew why. There were some legends that claimed it was used as path for pilgrimage, while others suggested it had something to do with early Guildsmen training. Regardless, it's initial purpose was cloaked in mystery and largely lost to time. All anyone knew was that it led from Animus Rock to Wraithswail and it was eighteen creeds long.

"There are exactly eighteen of these markers along the trail," Digory replied. "The last part is Wraithswail, herself."

"Nearly 19?" Ryd pinched his blonde brow. "Like the Moon year?"

"Exactly."

"That's why it's called Moon Trail?" Digory nodded. "Why though? Look, it doesn't even go in a straight line. It makes no sense." Ryd pointed ahead of them at the snaking path across flat grassland.

Digory shrugged. "Only Guildsmen know."

"Why?"

Digory shrugged again and didn't respond.

They continued in silence for quite a while. A crisp, metallic wind came from the west and met the men square on. Gusts lapped at their cloaks and manes of the horses. Reflexive watery tears pooled in the corners of their eyes.

Ryd turned to Digory again, wiping the wind from his face. "What's it like being a Guardsman?"

"What now?"

"You once said something about passing the time." He gestured ahead of him at a flat land of nothing—just seeded grass. "We have time to pass."

Digory sighed. "Alright."

"What's it like?"

Digory shifted his weight in the saddle. "It's life."

Ryd nodded.

"It's all I've known."

"Right," Ryd sighed, tired of Digory's walls. "You can just say you don't want to tell me." He shifted his weight to face forward again.

"I mean it," Digory turned in uncharacteristic sincerity. "Brochet is my life."

Ryd studied the man's hard expression. "What of your kin?"

Digory appeared to examine the landscape ahead but was in another place in his mind. Hearing the boy's screams. "You know the law."

"Sure," Ryd said. "That's why I ask."

"Speak plainly," Digory growled.

"I thought it was obvious."

"Well, out with it."

"You're a Guardsman so your father must have been one," Ryd said, like the sky is blue. He was met with silence. "Am I wrong?"

Digory didn't look at him. "You have me all figured out."

Ryd was surprised. "Your father wasn't a Guardsman?" All Guardsmen were to be descendants of one. It was Westerviolet law. Silence. "An uncle?" More silence. "How are you one, then?"

Pushed to break, Digory snapped his head towards Ryd. His red eyes flashed. "Why are you Stablemaster?"

"Because my father was before me."

"Wrong," Digory said quickly.

"What? No, but I…"

"You're wrong."

Ryd was confused. "What are you talking about?"

Digory shook his head and half smiled. "You really don't realize, do you?"

"Digory, what are you talking about?"

Digory spoke with cruel cadence. "You are Stablemaster because of Brochet. You exist because of Brochet. Everything that you have ever been and ever will be you owe to Brochet."

Ryd was struck. "My father taught us everything," he cried. "He was a smart, and good, and… and… an honourable man! How can you say I owe anything to the Lord?"

Digory shook his head. *He doesn't get it*, he thought.

"Tomas hunted my grandfather and tore my father from his care. I owe the Lord nothing." Ryd spat.

"I don't just mean Tomas," Digory said.

"Digory, what are you…"

He interrupted again. "Is there not a brand in the flesh on your hip?"

"That's not... that's not..." Ryd stuttered, completely caught off guard, fully insulted, when Digory interrupted a third time.

"Brochet owns you."

The words stunned Ryd and his inquest instantly ceased. He'd never considered it quite that way before. The men rode in silence again as Ryd frowned in pensive contemplation. Digory was hollowly pleased. Moments dragged together. Horses neighed or whinnied every so often. Neither man spoke.

The sun made an arch low across the sky beneath grey clouds. The wind increased, slightly at first, then with exponential intensity. It was not whipping or constant, rather, came in breath-taking, face-slapping gusts. Each burst forced the men to lower their heads and squint their eyes. Digory didn't mind because it gave him something other than Ryd's incessant questions to focus on. Progress slowed considerably.

Ryd finally broke the hours-long lull with a crack in his voice. "He made me promise."

"Hm?" Digory turned to him, snapped out of his own private thoughts. He'd gone to a place he frequented often, deep within his inner mind. He imagined he was holding Sybil, warm in a bed they shared together.

"He made me promise to protect him."

Digory frowned, image of Sybil's warm skin wrenched from his grasp. "What are you talking about?" He angrily turned to Ryd. "Who are you talking about?"

Ryd was distraught. "It was the last thing he said to me." He squinted and rubbed his face. Despite the gesture, his eyes obviously teared.

"Your father?"

"He made me promise," Ryd said softly, mostly to himself, "and he's gone." His voice broke and he hung his head. The silence had clearly weighed heavily on him. He looked like he was drowning in sorrow.

"Who?"

Angrily Ryd turned to Digory. "You never were going to help me find him, were you?" His almond eyes burned with tears.

"Wait." Digory's heart dropped into his stomach when he realized Ryd meant the stable boy. The shaky calm he'd cultivated for himself in the past hours was gone. "No... I..."

"Admit it," Ryd interrupted. "Admit that you used me. This was never about Col."

Hearing the name pricked Digory like a needle. "Ryd, no," he tried to explain without knowing what he would say, "that's not..."

"Admit it!" Ryd shouted at him.

"Ryd..." Digory turned his fully body to face his companion atop the saddle, but he wasn't listening.

"I failed him."

"You didn't fail him," Digory tried to comfort Ryd, although the sentiment was foreign. He'd never comforted anyone in his life. He'd never had a friend in his life. Sure, there were some of the better Guardsmen, like Gawen and Cador, who were easy to share mead with and sit by a fire. And Sybil had always been, in one way or another, a companion to him. But to have someone he truly cared for, and truly cared for him, was beyond anything he had ever anticipated. It got him thinking about why that was. "You've..."

"I did," Ryd interrupted. He looked to the curve in the path ahead with slumped shoulders. A blast of icy wind hit them hard.

"I don't have a father," Digory interjected.

"What?" Ryd was shaken from his self-pitying rut. "You don't? How?"

Digory stared forward, eyes narrowing into burning slits. "You asked about my father," he glanced at Ryd, then back straight ahead, "I don't have one."

Ryd smirked, thinking it was a joke. Digory glared at him. "What?" Ryd defended his own reaction. "Everyone has a father."

"I don't."

"A mother then?" Ryd asked, but Digory only shrugged.

"What then? You just appeared? Fell straight down from the Eighth Tower as a babe, is that it? Or rather, knowing you, you crawled up from the First."

"Funny," Digory said and turned to face ahead. He was just trying to make the ungrateful dolt feel better and did not deserve his disrespect. "Forget it."

"Tell me."

"Tell you what?"

"You can't say something like that and not explain."

Digory sighed. "It's not as interesting as it sounds." Ryd studied him. Digory's striking face was sallow. His expression, pained. Ryd had never seen this side of him before. "Farrah," Digory finally said. The name was obviously difficult for him to speak.

Ryd obviously knew of the infamous lost Vanguard lady. Everyone in Westerviolet did. Why, there was a whole holiday throughout the realm dedicated to her memory. "Lady Farrah?" he repeated.

"She found me," Digory told him.

"Found you?"

"In a basket in the Vanguard garden," he explained. "My mother abandoned me there. I was unapproved."

"I've only heard stories about her," Ryd admitted, reminiscing the legendary beauty with a heart of gemstones. She was a saint in Westerviolet for her kindness, known particularly for her affection for native children. Every year on the day celebrating her, each child was given a candied lemon in her memory—a luxury denied to them normally.

"She died young. Likely before you were born. I hardly remember her."

Ryd's eyes grew wide. "Lady Farrah *raised* you?"

Digory nodded once, sunlight catching on his scraggly beard as he scratched it. He still hadn't trimmed it throughout the whole journey. He was almost starting to like this uncouth Baneswood look and had considered growing it longer. "She saved me," he admitted. "Mothered me as an infant. But like I said, she died when I was young."

73

"How did she die?" Ryd asked. Westerviolet's customs forbade the people from discussing a Vanguard ancestor's death, but Westerviolet felt life a lifetime away on the gusty trail they currently rode.

"Raiders," Digory said. Ryd nodded solemnly. "Tomas hates me," Digory went on. "He was cruel to me as a boy, but didn't harm me, for I had Lady Farrah's protection. He's still cruel to me since I remind him of her, but I believe he has kept me around because of it. I was raised next to Sybil. Later, Tomas made me a Guardsman, to keep an eye on me I think." He exhaled. "And here we are."

A blast of cold wind from the west struck the pair head-on.

"And here we are," Ryd echoed quietly.

Iron grey cloud cover broke. The low dipped sun burned orange and large to the eye in the haze along stretched, flat horizon illuminating scattered wisps of clouds in magenta pink.

"Is that why you love her?"

"Who?"

"Sybil."

"What of her?"

"I just mean...I... I don't know." Digory didn't respond. "You don't have to tell me if you don't want to."

"I know."

Ryd rolled his eyes. "Fine," he said.

Digory scratched his beard. He didn't still respond.

The sun dropped lower and the magenta clouds burned red. At their backs, the sky turned deep purple, blue, and black in the wake of dusk. The dim light from the twilight hour cast an eerie mist-like glow across the land. The wind was unusually calm. It was warmer than before.

"Look at the grass," Ryd finally said.

"Hm," Digory grunted, lost in thought, the few memories he had of Lady Farrah floating around in his mind. Her thick hair, kind smile, and twinkling hazel eyes. The way her cold hands felt on his skin. Her lemon-scented breath on his neck as she held him close. Her sweet, slightly off-key voice as she sang him to sleep.

"The grass," Ryd said emphatically. He pointed at tall blades spinning up out of the ground. From afar, the mutation was indistinguishable, but upon close inspection, each blade grew in a corkscrew straight up. Even the seeds at the end the stems spiralled.

"What about it?"

"Look closely," Ryd urged, and Digory reluctantly squinted. "Did Sybil tell you anything about that?" He shook his head. "What do you think it is?"

"It's grass, Ryd."

"I'm serious."

"So am I."

Ryd frowned. "I didn't know it could do that, did you?" Digory shook his head a second time. "Why did the wind stop?" he asked abruptly, instantly noting the odd stillness of the air compared to the earlier gusts. Digory sighed loudly, about to make Ryd shut up by force if he wouldn't on his own.

"You aren't curious?"

Digory turned to him. "No," he said with finality.

Ryd scanned the horizon cautiously. "And there, look!"

Digory sighed loudly against the back of his throat. "What now?"

Dirt mounds piled high stuck up through the tall grass. Death beetles, insects with round bodies and spindly black legs with twisted feelers atop their brows, scurried in dozens of uniform lines. Just like the grass, the mounds of dirt and bugs' appendages were spiralled too. They were disgusting and a bit terrifying.

"Hm," Digory said.

"That's it? You don't care? It's…it's incredible."

"It's strange, but not amazing."

"Do you hear that?"

"Hear what?"

"That." Ryd looked from side to side. He searched for the source of a low, crunching hum.

"I don't hear anything."

"Why does everything look like that, Digory?"

75

"I've created a defix," Digory sighed to himself.

"What did you say?"

"Nothing," Digory said. "Nothing."

As Ryd scanned for more abnormalities he asked, "How much further?"

"Hm?"

"I said, how much further?" No response. "Where are we?" Nothing. "Hey."

Digory barked like a dog. "What do you want?"

"Forget it," Ryd mirrored the tone.

Digory sighed. "What is it?"

"I said, forget it."

Digory softened again. "You asked how much further?" Ryd nodded. "It's nearly dark," he said under his breath.

"I can see that."

"Quiet, I'm thinking." Digory paused. "It's nearly dark so we should nearly be to Wind Valley."

Ryd's eyes grew wide and Digory knew why. Everyone had heard the tales. Lost caravans, unexplained disappearances. Only Wind Runners made the trip with any regularity, bringing caravans of spices from Graceview, and they were said to be a particularly hardened group of merchants who notoriously didn't speak and only made the trek once a moon, when it was new. It was also a large part of why Graceview spices were so expensive. "Is that why the grass is like that? It must be, right?" Digory shrugged. "What's the truth of this place?" he looked again from side to side. Digory kept eyes forward. The only sunlight now came from the west in a thin, yellow line amidst dark blue and black. "What have you heard?" Ryd pressed.

"To stay away," Digory said. "Those who cross never return. The ones who do are never the same. No one speaks of it, even the wind runners. Especially the wind runners." He squinted. "Why? What have you heard?"

"The same," Ryd said. "Why make a road through it? Is it the only way to Graceview? Or Ironbark? Or to Wraithswail?" Digory shrugged. He wasn't in the mood for this. "The Vanguards don't know more about it?"

"Why do you ask me?"

"You just told me that... You always... Well..." Ryd sighed. "Never mind."

Digory side-eyed him, then chuckled. "I don't know much," he offered. "Rumors mostly." Ryd listened in anticipation. He knew Digory knew something. He always did. "It's what made Hastein Thorne, Hastein Thorne."

"Really?" Ryd was instantly impressed. The infamous philosopher was revered in Westerviolet as a key advisor of Brochet. He was as highly regarded as the Ancestors themselves.

Digory nodded. "That's the story."

"How?"

"Traveling from Graceview to Animus with Omer."

Ryd hadn't heard that name before. "Who's Omer?"

"Omer Thorne."

"Who's he?"

"He was Hastien's only male Thorne cousin," Digory told Ryd. "The last Thorne Guildsman."

"The last one?"

"Well," Digory said, "there hasn't been one since he disappeared."

"Disappeared?"

Digory sighed, scratched his beard, then explained. "The pair left Graceview together. Hastein arrived at Animus Rock alone."

"When was this?"

"Right before the Uprising, I think."

Ryd frowned. It sounded like all the other stories he'd heard about Wind Valley. "What happened to them?"

"Your guess is as good as mine," Digory said.

"Was Hastein Thorne not always..." he trailed off, "Hastein Thorne?"

Digory turned his head and knowingly met Ryd's eyes. "Hard to believe, right?"

"This valley made him that way?"

"Seems so," Digory said, then paused with a glint in his eyes.

"Do you want to know what I think?"

"Yes," Ryd said quickly. He'd obviously been waiting to hear what Digory thought all afternoon and was pleased that he'd finally engaged him.

"I think Hastein made it all up." Ryd made a face. "Go with me on this. I think he killed Omer. I think he started the rumors about this place to scare the others away into never finding the body."

"Why would he do that?" Ryd was aghast. "That's the opposite of his Teachings."

Digory half-smiled and shook his head, having little regard for any kind of creed that dictated how he was meant to live his life. "Or that's what he wants you to think."

"But... but he's the smartest man in the whole Kingdom!" Ryd cried.

"Smart men don't murder?"

"What reason would he have?"

Digory sighed. *What reason wouldn't he have*, Digory thought. "Do you know anything about Thorne?"

"Not really." Digory gave him a sceptical look. "No, you're right. Nothing," Ryd conceded.

Digory began to explain. "There were four Thorne men before the Uprising: Gudrik, Hastein, Ustin, and Omer," he said as horseshoes clopped underfoot. "Gudrik, Hastein and Ustin Thorne were brothers. Omer Thorne was their cousin. Gudrik and Hastein were politically aligned New, as Ustin and Omer were aligned Old, creating a split down Thorne." *The pairs hated each other*, Digory thought, *despite working so closely*, knowing of them because of their visit to Westerviolet long, long ago, when he was just a boy. He remembered observing the strange, tall, green-eyed men nearly come to a duel from behind a tapestry. "Gudrik became elder after the untimely death of his father Miles," he told Ryd. "The four men were close and in practice ruled Graceview as one. The four Thornes, as they were known. They played both sides." Ryd nodded as he listened. Digory continued, adding with knowing inflection, "Until Gudrik Thorne became friends with

Leander."

"Who?"

Digory sighed loudly. He was tired of having to explain every little thing. "I forget that you..." he sighed again. "Never mind. Norland. Leander Norland."

"Oh."

"Leander Norland was wed to their sister Grima," Digory said, realizing that there were many names and it was hard for even he himself, at times, to keep them all straight. "Grima Thorne," he added. Ryd nodded. "Eldest Gudrik Thorne held elderclaim and ran the realm. Hastian Thorne, the second eldest brother, founded the Bank."

"I didn't know that was him."

Digory nodded. "Most give credit to his son."

"Who?"

"Wallace."

"I've heard that name before," Ryd admitted, falling into thought.

"You're right," Digory offered, nearly chuckling.

"Where do I know that name from?" Ryd asked almost rhetorically, searching his memory as he crunched his eyebrows.

"The green-eyed curse back at the Villas."

"Who?"

"The one with Sybil," Digory clarified. "With a man's body and a boy's face. Called himself Thorne. Said he was Wallace's bastard."

Ryd nodded as recognition flooded in. "That's right."

"Gudrik and Hastein had a third, youngest brother named Ustin Thorne," Digory went on. "He was raised at Animus Rock and turned progressive. Voted New. Sat on Council. Even married an *earth*..." Digory caught himself. "I mean native. He and the Lord are friends."

"Lord Tomas?" Ryd asked with wide eyes. Digory nodded and scratched his beard. "You still haven't said," Ryd was unrelenting, "why do you think Hastein Thorne killed his cousin?"

"Sybil told me the story goes that the pair travelled to Animus Rock for emergency Council right before Omer disappeared."

"Emergency?"

"It was right before the Uprising," Digory said, then frowned, flustered he didn't have the full story. "I don't know, but Omer was notoriously New and Hastein was Old."

"Oh."

"Yes," Digory said wearily, knowing Ryd made the same connection he had.

Ryd frowned. "I can't believe Hastian Thorne would do that."

Digory shrugged. "It's either that or this place made one man a god and swallowed the other whole." He gestured around the dim lit valley. "You decide."

"How much further to Graceview?"

"A day, maybe less."

"What's it like?" Ryd asked.

Digory paused and thought about it. He didn't know much. Graceview was mainly known for its coin and spices. Little was known about the natives themselves, apart from the notion that they were extremely xenophobic and preferred to stay in their own realm. Vanguard Thornes, according to Sybil, were opportunistic and manipulative. "I've heard it's an Old realm pretending to be New," he said.

"I can't imagine..." Ryd trailed off. His curiosity was like a flame, small at first but growing with each new piece of information he learned. He couldn't get enough. "What else?"

Digory shrugged. Unlike Ryd, he was growing weary of the Kingdom and her stories. They all started to sound the same to him after a while. Betrayal after betrayal. "I don't know much," he said. "We'll find out soon," he added to end the questioning.

It didn't work.

"Why do they call it 'Wind Valley? There's less wind here than anywhere." He paused. "I don't get it."

Digory needed time with his thoughts. Enough of Ryd's chattering. "We should make camp," he said loudly, ignoring

Ryd's speculation. "The light's nearly through. And I was raised in day."

"Here?"

"Where else?"

"I don't know," Ryd said defensively, "but we don't even know what this place is."

It was dark now with only the memory of light on the western horizon in a slightly lighter black than the rest of the sky. Shimmering stars poked through the evening veil, one by one.

"Will your beasts make it another day without sleep?"

Ryd sighed then conceded, "No, they will not."

"We camp on the path," Digory commanded, reasoning out loud to himself. "We haven't passed another in more than a day's journey. That strange grass should burn the same as the regular kind, likely better. It looks thicker, more like branches than grass," Digory said, pulling Chester to stop. He dismounted.

Ryd was wary. He didn't have a good feeling about this yet dutifully followed Digory's lead and dismounted. He removed dry feed from a saddlebag. The horses ate hungrily.

Meanwhile, Digory used a dagger to hack away large portions of the grass in the darkness. It was thicker and tougher than typical grass and much taller than it appeared from a distance. He took fistfuls of hardened twisted stems and tossed them onto the road. As he handled the odd grass, he noted how similar each stalk was to the truck of a tree, with delicate bark and everything. He slipped a small piece of it into his trouser pocket for later inspection by Hudde. Soon, he'd organized the odd kindling into a neat pile, made a spark, and produced a hearty fire in the middle of the Moon Trail. He was pleased by how well it burned.

The exhausted men ate their rations quickly and silently, huddled near to the crackling flames. The strange grass burned seemingly hotter than typical wood and louder in deafening cracks and pops. At the center was a heart of bright green instead of red, orange, or blue. It gave off a heavy matte white smoke, tinged emerald at the edges. The air filled with an organic, putrid scent.

Digory sniffed.

"I like it," Ryd said. Digory stifled a chuckle. "What?" Ryd frowned.

"You've never," Digory said, then paused. "Well, I guess you haven't," he seemingly answered himself. "Sun rot does not count."

Ryd was lost. "What are you talking about, Digory?"

Digory smirked and raised his eyebrows, then kicked a pebble with his boot. "Nothing," he said.

"It smells nice."

Digory grinned. "I didn't say anything."

Ryd hated when Digory did this. "Will you just tell me?"

Digory turned slowly, shifting his weight so that his shoulders and body faced Ryd. "It smells like a dead body," he said, then paused with a half-grin, "rotting in still water."

Ryd was disgusted. "How do you..." he trailed off, then sighed. "I don't want to know."

Digory turned back to face the unusual flames and smoke. He watched shadows dance on the matte white clouds, glad he'd shut Ryd up, at least for the time being.

On either side of the trail, the corkscrew grass towered over the pair and their fire. The Moon Trail was wide enough for two carts to pass with ease so there was large buffer on either side. Either man could stretch out across the hard-packed dirt and pebbles in any direction apart the one facing the fire and meet no obstruction. The horses, tethered to long ropes tied to a post driven into the ground, rested in the near background. The grass lined thick and high right up to the road in all directions apart from where Digory had just hacked some of it away. It stopped perfectly at the edge of the trail no matter where inspected, as if magically maintained, now illuminated with flames from its brethren on fire.

Without warning, Digory gasped and jumped into a defensive position.

"What is it!?" Ryd gawked, spinning his head, searching for attackers.

"What the curses!? Is this a jest?" Digory looked from Ryd to an empty spot through the flames then back, panicked like an animal caught in a trap.

Ryd shifted upright slowly, instantly alarmed, pressing his palms into the dirt-packed trail to sit up. "W... what's going on? Are you okay?" He studied his companion and was immediately concerned. Digory's red eyes burned and beads of sweat pooled on his brow. His gaze darted. "Digory..." Ryd said, this time with more concern than fear.

Digory's gaze was focused on the empty spot. He spoke to it in confused, trailing bursts. "But... I saw you... There's... no way..."

"Your eyes," Ryd said. He moved to stand. "Digory," he said more forcefully as the man's pupils grew larger and larger until they blocked the red of his iris completely. Quickly, too, his gaze glossed over as he glared at the empty spot through the flames.

"Stay away from me!" Digory bellowed, holding his hands up. "Defix!" he cried, never breaking his eyes from the empty spot, until finally acknowledging Ryd with wrathful fury in a shout. "What the curses did you do to me?!" he cried.

"Me!? Digory..." Ryd pleaded. "Something's not right..."

"That's for cursed sure," Digory interrupted loudly then devolved into a fit of nonsensical chuckling. He looked from side to side like a cornered hare with eyes peeled impossibly wide. He scratched at his beard obsessively with his hand, holding his Guardsman dagger out in front of him with his shaking other. The light shone through the pale green glass like it was reflecting through a stream.

"What the curse is this," he whispered under his breath with a grin, and terror in his eyes. The firelight illuminated the sharp angles of his face with whetted shadows. "I killed you!" he shouted with all the air in his chest at nothing, to Ryd's horrified dismay. "I cursed saw you..." his voice croaked, "curses," he swallowed. "I heard your chest crack, you little bastard. I saw the blood." His voice broke again and Digory pulsed his jaw. "I saw it."

Shocked, fearing for his life and Digory's, Ryd backed away.

Digory's voice buckled again. "What are you..." he paused, inhumanely dilated eyes in a furious stare, unblinking. "How can you be..." Digory trailed off again in shocked wonderment. "Don't look at me like that," he said. "Stop it. I didn't know! I didn't know, okay? I didn't know," he said defensively.

Ryd stared, stunned.

"It wasn't about you!" Digory shouted. It was like he was having a conversation. "Did you think about that?" He paused, as if listening. "No." He paused again, then shook his head furiously. "No, I swear it!" he pleaded at the empty spot. "Never!"

"What do you see?" Ryd tried to break the trance. Digory ignored him. "Who do you see?" Ryd tried again. Nothing.

Instead Digory growled, still at the empty spot, "You know what? Curse you. I'm happy I killed you. Ha!" He fake laughed loudly as he pointed accusingly through the flames with eyes wide.

"Digory, watch out!" Ryd cried as an attacker darted towards him, out of the winding grass. "Raiders!" He launched to hide. Digory turned, now with huge black pupils for eyes. He laughed again, genuine this time.

"Hear that, kid?" Digory turned and said to nothing. "He's crazy."

"Me?!" Ryd exclaimed, wide-eyed in panic, wishing he'd grabbed a weapon, worried for Digory. Digory laughed again, as if drunk. He obviously wasn't being attacked. Ryd poked his head from the grass slowly to investigate.

"Ah!" Ryd shouted and jumped back into the grass again, seeing a skinny raider with a bow and arrow stalking him.

At Ryd's comical actions, caused by nothing Digory could see, Digory burst into a fit of laughter that knocked him to the ground. He rolled in the dirt of the path.

"What is so funny?!"

"You look like a bird!"

"A bird..." Ryd trailed off, eyes wild, drenched in confusion.

His head felt unnaturally heavy. "What the curse are you talking about there is no time for..."

Digory was delirious, wobbling, a fearsome sight amidst white smoke and casted firelight. "Your eyes, you curse! No white!"

Ryd rubbed his brow and yawned. He tried to stand, stumbling out of the grass in tilted vertigo, then he gasped as he realized. "He's not there," Ryd said under his breath. "He's not there," Ryd squinted, and repeated. "He's not there," the young man whispered a third time, realizing exactly what was happening. A poison causing hallucinations. Some kind of toxin in the smoke!

"What are you doing?" Digory turned. "What's he doing?" he asked the shadows of the flames.

"I figured it out!" Ryd shouted. He shut his eyes tight. "Digory, whatever you're seeing. It's not real! It's not there!"

"What? But, the boy is right..." he slurred.

"Who? What boy? Digory, listen to me," Ryd said, eyes clenched tight, mentally reeling yet trying to stay calm. "It's not there! You have to trust me."

Digory moved his hand across the dirt path until it found his familiar dagger, dropped during his fit. He held it up, in front of him at first, then slowly angled to his own neck. "He's right, you know."

"Digory!" Ryd shouted desperately.

"I killed him though, Ryd," he said with a croak. His eyes were teary. "I killed him."

"You've killed a lot of men. I've killed too," Ryd said, then swallowed. "It's okay, I'm sure it was for..."

"It wasn't," Digory interrupted. "I didn't have to. I wanted to." He paused and raised his head to look at Ryd. He was crying now. "I am so sorry."

"Sorry, for what?"

Digory turned back to the spot past the flames. "No," he replied to nothing. "No!" he shouted as if in reply again. Ryd was so confused. Who was he speaking to? Who did he see? "I won't. Can't you see I've changed? I'm different!" He paused and frowned. "Don't say that," Digory whispered. He shook his head. "Don't." He paused for the longest yet, then almost appeared to nod as if in response to the invisible speaker.

He took a deep breath and hung his head with tears in his eyes, then looked up. "You're right, but not if I'm dead," Digory said, as if in spite.

Then, he pushed his dagger forcefully to his own neck.

"Stop!" Ryd screamed, lunging towards him. He tackled Digory. In the chaos he knocked the dagger away.

After the ordeal, they each collapsed to their knees in exhaustion. Ryd felt near tears. He put his hands on Digory's wide shoulders. The man heaved in restrained sobs; eyes locked on the dirt. In pity, Ryd brought Digory close to his chest and they held onto one another, sobbing together in the dimming firelight. The experience was surreal, like a nightmare come alive.

Then, as if snapped awake from dreaming, Digory tore out of the embrace. He stood without a word, walked ten paces away, and sat with his back to Ryd in a thump.

Ryd sighed, then looked warily over his shoulder. "You're not there," he whispered at the visage of the raider he'd killed along Narrow Road, waving at him, smiling menacingly at him, before crumpling into a ball. He fell into a fitful, dreamless sleep.

Ryd woke at first light. He yawned, ready for a fresh day, hazy memories of the past evening flooding in slowly like molasses. He moved leisurely and went to stretch, then craned his head. To his surprise, everything was already packed. Digory was dressed and supped and had already brushed away all evidence there was a fire on the trail. The horses were saddled.

He could understand the man's need to get away from whatever happened last night, as curious as it was. Ryd pondered on this while watching the morning sky. In the east it was periwinkle and lapis blue, streaked with neon pinks and vibrant oranges from the sun peeking through intermittent cloud cover. The west was still cloaked in the blackness of dawn.

From already atop Chester, Digory shouted, "Are you coming?" with a professional bite.

Ryd scrambled to stand. After he relieved himself, quickly, the men were on their journey again.

The light on this crisp clear day was brilliant. The pair rode with beaming rays on their backs. Ahead of them the fluffy white clouds painted in ethereal yellow from the rising sun. It was silent apart from occasional caws from birds or the humming sound Ryd had pointed out earlier, now familiar.

"What is that?" Ryd finally said after the sun was nearly at full height in the sky.

"What is what?"

"That sound."

"I don't know."

Ryd set his jaw and stared ahead. "I couldn't sleep last night…" he paused. "That sound."

"I didn't notice it."

"Hey, Digory."

"What now?"

"What is that?" Ryd pointed ahead. "Is that? Oh no…" he trailed off, in horror.

There was a body in the distance. It lay face-down on the trail, beneath a pool of dried blood, next to an overturned cart of spices, recently burned. It had to be a body, yet it was nearly unrecognizable beneath a squirming layer of spindly bodies, crunching on limbs, systematically devouring it.

ANIMUS ROCK CASTLE

S ybil paced the enormous Animus Rock castle halls in frustration. She had searched for moons and still, found nothing of note.

She never spoke of the forbidden Westerviolet East Tower, or the small handwritten books she discovered within it to anyone. Nor the strange ghost bell she heard ringing so many moons ago. She continually read through the book she'd brought with her to Animus Rock, studying it. It led her to hidden passageways through the castle and rooms that only revealed themselves at dawn or dusk. Most were largely empty and uninteresting, barring a few old paintings or tapestries and weapons stored ceremonially on the walls. Nothing of note.

Only one hidden chamber she found piqued her interest. It required her to spin around three times, then touch a particular stone before the wall shifted open for her magically. When she first entered it, it was in disarray. Furniture strewn about, mirrors smashed and tapestries ripped into ribbons. There were even splashes of blood on the walls. This intrigued her greatly, and she spent time searching it for clues as to what it was and what had occurred within it but came up wanting. Later that moon, she visited the chamber again, and it was in proper order, to the point the mirrors were restored and placed back on the stone walls. She puzzled over this phenomenon, visiting the chamber time and time again, finding it always in different states, until she realized something. It reflected the state of her mind. If she was anxious, distraught or even murderous, so was the chamber. If she was calm, confident or peaceful, it was as well. The small book called it, "The Tempered Hall," but nowhere could she find what it's intended purpose was.

The small book was filled with complicated annotations that she could often barely make out, just adding to its allure. It had no author, nor date that it was written inside or out. It was a mystery completely where all the books came from, but it turned out they were trustworthy. Or, at least this one was. Each time she followed a map, it led her where it said it would, even when she did not see a way forward.

Sybil wished that she had paid more attention to the rest of the books, only vaguely remembering their contents. One had various blessings and another curses. Another still outlined procedures for handling various beasts that she thought were only legend, like the Bellamine griffins. Several others outlined the magical uses for plants that she had never heard of, like oathvine, said to tighten when a lie was spoken nearby. Sybil told herself there was time. She would collect them next she returned to Westerviolet.

She perpetually tried to find the way to the Ninth Tower but was left wanting. It was now cold outside, and she still was not any further towards her new goal.

Although, she was closer to her initial one. Her plans with Hector were underway. In mere days, the results of her manipulation would become clear, and then she would have a path forward. She was just a stone's throw from the Tourmaline Throne.

Sybil formulated a theory as she roamed the reaches of Animus Rock, that the Ninth Tower only revealed itself to the true ruler of the Kingdom. She thought that once she was Queen, the hidden Ninth Tower would surely accept her. Now, she wanted it more than she did before. More than her yearning to know about the forgotten Vanguard powers, potentially harnessing them for herself. More, even, than her yearning for her lost love Rosen that she buried deep in her heart. So deep, she barely felt it anymore.

She had a new dream. She wanted the Ninth Tower. She wanted to go higher than anyone in the Kingdom's memory had gone before.

She intended to make her dream a reality, by any means necessary. Except, she thought to herself, sacrificing her daughter. Sybil would not betray Rose like her own mother had betrayed her.

THE VANGUARD SHIP, SPACE

About 2000 years ago…

Reynold, now the elder of the Graves bloodline, with Junia by his side, addressed the entirety of the Vanguard crew, hullhands and all.

"We are prepared to reveal our research," he said, "finally, after all this time."

A resounding cheer reverberated about the mess hall.

"Tell us Graves!" Xenon Regnard shouted from his bloodline's table. He was an old rival of Reynold's from childhood. He perpetually tried to bait Reynold into a feud, but Reynold's preoccupation with his visions left Xenon wanting.

"My wife and I have dedicated our lives to mapping the future."

"As we are not able to contribute biologically," Junia said with far more poise than she felt, "this is our way to give back to the Mission. To further our causes."

"We are intrigued," Morfit elder Herelius said from his seat. Grunts, nods and "Yes, tell us more!" heralded from the other bloodline tables.

"Though our experimentation," Reynold said carefully, "I have developed a way to view the future. I cannot grasp it, but I have mapped it."

"Fascinating!" someone shouted.

"Unbelievable," grumbled another.

"Graves lies!" said a disembodied third.

"Our notes will be made available in due time," Junia said, lying, but you must believe us. We speak the truth."

"The future I am inextricably linked to, for reasons beyond my comprehension," Reynold added under his breath, "has a healed Earth."

"Healed? Xenon said. "Poppycock! There is no way. The drones report that…"

"The drones only report on the present, Xenon," Junia said pleasantly. We speak of the future."

"Yes, but the date extrapolated from the condition of the planet gives us a likelihood of less than a single percent that it will be hospitable for us in the next ten thousand years. By that time, our ship will be long deteriorated. We, and our descendants, will all die up here."

"I am well aware of bloodline Bellamine's predictions," Reynold said. "As you mentioned, there is a chance. A 0.42% chance at that."

"Yes, but those are ridiculous odds. You're telling me you have somehow discovered how to visit this unlikely future. A future where the planet heals?"

"More than that, old friend," Reynold said, to a grumble from the others of the Graves bloodline, "The Earth is not only healed in this future. The Earth is populated. By us."

An uproar began. Shouts of, "Absurd!" and "Graves lies!"

Then, large-eared Vasyla Bellamine stood. A hush fell over the tempestuous crowd. She was the most brilliant scientist of all, the sister of the captain and daughter of the captain before, Cormac Bellamine.

"He does not lie," she said. "Many of you have heard of our Soul-Travel technology. The walls of this ship have ears." A round of chuckles. "But what you have not heard is that we are all but ready to begin trial testing. Our technology is nearly complete."

Reynold squeezed Junia's hand, hard.

ANIMUS ROCK FOURTH TOWER

Present Day

"How rude," Sybil said quietly, under her breath, to the side, tapping her foot as if she'd been forced to wait to enter a ball. "To stall us."

Monty repressed a smile as he caught a whiff of Sybil's musky, citrus noted breath mixed with the scent of violet oil on her skin when she leaned a bit towards him to speak. Today she was as beautiful and daunting as ever, dressed in a blood-red gown tight to her frame to match her lip stain. "Herman isn't here yet either," he said. "We can't start anyway."

"Still," she said with a side eye, twirling a plait of her hair. It had escaped from her high head style tipped in red gems to match her gown.

"I'm sure she has a good reason," he added, defending his tortured friend. "You just don't know her very well." Sybil frowned, displeased he was siding with Galla. She didn't respond. "Galla is difficult, I admit, but once you know her she is…"

"I don't care to get to know her."

Monty side-eyed Sybil and half smiled.

Meanwhile, the sun passed over the lip of the Council Hall walls, spilling through the legendary glass dome that capped it. Per usual, each Vanguard mural sparkled and shimmered in the climbing light. Atypically, the Council session had not started. Various Vanguards and High Natives alike milled about the expansive space in confusion and frustration. Disgruntled murmurs permeated the hall like chirping evening crickets.

"Where is he!?" King Humphry shouted over the humming din. From the expansive distance across the room, Hector

Graves's icy eyes met the King's red glare. Hector shrugged. "Someone find him!" Humphry shouted again, pouting in a fit, swinging his head around. "Where is my Second? Find him!" he tantrumed, crossing his arms mulishly at his chest, bucking the sleeves of his white-pelt cloak dyed Bellamine burgundy overtop of an intricately embroidered tunic left long. His beady, close-set eyes glared.

The Queen sat aside the King in pure white robes knotted and looped around her neck, as was fashionable in the North. Her shoulders were bare, despite the chill in the hall, and blond curls cascaded down upon them. As typical of those from the North, she was particularly resistant to cold. Per usual, the Queen had an unimpressed expression on her exotic, doll-like face. She rolled her slitted red eyes.

Beneath his blood emblem, Hector watched all in the hall with a razor gaze to match his hawk's, perched on his shoulder. He smiled, enjoying the Kingdom's final moments of naiveite as he waited for the impending theatrics to begin. It was only a matter of time. Behind him, his wife, a ghostly pale woman with mousy hair and dead expression sat. Millie Busk. She sipped from an iron goblet and studied the floor.

Meanwhile, Rupert Morfit leaned into the group he sat huddled with beneath the Regnard emblem, speaking in quiet confidence, halfway across the chamber from Hector. He sat with his legs wide, elbows resting on each. His twin blades flashed from his hips with his every movement.

"How many?" he asked Ogo Regnard.

"Nearly half," Ogo replied in hush. He'd arrived at Animus the day before, greeted by endless whispers, followed by rumors of Lyonshall's fall.

"Provisions?" Rupert asked next.

"Six moons, maybe less," Ogo replied. Ogo Regnard's flaxen hair was to his ears, combed back. He sat with a straight back wearing silver armor emblazoned with a rose underneath a burgundy red cloak. He chewed on a fingernail.

Rupert frowned, already knowing the truth, needing Ogo to admit it outright. "There should have been more."

"There was more," Ogo said quickly.

"How?" Ogo's son, Gachan Regnard, asked. "Where are they now?"

Ogo sighed. He was not ready to face his sins. Not at all. In the prominent overhead daylight, his normally handsome and striking features inherited from his Thorne mother made him look old. He rubbed his eye with his finger wearily. The shimmering Regnard bear bore its fearsome teeth and claws in the mural behind him. "Burned," Ogo he finally said in a sigh, unable to meet Gachan's eyes. He knew he must own what had been done, but in the bright light of day, his decision hung far heavier on him than he thought it would.

"The rumors are true then."

"Speak plainly son," Ogo commanded, glaring in fear masked with indignation.

"Our blood home is gone," Gachan said hollowly, hoping it wasn't true but knowing it was at his father's expression.

Rupert sat backwards in his chair and crossed his arms in front of himself as Ogo sat forward with intensity. He glared in fury at the younger, yet nearly identical man. The son was a copy of his father, apart from brilliant red eyes.

"Gachan," Ogo growled. "That was no home."

Gachan knew he should have insisted he march with Father. He knew Father and his temper couldn't be trusted. *Lyonshall's loss is on me*, he thought sadly. "Why wouldn't you save it? Once the tyrant was dead, why let it burn? The castle was history," he added seriously, hoping the words pierced like he meant them to. "Ours. And what of the natives, enslaved at no fault of their own?"

Ogo felt a lash of shame. He'd commanded his troops burn everything, including the mines with the natives inside. Not only did he destroy his blood home, but he crippled the entire livelihood of the realm. "Do not question me," he boomed, startling several nearby attendants and high natives in the hall.

Rupert knowingly watched the back and forth between father and son.

"Father, you said it yourself," Gachan went on, "You ruined

Lyonshall, her provisions too." He paused, narrowing his red eyes. "Why?"

"I said…" Ogo began angrily, embarrassed to be questioned by his son in front of a Morfit.

"He has a point," Rupert interjected stoically from his comfortable seat. Ogo was an old, dear friend and that was how Rupert knew he tended to be rash, vindictive, and irrational when wronged.

"I know what I'm doing."

Rupert sat upright. "Do you?"

Ogo looked away.

Then, as everyone was still waiting for Council to begin, a spine-tingling, ear-piercing scream cut the room.

Verity sprinted into the hall, draped gown highlighting her rounding belly, flowing out behind her like blood and bile from a wound. Her face was smeared in painful tears marked by the dripping blackness around her coal-lined eyes. She collapsed into Queen Gracea's outstretched arms.

Gracea stroked Verity's sweat-covered brow. "Shhh, it's alright," she cooed with her heavy Northern accent. Verity shook, clinging to the pale, smaller woman as if she let go, she would drown.

The King stood in astonishment. "What…" he paused, "what is this!?" he yelled over the sobs.

"Herman!" Verity wailed. Queen Gracea rocked her like a child.

At the mention of his brother's name, as if on cue, Hector Graves leapt from his chair. He ran across the hall in long bounds. It was time. His terrifying hawk cawed loudly overhead, gilding to stay at her master's side. Hector towered over Verity in an instant.

"My brother?!" he bellowed.

"He's dead!" she cried.

"What?!" Hector spun. "No," he whispered, eyes narrowed, inwardly rejoicing that all was going according to plan. "It can't be," he said louder. "No!" he shouted and Verity wailed once more. "Are you sure?" he pressed intensely.

Hyperventilating, she nodded again.

In the meantime, all others in the hall gathered around. Prihim Minney and Rupert Morfit from opposite sides of the hall pushed their way through endless gawking high natives to stand right by Verity.

Prihim got down on his knees next to the women on the floor. "What has happened?" he shouted earnestly, oozing panic, brown eyes impossibly wide. "Is she with him?" he pled.

From where she watched in the shadows, Sybil chuckled. She almost felt sorry for the man. Almost.

Then, Hector lunged forward with unexpected speed and grabbed Prihim by the arm with long fingers, surely bruising where he gripped him. "Get away from them!" he chided, picking Prihim up as if he was an irritating child and tossed him aside just as easily. Prihim stumbled and tripped and slid across the floor.

"No!" Prihim objected, crumpled in defeat. "Is she with him?" he asked again, scooting across the floor, wildly worried about his love, heart in his stomach, refusing to think the worst. Galla hadn't returned in almost a fortnight. Today was the last session of fall Council and Galla wouldn't miss it. She lived for Council. She lived for her duty. "Do you know what happened to her Verity?"

Verity looked towards Prihim in confusion, as if snapped from a dream. She turned her tear-stained face towards him. "Who?"

"Galla!"

At his outburst, Hector laughed loudly, thinking to himself how well the Minney man played his intended role. Then, still smiling wide, he gestured around with open palm hands, addressing the crowd ostentatiously.

"Don't you see through his game?" he asked loudly, gesturing to Prihim. "Do you really think he doesn't know where his woman is?" he asked again, casting a spell over the onlookers with his words. "It's misdirection!"

The hall filled with whispers and gasps. Several High Natives nodded and murmured amongst themselves in agreement with

Hector. Others put their hands to their mouths or deeply frowned.

Prihim held up his hands. "No," he shook his balding head at storming looks and brooding scowls. "I... I... I haven't been able to find her. I... I think something's wrong. Has anyone else seen her?" he asked pitifully, looking around at the hovering crowd of onlookers in fine robes and jewel-tone gowns. "I'm worried!"

Concerned, Rupert took a step forward, glancing back and forth between Hector's svelte frame and the crumpled, defeated Prihim. He had not seen his sister either. He'd assumed she was still cross and was avoiding him, until now.

"Herman!" Verity wailed into Gracea's breast. Her heavy black makeup stained the Queen's gown with dark smudges across the chest, but the queen didn't seem to notice. Instead Gracea rocked and held the crazed Verity gently, humming a foreign tune into her hear to calm her, as Hector pontificated on.

"Look at his eyes shift," Hector said accusingly as he stormed closer to where Prihim lay. He pointed at him dramatically. Many high natives nodded knowingly. "He lies!" Hector shouted at Prihim. "What have you and the *bare* done to my brother?"

"Hector!" Rupert warned in defence of his twin. The crowd all around mumbled in growing discontent and agreement. The sun had climbed high and already the shadow on the floor approached the next mark. The whole hall was filled with light.

"Hey, wait," Prihim said while scooting backwards, kicking his heels against the floor as most in the room instinctually inched towards him, crowding around him. Monty stepped back with arms crossed then glanced to Sybil at his side, biting her lip with dark eyes on the unfolding scene, engrossed and unblinking. She didn't seem surprised. This was suspicious, Monty thought. As if she had expected this. And was enjoying it.

"Herman, Herman!" Verity wailed over and over.

"Shhh," Gracea hushed as she rocked her.

"Stop cursed crying," Humphry said angrily from his perch. She didn't. "Stop it! Stop it stop it stop it!" the King fumed, brown face turning red, shouting in unbridled emotion. He couldn't stand to see his big sister cry. In a dramatic display he spun and flipped over a chair. It crashed to the hard floor and splintered in every direction, causing many High Natives to squeal and scatter, colourful robes flashing like beetles caught in the light.

Rupert watched the unfolding scene with analytical round eyes and was disturbed at best. The way that Hector swooped in and spun everyone up in his web so easily made Rupert think the whole thing was choreographed. "Tell us what happened," Rupert stoically commanded Verity, trying to get to the bottom of the mystery.

"He... he... he..." she gasped over and over.

Humphry had already lost what little patience he had. It was disconcerting for him to see his normally strong sister in such a state. "VERITY!" Humphry bellowed at her. An unexpected hush washed over the woman at his outburst. She struggled with her breath and sniffled from dripped mucus and tears then, finally, calmed enough to speak.

"So much blood," she whispered into Gracea's breast, then turned her head. "He... he..." she started, then paused, failing to find words to describe something so horrible. She still didn't believe it was true and wondered when she would wake from this nightmare. She unconsciously clutched her belly, thinking of the babe yet to be born, without a father. "I don't know how to say it," she added solemnly as she met tear-filled eyes with her brother. At his reaction, and the bated breath of the rest in the hall, Verity knew she must respond. She swallowed hard.

"He tore off his own face," Verity told them.

The hall collectively gasped.

"How can that be?" Ogo interjected. He stepped forward, biting on his thumb nail out of habit.

"Cuthbert," Hector spun and shouted.

'Aye," the old man replied with a bark. Only he still sat, reclined with feet up under Norland's aubergine-tiled emblem.

"Is Alain at the Rock?"

"Aye," the old man barked again, then fell into a fit of hacking.

"Hector, what are you..." Ogo started, trying to take command, but Hector held up his hand.

"I will oversee the investigation," Hector replied to Ogo cooly. "You are in line for a Magistrate hearing. Your involvement would not be proper."

Ogo was struck by the insult. He took another step forward to confront Hector, glancing upwards at the slightly taller man. "We have not disc..."

"It is my blood," Hector interrupted in monotone, as if speaking to an earthblood slave. "That wasn't a question," he added with a coyly raised brow and the slightest hint of a smile. Hector could feel his insult slicing the man's poise like a knife. This pleased him greatly.

Caught off guard, not wanting to insult Graves in front of the whole Kingdom, Ogo took a step back and frowned. He bit his cuticle bloody but didn't respond. He felt as if they were back at Lower Academy. Nothing had changed since then.

Hector cooly turned back to Cuthbert Norland. "Alain will do," he told the fat man.

Cuthbert scrunched his face. "As First Warman he shouldn't..." he began to protest but was interrupted loudly.

"Cuthbert!" Hector bellowed, shocking everyone to jump just like when his hawk cawed loudly. "Alain to investigate. That is command." Hector's grey gaze was like ice spears, as cool as the weather outside. Cuthbert obediently lowered his head, blinking in agreement despite his misgivings at sending such a high-ranking officer, much less a Vanguard, out on such a task.

The rest in the hall continued to murmur, this time about Hector's role. Hector sensed this and put an end to it quickly. Without his brother in the way it would be simple. "As I'm sure his Eminence himself would have commanded," he looked at Humphry for confirmation. "Truth?"

"Just fix it!" Humphry shouted, at the brink of tears himself.

He stormed out of the hall in a rush followed by an avalanche of attendants.

The Fourth Tower was in an uproar. It was chaos. Natives and Vanguards alike gossiped loudly back and forth, speculating wildly over what just occurred. Amidst the commotion, Hector turned to Verity, looking down at her over his sharply manicured, salt and pepper beard.

"Where is the body?" he asked her pointedly.

At that, Verity wailed again, burrowing her face deeper in Queen Gracea's chest. Between the coal from Verity's eyes and the oil from her hair, the Queen's gown was completely ruined. The jewels in Verity's earlobes crashed together as she shuttered and sobbed. Hector rolled his eyes. "Woman!" he shouted theatrically, "Where?!"

"B... b... bedchamber," she said quietly, tears still streaming, whole face smeared black from her eyes. "Graveshold," she added in a breathy whisper.

Wordlessly, Hector snapped in Cuthbert's direction. His hawk screeched.

"Yes, my Lord," Cuthbert nodded, chins jiggling. "I'll send him," he added quickly and sat upright in his seat as best as his belly would allow, "Right away."

"We will discover the villain," Hector said with bolstered sincerity to Verity as he turned back to look at her. "I swear it." High Natives and various Vanguards around the hall nodded. At the same moment, his amber-feathered hawk again cried out in a screech from his shoulder, as if in agreement, to a few gasps in the hall. *Good girl*, Hector thought.

"Thank you, Hector," Verity genuinely replied. "Thank you," she whispered in a sob to Gracea's chest. The Nomad Queen had stayed still and calm, comforting the panicked woman with unbelievable poise. Gracea still hummed a foreign lullaby that reminded her of home in Verity's ear to calm her. It seemed to sooth the woman considerably.

As the commotion dwindled and several onlookers moved to rest against the tiled walls or sat back down to witness the fallout of Verity's horrific sadness, the hall was met with another jarring interruption.

"Help!" a higher-pitched cry came from the opposite end of the hall. "Someone, anyone!!!" the panicked shouts wailed, "HELP HER!"

Heads turned in confusion.

"Over here!" Aftea Regnard screamed, flailing fleshy arms at the others. "Help! Help! Millie! No!" She shrieked. "Stop! No!" Aftea waved her arms in helpless panic. She was the first to notice what was going on.

Soon, the whole hall turned to investigate.

Mouths gaped open as Millie Busk's thin body bucked and seize underneath her high-neck, long sleeve modest brown gown and cloak, convulsing at the foot of her chair. Sunlight poured into the hall casting dancing sparkles over her, reflected from the Gravesblood skull emblem behind her. Healed wounds, bruises, and welts were obvious across her body as her robes shifted during the fit, but Millie's old scars paled in comparison to her latest.

The juxtaposition of beautiful glinting light against the disgusting scene made the reveal that much more terrible.

Shockingly, to the witnesses' horror, all the flesh around her sunken eyes had been picked away. The skin around her mouth, lips, and cheeks too was tattered or missing. Red sinewy muscle fibres of her face and porcelain white jawbone were exposed. Her tongue flopped out of the side of her cheek through her teeth like a large worm. The woman was unrecognizable. As she convulsed Millie clamped down hard, biting her tongue in two, gushing a torrent of blood as the severed piece flopped on the floor. She lay amidst a river of gore. Her hands, especially her fingertips, were stained red to match Sybil's gown.

Sybil's hand jumped to her mouth to hide a smile from where she observed amidst the concerned crowd. She watched Millie twitch in death on the floor. She'd never seen someone die from mad honey before.

How fascinating, she thought.

"In the commotion, no one saw her," Faye said then paused, eyes shiny. "No one noticed her." She adjusted her draped black garment with long sleeves and a high neck, traditional mourning attire. Red boots peeped from beneath with each step leaving dainty footsteps in the sand. "She died alone," the wilted woman added with a crack.

"When will they announce, do you think?"

Faye's green gaze glassed over. "Tomorrow probably," she said quietly.

Sybil leaned in, pulling her black shawl tighter as she paced through Eden's garden aside Faye. The Kingdom was shaken in the wake of Herman's death. The final Council session had been suspended until the mourning period was over, giving Sybil an exorbitant amount of free time. Today, her and Faye were on a causal stroll through Eden before she collected Rose from Academy. Although other Vanguards tended to send natives for their children, Sybil preferred to do it herself. "How is Aftea?" Sybil asked her with mock-concern.

Sybil wore a black, low-cut gown underneath her black veil-like mourning shawl. Her gown flowed down her body, pooling behind her gait like a river of tar. Her hair was loose in a knot low at the base of her head, stuck with pins tipped in black diamonds. Hanging between the youthful crease of her breast, per usual, was Sybil's green-gem emblem pendant, catching the bright early afternoon sunlight in luxuriant glistens. As customary, red firefang leather boots peeped underneath her garments as she strolled.

"It's so sad." Faye's eyes focused on the path ahead. A scorpion scurried to escape them, as if the pair was chasing it knowingly. Faye watched the spindly body wriggle across the sand. "She died alone," she said.

"Dear," Sybil spoke softly with shrill undertone. "You sully the memory of Millie's life with the stain of her demise."

Faye balked. "Life? What life for is there a defix's wife?"

"Oh now, Faye."

"Don't act like you didn't see her scars."

"None of our business," Sybil replied sweetly. "Besides," she added, eyes flashing like black mirrors, "she was no one."

"Sybil!" Faye exclaimed, horrified anyone could say such a thing. Faye was born and raised at Animus, away from the Regnard blood traditions, and held all life in high regard.

"You didn't let me finish," Sybil added quickly, taking Faye's soft arm under hers. "She was no one to us," she added, but Faye still huffed. Noticing her reaction, Sybil tried to recover. "I mean to say she was no friend of yours nor mine." She paused. "Do you deny it?"

Faye looked as if she was going to argue, then sighed. "I always meant to speak to her," she conceded. "To invite her to walk with us," she added sadly.

"But," Sybil said, pleased she'd manipulated the poor woman so easily, "you didn't." Faye stopped pacing. Her silence was sombre. Sybil walked behind her wilted friend then wrapped her thin, pale arms around her. She rested her head on Faye's shoulder. "We care for the friends that we do have," Sybil whispered into her ear, then asked again, "How is Aftea?" to distract her.

Faye took a deep breath and with feigned cheer said, "Good, I think."

"I know you better than that."

"You're right, it's terrible," Faye admitted, glancing to Sybil quickly. "She's doing terribly."

"Oh no," Sybil whispered as if she was concerned. "That bad?"

"She thinks it's her fault and I've tried to tell her, if it's her fault it's all of ours, too," Faye said. "We were all right there and no one else noticed her either." She felt horribly guilty she'd not done anything herself to stop it. "She died alone," Faye said quietly. "Poor Millie."

"Faye," Sybil said with a commanding bite. "Do not forget she lived alone too."

Faye spun her head, half-weepy, half-indignant. "What did

you say?"

Realizing she'd nearly been too forthcoming about her true nature, Sybil waved her hand. "Forget it, forget it," she said dismissively, irritated fully at Faye's weakness and impracticality. "Forget about her Faye. She's gone."

"Why are you being so cold?" she asked with a frown.

Sybil's jaw flexed. She took a breath. "I chose the wrong words…" she trailed of, internally sneering, "in my sadness," she finally added. "I mean to say there's no helping her now."

"How do you mean?"

"I don't believe in wasting grief on the dead."

Faye crossed her arms; shawl wrapped around her elbows. "What, then?"

"I say we should mourn the living."

The words hung in the air as the women paced through this portion of Eden's maze. A series of plump Rock birds, greyish-brown fowl like looked very much like rocks, why they got their name, wandered out of a spiky bush, squawking as they pecked at the sand, the only sound apart from the women's footfalls.

Then, unexpectedly, Sybil chuckled with contagious warmth and leaned towards Faye. "Forgive me," she said, smiling wide. "I am so poor at knowing what to say." She offered her hand.

Faye easily relented and matched the grin, accepting the sentiment. "You are so strange, Sybil," she said, almost in awe of her. "The best part is," she added offhandedly, "no one would think it to look at you."

You have no idea, Sybil thought as she adjusted a pin in her hair.

"It is murder, you know," Faye lowered her voice to a breathy whisper. "The same culprit, both."

"Hard to say," Sybil replied, bored already. She was tired of the Kingdom's incessant speculation over Herman and Millie's deaths. It had not yet been a moon and already there was gossip swirling that the deed was done by every single bloodline in the realm. Each day, a new Vanguard or High Native accused in the streets. *No one knows a thing*, she thought.

"No, no," Faye said excitedly, loving women's speak,

particularly when she was the one to spread the news. "It wasn't a question. I wasn't asking you, Sybil. I am telling you."

This caught her attention. "What is?" Sybil asked quickly, spinning her head. With the movement she lost a gem from her hair, deep into a bank of sand. She glanced to the spot wistfully for an instant, then back to Faye. Gemstones could be replaced, she thought. This could not wait.

Faye lowered her tone even more. "Herman and Millie were both poisoned," she said in a hush.

Sybil frowned. *Did Faye know? Nonsense,* she assured herself quickly. "I don't understand," she said.

"The poison was not intended for Millie but meant for Hector instead!"

"Faye!" Sybil gasped predictably, instantly relieved. "Could it be true?" She leaned in. "I hadn't considered…" she trailed off. "Are we sure the poison matches both deaths?" Faye nodded slowly. "Results from Alain's investigation already?" Faye continued to nod. "Really?"

"In truth," Faye confirmed, proud to hold Sybil's interest.

"We're not supposed to know until the…" Sybil widened her eyes, playing her part beautifully. "How does Rupert know?" Faye shook her head. "Faye," Sybil prodded knowingly.

Faye quickly caved. "Oh, he made me promise, Sybil."

Sybil smiled. "Don't worry," she said sweetly. "You know I won't say anything," she lied. "We're friends," she added, wanting to gag inwardly.

Faye again returned the smile then lowered her voice in confidence. The women leaned toward each other, as most tend to do during women's speak. "My brother," she said softly.

"Gachan?"

Faye nodded. "Friends with Alain," she said, "from time spent on the Dead Line."

"I see," Sybil replied, genuinely surprised, not realizing Alain Norland was in any way allied with the New. She pulled her shawl tighter. "I didn't know."

"They don't publicize their alliance, but Gachan assures

they're close," Faye told her.

Interesting, Sybil thought. "What has he found?" she asked.

"As Verity described."

"Just like Millie?"

"Worse," she said. "Flesh from Herman's throat and neck gone, too." Sybil's hand leapt to her mouth to hide a smile. "Awful, I know, but you asked."

"Who could have done such a thing?" Sybil asked in feigned horror. She enjoyed this game greatly.

"That's the scandal," Faye said excitedly, stopping her pace. She met Sybil's glare.

Sybil stopped too. "Tell me," she commanded.

"It stems from the poison."

"They know the type already?"

"Turns out, by chance," Faye told her. "Alain is familiar."

"Really?" Sybil said, hoping she sounded genuinely surprised. "What poison makes you tear away your own face?"

"He's investigated it already in the small villages along the Bones. Some kind of new drug," Faye said.

"Earthblood take that..." Sybil said, then paused, "...for fun? Why?"

"Rupert says the..." Faye paused in search of a word, "*reaction* only happens if you take too much."

"So, what is it then?"

"That's the thing," Faye began. "You must not say anything, Sybil, until they know for sure, but, well, it doesn't look good. If Rupert knew that I told you he wou..."

"My dear," Sybil interrupted sweetly, white teeth flashing like a ruby fox's amongst hens. "You have nothing to fear. We are friends. You can trust me."

"Thank you, Sybil. You are too kind to me. Such a dear friend."

Sybil tried her hardest not to roll her eyes. "So?"

Faye took a step toward Sybil and glanced from side to side, ensuring they were completely alone on the path before she spoke. The cluster of small rock birds followed far behind him, squawking every so often in the background. "Mad honey," she finally said with a twinkle in her eye.

Sybil chuckled. "You must be in jest," she said in mock disbelief, feeling a pang of adrenaline. The plan really was working. Part of her could hardly believe it, while part of her was knowingly smug. "You're not?"

"I'm not Sybil," Faye said excitedly, "it's true."

"That can't be. Why, it's all gone! A tale from history, nothing more."

"It's not," Faye shook her head adamantly. "It's back. It's even here, at Animus."

Sybil pulled her shawl tighter. "That's awful. Terrible," she added hollowly. Faye nodded in agreement. "Who is polluting our Kingdom? That's what I want to know."

"Sybil. It's Littlebell," she said in an even lower breath of a whisper.

"Minney?" she asked, trying her hardest not to smile. "Why would..."

"Prihim," Faye interrupted. "It has to be Prihim."

"But, I don't understand," Sybil furrowed her brow again, deeply pleased internally. "Why?"

"You must swear not to say anything."

"Faye, just tell me."

"Rupert thinks it was really Galla."

"What?!" Sybil whispered in a gasp, pulling her black shawl tight to her chest. *Everything is going so well, almost too well,* she thought happily.

"She's been missing," Faye said. "She disappeared after a fight at Graveshold with Rupert and Herman, saying that she deserved more."

"Oh my."

"It's far-fetched I know," Faye began defensively, thinking the accusations ridiculous, yet she was swayed by the evidence. Prihim and Galla had too much to gain from Herman's demise. "Gachan thinks they want the Second chair for themselves," she said. "The woman is fanatical," she added. "You were so right about her, Sybil. So right about her if this is true. And, it must be true. Prihim wouldn't have done it alone. He never does anything alone."

"How are you so sure?" Sybil wanted to see just how strong this story was. "I can maybe understand why Galla would murder Herman, if they wanted his seat next to the King for Prihim. But, why harm innocent Millie?"

Faye bristled with excitement. She loved to be the first to break a story. "It was meant for Hector," she told Sybil pointedly. "It is as I told you!"

Sybil half smiled and side-eyed Faye, then glanced down and kicked a bit of sand with her red boot. "You say that like you're so sure."

"Rupert thinks so."

Sybil pulled at her shawl, picking at a seam between her pointer finger and thumb. "Let's see what the investigation finds."

Faye was a bit taken aback. "You don't think it was Prihim?" Sybil was so smart. If Sybil didn't agree she may have to rethink the theory, Faye thought. Sybil shrugged. "Oh please," Faye prodded. "I know you can connect the stars as I can."

"I'm trying to be fair," Sybil said. "To wait for evidence." Faye stared knowingly at her. "It was probably him," Sybil conceded with a warm grin.

"Thank you!" Faye cheered.

The women giggled together.

Frost lapped at his warm breath. Dark clouds wrapped the sky and shone like a translucent gemstone; sparkling with long, shimmery parallel ripples that blended perfectly with the dark stone Animus Rock Towers.

Prihim internalized the last sky he would ever see. He was only outside for a short while in route to the First Tower, but he did his best to soak that moment up for an eternity in his memory.

Two hulking men in dark armor stood at each of Prihim's shoulders. Hateful boos and taunts echoed from the indignant crowd at their backs. A furious chant of "Herman! Herman! Avenge Herman!" erupted and faded behind them before disappearing with the clank of heavy doors.

Prihim studied his captors after entering the First Tower, heart thumping in his chest, cool stone beneath his feet bare feet.

The men's forearms bulged and their shoulders were like boulders. Their necks were so wide that they disappeared completely. Their chins and heads were clean-shaven. Each man's face had largely distorted brows and sharply cleft chins. Each man's skin shade varied from the other, one was olive-toned and the other red, and each had dim, bloodshot eyes. Both had a device sewn into the flesh where their head met their spine. One was healing with a thick, white scar at the outline. The other oozed infection in green and yellow puss. Both men smelled terrible.

Hearing the dwindling hateful boos and cries behind him, Prihim hung his head. His hands were bound behind him. He was nude. He'd never felt so defeated and alone. How could everyone hate him so? He'd not done anything. He'd never imagined this could come to pass, he thought as he studied the welts on his wrists and across the rest of his body. All he wanted was to find his love, Galla.

The Warmen dragged him down countless dim-lit corridors as they descended deeper and deeper into the First. Cries for water, angry shouts and inhuman screeching curled all around him.

Once in the stale, musty, unlit belly of the tower, they tossed Prihim Minney in a cold, windowless cell.

Then, an iron gate clanked with chilling finality behind him.

BLACKWOOD FOREST

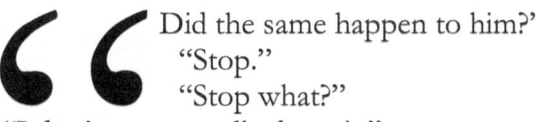

"Did the same happen to him?"

"Stop."

"Stop what?"

"I don't want to talk about it."

"It had to be that," Ryd said under his breath. "What else would make a man..." He trailed off. What were those things eating the body?

Hours back Digory and Ryd had forked off the Moon Trail headed southeast towards Graceview instead of south to Wraithswail. They needed provisions. And this was a faster way to Littlebell. This path was narrower than the last and transitioned to finer, lighter silt and sand instead of hard-packed dirt and pebbles. Digory and Ryd left the spiralled grass behind. Now an arid expanse stretched out ahead. Tufts of rough shrubbery, cacti, and starved trees dotted the landscape. Everything here looked as if it was barely alive.

"I told you I heard something," Ryd said, remembering the crunching sound. "I just didn't think it was..."

"I said," Digory's eyes were locked on the horizon ahead. "I don't want to talk about it."

"What did you see?"

Digory growled like beast about to pounce. "Ryd."

"In the Valley." Ryd spoke like an excited child. "Last night. What did you see?" The men rode in a line. Digory in front. Ryd behind. He craned his body to the side, hoping to catch Digory's prereferral. "Why won't you tell me?"

A black and green snake twice as long as a man slithered in the wake of sand beside them, as if it was eavesdropping on their conversation.

Digory was on autopilot. He couldn't get the stable boy's face out of his head. He felt as if he was reliving the instant the child died over and over. "It's not important," he said. He hadn't spoken more than a few words since they'd left camp and only when pressed by Ryd.

"It seemed pretty important last night."

Digory sighed. He isn't going to shut up, he thought. "Well," Digory half turned backwards, "what did you see?"

"The raider I killed," Ryd said simply. He saw the man's face in his mind's eye. "It's strange to say out loud." Digory silently rolled his eyes, jostling back and forth with Chester's gait. "I can't believe I killed a man," Ryd said, mostly to himself, then was quiet for quite a time. "What did you see?"

Digory moaned. "Enough." He half turned to Ryd, then forward again. "Enough, alright?"

"What's your problem?"

"You don't want to know."

"That bad?" Ryd wondered what could shake his unshakeable companion.

Digory sighed. "I liked you better before."

"Before?"

"You talked less."

Ryd sighed. "Right."

The sky overhead was clear blue with no clouds and the air was stagnant and dry. A V-formation of honking fowl flew above them, headed south. The sun dropped on their right and bright sunbeams beat at their arms and shoulders. They were being hugged by the light.

"Thank you," Digory said unexpectedly.

"Thank who? For what?

Digory glanced backwards what he hoped was sincerely at Ryd. "You saved me." He thought back to the burning Arena. He owed the man his life and that debt was weighing heavily on him. Never before had he been cared for in such a way by another. "Thank you." Ryd blinked several times, stunned. Before he could respond, Digory turned forward in the saddle again. "They need water soon," he added.

As unexpectedly as Digory's warmth had come, it was gone.

"Water?"

"Your beasts."

"Oh." Ryd paused. "They do." He looked around as he rubbed Mable's neck with his wide palm. "Should we worry?"

"No."

"No?"

"We're close." Digory pointed.

Graceview loomed on the horizon.

As if out of nowhere, an overgrown paradise rose up from dry earth. Trees that would tower over the height of the Animus Rock fortress wall stood in precise formation with unusual coal-black bark that shone in the light. Amazingly, the bark appeared to move or flow like tar on the trunks as if dripping down the branches from the leaves. The trees shot straight up until the highest branches snaked out horizontally at premium sunlight. Perfectly round, grey leaves tipped these high snaking branches in multitude. Each leaf had one matte side and one glimmering one.

Rows of the remarkable foliage painted the skyline in grey glitter. It sparkled like a pile of stars.

There was only a hint of the Graceview castle's monstrosity far beyond the odd forest. High above the tree line rose a breath-taking structure completely engulfed in vines and leaves, only visible when one squinted, it was so distant. The traditional castle was apparent underneath the overgrowth, however, only in form. Not one piece of granite or stone could be seen, like the castle was built from the garden herself. The flute vines that covered most of it were thick and pointed with furious black thorns and pale green flowers with tiny spiky petals, said to curse anyone who was pricked by their thorns with hearing music endlessly, to the point it drove them mad. Emerald-dark frilled ivy with palm-size leaves and delicate light blue vines filled the cracks. Various other exotic plants crowded up to the base of the structure and climbed the walls in an arabesque of greens, and yellows, with pops of violet from amethyst flowers with oblong-petaled blooms. It was a breath-taking sight to behold, particularly once one stood at the foot of it.

However, today, Graceview's castle only had two towers visible from Digory and Ryd's distance away. They were heptagonal, with seven sides in total on each. Seven-sided windows dotted the towers at inexplicable intervals as well. At the top were rectangular structures for decoration, long-ago covered with green and black vines. Each tower had a balcony at the highest point that went fully around. Both balconies too, were overgrown.

It looked as if a garden swallowed the castle whole. Ryd studied the horizon with ever-widening eyes. He didn't realize how large Graceview was.

Digory and Ryd pulled their steeds slower when they reached the lip of the trees.

"Oh no, not this again," Ryd groaned, pointing at the oil-black trunks.

Brown fang vines encircled each one, wrapping from the bases upwards, all in the same direction. It doesn't look natural, Ryd thought. Some bark bulged beneath time-pressured squeeze of the vines, as if suffocating beneath their grip.

"What are you talking about?" Digory said, trotting brazenly into the shimmering forest canopy. It didn't matter what he was about to face. His inner storm was battle enough.

"It looks like the grass, Digory," Ryd said warily, heeling Mable to trot. He hurried to Digory's side, then glanced at his companion.

Digory scoffed. "That's different."

"How?"

Digory shrugged. He couldn't think about it. "Vines do that," he said.

Ryd frowned. "I still don't like it," he said as they slowly entered the cool shade. "Look," Ryd pointed again.

"What?"

The young man gestured at the trees. "They're too even."

Digory turned his head. From beneath tree coverage, light

was dim. Squinting, he studied the formation. It looked like they had been planted. The trees were placed identical distances apart from every angle. The grid-like pattern was clear and tight enough to inhibit travel on horse or cart, even walking through it would prove challenging. Because of the trees, the only way to reach Graceview was on the path they took.

Digory didn't care. He shrugged again.

"It looks like someone put them there," Ryd said.

"They probably did."

"How?" Ryd asked quickly.

"You care about their trees," Digory said, rolling his eyes, "yet you've never thought how they built the cursed things at all?"

"What things?"

"The castles," Digory said in a loathing spat. Ryd realized he'd never thought about it. "How did they move those stones? You remember Anstout, don't you? All the way on a mountain top, built with boulder-size rocks." The younger man nodded. "What about Westerviolet? What about Animus Rock?" Digory pressed, gaining momentum. "The towers? What builder today can match it?"

Ryd stuttered, "I... I... I don't know. I figured that..."

"No," Digory interrupted loudly. "Stop. You already said it. You don't know."

"But..."

"You don't think," Digory snapped.

"Hey," Ryd protested. "That's not fair."

"There is so much," Digory started, thinking of the Vanguard lore Sybil had told him bits and pieces of before swearing him to secrecy, then he paused. "Forget it," Digory said through a sigh. It wasn't worth it.

"What's gotten into you?"

Digory ignored him, pulling his cloak tighter in the chill of the forest.

"Curse you, you know that?" Ryd said angrily at Digory.

"Ryd..."

"No!" Ryd shouted at him, pushed to his limit. He couldn't take the abuse any longer. "What's your problem? One moment you're this, the next you're that. What the curses, Digory?"

Both pulled their horses to a halt. This path through the forest to Graceview was much wider than through the arid land. There was also company this close to the city. A trickle of merchants, beggars, and costermongers milled about, all dressed in nondescript brown to beige robes in varying levels of threadbare. They seemed to live in shoddy hovels clustered around the lip of Blackwood.

"You, what the curses?!" Digory shouted back.

From atop Mable, anger masking hurt feelings, Ryd shoved Digory. Digory shoved back, hard. Ryd half toppled then clumsily tried to save the dismount. His foot stuck in his saddle and he had to jump for an uncomfortable second to get free, flailing miserably as he hopped awkwardly to unloop his ankle.

Digory laughed at him.

Embarrassed and insulted Ryd shouted a guttural "Ahh!" and ran for Digory. He tackled then dragged Digory off Chester.

The young men fell into a dust cloud of fists, knees, and elbows. Ryd swung as Digory tried to hug him calm, knowing the Stablemaster had no chance at besting an elite trained Guardsman. Then, Ryd bucked and hit Digory's lip and nose with his skull. Infuriated, Digory punched him in the jaw, although resisted the urge to reach for his dagger. As they tussled a small crowd gathered. A few even seemed to be taking bets, whispering to each other and kicking out their feet in a strange, unfamiliar fashion.

Eventually, the tussling pair slowed from exhaustion and lack of proper sup or sleep. They stopped when Digory sat on Ryd and held his arms to his torso. The left side of Ryd's face swelled in a black and green bruise, adding to his wounds picked up in the Confines. Digory's nose and lip bled.

Both panted in exhaustion.

Finally, Digory rolled over to lay with his back on the dirt next to his companion. They looked up at the glittering leaves from below together, breathing heavily, nearly smiling. Meanwhile, the small crowd had dissipated except one. A young man hung back, watching them from the tree line.

Without a word, Digory stood and offered his hand to Ryd. Without hesitation, Ryd took it. They met eyes briefly and nodded, peace silently struck, then mounted their prospective horses.

This is my chance, Sieffre thought to himself. Just one more mark, and I am elevated, as the Great Thorne deigned so. He took a deep breath, steeling himself to his purpose. *Just one more mark*, he thought. *Then all will be worth it.*

"Wait," the onlooker said as he walked out of the shadows.

"Who are you?" Digory barked. "What do you want?" His hand hovered over his dagger instinctually.

Sieffre raised his hands. "I'm friend," he said eagerly.

"We don't need friends," Ryd retorted back.

Digory smirked, a bit proud. "He's right," he said, low and deep. "We don't."

"Hear me out," the man went on, accent complex and strange. "Graceview is difficult." He took a step forward. "I offer my services."

"Services?" Ryd asked.

"Come on, let's go," Digory told Ryd. He'd seen men like this before, waiting to prey on unsuspecting natives outside of strange realms. "It's a ploy."

"It's not!" Sieffre stepped forward another pace.

"Stop where you are," Digory commanded loudly. The young man widened his eyes and froze at Digory's practiced tone.

"What services?" Ryd asked curiously, ignoring Digory, intrigued by the man's earnest expression.

"Ignore him," Digory warned. "He wants coin."

"I want to help you," Sieffre said angrily.

"You want to help us for free?"

"No," he said, then paused and raised his eyebrows, "but..."

"There, you see." Digory turned to Ryd. "He wants coin."

"I want opportunity," the man interjected, skipping a few paces to stand immediately in front of both Mable and Chester, "nothing more."

"Hear what he has to say," Ryd pleaded Digory.

Digory sighed loudly against the back of his throat. "Fine," he said, then quickly shouted, "What!?"

Startled, Sieffre jumped as tiny flecks of Digory's blood spattered his robes.

Ryd gave him a better look. The young man had brown skin and mid-length wavy dark-brown hair pulled into ponytail behind his head, in line with the rest of the men they'd witnessed this close to Graceview. He was on the tall side and soft around his midsection. His eyes were sunken and red, with heavy bags. His face was long, with a clef chin, and his lips were naturally curved down, as if he was always frowning. And he spoke with an off-putting, unfamiliar dialect.

"You have never been to Graceview."

"How do you know?" Digory said.

"It is clear," he said with a knowing smirk, looking them up and down.

"But, how?" Ryd asked, but the man only shook his head and smiled. "How?" Ryd asked again.

"For start," Sieffre said, "your mounts."

Ryd blinked twice. "Really?" he asked, not following, although the stars began to align for Digory. He'd heard something about the rarity of steeds West of the Missi, however, hadn't given it much thought until now.

The stranger chuckled loudly and took a confident step, hands held in front of him in peace. "You prove me true," he said, then paused. "You will see. You need me."

"Not enough," Digory replied, unimpressed.

"Why do we need you? What is your name?" Ryd asked. "Let's start there."

"Sieffre," the young man slightly bowed his pony-tail head. "Call me Sieff."

"Okay, Sieff," Digory said dryly. "Explain yourself. Now."

Sieff sighed, annoyed. These strange men were proving far more difficult than he'd anticipated they'd be. The Great Thorne had not indicated they would be so challenging. So resistant to aid. "I'm trying to help you," he said then paused and looked them up and down again. He rolled his eyes and said under his breath, "I cannot believe it is not clear."

"Out with it," Digory said.

"You're targets!" Sieff yelled. "You made a display of how stupid you are." He added ominously, "They'll be ready."

Ryd didn't like how that sounded. "Who?"

"Not important now."

"What is, then?" Ryd asked.

At that, Sieff smiled wide and opened his arms. "I guide you," he said warmly. "You won't be safe without me."

Digory and Ryd, together, chuckled. "You don't know us," Digory said.

"There is much that you don't know," Sieff warned. *The Great Thorne told me everything,* he thought.

"Hold on," Ryd held his hand to the stranger then pulled Mable closer, so he could confer with Digory. They lowered to a whisper. "What if he's right?" Ryd asked Digory with a tinge of worry.

"Or he says that to all doltish enough to listen," Digory replied. "He's a con."

"I believe him," Ryd said.

Digory studied Ryd's serious expression, then he sighed. He couldn't believe he was entertaining this. "Why?" he asked.

"Digory, our horses."

"What about them?"

Ryd's eyes scanned the path on either side of them, glancing from meagre dressed native to the next, all on foot. "Have you seen any others?"

"Pulling the cart that passed not long ago?"

"No horse," Ryd said, shaking his head. "Mule." Digory frowned, realizing his companion was onto something. "Not one," Ryd added.

"So, no horses?" Digory said rhetorically. "Coincidence." He wasn't sure he meant that. Ryd may be right.

Ryd shook his head "no" again. Digory paused and out of the corner of his eye studied the stranger. He seemed harmless enough.

"Let's take him with us," Ryd said. "Once we're through the forest, once we've actually made it to Graceview, we decide."

"If we don't trust him, part at the gate?" Digory asked rhetorically. "Fine," he conceded.

Both men turned to address the stranger.

"Accompany us," Digory told Sieff, "and explain yourself," he said then paused. "Properly," he added with threatening tone.

Sieff nodded furiously. "You have my word Lords, my word."

Digory chuckled. He scratched his beard. "Lords, huh?" Sieff slightly bowed his head. He offered no explanation. "I like Graceview so far," Digory said to Ryd. "I like the way Lord sounds. Could get used to that, couldn't you?"

Ryd shook his head at Digory as they urged the horses off and made way to Graceview. While Mable and Chester trotted, Sieff double-stepped next to them to keep up. His cheeks burned red.

"You said 'opportunity'," Digory said to Sieff, scratching his beard. "What was your meaning?"

"Men of your stature have great sway here," Sieff said through heavy breaths. "I only ask a small favour of you."

"Here we go," Digory mumbled. No one offers kindness in this Kingdom without want of reward, he thought.

"Elevate me," Sieff said, face tilted up toward Digory and Ryd like a believer at the stream.

Ryd wasn't sure he heard the man correctly. "Elevate you to what?"

Digory smirked. "What's he talking about?"

"I am so close. I need only one more mark then I'll have steeds of my very own," he said whimsically. "And a woman I choose."

"What are you talking about?" Ryd asked. He sighed. He was tired of being in the dark. And he was tired in general.

"Why, only one more," the young man said, pulling his left sleeve to showcase countless ticks in glinting silver to match the leaves of the trees, tattooed in precise lines. Then, he showed his right forearm. Covered in tattoos the same.

"What the curses?" Digory leaned over to inspect.

Sieff beamed proudly. "Only one more."

"How does it work?" Ryd asked in a hush, befuddled by the strange markings. "What does it mean?"

"You're my final task," he said assuredly. "Two strangers. In Blackwood. On horses."

"Mission?"

"I am young to be this elevated, you know."

"He's insane," Digory said to Ryd.

"I wouldn't speak like that if I were you."

Digory sighed loudly. "I'm already getting sick of him."

"The Great Thorne wouldn't like it," Sieff added ominously.

"Great Thorne?" Digory said, then smiled. He'd heard a bit about this. The natives of Graceview were said to praise and adore Hastein Thorne above all other Thorne Vanguards, alive or dead. Weak ones and their weak beliefs, he thought. He shook his head and scratched his beard.

The man lowered his voice to a whisper. "I warn you, do not speak that way. Not of Hastein the Great."

"Hastein Thorne?" Ryd asked.

"The Great Thorne," the young man spat. "Such disrespect," he added, shaking his head in disgust.

"You think he's a god, huh?" Digory said, looking down. The man silently frowned and looked forward. "Thorne tells you what to do, then you do it?"

"Great Thorne," Sieff corrected angrily, snapping his head around, "He reads life's mission."

"Oh of course," Digory said. "Life's mission. Sure." Hastein Thorne had been dead for years. Whoever this man prayed to was no god, he thought. Just a silly distraction, as the Brochet Ancestors were for the people of Westerviolet.

"Do not jest," Sieff challenged him. "He knows."

"Hmm." Digory was unimpressed and about to stop listening to him entirely.

"Once we've moved forward on our mission," Sieff said,

wanting to prove himself, not understanding why these extinct were fighting him so, "we're blessed with a mark." He held out his arm. "Enough marks elevate."

Ryd furrowed his brow. "Elevate to what?"

"Where are you from?" Sieff countered. "I must know a bit about you, to make it easier."

"Make what easier?"

"Why, your concealment."

"Concealment?" Ryd asked nervously.

"Did you think you could walk right through the Marks just as you are?" Sieff laughed loud like a tickled child. He wiped a tear from his eye. "I told you. You need me."

"It doesn't matter where we're from," Digory dismissed outwardly, although inwardly unnerved by the odd man's reaction. "We are just passing through."

There was a shocking lack of plant life in this forest. Only a scattering of small sunbloom caps in pale yellows around the bases of the trees. It was unlike any forest Ryd had ever seen.

"Why did you come here?" Sieff asked.

Digory gestured to Ryd. "Someone is afraid of water."

"Avoiding the Missi?"

"Littlebell," Ryd added.

Sieff nodded knowingly. "A mistake made by many."

"Mistake?"

"You are fortunate for your steeds," he said happily, then smiled wide. "You don't even know."

Digory's curiosity perked. "Enlighten us," he said.

"When you come to Blackwood," Sieff gestured around at the spiral-vined black forest, "the Kingdom falls away. It is gone. But," he paused. "I've heard tales from the few," he lowered his voice to a whisper. "The things they claim," he paused again. "It's unbelievable." He looked to the men on horseback. Although discouraged from broaching this topic, his curiosity was brimming. "Tell me what it's like," he whispered.

Ryd turned. "What is what like?"

Sieff's eyes pled. "Anywhere else." Ryd felt his stomach knot for the man, but he wasn't sure why.

Digory felt no such pity. "Who is 'they'?"

"The worthy are chosen," Sieff replied, tone flipping to defense. "It is an honor to be chosen, to be sure. They ensure we're pure, you see." He spoke with such a heavy accent at times he was difficult to understand. Neither Digory nor Ryd had any idea what he was talking about.

"Chosen?" Ryd asked. "Pure? Should we just turn back?"

"No, it would be a waste of time. And we need provisions." Digory couldn't stand riddles. "Who the curse is 'they'?!" he shouted at Sieff.

Sieff was taken aback. "Why, Thorne Watch."

"Ah," Digory sat back in his saddle.

"Who?" Ryd asked. "What's he talking about, Digory?"

"It's like Guardsmen for Thornesblood." Digory said. "Ryd," he whispered, "he's talking about Vanguards."

"Oh..." Ryd trailed off. He rubbed his temple trying to digest this strange encounter, imagining all the fearsome unknowns up ahead.

Sieff walked double-pace proudly, to the side, just out of earshot.

Nearly two days travel through Blackwood Forest brought them to the wake of Graceview's city.

Shops, stalls, and carts popped up along the path, nestled into the first row of the tree-grid on either side. Some merchants utilized the trees themselves, hanging wares from ropes tied across. Others nailed boards to the black trunks like makeshift countertops. Some shops were two or three stories high. Ladders rested against dark trunks between floors. Hovels and shacks seemed to be built into some of the tree-grid behind the first row of shops and nondescript natives filtered in and out.

The air churned with spice, collagen and fat. Fluffy white sky squirrels with black tails leapt from branch to branch overhead.

The scent of charred vegetables, boiling stock, and frying meat bombarded both Digory and Ryd. Both salivated hungrily.

Most of the stalls had food of some kind. The others were overwhelmingly piled with mounds of fine-ground wares in reds, burnt-orange, greens, blacks, and yellows.

The pungent aroma of each stand was stronger than the last. It overwhelmed the senses.

"What is all of this?" Ryd asked in awe.

"The true heart of Graceview," Sieff said, beaming, gesturing down the line. "Fill the belly, fill the soul." He smiled wide. "That is what we say."

They'd slowed pace considerably with the makeshift market's hubbub.

All around them milled near-copies of Sieff. All wore matching robes of practical brown or beige wool in varied degree of tatter, with hair cut mid-length, male or female. Men wore it pulled back loosely as Sieff did, tied with a piece of twine. Women's hair was braided into severe mid-height buns. None wore ornamentation or face paint either. There were also surprisingly few children. Most were elderly, sickly, or deformed.

In stark contrast to the variety of tone and coloring of the people at Animus Rock, like in Westerviolet, the natives were the same shade and hue of brown. Hair color varied from medium brown to black, but all shared the same texture and wave. Faces were long and red eyes were sunken with dark bags. Most seemed to carry extra weight, particularly around the midsection. Everyone looked the same.

"Sup here is good?" Digory asked.

"The best!" Sieff exclaimed. "Top spices in all the lands."

"That's what the smell is?" Ryd asked, sniffing the air. He'd never smelled anything so wonderful. Unlike his first encounter with strange food in the dens beneath Littlebell, these wares seemed delicious. His mouth watered.

"You are in for a treat," Sieff said. He gestured and led Digory and Ryd aside to a stall under a hanging piece of ragged brown cloth, in mimic of an awning.

Three ropes were tied between the two trees directly behind the stall and each had unfamiliar dried plants hung from them. The top, a long greenish black leaf—wild Fernleaf—delicious when rubbed on boar, said to enhance eyesight. The middle, tiny dried yellow flowers on wilted vines—thimbleberry flowers looped into circles, used in soups to enhance color and flavour, rumoured to bolster confidence. From the bottom hung dried bunches of red and lavender berries—Devil's juniper, usually dried and ground and sprinkled on all matter of dishes to enhance the spice, allegedly enhancing passion as well. All were unfamiliar to both Digory and Ryd.

Behind the stall, a small fire burned. A sky squirrel, now just roasted meat and bone, dripped juices from a spit.

Tray after tray with torn pieces of roasted meat doused in different combinations of spices lay on a crafted wooden table underneath the brown cloth awning. Behind the trays were identical glass jars with long wooden ladles in sauces of varying consistencies and colors.

Digory and Ryd looked warily at the strange food. Neither dismounted. Both watched the unfolding interaction curiously.

Sieff's natural frown rose in a friendly grin as he greeted the stall's merchant, a slouched middle-years man of similar appearance. Each held arms out at an upwards angle to the other with hands clenched in fists. The gesture forced sleeves to the elbows, exposing the brilliance of silver on Sieff's arms in stark contrast to unmarked arms of the other man.

The merchant eyed Sieff with reverence then hurried to fix a large plate, bowing and scraping as he did it. Neither said a word. Digory and Ryd looked at each other, confused, then back to the exchange.

Sieff grunted and pointed to several trays, then glass jars. The merchant worked quickly then handed Sieff a rectangular clay plate with high-lipped edges piled stacks of charred meat doused in the variety of spices. Dripping fat leaked from the loin and pooled beneath it like gravy. Atop the meats were drizzled lines of sauce in white, vibrant green, and deep red.

"Three spears, please," Sieff added.

The man handed him three carved sticks with corkscrew points of the end, mimicking the odd grass and spiralled vines. The sticks were long enough to grip the smooth part between one's fingers and thumb, leaving the sharp-tipped end free.

Ryd noted the merchant. Unlike Sieff, in boots, his feet were clad in strappy sandals crafted from leather and wood. However, like Sieff's forearms, his feet were dashed in silver lines. They glinted on his walk back into the stall.

Sieff approached Digory and Ryd with the platter in one hand and the odd "spears" in the other. He dropped two spears on the plate, leaving a third in his palm.

"What is that?" Ryd asked.

"Come down," Sieff told him, beckoning with a grin. "Try for yourself."

"You're really going to…" Digory started. He paused to watch Ryd happily dismount. "Really?"

"Here," Ryd thrust Mable's reigns up at him. "Hold her." He joined Sieff with the plate. The taller man smiled wide.

"Take a spear," he said. Ryd picked up the unfamiliar implement. "Like this," Sieff demonstrated.

It is probably poison, Digory thought. *Either that or disgusting.* He ignored his mouth watering. "What are you doing?"

Ryd ignored Digory as he flexed the finely carved spear between his fingers. Like their guide demonstrated, Ryd spun the implement towards the high-lipped platter, skewering two pieces of the roasted meat covered in sauce and juice.

Meanwhile, Sieff lifted his spear up to his mouth and removed the meat with his teeth.

Ryd watched him closely, studying the drip of white, green, and red sauce from the roast squirrel mixing on his plate. He took a breath, held the meat up to his mouth, and copied Sieff. He ate with bared teeth. Ryd chewed timidly at first, then with growing enthusiasm, mouth exploding from flavour. He'd never tasted anything so wonderful. Before he finished, he smiled wide.

"Digory," he said though chewing, his teeth covered in dark spices. "You have to try this!"

Digory shook his head.

"Didn't I tell you?" Sieff nodded proudly. He turned and lifted his hand with the spear upwards. The merchant smiled in thanks at the apparent gesture of praise. Even under the shadow of Blackwood's canopy, Sieff's forearm glinted brilliantly.

The end of the Blackwood Forest was in sight. Light broke through round leaves.

Something had been bothering Digory since they left the merchant stalls half a day's travel ago. He turned his head to look at their guide. "Why didn't you pay him?" he asked quizzically. "The man with the meal."

Sieff walked between Mable and Chester. He glanced up. "No coin here," he said.

Ryd frowned when his thoughts about Col were interrupted, yet, he was intrigued. "But, then," he asked, "why did he serve you?"

"I am doing the Great Thorne's work, of course."

Digory chuckled. "No coin? Impossible. The Kingdom runs on coin." Sieff looked at him like he was stupid. He held his arm out and upwards in a fist, exposing his tattoos.

"Beautiful," Digory said dryly.

Sieff scowled. "This means a great deal," he spat, lowering his arm. "Do you see others with the marks I have?"

"Everyone's in long robes," Digory retorted. "So, no."

Sieff shook his head, drab ponytail flapping from side to side. "Extinct," he muttered.

Digory chuckled again, amused he'd ruffled the man's feathers. "What now?" he asked in a smirking smile.

"You know nothing."

"Don't insult him," Ryd chided in a whisper, but Digory only laughed. "There's really no coin here?" Ryd asked Sieff more gently than Digory had.

Sieff looked up and met Ryd's kind eyes. "No coin," he repeated sharply.

"But…" Ryd started, then trailed off. He thought Creed Coins were Kingdom-wide. Did Graceview use something else? Didn't Creed Coins come from Thorne? Hadn't he heard something about that? He wanted to ask but then felt silly not knowing where to start, so he retreated into silence.

"What is it you speak?" Sieff pressed him, intrigued by the inflection at the start of his sentence.

Ryd turned to Digory, unsure, as if asking for help. Digory slightly nodded.

"Graceview is the Bank." Digory said to Sieff, speaking for Ryd. "For the Kingdom," he added, then hesitated when Sieff didn't respond. "Isn't it?"

Horseshoe clops and three-burst chirping birds in the trees high above were the only sounds other than the foreign cacophony of voices on the trail. The wind picked up and jostled all the leaves overhead in a whoosh. Ryd glanced up, in awe of the sparking natural awning.

Sieff smirked like he knew something Digory didn't, then replied, "The weak need coin."

"Creed Coins are minted in Graceview," Digory retorted. He knew that was fact.

"It matters not."

Digory was taken aback. "How does that not matter?"

Sieff's sunken red eyes held Digory's intense gaze. "It matters not to the Elevated." He used a particular diction for the last word, as if it was sacred,

"Ah," Digory said, turning forward in his saddle, "that again."

"You have more lines on your arms, so he gave you food?" Ryd said.

Sieff laughed. "It sounds as nonsense when you speak it like that."

"But…" Ryd began, until he was interrupted.

Sieff loudly chuckled more. "Lines," he said, repeating Ryd's term. "You are a funny man," he added with a grin. "Lines," he muttered, shaking his head.

"Well, what do you call them?"

"It is my Silver," Sieff replied proudly, showcasing his left forearm for the men to study. "Silver marks."

"Mark is the same as line," Digory said under his breath, eyeing the brilliant tattoos like dainty shining scars covering the man's dusky skin. Sieff ignored him, still walking with head held high. Ahead, the forest's exit light grew brighter.

"Let's stay with him," Ryd leaned to Digory.

Digory moaned. "He's the worst."

"He has honest eyes," Ryd countered, trusting the man without being able to explain why.

"They're red, the same as yours and mine."

"Still," Ryd argued, "it's clear there's much we don't know about this place. He could be useful. And we've made it too far now to turn back and attempt to go through Wraithswail to Littlebell. You know I'm right," he added perceptively, seeing it in Digory's expression.

"Ugh," Digory relented as he knew little about Graceview himself, and a guide would be likely helpful. Besides, this man was harmless. If needed, he knew he could best him in less time than it took to say *silver mark*. "Until he proves otherwise, fine."

The group slowed as they approached Graceview's massive entry.

Ahead, the tree line broke in a grand twisted archway made from the trees and their branches themselves, pulling together the seams between the tar-like trunks at the closest point to Graceview's titanic city. Wide, brown fang vines latched this massive natural archway to the earth. Both Ryd and Digory marvelled at the grandeur.

To Digory's surprise having heard Graceview was impenetrable, there was no wall. Not a constructed one anyway. No man-made fortifications at all. Instead, the row of trunks closest to the city grew wider than the others and together seemingly in a natural fence, as if one massive tree encircled it. The enormity was mindboggling.

Here, clustered around the natural archway, were bunches

hovels built into the grid of trees, just as they had been the whole length of this trail through Blackwood. The natives here were slouched, underfed, and sandal clad as the merchant earlier on had been. There were several decrepit looking souls with crumpled legs, or under-developed arms. Men and women in drab robes pulsed in and out of Graceview via the natural arch, uninterrupted. It was a sorry looking bunch.

"No guards?" Ryd asked Sieff at the sight of the empty archway. Every realm he'd been to so far, except the lawless Confines, had guards at the gate. Even Littlebell.

"Guards?" Sieff asked, frowning at the unfamiliar word.

"Thorne Watch," Digory added, translating for Ryd.

"Oh, why didn't you say so?" Sieff shook his head. "Not here. They see no reason to keep eye on the Lowmarks. Come," he gestured.

Digory and Ryd exchanged a look, then followed Sieff into Graceview on horseback. Stinking bodies covered in dirt from the fields or silt from the mines buzzed about each other until they saw Digory and Ryd, then the chaotic crowd split as if by magic.

"What's going on?" Digory asked warily.

Sieff turned to him with a knowing smile. "Your mounts."

Graceview's roads were winding, like branches of a tree. They darted back and forth and connected nonsensically at intersections of three, four, or even five ways. Compared to the Capital, these roads were narrow. Unlike the cobblestone streets of Animus, though, these were unpaved. These sandy streets were marked with deep wheel-worn paths. Somehow, despite no clear indications of direction, Sieff walked confidently, completely sure of where he was going. The pair followed closely behind him.

Everywhere they went in the city, natives reacted the same way, parting for Digory and Ryd on their horses, bowing their mousy heads low. Sieff walked ahead of them, head held high, the whole-time beaming.

"How big is this place?" Ryd asked as his eyes swooped side to side, wide in excitement. A deep crevice was carved off the side of the road, on the left. The buildings along that side each had makeshift arched bridges over the ditch. The streets were angled down slightly towards it. He wondered what it was for.

"Twice as wide as the forest is long," Sieff replied.

"That's..." Ryd paused. He squinted. "That's huge," he finally said, raising his eyebrows as he turned his head.

"That can't be," Digory said.

"Why not?" Sieff turned to him, slowing his pace to walk next to Digory, instead of in front.

"Because that would make it nearly fifty creeds wide!" Digory exclaimed. "It just can't be," he added knowingly, but Sieff smirked at him. "Curse you," Digory said to the guide.

Sieff frowned, turned, and doubled his step. He walked a good bit ahead of them now.

"Your fault," Digory turned to Ryd.

"Me!?"

"If we'd taken the river," Digory accused, "we'd have your bare woman by now."

"Hey," Ryd warned.

But Digory couldn't stop. "We wouldn't be in this cursed place, following this cursed asshole," he grumbled.

"Quiet!" Ryd said in a shouting whisper, glancing over his shoulder anxiously, then back to glare at Digory as if he was a misbehaving child. "What if he heard you?"

"I hope he does," Digory said, then lifted his hand up in a fist, in mock of the earlier gesture. "Curse you, man."

"Digory!" Ryd shouted.

A few in the crowd looked up and frowned in passing. Digory lowered his hand and rolled his eyes. If Sieff heard, he didn't indicate it.

Ryd raised his voice, "Respectfully," he said, addressing Sieff, ignoring Digory. "Where is the Bank?"

Sieff turned and chuckled pleasantly as if the previous interaction never happened. He knew better than to concern himself with griping of the Extinct. He pointed to the castle, in the far center of the monstrous city. The landscape was flat and buildings were squat. The towers were all that could be seen above the skyline.

"The Bank is in the castle?" Ryd asked.

"It's at the base."

"What's it like?"

"Topped in a copper dome," Sieff said, then paused. "This dome is very famous," he added.

"Why?"

"It is enchanted."

"Really?" Digory challenged.

"Oh yes," Sieff replied.

"How?"

"The copper does not tarnish or darken," Sieff said. "It is immortal. It is proof of elevation, if one can so achieve."

"Oh, right," Digory said, smirking, "of course. Sure."

"Digory," Ryd whispered harshly, but Sieff was unfazed. His sleeves moved as he walked. His wrists glinted with beams of passing sunlight, like scales do underwater.

"The dome tops the Bank," Sieff went on, "but my favorite, personally, is the Coral."

"The what?" Ryd asked.

"'The Coral Gate," Sieff said.

"What is it? Coral?"

"The entry to the bank," Sieff replied. "One of two to the castle."

Ryd liked how excited Sieff got. How the man's eyes lit up as he spoke of it. Like a child's. "Why is it your favorite?" Ryd asked.

"It's miraculous," Sieff said. "Gigantic as if a defix one hundred times the height of a man placed the slabs there. Heavy as boulders and made from solid coral."

There was that unfamiliar word again. "Coral?" Ryd repeated.

"It is from the ocean," Sieff said.

Before Ryd could ask, the man added, "I can tell you are heathens, unfamiliar with the Teachings, so I will explain. The ocean is also called the 'Cursed Waters'. It's more water, without an end, and salted. Wraithswail is not far from it."

"No," Ryd half smiled. *How absurd*, he thought. "Really?"

"Truth," Sieff assured confidently.

"How do you know?"

"It is in the Teachings," Sieff said.

Digory smirked and shook his head.

"Say it's true," Ryd entertained, entranced by the idea. "How did they get it here? The..." he paused, fumbling with the foreign word, "coral. How was it done?"

Sieff smiled wide. "Someday I will know that answer. I hope," he added cryptically, "soon."

"Ugh," Digory muttered, fully sick of this man's riddles as Ryd shot him a glare as if to say, 'be nice'. The sky was still cloudless and the sun beamed uninterrupted down as they paced the city. Digory was hot, uncomfortable, and now irritated to boot. "How far?" he barked at Sieff.

Meanwhile, Ryd was entranced by this strange city. The buildings they passed by were freestanding, not town homes, with wide alleys cutting between rectangular blocks of red rock, built from some kind of clay. Structures were single story with no windows apart from a circular face-sized one in the rectangular door. Roofs were flat platforms sprung to life with dynamic, plush dark-green foliage. Each and every building was topped with a garden, like leaves sprouted from red-brick roots. From overhead it likely looked like patches of greenery, Ryd thought to himself, in wonderment. He'd never imagined such a place could exist.

"We're nearly out of the Lowmarks," Sieff told Digory.

Ryd looked at Digory, having no idea what 'lowmarks' meant. Digory silently shrugged back.

All the buildings they passed here seemed to be residential. Natives with identically hued skin and nondescript, threadbare robes walked in neat lines. Several pulled carts by hand in worn divots through the mud. Carts were covered tightly in burlap, however some wares spilled free. One particularly shoddy cart pulled by a wrinkled, slouched woman trailed a thin line of orange-ground carnelian spice on the dirt behind her.

Unlike in the forest outside the gate, the natives here appeared to be in far better health. And they were quiet.

Conversations were spoken low. Heads and eyes were cast down. Everyone wore sandals. Some flesh was more tattooed than others. Together, the feet of the crowd glittered like the Blackwood leaves.

Finally, Sieff slowed after hours on circuitous paths through the overgrown city. He called for them to rest their horses aside a notable building, much longer than the rest positioned at the back loop of a cul-de-sac. Unlike the windowless others, this one had round glass spread uniformly across each wall in mirrored black. The rectangular-cut bricks of the outfacing walls were painted black to match. On the roof, instead of a green garden grew a floral one bursting with petals of competing color, scent, size, and beauty. Amongst a sea of green, this colorful arabesque made a clear impression. And it smelled wonderful.

The front door frame was high, arched, and lined in round red-tone stones. The door itself was dark grey metal with hammered details, and red diamond-shaped windows.

To Ryd, the building looked like a defix with wrathful eyes. It was equally intimidating.

"Wait here," Sieff said.

He left Digory and Ryd in the middle of the road and went to the arched front door. He knocked seven times. After an uncomfortably long wait, the right diamond opened to a man in a red hood's face. Ryd thought it seemed like the defix winked. Sieff conferred in unintelligible whispers as Digory and Ryd watched on.

"Hey," Ryd said to the side to Digory without taking eyes off the interaction.

"What is it?" Digory asked back absently, studying the exchange closely.

"I've seen those robes before." Ryd narrowed his eyes, memory flashing back to that horrible black building.

"The red ones?"

"The Confines," Ryd said surely. "I saw them at the Dark Arena," he added. A fearful shiver ran down his spine.

"Viccouri," Digory said to the side, not taking his eyes off

Sieff either.

Ryd frowned. "What did you say?"

"They're called Viccouri," Digory repeated without any further explanation. He was tired of explaining things. He was tired in general.

"How do you know that?" Ryd asked eagerly, titillated by new information despite his traumatic associations. Remembering Lys, feeling a painful stab in his chest, Digory only sighed. "What?" Ryd asked sharply, noting his pained reaction.

Digory exhaled loudly against the back of his throat, swallowed, then turned to meet Ryd's questioning look. "Remember the girl I told you about?"

"The one you didn't go back for?"

Digory glared at Ryd. "Yeah," he said. "Her."

"I don't understand," Ryd said, not knowing what that girl had to do with anything. "What are the red robes for?"

"Bookkeepers at the Arena," Digory spat. "Curses if I know why they're here." Ryd nodded. "He really is taking his time," Digory changed the subject to complain, feeling sweat beat on his brow, "letting us roast in the sun."

"It looks like he's coming back over here now," Ryd said lightly, hopelessly positive.

Sure enough, just as Ryd spoke, Sieff wrapped up his conversation and walked back over to where they stood beside Mable and Chester. Digory slouched against the side of a building with his satchel on his shoulder while Ryd stayed by the horses, patting Mable's strong neck.

"It is best case," Sieff said as he strode.

"Oh?" Digory challenged, crossing his arms. The sarcasm was lost on Sieff.

"Yes!" Sieff exclaimed happily. "The Viccouri are willing to mark barter."

Digory frowned. This was the catch he was waiting for, he thought. "Mark barter?" he asked for clarification, standing upright, lowering crossed arms to hover at the ready beside his concealed dagger. "Why do we need these Viccouri anyway?"

"Viccouri," Sieff corrected his pronunciation. "Mark barter

is not always acceptable," he added with a wide smile, "but I explained to them your worth. Your importance." He turned to meet Ryd's confused look. "The mission," he added with pride.

"What does 'mark barter' mean, Sieffre?" Ryd asked in a serious tone.

"It is the price that must be paid, I'm afraid," Sieff said with contrite eyes. "And call me Sieff."

"Sieff," Ryd said quickly, fearing the worst, feeling Mable's steady heartbeat beneath his hand. "What price Sieff?"

The man's smile dropped. "Your mounts, my Lords," he whispered.

"What!" Ryd took three steps forward and bellowed. "Never!" he shouted with fury. "Digory?!" he turned with pleading eyes. "Did you hear that?"

Digory instantly felt a compulsion to protect his companion and removed his heavy satchel from his shoulder. The ostentatious, now tattered hat picked up before Anstout clung to the outside. Digory unfastened the hat as he set the satchel down.

Sieff chuckled. "That fashion is no use here," he said, eyeing the hat. "Ridiculous. They will never accept..."

Digory interrupted, "No," loudly. He sat the hat into the sand while digging further into the pack.

Sieff lost interest. He looked at Ryd. "You will never make it to the tunnels with them," he said, gesturing to the horses with his head.

"Tunnels? What are you talking about?" Ryd asked, distraught. "Digory is right. You're trying to con us," he accused. "Steal them," he added as four hooded, red-robe clad men scurried out of the cracked front door. They approached Mable and Chester. "Oh no," Ryd took one step, then another, positioning his body between the horses and himself. "I see what this is!"

"Ryd hold on," Digory shouted over, still fumbling with something in his bag.

"Hold what on?!" Ryd shouted back at Digory, hysterical, not understanding why he wasn't helping. "Look, they're taking them! Sieff…" he pleaded, voice cracking, eyes near tears. He loved those horses with everything in him. They were all he had left of home, until he found Col.

"I am sorry," Sieff said sadly, looking down as if he couldn't bear to see Ryd's face. "It is the only way," he added and glanced up.

"But," Ryd asked, stunned, "why?" as the four red-robed men with hoods ominously up reached the steeds.

"Hold the curses on," Digory said loud and deep. All looked up to see him with crossbow in deadly aim. "What did you mean 'tunnel'?" He asked, pointing the weapon at Sieff.

"There… there… there is a tunnel," Sieff said, stuttering, sunken eyes wide with fear. "You must not take the Gate."

Digory glared at their strange guide. "Which gate?"

"The Middle Gate."

What the curses is the Middle Gate, Digory thought. "Why not?" he asked.

"The Watch," Sieff said surely. "You'd be spotted immediately. With your mounts, you'll be struck down on sight."

"Thorne Watch?" Digory asked, already knowing the answer, hesitating slightly. He'd heard from Sybil of the ruthless nature of Thorneblood's version of the Westerviolet Guardsmen. She told him it was unlike anything he could ever imagine; it was so horrid. He didn't want to find out what that meant.

"They are all over the middlemarks," Sieff said, swallowing in a gulp, eyeing Digory's strange weapon nervously.

Meanwhile, the Viccouri hovered aside Ryd and the horses, ominously unmoving, faces shadowed behind pulled red hoods. Ryd didn't like them at all.

"If you're on Hastein Thorne's mission, as you say, why would Thorne Watch prevent you from it?" Digory pressed with sharp eyebrows. "What the curse are you talking about?" he added in a growl. "Middlemarks means nothing to me."

Sieff leaned back far where he stood. "We must go under the Poison."

"Say one more incomprehensible doltish phrase and I'm firing this through your eye."

"I've seen him do it," Ryd chimed in.

Sieff sighed in frustration. "The Poison Wall, splitting the lowmarks and the middlemarks." This is why the Great Thorne gave me this task, he thought to himself. I'm able to handle the idiocy of the Extinct. "We must not take the Gate, for there is Thorne Watch. And we cannot go over the wall."

"Why not?"

"It has its name for a reason."

Both Digory and Ryd nodded, understanding his meaning fully.

"If not clear," Sieff added. "You cannot touch it."

"Get away from them," Digory barked at Viccouri inching towards the horses. At his command the men in red robes jumped and scurried back into the depths of the black building. Digory followed them with arrow's bead the whole time. Then, he turned his aim back to Sieff.

"Explain," he said slowly.

"I have," Sieff spat. "You have no marks. You are not of Graceview. Thus, you must barter for the protection of the Viccouri." He paused hotly. "If this didn't benefit me greatly I would have been rid of you long ago," he muttered under his breath. I must be strong for the Great Thorne, he thought.

"At least we agree on that," Digory said, gesturing with the crossbow.

"Will you put that down?" Ryd asked Digory, seeing Sieff was no threat now that the red-robed men were gone.

Digory ignored him. "Why go through the heart of the city?" he asked Sieff. "Is there not another way to Littlebell?" Sieff opened his eyes slowly as if he'd heard something unbelievable, then began to laugh. "What?" Digory asked, insecurity bubbling in his throat like bile.

"You really don't know," Sieff said, smiling still. "I suspected you would have realized by now." He added with a smirk, "Most do."

Digory hit his limit. He was surprised he hadn't already shot the bastard. "What is your meaning?!" he screamed at the Seiff. A flurry of strange fowl squawked in protest at his reaction and flew from their perch atop a nearby building

Sieff lurched backwards as if hit with a strong wind. "There is no way to Littlebell," he blurted loudly. No way out at all. Not without the Great Thorne's protection and blessing. Without my help." He said loudly. "I... I... I thought you knew!"

"No way out?" Digory growled.

"To come here on mounts why, why you must have known! Why else would you follow me? I..." Sieff stuttered for his life, "I thought you knew!" The Great Thorne had not warned Sieff of their ineptitude, but it must be for a purpose. Everything the Great Thorne does is for a purpose, he thought. He steeled himself to stay loyal to the mission at hand.

"Digory what does he mean," Ryd asked with nervous inflection from where he stood between Chester and Mable, one hand on each mostly to steady himself amidst the drama.

Digory ignored him. Instead, he stepped forward with weapon ready.

Sieff, with wide-panic eyes, explained. Or, tried to. "Y... y... you're extinct," he stammered out, taking slow hunched steps backwards under the weight of Digory's crossbow aim. In the background, the Viccouri peered out of both front door's defix-like windows, panels open for viewing.

"What the curses," Digory grumbled. "Why do you keep saying that?"

"You exist to serve the Great Thorne," Sieff said, "as we all do. That is our purpose. Although you know what you are, you do not believe in the Mission, there as you will never achieve elevation. Your Mission is dead. Extinct."

"Get to the point," Digory gestured the crossbow.

Sieff lowered his voice. "Visitors do not leave," he said, "because the Extinct are dead anyway."

"That doesn't sound good," Digory replied.

"Only Vanguards are allowed passage," Sieff conceded as if it pained him to say it, bowing his head, "and that occurrence is rare."

"Thorne Watch takes every visiting native where?" Ryd questioned. "Where, Sieff?" he added, although he already knew the truth in the pit of his stomach.

Sieff shrugged. "Away."

Digory frowned, racking his brain for a hint of warning from Sybil. Some bit of knowledge about Graceview to indicate it was like this. "What the curse does that mean?!" he shouted, already knowing deep down he'd ridden them into a trap.

"Did you know about this?" Ryd turned angrily to him. "Before we came here?"

"No!"

"I presume it is well hidden," Sieff added.

"Then how the curses were we supposed to know?! This is the way to Littlebell in the west. The Moon trail, through Graceview, then across the River to Littlebell. I've heard it spoken dozens of times. How the curses could they keep something like this secret!?" Digory shouted with red eyes glaringly wide. Sieff blinked and looked between the men. "What?!"

"The Moon Trail claims many lives," Sieff said with meaning, "but not all." All the lives lost to Graceview were blamed on Wind Valley, it seemed.

"What do we do?" Ryd said in a hush to Digory as he slowly lowered the crossbow in one hand to his side. "We can't just leave them here," Ryd added as he looked towards Mable and Chester's pleading red eyes. "Hey, Digory," he shouted in a whisper, but Digory stood solemnly.

"Thank you," Sieff nodded to Digory as he lowered his weapon. "I need your mounts," he added, nodding to Mable and Chester.

Digory returned the nod.

"Digory, we can't!" Ryd cried out. Digory shot him a look. Ryd knew he was alone. "What happens to them if I give them to you?" Ryd patted their flanks, realizing he might have to let them go.

"To be true," Sieff stepped forward. "I have a bid."

"A bid?" Ryd frowned and scratched the back of his neck.

"They enter the stable and I am only one mark away. I can request bid. When I am elevated, of course."

"Of course," Ryd sighed. "This was your plan," he said, defeated.

"It was life's plan," Sieff confidently replied. "Mission," he added.

"Ugh," Digory moaned, not wanting this irritating man to benefit from Ryd's misfortune. "Is there no other way? We pay a Wind Runner to take the horses back to Animus for us? Come for them later?"

Sieff shook his head 'no'. "The Viccouri will only take us if you surrender them."

"Remind me why we need them to take us anywhere at all?" Digory asked. "Why can we not turn back?" He felt sorry for Ryd. However little he understood the man's attachment to those beasts, Digory felt compelled to defend him. Besides, why trust Sieff? True, it would be a gruelling journey to return the way they came, and Digory wasn't keen on passing through Wind Valley again, but anything would be better than capture by Thorne Watch. Digory knew enough about Thorneblood from Sybil to know that.

Sieff sighed again and rolled his eyes. "I am telling you, Thorne Watch will find you. You are extinct and you will disappear. They all disappear. There will be no escape. No Littlebell, no rest of the Kingdom. There will be nothing!" he shouted, surprising both Digory and Ryd. "And, don't forget about me, your good Sieff," he added goadingly. "It is my last Mission, appointed by the Great Thorne himself, but noo that is not worthy of your attention or respect." Sieff spat at the sand. "It is not just your life that hangs on this passage, Lords. It is mine as well."

Ryd believed him. He trusted the look in his eye.

"How do we know you aren't taking us to Thorne Watch yourself for a prize?" Digory asked sceptically. He didn't know what to think.

Sieff was at the end of his rope and stormed to confront

Digory where he stood. He thrust out his right arm.

"Beautiful, I told you already," Digory sneered.

"No, no," Sieff said, shaking his head, brining attention to his pinkie finger of his right hand. It was the only space other than his neck and face that was not tattooed with silver lines. "Just one more," Sieff repeated slowly, meeting Digory's eyes. "Please, my Lord," he begged. "This is my only chance for happiness."

Digory ground his jaw and swallowed. "For happiness, huh?" he asked. "Your last chance?" he added. Sieff nodded seriously and Digory believed him. He sighed loudly and looked at Ryd.

"What? No. You really expect me to..." Ryd paused, panicked, gutted at the thought of losing his steeds. "They have been with us since the beginning."

"I know," Digory started, "but Ryd..." he trailed off, knowing Ryd understood. They had no choice.

"They're all I have left," Ryd said sadly. He stroked Chester's flank.

Digory shook his head. He stomped over. "Just agree, will you? We can get others," he said. "I want to get the curses out of this place."

"You said it yourself this was a scam," Ryd defended under an angry blond glare. "Now you press me to agree?"

Digory rubbed his beard. He gestured around. "Look at this," he said.

Sieff waited as his future hung in the balance, listening between the men, head winging back and forth like a wind vane.

"I have!" Ryd shouted in defense. "I have been looking..."

"No, you've been basking in it," Digory interrupted loudly. "Looking from one rousing thing to the next. Did you notice how they all keep their eyes down, pressed to the path as if illegal to meet gaze with another? Everyone walks in straight lines, as if trained to do so. Did you notice that?" Ryd slowly shook his head, realizing he didn't. "Does it remind you of any other realms?" he added sharply, thinking of Westerviolet. "Did you see any of the posters?" Digory prodded next.

"I didn't stop to look I…"

"Men with thorns through their necks," he recounted. "Some kind of cursed propaganda."

"Oh," Ryd replied hollowly.

"Yeah, oh. And don't get me started on the tattoos." Digory lowered his voice to a whisper, wondering what kind of terrible weapon those silver marks were against Graceview's people. "They are Thorne's slaves and thankful for it." He shook his head. "It is so cursed."

"What is your point?"

"I believe him."

"You should believe me," Sieff interjected, listening clearly to every word.

"Quiet," Digory spat at Sieff then looked back to Ryd. "I believe him. He's right." He took a breath, then sighed, hating to admit it, but knowing the truth in the pit of his stomach. "This place is a trap."

ANIMUS ROCK'S THIRD TOWER

S
he hadn't slept since she learned of the tragedy. Everything good and righteous about the Kingdom seemed to snuff out overnight. Nothing about Rotrude's proud Animus Rock felt the same as it had been before. The people were reckless, lawless even, during this time of unrest.

"It is a tragedy when any Vanguard is lost," Rotrude said, sniffling as she paced. She thought back to the eve she heard the news that their Kingdom's beloved advocate was gone. How broken hearted she was. Her mind then leapt to last night. She was there at the traitor's trial in the courtyard, angry-faced and crying like the rest of the crowd. "Herman was one of the best," she said truthfully as she dried her tear-filled eyes on a tattered handkerchief. "But the mourning time is over. Life must move on. Lessons must resume," she said, as she had been instructed to do. She blew her nose on the cloth.

Instead of her typical Tower robes, Rotrude wore black with customary red boots. Although, given her modest income, they were berry stained, not crafted of firefang leather. On her head–a humble black net veil, once torn and since carefully patched with thin grey thread. She wore the stitch towards the back over her pale oiled hair to hide it from scrutiny of the Higher natives of Animus. Due to her heritage and lack of generational wealth, Rotrude was never fully accepted, although she tried diligently to change perceptions. To her disadvantage, she was quite the sight, towering in front of the Lessonroom with bright white hair slicked back so flat it accentuated her bulbous head and unbelievably small ears. And Rotrude's red eyes were unlined and puffy from crying. Her nose dripped to her top lip.

As Rotrude addressed the hall of children, she leaned with her hip against her desk with the fire roaring behind her. She appreciated the huge fireplace greatly at this time of year, for it was sunny outside but far below freezing, showing in frost on the windowpanes. The children bundled in extra layers of cloaks and muffs because the Lessonroom's fire was no match for the bitter cold. Anyone sitting on the far end, or near the windows, away from the flames, could see their breath when they spoke.

Some children fidgeted and others whispered amongst themselves. Rotrude eyed them all carefully, preparing to delve into the details of The Uprising.

"Life was good for the most part," she said as if casting bait from beneath her black mourning veil, "in the wake of the Blood Wars." The children hushed, a bit. "The savior Ueli Bellamine proved to be the King that all hoped for. The early 3900s were prosperous, for trade opened between all realms for the first time in half a century. The worst abuses were done away with and life as a native improved dramatically. It would have been utopic," she added, "if not for one small problem."

The children stopped fidgeting and leaned forward, interest piqued. Rotrude stood and began to pace.

"The Kingdom was in massive debt." Coin is the root of all misfortune, she thought. "Every realm suffered in one form or another."

Malla raised her hand and Rotrude called on her.

"Everyone owed coin?" she asked loudly. Frosty breath escaped when she spoke.

"Yes," Rotrude said with a nod. "And, back then, there were more than just Creed Coins."

The children collectively denied with a giggle, shaking their small heads and whispering among themselves.

"It's true!" Rotrude refuted. "Each bloodline had their own form of coin until about one hundred years ago. For instance, Pre-Plague Calvanese traded crystals collected from deep in the Duskfang caverns. They would engrave each with their emblem to mark them as currency. Interesting to note, these stones became priceless in the wake of their demise. The wealthy collect them now." She thought back to the Lady Regnard's collection, how the precious stones called to her from the mantle when she was a young child. She pushed the distant memory from her mind.

"After the Blood Wars," Rotrude went on, "many of the realms tried to create more and more coin to pay off their debts but this didn't have the desired effect, I'm afraid. Instead of alleviating problems, it just made things worse."

"The economy spiralled out of control because inflation was such a colossal issue. Sometimes, buckets or sacks had to be used to carry enough coin to buy just bread, or a piece of loin. That is how little the coin was worth after they made too much of it, you see." She'd heard stories from the camp elders about the struggles, passed down generationally.

The children shook their heads in disbelief, but Rotrude nodded with truthful eyes as if to wordlessly say, *believe it.*

Avina was concerned and raised her hand. "How did they fix it?"

"After years of chaos," Rotrude told her, then turned to glance at the icy threesome. "Thorne presented a solution." Orosia and her pale copies beamed through pursed lip smiles, crystal crowns glinting like the frost outside.

Malla raised her hand. The gem from her throat sparkled. "Why did anyone listen to them?" she said hotly. She glared in the other girls' direction, thinking them no good backstabbing traitors, just as her father told her all Thornes were.

The icy blondes glared back.

"Malla," Rotrude warned. "Because of how much the Kingdom owed Thorne. Instead of deal with all the competing currencies, Thorne proposed an alternative."

"Thorne unified the Kingdom through coin," she said, watching the children, especially those further back in the hall, shiver in their seats. She assessed all the young faces. They were so different and yet so innocent, just beginning to comprehend the massive divides between them yet. Give it time, she thought to herself. In her experience, Vanguard innocence faded quickly. "Hastein Thorne and young son Wallace presented it to a dying King Ueli, who loved the proposal and agreed. It was his last decree, in fact, that any competing currency used as coin other than Creed Coins declares its holder a traitor. The Kingdom's bank to sit in Graceview. Thorne was appointed to oversee the mass conversion to the newly minted Creed Coins that we all know today."

Rotrude pulled one of the familiar coins out of her pocket. Copper, pressed with a masculine crowned profile on one side and Bellamine griffin on the other. It was eight-sided, with silver grooves cut into the edge and a perforation four ways, to split the creed coin into creed ques if needed to make change.

"Do you see this, here?" Rotrude held the coin out to the children. "These little silver lines?" They leaned in to see. "These lines make it impossible to edge the coins properly. Does anyone know what that is?"

No hands raised. Faces were blank.

Rotrude explained. "Before the standardization of currency, edging was a common practice. Take, Lyonshall Reddies." She pulled a red-tone coin twice the size of the other and held it for comparison. One side was the stylized outline of Lyonshall castle. On the other, a roaring rosebear. Edges were smooth.

"True, the metal was dyed red to give the coins distinctive appearance, but they were still rounded with smooth sides. Therefore, anyone wanting to counterfeit coins could simply slice a thin edge off of many, undetected. After a while, they would have enough of the unique red metal to press their own fake coins."

Tiphanie raised her hand. Rotrude called on her. "Isn't that against the rules?" The girl wore a rosebear pelt hat and matching scarf, both bigger than she was. Fur engulfed her.

"Yes," Rotrude said. "Very much so, but they did it anyway. That's why the Creed Coins were better and why they were introduced incrementally each year until completely taking over the economy after adoption in all realms by 3985. Baneswood was the last to comply. That was after an embargo was put in against them to force it, ordered by the King. Before that point, Baneswood only bartered. But the embargo drove Dale away from the crown and further fuelled the climate for war."

She paced.

"That leads me to the other key catalysts of the Uprising."

Lucette meekly raised a hand.

"Yes?"

"What does *catalyst* mean?" she asked softly.

"Cause, Lady."

Lucette nodded. She sunk into her chair after cruel snickers, hiding behind her stringy hair.

"Quiet," Rotrude chided. The room hushed instantly. She started to pace again, speaking with her hands as she described the next gruesome piece. "Gauthier Norland, son of the Blood Wars, was in his ninety-years when his much younger wife Sylvia Thorne, descendant of survivor Allen Thorne, finally birthed a living son named Bin." She paused and took a breath. "Bin Norland, born in 3918, was an instrumental force during the Uprising." Her spine shivered just to say the name. "And he committed one of the most horrific atrocities in modern history."

The children leaned forward, listening intently, mostly looking concerned. Evia shifted in her chair feeling hot attention for what her bloodline had done, half beaming pride, the other guilt. It was a confusing emotion, to be sure.

Jole, or Jire (for it was impossible to tell them apart) shouted, "What'd he do!?" in excitement.

Rotrude frowned. "It was not exciting. Not at all. Remind yourself about the lesson of the poor Beaumont girl, snatched from Littlebell at Minney wedding before the Plague, decades before. Remind yourself how history repeats itself."

The children mostly frowned.

Rose leaned to Evia. "I know what he did."

Evia looked at her in twisted delight, "Really!?" She'd not been given any instruction in the history of her forefathers. Her mother emphasized the future, not the past, in their lessons.

"Hush," Rose said, wary of the Lessonmaster.

But it was too late. Rotrude heard the girls' and turned. "Ladies," she said shrilly. "Share with the class."

Rose and Evia together blushed burgundy.

"It's nothing!" Evia said. Rose nodded in agreement, dark curls bouncing over her shoulders.

Rotrude frowned. "Do you think this is funny?" she asked, putting a hand on her hip. She stepped towards the oldblood girls.

Evia's hand leapt to her mouth and she snorted, pleased with any kind of attention and her ability to get a rise out of the Lessonmaster. She had little respect for Rotrude, given her family's beliefs, and her dislike of the earthblood woman grew by the day.

"Stop that right now!" Rotrude chided. "Disgraceful." Rotrude pointed at Evia. "Stop!"

"Yes Lessonmaster."

Not wanting to provoke Rotrude, Rose kept her head down. She'd learned a few things over the past moons, one of which, it was better to stay quiet.

"Anything from you, Lady?"

Rose looked up with a burning scowl, thinking Rotrude was a bully. Her mother would not like this Lessonmaster at all. She decided she didn't either. She shook her head slowly, 'no'.

"Good," Rotrude said, then turned and walked to hover in front of the roaring fireplace. The girls were left breathing icy air.

"In 3960, Bin Norland kidnapped Lilli Minney."

The children mostly gasped.

"Why!?" a few yelled.

Rotrude's tone had lost its softness, as she was irritated by the oldblood girls. "Lilli left herself open to it. She strayed far from home and thus was vulnerable to kidnap." Upon seeing the hurt faces, especially of the newblood girls, Rotrude added, "She should have been more careful. Her actions completely ruined her bloodline."

It was true, Rotrude thought. Why would one risk all simply to be alone with one's thoughts? When you're a princess of a realm, that is selfish. Selfish and mad.

"To capture her," she said to the children aloud, "Bin Norland marched along with Busk and burned Littlebell." The fire cracked behind her. "The girl was foolish," Rotrude added harshly, gaze cast towards the loudly dancing flames, believing it fully. "It was her fault."

Avina had glassy tears in her doe-brown eyes. She raised a hand slowly.

"Yes?" Rotrude called on her impatiently then hesitated when she looked at the girl, realizing she spoke of her kin. "Oh, dear...I'm..."

"Why her? What did she do wrong?"

"Don't worry yourself..."

"Tell me."

Rotrude sighed and rubbed her temple. "We are encouraged by your kin to leave this part vague," she admitted honestly, in protest of the decree internally. She thought the Vanguards should know everything about their history, including the power that ran rampant in their blood however, the Guild forbade it expressly.

"My kin? Vague? Lessonmaster," Avina said, "I don't understand."

Neither did Rotrude. But she couldn't tell the child that. "A great deal is donated yearly," she told her grimly, "and those donors are entitled...." She trailed off in search of a word to describe the horrible reality correctly, "input on lesson planning."

"Lessonmaster, that does not..."

"Avina!" Rotrude nearly shouted, startling her and most of the others as words escaped her mouth. "If you wish for a change in the lessons, have your father go to the Council and see to it there. It cannot be through me," she added with a bitter bite.

"But... but..."

"Avina," Rotrude was shrill. "Not today. I've had it today."

After that, Avina sulked in her chair. Malla leaned over to console her as soft tears fell on her rounded, dark cheeks. Her blonde waves flowed with the scent of river silt. Avina's hair, in comparison, was styled per-usual in a dramatic golden braid. It smelled of purplecress and moon flowers.

Across the room, Rose's eyes met Evia's.

'You know why?' Evia mouthed without making sound.

Rose nodded. Dark ringlets bounced. Evia's close-set green eyes widened.

'Later,' Rose mouthed back. Evia nodded with a knowing smile.

Fortunate for the girls, Rotrude missed Evia and Rose's interlude, because she spoke facing the other way and met Avina's eyes. She felt that she owed the little Minney girl this much. "Bin Norland took Lilli Minney back to Ravenshroud as his prisoner where he probably hurt her very badly," she said gently to the doe eyed girl. "Dissatisfied with her ability to produce a male heir, Bin Norland killed Lilli."

The children gasped.

"The Kingdom, naturally, was outraged. Sia Minney, Lilli's mother, went to the King and demanded punishment and retribution for what Norland had done to her daughter, but her outcry went unheard. This left a bruise on the New for harming the defenceless Minney bloodline without provocation. The Old proved they went too far. Something had to be done. And, it was, thirty years later." Rotrude lowered her voice and turned. "However, it took more than just one injustice to spark the New to rise up against oppression, again."

She paced.

"In 3960, Xerman Regnard, elder of the bloodline at the time, married his only daughter Cateurxa to Valentin Graves, Xerman's own brother-in-law and the girl's uncle on her mother's side. He did this to strengthen Regnard's political alliance with Graves, but it backfired horribly. Valentin's elderclaim had been long ago removed, so politically, the alliance was moot and thought an ill-move by all. Worse, Xerman's only son and brother of Cateurxa, Xabob Regnard, later rebelled against his father for what had been done, horrified that his sister was forced to marry Gravesblood, despite the lack of dead blood in the man's veins. Then, Xabob committed the highest sin in his father's eyes. To spite his father, he broke Regnard tradition. He married a native. In 3980, with his part-native children, Xoel and Xabier, Xabob took Lyonshall from his father in order to ally Regnard with the New."

Tiphanie beamed proudly from her pile of furs. "See," she taunted Malla and Avina.

The girls rolled their eyes at her, together. "Quiet," Malla shushed Tiphanie. Tiphanie sulked down into her coat. Only her eyes peeped over the top of the fur as if a wild beast ate the small, white-haired girl.

Rotrude noticed the fire burning low and took intermission to fuel it. She tossed on two hefty logs. Sparks erupted as the cool logs sizzled in the flames.

"Hjalmar Graves fell in love," she continued with command as the fire roared again.

Malla shouted in singsong, "Dead-blood can't love!" and all the children giggled together.

"Quiet!" Rotrude bellowed at them. Her head was killing her. She was in no mood for the brash Demos girl as she rubbed her temple again. The headaches had started when she was just a child, around the time she had to enter the mines, and now in adult life even so far from Lyonshall they occurred frequently. Especially when the temperature chilled. Especially after long lessons.

The children jumped and settled immediately at Rotrude's chiding. Malla sheepishly looked down while patting her hair flat, a nervous habit that her father hated, but she couldn't help it.

"As I was saying," Rotrude straightened herself, "Hjalmar Graves, born in 3948, current elder of the Graves bloodline, in fact, fell in love. When he was quite young. This is documented," she added, responding to disbelieving gazes. "There are letters he wrote to Anna Demos herself preserved here at Animus Rock." Rotrude spoke with authority since she had read them herself. Had she not seen these letters personally, she would not have believed it. "The union was forbidden by his traditional father and elder of the bloodline, Haulfrun Graves, yet Hjalmar pursued it nonetheless."

A few gasped. Most also shivered, understanding what disobeying Graves might mean. All knew it couldn't be good.

"For reference, Haulfrun was Harrye Graves's son, if you remember him from earlier. He is thought to be the first deadblood Vanguard." Children nodded at Rotrude's wide frame backlit by the roaring fire.

"Anna Demos was the object of Hjalmar's affection. She was known for her looks, possessing the Demos's legendary beauty. "Like you Malla," Rotrude said offhandedly. Although not outwardly an insult, it sounded that way, and Malla sank all the same.

"She's just jealous of you," Avina whispered to Malla. Malla nodded resolutely.

Orosia raised a slender hand. "How did they meet? If he was Old and she was New."

"At Animus." Rotrude offered no further explanation, leading the children to assume it was at Academy. Where else would Old and New bloods meet? She wasn't permitted to detail their true meeting place.

Tiphanie raised a confident hand next. Rotrude called on her. "If he really loved Anna, what happened that was so bad? If he loved her, then why?" In young Tiphanie's mind, love conquered all.

"I assure you he really did love her, but love can't change evil."

She took a deep breath and sighed with tired eyes as her head throbbed.

"He ran away with her in 3985," Rotrude told Tiphanie, "and the couple took refuge at Hellswater with her Demos kin. Despite threats from his father, the young Hjalmar would not betray his new bride and in-laws by reneging on the union. So, in 3988, sixty-three years ago, Haulfrun Graves marched on Demos." Outside, wind whipped in loud, metallic gusts. "The evil Haulfrun burned every vessel in Rysp Bay to get to his son," Rotrude said. "Hundreds of ships, destroyed. The fleet was decimated and Hellswater was left in ruins. The assault lasted days until Hjalmar and his bride Anna were finally captured. Haulfrun brought them back to Anstout." She paused again and pulled her mourning shall tighter. So much death. *This Kingdom never changes*, she thought sadly. "There, to teach his son a lesson," she told the Lessonroom, "he forced Hjalmar to kill Anna."

Malla clenched her jaw, already familiar with the tale, infamous in her realm.

"No!" Avina interjected amidst other children's frowns and gasps.

"Why?" Rose asked sharply.

"Why what?" Rotrude shot back. Her patience was parchment thin.

"If he was already home, if Haulfrun got what he wanted," Rose asked with black-pupil eyes, "why kill Anna Demos?"

"We don't know why, just that it was done," Rotrude replied without warmth. Would this cursed lesson ever be over?

Rose frowned, fully unsatisfied with that answer. There was always a *why*, she thought as Rotrude turned.

"Afterwards, a decree went out," Rotrude said loudly. The fire danced and leapt behind her with each chilly gust down the chimney. "The atrocity, what happened to Anna Demos, was outlined in detail, sent by Haulfrun to the Vanguard Council himself," she told the children, unable to comprehend anyone was ever as evil as that man was. "This was the final blow and the act that many argue spurred the New bloodlines into action," she explained. "There was, however, one more notable, dare I say, key aspect of the political climate that led up to the Uprising."

Rotrude warmed her hands on the fire. "One woman nearly brought the Kingdom to its knees."

This was Rotrude's absolute favorite part of Lower Academy lessons. After the entire autumn session, she'd finally reached the story of one of her most revered idols. One of the most tragic figures in the Vanguard's recent history.

The children listened intently as frosted breath blew from their nostrils like pale smoke.

"Upon King Ueli's death, his son Bastien became king," Rotrude said. "Bastien was crowned in 3933, in his mid-twenty years, then married a native from the Anstout realm named Jade. Chosen for him by his Council, pushed upon him particularly by Graves, she was touted to be of superior breeding and thus a worthy mother for a future king. In 3939, Queen Jade gave birth to King Bastein's son and heir to the throne, Orell Bellamine."

Despite the long lesson, the children hung on Rotrude's words.

"Bastien Bellamine's reign began with promise but quickly devolved. He proved to be of similar mind to his late grandfather, King Danil, the brute Boy King of the Blood Wars."

"Oh no," Avina whispered what many of the others thought, aloud.

"Bastien fell in line with Haulfrun Graves, Bin Norland, and Bin's cousin Lucien Brochet. The four men slowly plucked away the rights of the natives at Animus Rock, in their respective realms, and in all neutral zones, one by one. King Bastien was lenient on Vanguard lawbreakers but persecuted natives for the slightest offense, toppling the shaky peace struck by his father at the end of the Blood Wars. It was horrid," she couldn't help but add honestly. That was the world she was born into. "King Bastien's reign was an enormous backslide economically, not to mention, culturally. It was terrible how much of the native culture kingdom-wide was destroyed or outlawed by those men and later lost. This was part of why the economy fell to ruin, plus, all of the unregulated, unaligned currencies I discussed earlier. It took decades to implement the universality of Creed Coins, even though expressly approved by the late King Ueli. During Bastien's command, the Kingdom was in shambles."

Rotrude returned to the fire and warmed her hands, then, continued, in a raised voice over her shoulder.

"In 3980, King Bastien died of natural means. He was seventy-one years. His first-born son Orell was in his middle-years and overly prepared to take the throne. He was reported to be disciplined and intelligent. The man, however, was not handsome. Actually, there are many old ballads that speak of his acute ugliness. Orell the Ugly, many called him." The children giggled. "Despite that," Rotrude continued with a half-smile despite her pounding head, "he was good and ready to be king." She paused. "But there was a problem."

"What problem?" Malla interjected loudly.

"Malla," Rotrude warned with a side-eyed glare. The girl buried into her cloak made of foreign hide that looked like shiny black skin.

"Old King Bastien kept a secret. He had an elder child. A contest for heir."

The children murmured in growing excitement.

"A woman interrupted the session, tall and commanding with Bastein's large ears and strong features yet also Warnblood coloring. She was green-eyed and beautifully striking, even past middle years. The woman's name was Claudie Bellamine-Warn, daughter of Maryse Warn, so, granddaughter of Erik Warn, the only Warn Plague survivor. She claimed that her mother had an affair with Bastien Bellamine when they attended Upper many years before. Her family concealed her from Bastein's knowledge and views, instead raising her in her mother's newblood Warn traditions."

Rotrude adored this tale, despite its tragic ending. Claudie was one of her most beloved heroes.

"Claudie Warn quickly amassed the support of all bloodlines dissatisfied with Bastein's rule and apprehensive of a repeat from his son," Rotrude said." Because she was King Bastein's eldest child, it was legally justified. She amassed support of Warn, Morfit, Minney, Demos, as well as a reluctant Dale. Claudie, with claim of her birth and the support of these bloodlines, demanded the throne for herself. Orell the Ugly, with counsel from his father's closest advisers, declared her a traitor. After, there was a chaotic scuffle, most of the New troops in her accompaniment were slaughtered, and Claudie Warn was seized."

Rotrude rubbed her hands together then blew on them for warmth. The children listened closely in horror.

"Orell ordered the Animus fortress wall barricaded before any New realms could send reinforcements to help Claudie's cause," Rotrude said gravely, smudged black-lined eyes narrowing. "Within days' time there were over ten thousand troops across the varying New realms camped at the ready outside." She took a deep breath before explaining the next part. It still pained her today to consider the events that befell the Kingdom's rightful queen. How different the Kingdom would look today if alternative events had transpired. "King Orell imprisoned Claudie to keep her from power," Rotrude said with a crack in her throat. "He threw her into the depths of the First Tower."

"Oh no," Avina mumbled again. Malla rubbed her delicate friend's arm in consolation. The pair had gotten quite close.

Orosia Thorne had held her patience throughout every lesson, never correcting the information once. She listened dutifully to the information taught to her, despite its inaccuracies. Her kin had revealed to her the true Vanguard History. And, to give her and her sisters more power and control as they grew older, they were never to speak of it. But, to keep herself entertained, she asked questions to test the Lessonmaster from time to time. She adjusted her crystal crown, then raised her hand slowly.

"Yes?" Rotrude asked sharply. She certainly sounded annoyed, but Orosia wasn't fazed. She wasn't afraid of earthblood.

"What's the First Tower like?" Orosia asked, pale green eyes locked on Rotrude's red.

The Thorne girl's unblinking glare was as cutting as a legendary green Guardsman dagger. Just like Rose Brochet's gaze, Rotrude couldn't hold it. These young Vanguards are particularly potent, oldblood or new, she thought to herself. More so than any she had instructed before. It worried her.

"The First is Animus Rock's torture chamber and dungeon," she told Orosia as she glanced away, eyes sweeping the rest of the children. "It is important to have a way to teach the bad men a lesson," she said, mind flashing to Prihim the betrayer just last eve. "That is why we have the First Tower. It's where the ones who do wrong can…" she trailed off, imagining the horrors, "…learn," she finally said. Rotrude sniffled and wiped her nose with a kerchief, lost in thought a moment. "It was not meant for Claudie Warn," Rotrude added surely, back on point. Orosia frowned slightly as her question wasn't answered at all. This proved the Lessonmaster's ineptitude. She would surely tell her father. "She did nothing wrong," Rotrude went on. "Worse, she was imprisoned for ten long years." The children's eyes widened. "Claudie certainly did not deserve that."

Malla raised her hand, eying distraught Avina. "For ten whole years? Why? Why didn't anyone save her?"

"The New? They tried. Thousands of troops laid siege to Animus but were no match for the fortress wall. Too soon, winter drew near and they retreated, lest starve," Rotrude said sadly. "The assault halved every army there, not to mention, destroyed most of the Animus Realm economy. Eventually, the New realms crawled back to their prospective areas of the Kingdom to plot and lick their wounds."

The fire dimmed again behind her. Rotrude tossed on a fat, splintery log.

"By 3990, almost exactly 60 years ago, the New and Old armies were built up again. Tensions were high in light of all the other catalysts I've just reviewed, especially. It was then, days before the Spring Solstice, the New laid siege to Animus. New came from all over the Kingdom in competing armor and weapons, all fighting for the same cause. All there to rescue and crown their chosen Queen." She took a deep breath and assessed the children briefly, then exhaled against the back of her throat. Part of her hated that she had to rob these young minds of their innocence, but that was the state of the Kingdom they lived in. And it was the duty of her honoured position.

"King Orell ordered that the bedraggled Claudie, ten years imprisoned, be carried to the cusp of the wall, in view of everyone below," Rotrude said, and looked from side to side. The children waited, listening. "To his credit, King Orell stood right there on the wall next to her as he ordered the execution himself."

"They killed her!" Avina shouted.

"Yes," Rotrude said flatly. "Hung her in front of all." She put her finger at the bridge of her nose and squinted at the pulse in her head. She took a breath, noting the children uncomfortably wiggle in their seats.

"I know it's cold and this lesson is lengthy." She sighed and rubbed her temple. "My head is killing me," she confessed. "I'll mention one last thing, then you're free to go."

The children collectively cheered.

For the first time all morning, Rotrude broke into a pleasant, albeit weary, smile. She pushed her fingers to her temple and squinted her eyes, but persevered.

"In the 3960s, Thor Morfit, eldest brother of Andren Morfit and expected heir to elderclaim for Croft Hold, was cast out of his blood home by their father Myles after wedding Karin Norland. Together at Animus Rock they had one son named Eugene. This branch of the bloodline was neutral throughout the majority of fighting and stayed in the refuge of the Animus castle." She paced and rubbed her hands together. "We will go over all of this in detail to come," she assured, "especially once you're in Upper. But, remember Thor Morfit. He was one of the two keys to end the war, the other I'll cover later."

She cleared her throat.

"While Thor Morfit and his family were safe here at the Capital," Rotrude gestured around, "Myles Morfit, his father, his younger brother Andren, heir to elderclaim, and Andren's three sons lived at Croft. It was 4001, eleven years into the Uprising."

The children collectively leaned forward in anticipation.

"The Old attacked Croft Hold in a brilliant surprise siege,"

Rotrude explained. "Everyone there was killed."

"Oh no," Avina said a final time, fully defeated.

Malla raised her hand.

"Yes?"

"Didn't that happen during the Blood Wars?"

"The Silent Siege? Good memory," Rotrude nodded in approval. "Sadly, it happened again nearly a hundred years later. This time, referred to as the Croft Massacre."

The children nodded.

"The only surviving Morfits were Thor and his family, as well as his nephew Elias's children, daughters Leah and Sheila Morfit, sheltered at Hellswater with their mother Sama Demos. Since Miles and Andren were dead and the part-Demosblood girls gave no contest for Morfit elderclaim, Thor regained his title. After the destruction was cleared away, Thor moved his family to Croft. He obtained command of all of the New realms' armies as his brother had."

She paced and went on.

"Many initially were concerned about where Thor's allegiances lay, especially with his marriage to Norland in the midst of conflict. He did, however, prove to be faithful to the cause." That fact never sat right with Rotrude, but who was she to question what she'd been taught? "Unfortunately," she said, "he was a terrible strategist. In a series of crushing blows, he ran the New right into the ground." The children's faces were clouded, like a sky about to rain. "If you blame anyone directly for the outcome of the Uprising, it is Thor Morfit." Rotrude shook her head sadly. "Him, and Lachlan Regnard."

She spat at the flames.

GRACEVIEW

Ryd could feel his heart pounding in his chest, begging him to fight. To argue. To cling to his beloved companions. But he knew he could not. He and Digory had gotten into a predicament that only Mable and Chester could get them out of now. He felt tremendous guilt. How could he leave his steeds?

"You swear you will care for them properly? Speak to them daily. No more than a fortnight for horseshoes. Chester likes extra hay. And Mable's mane grows a bit long, and needs to be trimmed every…"

"Yes," Sieff interrupted, then looked over his shoulder, smiling warmly. Torch light accentuated shadows and illuminated all the lines in his face. "Yes, truly. I will care well for your horses. They will soon be the most valuable possessions I own," he added sincerely, trying to ease Ryd's mind, but the thought didn't comfort him one bit.

"Right," Ryd said, sighing, defeated. Mable and Chester were priceless, he thought. His last connection to his father, his brother and the only home he ever knew. He hung his head, studying the tops of his borrowed boots, thinking how foreign they felt on his feet, following behind Sieff in single file.

"You did the right thing," Digory said to his back. Ryd grunted. It didn't feel like the right thing.

The group travelled through a natural tunnel system in close succession behind a torch-bearing Viccouro clad in typical red. The robed man held the flaming implement above him high to brighten the reaches of the cave. The stalactite cathedral dripped a time-laden layer of precision-terminated crystals. The clear quartz points threatened the party from above like sharp, melting ice. As with many fearsome things, the beauty was breathtaking.

"This is really all under the city?" Digory said in awe, unable to hold back his amazement assessed the crystals overhead.

"A secret of the Viccouri," Sieff offered half over his shoulder at Digory, at the far back of the line. "What you mark bartered for."

"Where does it lead?"

"The edge of the midmarks."

Digory exhaled in slight annoyance. "That means nothing to me."

Sieff sighed with frustration too while the Viccouro in lead ignored them totally. He still walked with torch high, never once turning back to listen to the group's conversation. His arm had to be exhausted, Digory thought. It was nearly inhuman.

"This," Sieff said as he gestured above at the sparkly crystal ceiling, "takes us underneath the fields and the Poison."

"Okay, fine," Digory said, sighing, remembering something about a wall of poison that had to be bypassed. "Fine, but what is the midmarks?"

"A place for common man."

"What's that mean?"

"Hardworking folk," Sieff told him with a bite of defensive pride. "A respectable elevation."

Ryd's interest piqued. "Elevation has to do with your lines?"

"Marks," Sieff corrected, "and, yes."

Curiosity brought Ryd out of his pouting lull. "How?" he asked.

"We are born with none," Sieff told him, half glancing back every so often. "As children we have many opportunities to elevate. As we grow, missions increase in length or difficulty. If we are young or unmotivated we only have marks on our legs and feet. This constitutes the lowmarks." His bootsteps scuffed against moist rocks underfoot, echoing about the ever-widening, fully engulfing crystal cave. "The hardworking and pious rise up," Sieff continued. "Those of the midmarks are rewarded for their marks with pleasures or leisure. It is why so many remain here, so far from the level of elevation I seek," Sieff added hotly. "They are unfocused by this world's means of control. It distracts from the mission," he said plainly. The Viccouro in front scoffed audibly. "More or less," Sieff defended. "It's much to explain, you do a better job," he challenged. The man in the red robe shrugged silently. It seemed he wanted to be left out of it.

"Fine, so the more marks, the better?" Digory asked, flexing his bearded jaw.

"What makes the lowmarks and the…" Ryd paused.

"Midmarks," Sieff offered.

"Midmarks different?" Ryd finished.

"Labor, factory, and field workers fill the lowmarks mostly. The Spice Walk in the far north," he said as he walked carefully over slick pebbles underfoot. "Groves are northwest and grain fields, vegetables, and livestock to the west edged right up to the Poison."

"Got it…" Digory said unsurely, grappling with Graceview's enormity. This city must be nearly as big as a whole realm, he thought.

"Then in the southwest, the low of the low," Sieff started, shaking his head.

"What's there?" Ryd asked.

"Copper mines," Sieff said woefully.

"Sounds awful," Ryd replied, mirroring their guide's tone.

Sieff shrugged. "Mostly children," he added, as if that was consolation.

Ryd frowned, stung, immediately thinking of Col. "That's worse."

"But they can get out, right?" Digory prodded. "Get more of your shiny lines to move up?"

"Marks," Sieff said sharply, then sighed and paused, too frustrated to speak, yet he forced himself to continue, as if compelled. "As I said, the lowmarks is for the young or useless. Anyone there too far into birthing years is pitiful."

Digory smirked but entertained the strange concept. It seemed Graceview had a caste system, albeit more ridged than he'd ever heard of. "Alright," he said, appreciating Graceview's judgmental mindset. "What about the middle place, then?"

"The midmarks? From here, to here," Sieff gestured from his hips up his abdomen to his neckline.

"No, no," Digory shook his head. "I got that's where the lines go, but are the midmarks like?"

The Viccouro chuckled underneath his blood-colored hood at Digory's placating tone but didn't turn.

Sieff sighed. "The midmarks, some call it the middlemarks, sits around the foremarks on the east and south sides," he said simply.

"Of course," Digory said, knowing Sieff knew he didn't know what that meant. "The foremarks. Sure."

Sieff continued, unfazed. "There are five districts. We'll enter in the fifth. Four Point."

"Four Point?" Digory asked, wondering why the fifth district only had four points. Sieff nodded to confirm.

"It is a market."

"Didn't we pass through it on the outskirts in the forest?" Ryd asked. He thought back to their interlude in Blackwood and his delicious meal. Silence followed. "Graceview has more than one market?"

Sieff and the Viccouro laughed out loud in harmony. When finished, Sieff said, "Oh yes," he half turned to speak over his shoulder, "Five."

"Five?" Ryd repeated.

"Really?" Digory added in surprise. "Westerviolet has three in her entire realm. And only one within the Westerviolet commons."

"It's true," Sieff affirmed. "If you count Blackwood. It is makeshift but functioning all the same."

"Why so many?" Ryd questioned.

"The midmarks is large and herself has two," Sieff told him. "Each is tailored to its district," he added.

"Today we go to... Four Point?" Ryd asked.

"Exactly." Sieff nodded. "The tunnel is there."

"Another tunnel?"

"To the castle gardens," Sieff said.

"Why do we care about a garden?" Digory challenged. "I told you we want to leave, not go to the cursed Vanguard castle."

Sieff's patience with Digory was thin and it was evident in his tone. "It has the only gate to the other side of the wall and forest. From there only a day's walk to Littlebell."

"I see," Digory replied, mulling the new information over slowly, realizing he was too far in now not to trust the man.

"He will help us," Sieff gestured to the Viccouro.

"He better," Ryd grumbled, missing Mable and Chester already, "after the price paid."

Digory leaned forward and patted his companion on the back of his shoulder. It was uncharacteristic, but he felt compelled to do it. "Like I said, the right thing."

"Hmph," Ryd mumbled. "Can't wait to walk the rest of the way."

"What was that?"

"Nothing, nothing," Ryd grumbled more, wallowing in self-pity. In single file, from behind, Digory shook his head silently.

As they progressed the cavern ceiling drew tighter and closer to them. The stalactites did not dull, instead, increased in grandeur. Soon the walls pulled together to where hands easily grazed each side without far reach at all. At times, one had to duck to avoid sharp nearly water-clear crystals. Torch light refracted off the quartz tunnel in a mirage of dainty rainbows. It was breath-taking to behold.

Eventually the cavern narrowed forcing travel to hands and knees for the final stretch before exiting to the surface. The rock directly beneath them was long ago polished smooth from overuse and the men only had to duck to avoid scraping foreheads and shoulders. The group crawled on an upwards incline for endless painstaking moments before the tunnel emptied into a finished chamber.

The walls were papered black and the floor was lined with expensive-looking red-tone woven rugs. There were no windows and one low-burned fire. A staircase at the far end led upstairs towards a hint of light.

After they'd all tumbled into the chamber, the Viccouro gestured for Ryd and Digory to follow as he headed to the upper floor, robes kicking out with each step. They fell in line behind him. One by one they walked up the staircase into setting sun beams streaming in through black-tinted round windows. They were now in an identical building to the one they'd left behind in the Lowmarks. Digory and Ryd found themselves standing in a square room with modest furniture and drapery. Walls were mainly bare, apart from long tapestries each embroidered with an all-seeing red eye that appeared to watch you as you stared at it; The Viccouri emblem.

"Before we go," Sieff said, "take what he has for you."

"What more could there be?" Ryd turned to see the Viccouro holding two robes identical to Sieff's in one hand. In his other, two center-part ponytail wings in wavy dark brown.

"Oh no," Digory said.

"It is necessary," Sieff replied with a smirk.

Ryd sighed and approached the Viccouro. They'd come this far, why turn back now? He took the garment and hairpiece, then smelled each with trepidation.

Digory was dumbfounded. He couldn't be serious. "What are you doing?" he asked Ryd with a raised eyebrow.

"You heard him," Ryd gestured over his shoulder with his thumb to the guide. "Necessary."

"One more thing," Sieff said with full half grin now, natural frowning face obviously pleased. He withdrew a sharp, thornesblade from his breast pocket then unsheathed it to reveal the shine. "There are is no hair of the face here," he said as he approached Digory.

"Oh, curses no," Digory said, realizing their guide's intent as he backed up.

"But, you must," Sieff said as he raised his brows.

"You're enjoying this, aren't you?"

"They will spot you if not," Sieff defended hotly. "Don't dress and risk capture. Thorne Watch will surely spot you," he added cryptically with a hint of fear. "I only guide you. It's your path."

"Ugh," Digory moaned, tired of the man's inundated speech. Wondering if he wouldn't rather take on Thorne Watch instead.

Sieff took a few steps across the chamber and handed him the blade. "There is a bin there," he said, gesturing with his head to the side.

Digory wanted to fight back, to protest or complain, but Sieff was right. If the story held and no foreigners were present in Graceview, particularly so deep behind her fortifications, he would quickly be seen and given up. Begrudgingly Digory grunted to acknowledge Sieff's command as he half-heartedly shuffled towards the bin. Ryd watched Digory with wide eyes as he hacked at his beard. Course dark hair sprinkled the lip of the basin as his strong sharp jaw shone through.

"I can't believe you're doing it," Ryd said with awe.

"You got rid of the beasts."

Ryd shrugged and looked down.

Not long later, Digory was freshly shaven. His beardless face was sharply handsome, yet youthful; nearly innocent. Ryd couldn't stop staring at him.

"Am I too ugly for you?" Digory glared at him, but Ryd only blinked. Then Digory inspected his chin with his hand, feeling smooth skin there for the first time since he was a lad. "What?" he barked again. "Why are you staring at me?"

"Nothing, I've just…" Ryd said then trailed off, searching for the words. Digory looked like a different man. His regal jaw reminded Ryd of the legendary statues outside of Westerviolet on the Ancestor Walk. "I've not seen you without a beard is all," he finally said.

"Right," Digory grunted as he assessed his new appearance in a polished glass. "Does it look okay?" he asked over his shoulder quickly, then turned back to glare at the unfamiliar face staring back at him.

Ryd laughed loud, surprised the proud Digory showed any hint of insecurity. "You care what I think?"

"Forget it." Digory frowned as he recoiled. "Curse you," he

spat.

"Are you two finished?" Sieff assessed them, glancing up and down to study their new garb.

Digory and Ryd now both wore long dark robes somewhere between black and dark grey, however, clearly distinguishable color was long lost from years of use. Both garments smelled like sand and mildew. Ryd's was too long and bunched underfoot as he walked while Digory's was a bit short and stopped above his ankles. "Good. Put on your hairpieces," Sieff added. "There. Wonderful."

The matching ponytail wings appeared human, and stank as such too, Ryd thought, as he and Digory adjusted their attire.

"We look ridiculous," Ryd assessed dryly.

Sieff pointedly frowned at him, insulted, and silently gestured to the door. Ryd and Digory took the hint. As they walked out, Sieff turned head. He lowered his voice in warning. "Never reveal your fores," he said under his breath.

"Fores?" Ryd asked.

Sieff stuck out his arm in example. "You're unmarked," he said, like it was obvious. "Never remove the cloak at all," he added. Ryd nodded assuredly, taking the warning fully to heart.

"Got it," Digory said sarcastically. He couldn't stop rubbing his newly smooth chin over and over.

"It looks fine," Ryd told him. Digory mumbled an incoherent response. Ryd shrugged, then fell into silent observation as the group, including their silent red-robed Viccouro companion, exited the dark, squat structure.

They walked into the Midmarks.

"Wow," Ryd blurted, swinging his head from left to right, senses fully overwhelmed. They spilled into a bustling metropolis with the Viccouri's flower-topped building behind them. The air churned with a bouquet of the exotic floral blooms.

"Impressive, right?" Sieff said, grinning as his eyes swept across Four Point.

Ryd hesitated. "Not quite..." he trailed off as he noticed a gaggle of prisoners in cages, "the word."

"I was not expecting this," Digory said and nearly laughed, realizing instantly they'd stepped into a slave market.

"Is this..." Ryd started, then paused with questioning inflection.

"Four Point," Sieff finished quickly. "Yes," he added, nodding, smiling proudly.

"I thought you said it was a market," Ryd accused Sieff. Anger lapped at the confusion on his boyishly handsome face.

Sieff frowned in paramount puzzlement. "But, my Lords, it is," he said as he gestured out off to the right. "There, you see. Tomorrow's' wares for auction in morn."

Digory chuckled. "What the curses," he mumbled under his breath, shaking his head, amazed at the immorality. And he thought he was the evil one...

Four Point looked nothing like the Lowmarks. It was similarly constructed to the Lowmarks in that it was made of single-story buildings covered in gardens, but here, plants atop each roof were thin and spiked in light pale green. Buildings were constructed of darker brown instead of red. Bricks were cut smaller and mortared with black paste, instead of placed freely as in the Lowmarks, obviously of higher craftsmanship and quality. Alleys here were few, far-between, and well-hidden unlike the wider of the Lowmarks. Roads were small stone paved instead of hard-packed dirt. Buildings here were mostly connected town homes with curved faces and window panes to mirror the bends of the roads.

The Viccouri's building was exempt. as in the lowmarks, it was topped with a floral bouquet. This black structure was the apparent center of chaos here, with a large open square immediately in front of it. A spiral road sprung out from this piazza and encircled the whole building in a wide curve with all the darker brown brick town homes lining it.

Unlike how damp and still it was in the cavern, the air outside was dry, windy and hot as the sun dipped behind the only clouds, crowded up against the edge of the western skyline. Beams of light burst from behind them, much like the torch light off the earlier tunnel's crystals.

The natives here were dressed in identical attire but came and went freely, unlike those of the Lowmarks. The people here didn't walk with head down or in lines. There was, instead, an assaulting cacophony of yelling, shouting, and bartering. It was even louder than Littlebell, Ryd thought.

More than just the din reminded Ryd of Littlebell. The way they used their hands was reminiscent of the Minney's realm, but for widely different purpose, he figured. Nearly each native here spoke with swooping hand gestures, walked with wide arms, or gesticulated to one another in other various, dramatic ways to shake the sleeves free and reveal portions of their arms covered in silver marks. Most natives here too had their robes loose in front, sometimes with v-cut tunic below, to showcase marks on neck and chest.

Here the crowd glimmered above the waist, not below.

Most natives in the Midmarks carried more weight than in the Lowmarks, with hanging rounded bellies, lumped hips and ample chins. Men and women alike shared excess of adipose tissue. Teeth were notably darkened or yellow, or in many cases, missing entirely. Cheeks were mostly oily or pockmarked. Most had leather or cloth satchels slung over shoulder, indented into soft flesh. Most too carried some kind of spiced and skewered meat or fried bread in hand as they walked or shopped. Others drank from bulbous casks.

As in the Lowmarks, all were nearly identical with sunken eyes and naturally frowning expressions. The only differentiating feature between them, Ryd noticed on close inspection, was the type or number of rings on the hand. Most of the individuals here had dainty copper bands almost too thin to notice with hammered designs too delicate for Ryd to distinguish on their pinkies or thumbs. Much different from Littlebell's heavily jewelled fashions, worn primarily by men.

Also, notably, nearly everyone in the Midmarks wore boots. Actually, Ryd couldn't find someone without boots. The ground was dim in comparison to the flash of the lowmarks.

"Where is Thorne Watch?" Ryd asked Sieff's back. "I thought you said they're everywhere."

"They are," he said in a disbelieving hush.

"What's he talking about?" Ryd whispered to Digory. Digory shrugged, distracted by the sights of Graceview.

The square outside the Viccouri's black building was lined with crude carts much like the makeshift market through Blackwood, however more compact and portable with wheels to move stations from here to there, and far better built. Each sold the various wares that the larger natives carried and chomped on as they walked or waddled from station to station.

And Digory had thought Littlebell to be overrun with people, like vermin. However, Littlebell's city paled in comparison to Graceview's Midmarks, in his mind. So many people mindlessly consuming, flashing their silver lines at each other, like that makes them better than their neighbour. Digory shook his head, thinking of how so many were entrapped by the lies of Thorneblood. These people, although fat and happy, like suckling pigs, were prisoners. Prisoners of the worst kind, because they believed themselves to be free.

The buildings lining the square stood mostly as storefronts behind the carts. There were wide window panes, clear to expose rows and rows of various items for purchase, or rather, mark barter, within. One such store was lined with new, yet identical black cloth cloaks. Another was stocked with each imaginable size of the same brown leather boots. The next had hair products. Several shops had various herbs, dried mushrooms, flowers or leaves, all with signs in front of them bearing symbols indicating what they did. A few stores had living plants in pots in them, one with tiny, beautiful flowers with mouths and snapping teeth, that both Digory and Ryd eyed curiously. Some shops were filled with mounds of competing spices, others—meats, cheeses, breads, and so on. The mall of Four Point was fully alive with action. Within every shop natives shouted in barter, waving arms and fists furiously in the air.

Ryd peered inside one shop quickly as they walked past the bedlam. He listened to the throaty customer's voice barking with foreign inflection to the shopkeeper as she waved both fleshy arms over her head wildly. Then, his attention was caught by a sorry looking group to his far right.

At the far corner of the large square from the black structure was an open lot with a rectangular platform. Behind the platform were four rows of four towering cages. Inside each cage were dozens of men, women, and children in meagre rags or ripped cloaks, thin to the bone with sunken expressions. Men and women alike had unkempt hair, not styled in the Graceview ponytail or braided-bun fashions, but left loose and untamed. Most were bare of silver marks all together, although few had one or two on the tops of their feet. No more. The prisoners huddled in the corners of the cages against cold iron bars or shuttered in nightmare filled sleep.

A man identical to Sieff from a distance, except he was shorter with more weight around his middle, stood in guard of the cages. He had thick copper bands on his wrists held a black spear with arm-length polished pointed tip. As he patrolled, he barked nonsensically every so often, poking inside the cages threateningly, seemingly enjoying his brutish task.

Ryd cringed. "Is he Thorne Watch?" he asked Sieff.

Sieff chuckled. "No."

"What is this place?"

"You mean the Trade?" Sieff gestured over to the platform on the right. "Do not fret," he added, noting Ryd's troubled expression. "They're just Lowmarkers."

"But..." Ryd trailed off. He was stunned. "They're people," he finally said.

Sieff shrugged. "It is District Three's business."

"What is District Three?" Ryd asked, even more confused.

"The Overseers," Sieff said simply.

"Course," Digory replied. "Obviously, Ryd."

"It is their marks," Sieff added with a flat brow, tired of Digory's tone. "The Lowmarks is their responsibility."

"Sieff can you explain?" Ryd said as he loudly sighed. "You know we don't know what you're talking about," he added, footsteps pounding loudly on the path with black rocks pressed into the sandy pale dirt.

"Someone has to oversee them," Sieff said as he walked, obviously irritated, speaking as he would to a child. "They cannot be trusted to manage themselves, poor heathen-like souls. It's the task of those who reside in the Midmarks, in District Three." He gestured around at the chaos.

"To oversee the Lowmarks?" Ryd asked, finishing his statement. Sieff nodded approvingly.

Ryd was distraught. "What's that have to do with slavery?" he asked as he scratched the back of his neck with his hand. The gesture jostled his sleeve down to his wrist.

Instantly Sieff darted to Ryd's side and gripped his arm with unnerving strength, forcing it down. Sieff met Ryd's eyes and blinked once, as if holding his breath, waiting for an invisible force to swallow Ryd whole, but nothing happened. After a long confusing moment for both Ryd and Digory watching on, Sieff spoke. "Who said anything about slaves?" he asked and frowned, dropping Ryd's arm as if the interaction never occurred. He continued through Four Point.

"But... but..." Ryd started, then faltered. He looked again at the pitiful creatures locked up to his right. He felt his heart crack when he met eyes with a frail girl not much younger than Col, huddling in the arms of a woman that appeared to already be dead, head leaning backwards against cool metal bars with eyes and mouth agape.

"Come on," Digory prodded, stung by the same emotion Ryd was, just not as strongly. "Look," he urged, pointing at the four packed cages as the sun fell behind one of the two overgrown Graceview castle towers. Everything instantly cast in chilly shadow. Where Digory was pointing, bodies huddled in the corners of the cages. The ones not asleep had eyes wide in fear. "How can you say that?" he asked Sieff, nearly genuinely. "Caged. Like beasts. Just speak the truth of it. They're cursed slaves."

"You do not understand our ways," Sieff retorted as his face clouded. "Do not mock our culture."

"Wait... but..." Ryd started.

"It is great honor for them to be chosen for the Trade, but I waste breath." Sieff spat at the gravelly, sandy ground. "You are not worth it."

"Honor?" Ryd repeated indignantly, glancing at the prisoners again. "How?!"

Sieff seemed to barely hear him and sped up his pace to match that of the Viccouro, who up until now, had led the group from a good distance, seeming to want to stay out of the discussion entirely. "Extinct," Sieff muttered under his breath, barely audible to either Ryd or Digory.

"Hey, dolt," Digory spat at Sieff's back, "answer us!" but Sieff brooded in silence aside the red-robed Viccouro.

Ryd hung back and fell in line next to Digory. He looked from side to side then whispered, "Can you believe this place?"

Digory shook his head. He couldn't. "I'll admit I wasn't expecting," Digory paused, "this…" he trailed off. "I'm a bit impressed," he finally said. Ryd scowled at him. "They're totally brainwashed," Digory muttered, amazed by the brilliance of whoever was controlling them all, then chuckled to himself. He laughed louder.

"What?" Ryd asked finally, glancing to the side, still not used to Digory's beardless face. "What's so funny?"

Digory smiled wide as if drunk and shook his head. "Ryd," he started, then said in singsong, "pity not the dolt, but the man behind."

Unamused, wondering if Digory had gone mad, Ryd asked flatly, "What are you talking about?"

"Oh, you know… Duh-duh-duh, don't forget the rhyme," Digory sang the familiar tune off key. He hadn't thought about it in decades. Something about it made his heart flip in his chest but he couldn't remember why and shrugged that feeling aside.

Ryd smirked, surprised to hear Digory sing. "You never struck me as a bard."

"It's nothing," Digory paused, cheeks reddening, then added, "just a Westerviolet kid's ballad."

"Never heard it," Ryd said, boots scuffing against rocks. "Why sing now?" he asked, squinting at Digory.

"We're here judging Sieff, but we're following the dolt. What does that make us?"

Ryd frowned. "Bigger dolts," he sighed.

"This is all on you, you know," Digory accused glaringly. "If we'd cursed taken the Missi..."

Ryd shoved him. "Curse you, Digory," he said then stormed ahead. He fell in line next to Sieff.

Digory sighed. The Viccouro had hung back, forced to follow behind Sieff and Ryd due to the pulse of the crowd and walked only slightly ahead of him now. Digory leaned in a conversation attempt.

"He's a Vanguard castle, am I right?" Digory said, trying to commiserate with a smirking tone. But, face cloaked in shadow from his red cloth hood, true to form, the Viccouro didn't respond.

Meanwhile Ryd's gaze caught on a brilliant glinting light on the horizon between the pale green spiked roofed buildings. He realized quickly it was the Bank's glistening dome Sieff bragged of earlier. Its top curvature shone in taunting brilliance just as the sun dropped out of view, sending out an unnatural beam of light that swept the city, then disappeared in a flash.

When the sun was fully gone from the horizon and the two overgrown Graceview castle towers fell into darkness, an ethereal chill descended. The dry hot air felt instantly thick with moisture. A heavy, foggy dew set in. Mist settled into the curved streets and between the high-spiked leaves of the rooftop gardens. In well-orchestrated fashion, torches were lit on roofs as lanterns. One by one delicate lights popped on across the Midmarks, like a blanket of stars across the land, creeping towards Graceview's monstrous overgrown castle at its head.

The effect on the pale spiked roof-leaves was otherworldly. The eerie mist was illuminated just enough by the flaming lanterns that the spiked grasses cast massive dancing shadows across the building faces and roads. Ryd gaped in apprehensive awe at fog-laden landscape.

"We are nearly there," Sieff said, half turning head over his shoulder to look back at them. "And it could not be too soon," he added ominously as he turned back ahead.

"Why?" Ryd asked. "Too soon for what?"

"The Mist set in early." Sieff said gestured at the lantern-illuminated fog.

Ryd frowned. "What's that mean?" he asked, thinking it must be bad if it was anything as threatening as the setting presently looked.

"Soon comes the Pour," Sieff explained. "We must find shelter."

Ryd sighed loudly against the back of his throat. "Should I ask?"

"Ah, this is your first eve in Graceview," Sieff said as pace increased. Ryd matched it. "It rains nightly."

"Each eve?" Ryd asked with surprise. "For what purpose?"

"Yes, and it is," Sieff said then paused in thought for a moment, "difficult." He didn't answer the second part of Ryd's question, to his great annoyance. "Best we find shelter."

Ryd was puzzled. "But," he protested, "it is so dry here. And..." he added, trailing off to kick the pebbled dry dirt at his feet, ...sandy." He didn't understand what Sieff meant by Pour. Surely it didn't rain each eve in Graceview. Sieff must be mistaken, Ryd thought. "How?" he asked with unbelieving inflection.

"It's in the Teachings," Sieff replied with a shrug, obviously not interested in explaining further. "We must find shelter."

"Alright, alright," Ryd said. "Whatever," he sighed, pausing for an instant when he recognized deep sarcasm in his own tone, absorbed from Digory. "Lead the way," he added flatly, inwardly unnerved by his own inflection.

Digory skipped up to them after witnessing the exchange from behind. He couldn't hear a word, for the Midmarks was alive with chaotic bartering, shouting and the sound of wild animals at slaughter. He'd noted a butcher several paces back, swarmed by Graceview natives clamouring to purchase the apparently paramount wares. Unlike elsewhere in the Kingdom, even at Westerviolet, this butcher had living stock available. Amazing, it seemed like Graceview natives of the midmarks bartered with their marks for opportunity to slay a beast, that the butcher was to clean for them. He watched from a side-eye as a middle-years woman with drooping face, eager eyes and nearly as many marks as Sieff himself drove a dagger into the neck of a pristine white lamb. The woman broke into a wide smile and the rest of the onlookers clapped for her in an array of silver flashing arms and hands as deep red blood stained the young lamb's coat and it let out a final pitiful cry. "What'd he say?" Digory asked Ryd as he half watched Graceview's strange custom. It was still too crowded to walk freely or at each other's sides.

"Nothing," Ryd half turned, then looked ahead again.

Soon, the group broke away from the hubbub as Sieff followed the Viccouro down an alley hidden between two identical buildings with crumbling bricks. Ryd was amazed at the man's sense of direction. Everything looked the same to him in this part of the city. Dark brick building after dark brick building, each topped with the spikey grass, like square heads with wild hair, masked in a heavy cloak of fog, convoluted like a dream. If Ryd hadn't known the hidden alley was there, he wouldn't have been able to find it.

The alley spilled the group out onto another part of the midmarks, nearly identical to Four Point's market in a nautilus shape, however, this section had no caged prisoners. Instead, there were racks and racks of animals for purchase in addition to the typical wares of food and drink that they'd witnessed earlier. Ryd frowned as he noted costermongers quickly pack away their wares and pull under awnings, or inside buildings entirely. Storefronts slammed their doors. Everyone was moving hurriedly as if bracing for imminent attack. Ryd's stomach knotted in anticipation as all the hair on the back of his neck stood up, then a jolt of electricity ran down then up his spine. A resounding crack cut through the air in ear-piercing tone.

To his shock, an unbelievably huge bolt of red lightning lit up the sky, as if the clouds themselves threatened to bleed.

Digory instinctively jumped backwards and his hand

immediately went to hover over his concealed dagger. Ryd jumped too, but instead of crouching ready to fight, he cowered with a look of horror on his face. Both men relaxed slightly when they noticed neither Sieff nor the Viccouro flinched.

"The Pour," Sieff said casually over his shoulder at the startled men. "I attempted to explain to you," he added with half a smile as he tucked errant hairs behind his ears escaped from his ponytail from the charged air, seemingly pleased at Digory's reaction particularly. "This way," he added as he turned down a more narrow, dimmer alley.

Digory scowled at Sieff's hunched shoulders yet held back a retort and collected himself. He went to scratch his beard and hesitated when he gripped a smooth chin, then loudly sighed in frustration, wondering when he'd gone so soft. He barely recognized himself, physically or otherwise. Sybil would surely laugh at him for his troubles, he thought woefully.

"Where are you taking us?" Ryd demanded, voice fractured in fear as the sky lit up again with a cutting red bolt. It illuminated each of the men's faces in shadow and highlighted the spiked leaves.

"What the curse is that!?" Digory shouted upwards.

"Firebolts," Sieff said with a hint of amusement. "Why we shelter, if that is not obvious."

"Now it's cursed obvious," Digory muttered.

"Here," Sieff shouted over another firebolt's thunderous crack as he shot through a narrow-arched frame with no door.

Digory and Ryd exchanged a quick glance, then followed Sieff and the Viccouro inside. Anything was better than the firebolts, Ryd thought to himself, as he reluctantly stepped through the archway.

Ryd wasn't surprised to see that the archway led to a modest covered entryway with a tarnished reflecting glass, spanning one wall from top to bottom. The glass made the entire space appear twice as large. Two stone benches sat against the opposite wall facing the glass. At the far end of the corridor were long-ago cut stone stairs that led in a spiral downwards.

The entire space was overgrown from apparent disuse. If Ryd had come across this room on his own, he would have considered it abandoned.

Both Ryd and Digory entered with caution, not sure what to expect next, but given the extraordinary lightning outside, it was time to seek shelter.

The dark sky opened in terrible glory the moment the men entered the chamber. It exploded in glowing red bolts followed by roaring cracks, as if hundreds of ancient trunks snapped at once. Then, it poured what could only be explained as rain, for it was liquid and fell from the sky, but the drops, weren't really drops at all. Instead, the liquid was rounded in shape. Instead of water-clear, the round drops were tinted red to match the hue of the bolt-illuminated sky. Also, unlike typical rain, these odd drops were fist size and fell to the earth with shattering force. It was terrifying to behold.

The black rocks from the path outside exploded in miniature mushroom clouds each time a round drop landed there. The water collected quickly and pooled in flowing rivers. The black rocks worked to hold the path's integrity, while allowing runoff as well.

"This is why there is a ditch in the lowmarks," Ryd mumbled to himself. "I wondered." Sieff overheard and nodded.

From across the chamber, the Viccouro gestured and grunted at them. He pointed down the spiral stairs.

"It's a dead end," Ryd said, glancing down the stairwell. Sure enough, the stairs ended in a stone wall after the first bend.

"This is where we leave you," Sieff said. "Watch," he added as he handed Ryd a torch. Ryd took it and nodded in thanks.

The Viccouro, still standing at the lip of the stairs, began a series of hand movements fully unfamiliar to both Ryd and Digory. Then, he pressed his palm into a seemingly nondescript place on the wall. Soon, what appeared to be a dead end slid out of the way, revealing the continuation of the ancient spiral staircase, carved directly into stone.

"That doesn't look like a garden," Digory said flatly. He noticed now that the ground here was solid, unlike the sandy or pebbly paths of Graceview. Instead, it matched the tone of the cavern they'd crawled through to get to the midmarks. Digory wondered, could it be another cave?

"It will lead you through a tunnel," Sieff said as he glanced down at the staircase, already wet from the Pour's ominous runoff. "Continue until a ladder," he added succinctly. "Climb it and reach the Vanguard garden," he added with serious tone. "Head North with the towers at your back. Stay hidden and you will reach the gate. It shouldn't be well patrolled."

"Really?" Ryd asked with a frown. "No patrol at closest entry to the Vanguards?"

"Oh," Sieff said, "watch the trees, of course."

"Good to know," Digory replied. "When were you planning to tell us?" he added, stepping towards their guide in menace.

Sieff backed up. He glanced quickly at Digory's weapon, fast removed from his satchel and expertly built within moments. "I... I just told you," he said, voice faltering, staring down an arrow's point. "Please, please!" he added with widening eyes as Digory flexed his jaw and took a threatening step, like a ruby fox stalking prey. "I want you to succeed more than you do. Trust me. I need this."

Ryd sighed loudly, heart catching for their terrified guide. Sieff had helped them greatly, he believed, even if he had taken the horses. "Digory come on," Ryd said in a tired exhale as he walked over to the dark, descending staircase. "Let's go."

Digory held his pack over his shoulder and crossbow ready at side in right hand. "You really trust this guy?" he gestured with the weapon. Sieff held his hands up in peace.

"What choice do we have?" Ryd asked rhetorically, meeting Digory's intense glare. Knowingly, Digory exhaled and blinked. He lowered his guard slightly.

Meanwhile, the Viccouro, having done his job and already tired of it all, turned and walked to stand at the arched edge of the odd stone-floored chamber's entryway. From under shadowed hood, he watched streaks of red light illuminate black clouds with his back to the rest of the group.

Unexpectedly, red-tint water flooded inside and began to lap at their boots. Soon, it flowed in a modest stream through the chamber and down the spiral of the staircase with the rising storm outside.

"Great," Digory said, noting the river, irritated instantly, knowing he'd have to walk through it. He dropped his crossbow to his side in defeat. Sieff breathed a sigh of relief.

"Come on," Ryd urged Digory, not wanting Chester and Mable's sacrifice to be for nothing. He turned to face their guides. "Thank you," he said to Sieff and the Viccouro. "We would have been truly lost without you. If what you say is true," Ryd started, then paused. "If what you say is true," he repeated, "and our escape is that way, you've saved our lives."

"And you," Sieff half bowed his head. "You have no idea the blessing you have enacted on me. I will finally live to see my purpose fulfilled, honouring the Great Thorne and executing my work according to His plan," he said with a genuinely wide smile, almost speaking to himself, as if he'd imagined this moment for many years. "Go," he added, snapping out of his whimsy when another firebolt cracked loudly outside. "If you are swift, you'll reach the cusp by dawn, after the Pour has subsided. You should be too early for interruption. But still, be cautious."

Ryd nodded, still stung by the loss of his faithful steeds. "Mable..." he started sadly, "and Chester..."

"They are in good hands," Sieff assured, torch light dancing across his face, highlighting his sunken eyes. "You have my word." Ryd nodded once, wanting to believe him, then he started down the staircase with the red torrent lapping at his ankles.

After Digory had broken down his crossbow and repacked it into his satchel he reluctantly followed Ryd.

Sieff turned to the Viccouro after footsteps faded. "Do you think they will make it?" he asked.

Lightning cracked. The red-robed Viccouro shrugged.

The stairwell predictably dumped them into another cave.

Unlike the previous cave, this one was obviously man-made, cut with crude hacks through dull black stone. It was wide enough for one man, and tall enough for Ryd to walk comfortably. Digory was forced to crouch awkwardly as to not hit his head on the rock ceiling, feet squishing through mud, red-tone water lapping at his calves. Ryd held the torch out high in front of them, despite his arm shaking from the weight. Light bounced off the blunted rock-face.

"I keep telling myself she's worth it," Ryd said solemnly, thinking of Vera's chilling blue eyes. Remembering how he felt when he was near her. Like nothing could go wrong. Digory sighed. "What was that for?" Ryd half turned, provoked by his inflection.

"Just, why?"

"What is it you insult this time? Please just have your fun and be done quickly," Ryd said. "I really tire of this Digory."

"Come on," Digory jested with a provoking smile, nearly blinding when he was clean-shaven, unhidden by his dark beard. "I don't get it." He paused, then added, "I don't get you."

"What's your problem now?" Ryd paused aside a moist rock wall.

"You don't know her," Digory said plainly behind Ryd, forced to walk behind him through the narrow-chiselled tunnel. Each time either spoke, their voices echoed off the walls.

"I do," Ryd defended. "I do know her very well."

"How?" Digory smirked and scratched his bare chin out of habit. "How could you possibly?"

"You were near dead," Ryd retorted. "I don't expect you to remember."

"Hmph," Digory grunted. "You mean that horrid excuse for a kiss? Oh," he said, "I remember."

"Hey," Ryd warned loudly. "She's special. Truly, she's genuine light embodied."

"Aye," Digory said, nodding. "No argument there."

"I don't mean the blue eye thing," Ryd said quickly.

"Course," Digory retorted, nearly chuckling. "You mean the magic healing powers thing."

"Digory!" Ryd shouted in an uncharacteristic growl, turning to press him up against the rock wall. The gesture flung Digory's temple into the curved ceiling. Head throbbing, he deeply frowned. "You swore never to speak..." Ryd started, but Digory loudly interrupted, rubbing the pulsing welt on his head with the back of one hand, the other hovering over his dagger.

"Oh," Digory said with a hint of cheer despite his injury, delighted at Ryd's discomfort, "how could I not? You haven't thought of it?"

Ryd's instincts told him to stand firm, but he was tired and conceded. "I can't stop thinking about it," he admitted in a breath to Digory, remembering the swirling green and black pools of Vera's eyes as she healed him. "All of it." He exhaled then swallowed. "Her," he added.

The pair faced each other awkwardly in the carved tunnel, Digory crouched and Ryd standing with the tips of his coarse curls brushing the rock race.

Digory shook his head. He chuckled.

This infuriated Ryd and he took off again, not caring what the Guardsman did. He was going to rescue Vera and find Col without Digory, he thought angrily, to himself.

"Are you that blind, still, after all we've been through?" Digory taunted at his back. The words echoed around Ryd and continued to in his mind for long after he'd heard them. Instead of continuing the assault, Digory stopped and let silence permeate the cave.

After a while, Digory's neck and back were beginning to ache. He was tired of crouching and more tired still of the stale humid air and his irritating companion leading the way. That dolt will be a liability, he thought to himself, wondering how they were to make it through to the outside of Graceview.

"Why do you torture me!?" Ryd erupted without warning, jarring Digory from thought. "She's the only beam of light in my dark life. Why will you not leave it?!" He shouted with a tremor in his voice that warned he might cry.

Taken aback, Digory stopped, still crouched from the low

ceiling. He was stunned by the outburst in such a way he couldn't place it, half disgusted by the unruly show of emotion yet half brought to his knees. Digory was beginning to care for Ryd, and this unsettled him greatly.

Ryd didn't notice the pause until the cavern was notably quieter from one less pair of splashing footfalls. "Are you coming?" he asked, tone still angrily inflected as he turned backwards.

Digory shook his head like awoken from a dream. "Yeah," he said. He sounded defeated.

"What is it now?" Ryd kept walking, then paused when answered with silence. He was angry at Digory for taunting him, but still appreciated the man's company, despite himself. Digory was the closest thing to a friend he'd ever had. He didn't mean to insult him. He looked back. "Why do you pout?"

Digory furrowed his brow and frowned but said nothing. He ground his jaw; sharp line of bone and muscles clear now without obstruction of long-worn beard.

Ryd shook his head, accepting that Digory had his secrets. He sighed and continued on.

They came across a fork in the tunnel. One branch was man-made like where they came from, and the other appeared to be natural.

"Which way do we go?" Ryd asked.

Digory frowned. "Seiff didn't say anything about this."

A hiss came from the natural tunnel, so unexpected and terrifying that both men jumped.

"This one," Digory said, walking hastily down the man-made one.

"Aye," Ryd said warily, looking down the natural tunnel briefly. He caught the faintest glimpse of too many eyes. He hurried after Digory.

The rest of tunnel took all night. The torch went dim and extinguished to sad grey ash and puffs of smoke just as a series of bars embedded in the flat rock face ahead came into view. The pair didn't particularly need the torch as their eyes were genetically accustomed to darkness, yet, they spent so much of their lives in the day that they were more comfortable with ambient light at least. It was that way with all natives. They easily adapted to their conditions. If kept in darkness they grew to have impeccable vision at night yet lost ability to go into the light, and the opposite held true as well.

"The ladder," Ryd gestured with the ember-ended torch as tiny pieces fell onto wet rocks below, sizzling sadly before dying into nothing. "We made it," he said in a sigh of relief, mainly to himself.

"Finally," Digory said. His neck was on fire and his back was in nearly the same state. All he wanted was to stretch. If he could get out of this cursed realm.

Ryd ignored Digory's grumpy tone and ditched the torch at the base of the exit. It sizzled against cool wet stone and extinguished quickly. He gripped the first rung of the apparent ladder embedded into the rock and tugged a bit to make sure it was safe. It held strongly. Ryd took a deep breath and glanced upwards, steadying his nerves and setting his intention to make it out alive and return to save the ones he loved. He began up the ladder timidly, gripping the cool metal bars with all his might.

Digory made sure his satchel was secured then followed Ryd up the rungs closely.

As they approached the top of the claustrophobic tunnel, faint light crept through a mass above them. The closer Ryd got, the better visible the vines were. Black, with knots of green and thorns of brown with blooms donned by purple petaled-flowers with silver spikes in the center obstructed their exit. When the mass was within reach of his face, he paused.

"What do I do now?" Ryd shouted down at Digory.

"What!" Digory shouted back up. "I can't see anything. Your ass is in the way."

"Vines! Everywhere!"

"Is there a hinge?"

"A what?!" Ryd shouted downwards, heart thumping in his chest, thoughts racing. What if he was trapped there, at the top of the ladder? He was moments from fully panicking.

"Hinges!" Digory said. "Look at the edges. Check if it's a door."

Ryd nodded. With one hand clinging to the highest ladder rung, stomach churning, he poked at the vines with the other. Sure enough, as Digory suggested, they held as if thatched together. Green hinges to match the vines were embedded deep on one side. The vines easily swung away and allowed Ryd and Digory free. The pair climbed up into the private Vanguard gardens.

Ryd was unbelievably relieved.

As they emerged from the hidden tunnel, an earthy, mouldy aroma settled over them.

"Those look mean," Ryd whispered. He pointed at the nearby flowers' silver spikes, glinting in the first morning light.

"Then, stay away from them," Digory retorted.

"I'm not a fool," Ryd answered, straightening himself, trying to get his bearings. They'd found themselves in a garden as Sieff has said they would.

"Which way is it?" Digory asked sharply.

Ryd spun around to his gain bearings, then pointed in the opposite direction of the towers. North, like Sieff said.

Digory nodded. He walked that way.

"Hey!" Ryd yelled in a hush. "Wait," he whispered at Digory's back, stomach knotting in panic. Digory hung to shadows and moved from bush to brush like a wild animal, sulking in such a way he was practically invisible. Ryd skipped up to keep pace behind, crunching brutishly over delicate vines. "Wait for me!" he whispered loudly, nearly ignoring the plethora of strange foliage cascading out around them.

First light was nigh and cast the expansive gardens in sunrise orange. Plants of varied heights spread in descending color from dark to light green leaves. The layout looked like flowing water. The hedges sloped and hugged a precision-laid black-brick path grouted in black sand. Plants were primarily flowerless with leaves of competing size and shade. The only visible blooms came from the silver spiked flowers that dotted the fearsome vines that blanketed the unplanted ground like grass.

"Hey Digory," Ryd whispered to his back. No response. "Digory," he prodded.

"Why is it you chirp like a cursed bird?" Digory growled at him, slowly turning. When he met the young man's worried expression, he softened slightly. "What is it?" he grunted, mostly irritated at himself for caring.

"Nothing is wet."

"What are you talking about?"

"Look." Ryd paused, then pointed. "With the rain," he added, remembering the monsoon of red water the eve before. "How?"

Digory reached out to graze a face-size leaf in blue green, nearly turquoise, with his fingertips. It was waxy to the touch and completely dry. It seems Ryd might be right, he thought as he looked down. The vines in mimic of grass were so brittle they snapped or cracked underfoot.

"See?!" Ryd whispered loudly, half nervous and half excited, enchanted by the mystery, yet unnerved all the same.

"Quiet," Digory chided Ryd, remembering where they were. "But..."

"Be quiet, do you hear that?" Digory lowered his whisper even more. "Shh," he hushed as he brought a silent finger to his mouth.

Fortune was on their side, for they were just in time to blend into the garden's shadows and hum of waking fauna unnoticed. Unfamiliar birds chirped in whooping whistles all around them, nearly masking heavy footfalls.

Then, the sound became clear. Ryd's heart dropped into his stomach and his eyes opened wide with fear as he imagined all that could happen to them if they were captured. He knew how Lord Tomas treated anyone out of line at Westerviolet. The voices he heard sounded like they were contemporaries of his, with their accentuated annunciations and drawn-out pronunciations. A pair of these rich-tone voices belted through the early morn. Digory and Ryd scrambled behind a wide-leaf bush and held their breath as the group passed by.

Two elderly men wore finely tailored trousers tucked into high laced overly shined black riding boots. One had black pants, and the other brown. Their tunics were crisp white. They wore pale green, light fabric cloaks that billowed in the dawn time wind. Both hobbled slightly, shaking a bit as they walked.

One was bald with yellow-hue pale skin wrinkled like crumpled parchment, as well as tall and slender. His head was bulbous and his chin pointed. He had wide-set unkempt eyebrows and hooded red eyes. Ryd couldn't help but think that man was very ugly, an unfortunate crossbreed of native and Vanguard gone wrong.

The other man had a thick mop of blonde-greyed hair, strong jaw, and severe green eyes. His skin was wrinkled, thin, and icy pale. He had broad shoulders and commanding presence, despite his elderly gait. In comparison to the man with the bulbous head, this one was very striking, in part because his presence was so daunting, despite his obvious elderly age. And he was very handsome.

Behind the men was a wheeled seated cart pushed by a nondescript male native dressed just like Sieff. A gorgeous woman of middle-years with delicate features, slightly tan skin, pale green eyes and a snub nose slumped back in it, gazing out at nothing. Her hair was mousy brown and straight, left to grow long to below her breast, then hacked blunt. It was tucked behind her ears neatly. She bore a crystal crown settled atop her mane of hair. She was well groomed, from her modest robes to her buttoned boots, to her intricately fashioned scarf in northern craftsmanship tied around her neck.

The woman simply stared ahead as the native pushed the cart, not once turning to say a word or even adjust her position. Drool dripped from the corner of her crimson lip. She was fully unresponsive.

Digory and Ryd watched and listened from inside the bushes with breath held.

"He claims he is your bastard," the ugly man whined.

"Impossible," the commanding man said, shaking his head. "Lies," he growled.

"With respect," the ugly man with bulbous head added gently. "Wallace, are you sure?"

"Dugland…"

Yet Dugland Thorne pressed on, urged mainly by concern for his cousin's future. The news of an undocumented Vanguard had reached Graceview and he could only predict the outcome would be grim if the claim was not proven false immediately. "How many of the bare did you visit during the war?"

Wallace Thorne continued walking stoically, not even turning to glance at Dugland. "Makes no difference," he grunted. "Never once child sprung."

Dugland hobbled along at Wallace's strong strided side. "Are you sure, cousin?"

The cart groaned and bumped behind them.

Wallace slowed and lowered his voice. "You know my practice," he said pointedly.

The bald man swallowed hard. "Surely," he said, blinking his eyes, trying not to think of all the dead girls essentially no different from his own wife, put down by Wallace, "but each one? Each time?"

"It is how to ensure this complication not come to pass," Wallace replied plainly, clearly disgusted that his cousin would question him so. Dugland Thorne sighed, not knowing how to respond. "Is that it?" Wallace pressed, curious. "A fool claims my seed?"

"It is graver," Dugland said, lowering his voice.

"Explain."

The men continued pace, yet their voices echoed back to Ryd and Digory, who remained still, absorbing every word.

"He claimed it straight to Humphry," Dugland told Wallace. "Galla and Hector both caught winds. It was one of the first topics this session," he added, then lowered his head. He knew Wallace would not be pleased.

Wallace frowned in deep etching lines in his face and cheeks.

Despite his lively gait and quick wit, that was the one thing he couldn't change. He looked his age. Time wore on him.

Meanwhile, behind them, wheels of the cart squeaked loudly, breaking the early morning calm.

"What is your meaning?" Wallace finally said slowly, still frowning with his eyes.

"They call you to Magistrate."

Wallace sighed and ran his hand through his hair. "In all my years, this is a first."

Dugland nodded. "Don't worry. Ivor is prepared. He'll take care of it."

Wallace smiled wearily, but warmly. "I have no doubt, cousin," he said, softening to his beloved, although disgraceful and annoying kin. He turned to face the comatose woman. "Do you hear that, Olegaria, my love? Nothing to worry about at all."

Dugland watched Wallace speak to her with a worried frown, deeply disgusted yet unable to broach the subject, so he hid his revulsion totally.

Wallace turned to Dugland. "Where does the imposter bastard stay?"

"With Ustin's boy."

"I should have known," Wallace said slowly, knowing the child a bad seed the moment he sprung forth from a native loin, then paused. "Send the Prime," he finally commanded like a crack of thunder.

Dugland's heart leapt. The Prime was reserved for the most covert, unmentionable tasks. "But... my Lord," Dugland stuttered, eyes widening, mouth partly open. "Surely you mean just for the accuser..."

"Both of them. The imposter and Ustin's boy for harbouring him," Wallace interrupted cooly. "See it done," he added, chopping the executioner's blade. Dugland gulped. "It is what the traitors deserve," Wallace added heartlessly. "You know that is true."

"But."

"Cousin?"

"Your father," Dugland said timidly.

"What of him?"

"It is against his Teachings," Dugland argued, gaining momentum when he heard the words out loud. "He... he won't approve."

"My father doesn't have to know."

"I thought the man knew all," Dugland stopped and blinked at Wallace, stunned by his blasphemy.

Wallace glared sharply. He said with hollow inflection, "No man knows all."

With the sun rising in the east, Digory and Ryd carefully traversed the exotic gardens. They'd waited long moments until the Vanguards passed and the sun rose much higher before finally making moves towards the exit. By high-noon, an archway burst from tree-canopy in the distance. They could nearly taste escape.

"Do you think they made all of this?" Ryd whispered loudly at Digory's back, nearly forgetting himself.

"Hush," Digory shushed him, tired, hungry, and focused.

"The Vanguards, I mean," Ryd continued in whisper, leaning forward eagerly. The enchantment of Graceview's magical garden overwhelmed his fear and scepticism. He was amazed by the intimidating sharp blooms at his feet and the enormous leaves of most of the greenery, although he was careful not to touch anything. Plus, after nearly half a day without contest, he'd begun to relax. Unlike the frequently spotted guards at Westerviolet, he hadn't spotted any of the so-called Thorne Watch once. This relaxation had presently devolved into a fit of wonder that nearly made Digory sick. "Not just the castles," Ryd said, squinting his red almond eyes, glancing around, "but the plants and storms too. Did..." he trailed off, hardly believing it, yet the evidence was daunting, "did Thorne build this whole world?"

"Not now," Digory said over his shoulder harshly as he stepped behind a wide tree trunk, in wake of the tree wall ahead.

Ryd followed him but whined. "What are you doing? It's right there." He gestured to the overgrown exit. Shiny blue butterflies identical to glistening gems flitted right outside the opening where there should have been a gate.

"Look," Digory pointed to the tree line. Archers were well hidden. "Two," he said, then paused. "No. Four. There, do you see?"

Ryd nodded gravely, swallowing in a gulp, realizing he would have walked straight to his death if it had not been for Digory to stop it. This humbled him considerably.

Ryd watched as Digory licked his finger and held it up to the wind, squinting his eyes like he was thinking. Then he raised the crossbow. Ryd shut his eyes, knowingly, then counted four bodies falling from the trees in a series of moans and sickening thuds.

After that, Digory and Ryd walked out of Graceview freely amidst the flurry of jewel blue butterflies. Neither looked back. The ominous overgrown septogional towers were the only witness to their departure. The unlikely pair continued on foot to Littlebell.

ECHO'S OMEN

X avier was concerned about his brother's ambition, as always. He knew unbridled drive clouded the mind and he feared Basil was teetering at the edge of logic. Given the tumultuous state of the Kingdom, he was unsure Basil had the wherewithal to stand firm. To not react anxiously to the barking commands of Hector. True, Hector was blood and a brilliant strategist, but Xavier saw him for what he was. A spoiled, vengeful boy intent on making a name for himself, apart from his father.

He adjusted his dark ceremonial robe's heavy hood then tightened the green sash lashed at his mid-waist. It was hours past midnight in the early wake of the morn. A roaring fire blazed outside.

"Do you believe him?" Xavier asked Basil slowly. Despite his height, due to his hunch, Xavier and Basil were eye-level.

"What reason has he to lie? None," Basil dismissed. "Besides, it is as predicted."

"What is your meaning?"

Basil leaned in. "He played with fire. It was time he burned." He cleared his throat in a phlegmy gargle. "Herman had it coming."

It pained Xavier to think of his kin ending in such a way, without honor at all. "Yes, yes. But Galla, Prihim..." he trailed off, puzzled by the turn of events. "It makes little sense."

"Why?" Basil turned, moonlight shining off his white-blind eye. "It makes absolute sense. The earthblood cunt cuckolded her lover into it. Simple," he said, as if it were fact. Basil was not one to overthink a situation. The opposite, usually.

Still, the story didn't sit well with Xavier. "Where would she have run?" He'd never known a Morfit to be so rash. "And..."

he trailed off, "why? What purpose could she have?"

"Brother," Basil took a step, placing his hand on Xavier's broad, hunched shoulder. "Who cares?" he asked rhetorically with a yellowed smile. "One problem is done away with. Why does it matter *why*?"

Xavier didn't back down. "It seems too good to be...."

"Xavier," Basil interrupted loudly as his patience dwindled. He dropped his hand from his brother's shoulder to let it hang limp at his side. "If not Galla then another newblood curse to blame," he added as he shuffled away, dark robes dragging across the stone floor.

"How are you so sure?"

"Millie," Basil said, turning back, "of course."

Xavier closed his eyes. "Millie," he said through a sigh, hurt by the knowledge of what she had to endure, only to be met by such a tragic end. He'd always felt sorry for Ralph's homely daughter, although he'd never put a voice to the sentiment. "Poor girl," he added as he opened his eyes.

Basil laughed loud. "She's fortunate she finally escaped that bastard," he said with a gravelly bite, then chuckled to himself more, a proud of Hector rather than ashamed.

"What do you think about the rest of the news?" Xavier asked. It was shocking, nearly unbelievable, that Hector claimed betrothal to Tomas's own daughter, Sybil Brochet.

"Don't believe it," Basil barked.

"He writes it was her idea," Xavier countered. Basil waved his hand, yet Xavier continued, unnerved by the idea of a secret alliance, if what Hector wrote was true. To make a covenant of that magnitude without involving Tomas was a bold move, to put it mildly. "But..."

Basil frowned. "But what?"

Xavier took a limping step. "Hector assures it is truth," he said.

Basil met Xavier's eyes and shook his head. "Won't happen."

"Why not?"

"Tomas won't allow it." Basil knew that old bag to be stubborn as a blind mule. Xavier picked up on a hint of hesitation in his tone but didn't respond to it.

"We will see," Xavier said slowly, sighing. "Can you imagine, though?"

"Hector and Sybil?" Basil laughed again. "If true, it's the end of us all."

They stood in a modest closet with one high-placed window near a vaulted ceiling next to an assortment of chairs, ceremonial weapons, and other miscellaneous furniture shoved into a chaotic mess in the corner. The customary vestibule before any major Omen ceremony.

Basil sniffed the air and frowned. "This stink is Hector's doing," he said, scrunching and flaring his nostrils. "Even after the flames die it will be moons until we're rid of it."

"He was adamant that it was the only way." Xavier lowered his head, wanting to believe that true, knowing down deep it wasn't. "No traces to be left. Given the attention Cronog brought upon our newest recruit, it is safer to keep all activities covert, says Hector."

Basil waved his hand dismissively a third time while listening to the horde of deep voices buzzing in cacophony outside the door.

"The recruit," Basil grumbled. "Barely able to call him one. Hector aims to make that broken Dale boy an Omen Brother yet refuses to deliver him to us for assessment."

Xavier didn't know what to think of Hector's acquisition of Rhain Dale for their cause, however, he knew this wasn't the time to discuss it. "It sounds like the men are ready." He noted the familiar drone coming from the main hall. He cherished this time each year. The comradery, the power. It was all painfully poignant. He felt like he may cry from sheer overwhelmed blood pride. "The hour is nigh."

Basil nodded, drunk on power like his brother, intoxicated by the chanting just outside. He gestured to the high doorframe. "Shall we?"

Xavier bowed informally. "After you."

Together the eldest Graves brothers of Echo's Omen put their hoods up and exited into the Spire's massive hall.

From end to end, the impressive venue was packed with men in matching ceremonial robes also with green sashes identical to the ones Basil and Xavier wore, all humming together in the ceremonial chant. The robed men stood side by side in delineated rows encircling a group at the center. From overhead, their formation looked like a black nautilus swirl.

In the center of this robed swirl of men, seventy-five others were completely nude. Most cupped their exposed parts with cold hands in modesty. Most had welts and bruises. Brands of competing emblems on every hip were plainly visible.

The hum amplified upon Basil and Xavier's entry into the hall. All pulsed with anticipatory excitement at the sight of the Omen Elder. All the men matched each other's tone yet incrementally increased their intensity as if in competition with the volume of the next Brother. The whole hall buzzed like the earth after a lightning strike, lined with ceiling-high slits for windows on the east-face. Outside, a pungent fire burned, casting ominous shadows onto the opposing stone wall – the only light visible apart from the shiny glint of the moon in the hall.

Basil, followed by Xavier, walked through the mass of Brothers. Each stepped dutifully out of the way to allow them to pass until the old pair reached the pulsing center. The naked recruits, with welted bodies yet heads tilted upwards as if looking for absolution, parted for Basil and Xavier seamlessly, in unabashed awe of the grey-tone pair.

To them, the Graves men were living gods.

As Basil and Xavier approached, Quentin eagerly stepped out from the ranks of the robed. He stood in line with his father, hovering proudly to his left. Basil didn't acknowledge him.

Brothers Edwarde and Bertrand Norland silently stepped forward too and stood behind the older Vanguards. After a quick glance then nod to each other, the smaller Aron and Alec Graves followed suit. The two youngest Vanguard Brothers were dressed in the same ceremonial garb as the rest of the initiated, in standard length and size, so the bottoms of the robes pooled at the boys' feet and the arms covered their hands. All around them the hum from the droning wordless chant was deafening, as if one travelled into the center of a human-size beehive. Little Alec held hands to his ears to dampen the noise until Aron shot him a scowl and he dutifully dropped his hands to his hips to endure the painful noise stoically.

Basil surveyed the crowd with his one good eye. It was a ragged bunch this year, as it was every year, he thought to himself, craning his head against the bad crick in his neck to get a good look all around. Some from Hellswater there, stocky with wide brows and fisherman's gaits. And there, with their elongated necks, some of Anstout's skinwalkers, repressed of course, yet powerful, nonetheless. A gaggle from Lyonshall with white mop manes and coin-size ears, ugly fellows with roaring rosebears branded into their square hips. The most stubborn of brutes, but once broken, the best of slaves that do exactly as told. A sprinkling from the other realms of too, Ravenshroud and Westerviolet mostly, a few from Ironbark and Baneswood, all with the same battered appearance matched with eager, nonsensical grins. At first glance, all seemed to make expected additions to Basil's Brotherhood. He was pleased, smiling, feeding off the humming crowd. If what Hector wrote was true, it was more important now than ever to ensure a talented, ruthless fighting force. Today's ceremony was the first step towards that.

Each man tested grey, so naturally the next step was to remove them from their former name. Their old selves must die in order for them to assimilate into the oneness of Echo's Omen, to become a Brother in a sea of Brothers, none any better or less. Basil revelled in their storied tradition, feeling the inherent power of the time-honoured ritual.

"Now!" Basil bellowed. The massive hall silenced in a rapid hush. Shadows from the fire outside danced on the ceiling and walls. *"You* become death! Destroyer of worlds." He circled the recruits. It was quiet, eerily quiet apart from Basil's pontification, as if the men collectively held their breath. "You will die today," he said direly as he stopped, turning slowly to glare at the recruits.

"Mortuum," he muttered next. Basil walked down the line, making a point to gaze deep into the soul of each man, squinting his good eye at them. He could feel life's power pulsing behind their eager faces. "Mortuum," he spat. "Mortuum."

The recruits shifted nervously, unsure of what to expect. They'd made it through the most cursed First there was — Echo's Omen training — and they had no idea what awaited them on the other side.

A barely audible whisper arose behind Basil as he paced in a slow-beginning crescendo. All initiated Brothers began to follow him in the chant.

"Mortuum, mortuum," the collective repeated. The last 'm' of the word was drawn out in elongated hum. "Mortuum, mortuumm, mortuummm." Volume increased. "Mortuumm! Mortuummm! Mortuummmm!" All shouted now. The hall was emptied of décor, which enabled resounding acoustics. There were only brutish iron chandeliers left, hung low from the vaulted ceiling.

"Mortuumm! Mortuumm!"

The chant was chilling. Haunting. The recruits' faces were wild with anticipation mixed with instinctual fear.

Basil stopped at the last man the row, having made his way around the entire nautilus of seventy-odd men. This man was thin and had a triangle shaped face and a permanently pinched brow, as if he'd endured great hardship already in his short life. He was shaved bald and naked like the others, with a siren brand on his slight hip. Basil grabbed this final recruit by the shoulder. He threw him harshly to the floor.

"First to die," he said, pointing a gnarled finger. The chant devolved to a hum again. "First to die," Basil repeated.

From the ground, the Hellswater high native recruit trembled as he looked up at the ominously humming horde around him.

"Stand!" Basil commanded the man, shifting his pointed finger to another spot in the hall. "Go!" Eyes dated to follow Basil's point. It landed on a differently dressed Brother, entering from the far end of the hall. All Brothers seamlessly parted for the highly ranked Green Brother, allowing him to reach the center of the swirl with ease, as they had for Elder Basil and Xavier.

This Brother wore a fully green robe with hood drawn to hide his face in shadow, mostly where his position got its name. The Green Brother carried a leather satchel in one hand and a squat stool in the other. He placed the stool down in front of the recruits, in the center of the Brothers, and sat atop it before unpacking his bag. He withdrew a case filled with the tools of his trade.

The trembling recruit scurried to stand and hurried dutifully over to the Green Brother. The hum got louder.

"Begin," Basil growled with a creeping grin. He enjoyed this part of the ceremony very much.

The thin, naked man stepped bravely towards the Green Brother. The Green Brother clutched a polished blade. He gestured with it for the recruit to approach. Once the recruit reached him, the Green Brother unceremoniously grabbed the man's buttock and hip. The recruit looked down in reactive indignation but remained calm.

"Die," the Green Brother said from behind his shadow-filled hood, like rocks sliding down a craggy ledge.

"DIE!" the whole hall shouted in unison.

The Green Brother sawed the olive-toned recruit's branded skin away, as if carving fowl for sup.

The recruit began to cry out in a yelp of pain, then bit his lip with his teeth. Tears quietly pooled in his eyes but he remained still. The man knew his life depended on it.

"Good," Basil purred under his breath, catching a glance with Xavier. Both men nodded to each other. The first recruit's initiation was telling for the year to come. A stoic reaction was a fortunate omen indeed.

The Green Brother hacked at the recruit then tossed the tattooed flesh aside leaving a wide patch bleeding from the man's hip. He ignored the wound and instead turned the pain-shocked man around, so he was eye-level with his protruding ribs and thin chest.

The Green Brother withdrew a pointed implement from his bag then barked, "Be reborn," at the recruit as he lifted it to the man's ribs.

"REBORN!" the initiated Brothers resounded.

Basil bellowed over the chaos. "Be free of the chains that once bound you! Take from this land what is yours! The Omen is your soul now." He paused for emphasis, then shouted deep and drawn out, "One. Is. All!"

As Basil screamed with full-lunged intensity, good eye sweeping the hall, glaring at each, making every recruit feel he was staring right at them, the Green Brother put the pointed end to the recruit's skin, between his fourth and fifth rib, aimed upwards at his heart.

The hall erupted in the chant once more, "Mortuum! Mortuumm! Mortuummm!" as the Green Brother began to work.

When he pulled away from the recruit's ribcage, tattooed in black scrolls was:

(stylized tattoo lettering)

The young man shook from shock and excitement as the hall breathed in chant around him. The Green Brother held a round polished disk for the recruit to inspect the tattoo mirror-image:

mortem

Next, the green robed Brother took a syringe and uncapped the end to reveal a fearsome needle. He used it to withdraw dark liquid from a vial. Then he held it to the olive man's sullen flank and injected him.

"Is... is... is that it?" the recruit asked the Green Brother in a croak, feeling his vision fade in and out as his whole body tingled. He felt different; cold and hardened, as if ice encased his heart. The green-robe nodded once to him, still never revealing his face, simply gesturing his head off to the far wall, indicating he go there. The newly initiated brother, dazed and in pain, brain thumping from his newly gotten grey injection, stumbled away.

An anonymous Brother from the crowd with hood equally drawn thus face hidden in shadow emerged with a white cloak in his outstretched, upwards-faced palms. He bowed slightly to the bloody, dazed initiate and thrust the robe at him. A line of others with white robes in hand emerged behind him awaiting each newly initiated Brother with their own initiate robe.

The new Brother gratefully donned the white garment. Blood quickly pooled on his hip and bled through, leaving long, red stain down the side.

The chant went on and the initiation process continued down the line of men, in order, one by one, from the outside of the swirl of men to the inside, as if unwinding a length of string.

Aron yawned. He couldn't help it.

Edwarde eyed the Graves boy angrily. "Don't do that," he growled.

Bertrand turned to see what the fuss was about, silently raising an eyebrow disapprovingly.

"Yeah, don't," Alec added smartly.

"Shut up," Aron said to Alec.

"All of you," Quentin turned and barked, irritated he was relegated to children's keeper once again. "Silence!"

"How dare you?" Xavier turned in a hush to Quentin, eyes wide at his nephew's offense. "Do not disturb Initiation. Are you mad?"

The bickering boys hushed immediately and darted eyes unblinkingly forward beneath heavy hoods.

"I..." Quentin stuttered, "I am seeing to the children."

"They are Brothers," Xavier chided under his breath, "not children," glancing to Basil to ensure he was out of earshot. "They see to themselves. Stop attempting to control all, Quentin."

"I.. I.." Quentin's grey eyes widened, desperately wanting to defend himself. He paused, reminding himself of the futility. He sighed. "Never mind."

"Good, hush," Xavier chided. "If only your father heard

you," he added with a knowing look, then turned back to face the ceremony.

Quentin glared at Xavier from behind and crossed his robed arms in front of him. He anxiously awaited the day that he was the Elder and thus Master of Ceremony. He watched the rest of the proceedings with a hooded frown.

It was not yet first light and daybreak lapped at the western skyline in a pale green glow overlaid atop the star-filled black of night. The frosted scent of wind whipping through pine needles was the first thing to hit their young nostrils.

The pack of boys walked out of the Spire's massive hall, down the front stairs and into the cool air.

Aron yawned again. "Why do we do this so late?" he asked up at Edwarde as he rubbed a sleepy grey eye.

"It's when the veil is thinnest," Edwarde replied. "Don't you know anything?"

"Yeah huh I do."

Alec looked up at his big brother earnestly. "What's *veil* mean?"

"Shut up," Aron spat, not wanting to be embarrassed in front of the Norland boys. He didn't know either, though. He was just repeating what he'd heard.

Bertrand, who followed behind them, chuckled low and deep wordlessly. Edwarde glanced over his shoulder, pleased by the reaction, grateful for his silent companion. He smiled and met Bertrand's eyes. The brothers blinked together.

All four of the young men let their hoods drop behind them in the aftermath of the ceremony. Their pale cheeks were blotchy red and their hairlines were sweaty. Eyes drooped in need of rest.

"It makes the Grey work," Edwarde finally told the younger boys, as if it was obvious, but he didn't know either.

"Why didn't we have to get it?" Aron asked. "Did you?"

"Yeah?!" Alec added indignantly.

Bertrand chuckled in a belly-deep rumble. His wide shoulders bounced.

"The poor dolts," Edwarde shook his head, agreeing with Bertrand's silent judgement. "They have to know, right?" he looked back. Bertrand wordlessly chuckled, then smiled as he shrugged.

Edwarde faced the grey-skinned boys again, still walking in the direction of the barracks, a crisp wind chilling his sweaty brow. It was a cool evening. Wind flowed lazily down from white-topped mountains. The air smelled metallic. Snow started to dust. "Bertrand and I need the Grey," he said matter of fact to the Graves boys. "You both don't."

"Why not?" the older pressed.

"You're half-dead," Edwarde said. "Both of you."

"Nuh-uh!" Alec wined.

"Liar!" Aron shouted.

"Boys," Edwarde slowed and turned to them as the group reached the center courtyard. "If you don't believe me, ask Quentin yourselves."

The fire that illuminated the hall from outside still burned. The young men mostly ignored it as they walked, apart from wide steps over an occasional charred limb. The worst part was the smell of scorched skin, which the boys were all accustomed to by now. And the wind helped with it considerably.

Flames erupted from mounds of torsos, heads, feet, and other body parts ablaze. The morbid piles lined the whole pathway to the barracks, stacked two stories high. All bodies were male and all were unclothed, seemingly hacked up, tossed, kicked, and shovelled into piles, then lit on fire. The air roasted with crackled fat, singed hair, and burnt flesh.

The thousands of corpses outside of Echo's Omen Spire fuelled a brilliant bonfire that lit up the whole sky.

OUTSIDE LITTLEBELL

"Are you sure it's this way?" Ryd asked with a frown. He couldn't see anything, and he was tired of getting pricked. Digory ignored Ryd, focused on moving forward, hacking at tall, seeded grass ahead. "We should have stayed on the path," Ryd added smartly. Digory silently rolled his eyes and groaned while continuing to hack.

It was brutally cold, with little wind and high humidity. Fine snow misted over the sloped meadow. The pair's collective mood matched the weather, sullen after their encounters in Wind Valley and their ordeal in Graceview. They hadn't spoken so much as a few words in the last day, even as they left Graceview's writhing, vine-wrapped castle in their wake.

"Hey," Ryd whined. "Digory."

Digory stopped and turned with his green blade threateningly, half wanting to use it,

"Hey!" Ryd jumped back, caught off guard by the hate in Digory's eyes.

"I'm cursed tired, okay," Digory said with a sigh. "You've said that more times than there are flies. *We should have taken the First Cursed path*," he mocked. "If you wanted the path so cursed badly you should have taken it yourself."

"But," Ryd said, slightly confused and hurt by Digory's angry outburst after all they'd been through, "you still haven't said. Why do we hike through a swamp?"

Digory gritted his teeth. "It is not a swamp."

Ryd lifted his boot to inspect the muck beneath it. "Tell me why."

"This is faster," Digory said over his shoulder. He focused his effort back on his present task, hacking away through the irritatingly thick river grass. The grass was particularly ruthless because it bore fearsome briars that latched to Digory's flesh with each hack.

"But the bargeman said to go through the city."

"Yes," Digory said slowly and angrily. *The Bargeman doesn't know what I know,* Digory thought. "Because the bargeman doesn't have the stones to go this way."

"Why not through the city?"

"Ryd, enough."

"What are you hiding from?" Ryd asked, beginning to catch on. "Or, rather, who?"

"One more word and I might slip with this," Digory threatened with his dagger, then continued to hack. Ryd's astute observation unnerved him. True, he planned to avoid Littlebell, for he couldn't be seen there by any Minney bloods with Ryd. His plan with Sybil wouldn't allow for it. But Ryd didn't need to know that.

"Where did you go that night?"

"What night?"

"Littlebell."

Digory inhaled slowly, trying to keep a semblance of calm. "I told you already."

"Right, that's right," Ryd replied, trust wavering. "Theatre. Then after that."

"Who says I did anything after?"

"You looked like you hadn't slept," Ryd retorted, beginning to think he knew Digory a bit better than to believe his lies outright. Digory shrugged. "Come on, you can tell me."

Digory sighed, touched briefly by Ryd's sentiment. "You really want to know?" he asked. Ryd nodded expressively. "I told you I met the Minneys," Digory said. "Leon knows my face."

"And why would that matter? If I am to be with Vera, I suppose they all should know my face shortly," Ryd said. He broke into a goofy smile.

Digory frowned. "They cannot know our plan," he said low and deep.

Ryd balked. "Why not?"

"They'll try to stop us," he replied. That wasn't necessarily untrue, he thought.

"Digory what happened? Something happened with you and Leon that night."

"Leave it," Digory growled, knowing if he were to reveal the plot against Prihim, the entire web he was weaving around Ryd and Vera would unravel and he would lose his beloved Sybil because of it. Sybil was everything, he reminded himself. The prize he'd strove towards his entire life. Without her, his existence had no meaning. He did his best to cling to her memory, although thoughts of the stable boy continued to pop up in his mind.

"That's why we go around?"

Digory nodded curtly.

Ryd sighed in acceptance as he glanced about. "Just admit it if we're lost," he said.

"We're. Not. Lost."

"What then? How far?"

"We're close. Will you shut up now?"

"How close is..."

"Quiet!" Digory shouted, spinning, thrusting his dagger forward. He felt time get drippy and slow as if it was pulsing through his weapon's blade, just like every time he gripped it. "This is for your cursed benefit."

"That is horse shit and you know it," Ryd shouted back, leaning away from the dagger. "This is for you. For Sybil."

"Hey," Digory barked. "Show respect," he added as he turned away from the cowering man. He re-sheathed the dagger. "I'm taking you to your bare."

"Don't call her that! *You* show respect! She saved your life!"

Digory sighed, deciding to be rid of his pest. The best way he knew how was to distance himself, so he lowered his head to face the brunt of the spiky seeded grass. He charged in.

"Hey, wait!" Ryd shouted, but Digory had fully disappeared into the grass. Ryd darted after him.

It was sunset when they finally reached the Narrow, welcome familiar territory indeed. The sky above the pair was cool like armour, matte grey darkened to blue and black. Light snow dusted them from every angle and covered the landscape in a fine power.

The men were riddled in scrapes from the spores of the grass they'd passed through to get there, in order to avoid Littlebell's city. The injuries from the rest of their journey didn't help their haggard appearances either. Ryd's face was still healing from his ordeal in the Confines and the fight in Blackwood while Digory's top lip was swollen slightly, quite obvious now since he had no beard. With a bare face, he'd never felt so exposed.

"I recognize this!" Ryd exclaimed, brightening as they rounded a shadowed bend. "We've been here."

Digory grumbled wordlessly. *We've been down the whole cursed road, nearly twice now*, he thought.

"There, do you see?" Ryd turned and pointed towards Littlebell's sprawling city brightening in the distance. Thousands of modest hovels illuminated along the dark horizon, crowded around the Bell Tower and up against the wide brown Missi.

"Okay lover boy," Digory taunted, "which way?"

Ryd furrowed his brow. "The view was different from atop a horse."

"Funny," Digory said. "You claimed to remember. Now's your chance to prove it."

"I thought we'd go the way we came, not through your swamp. I'm turned around."

"Do you know or don't you?"

Ryd paused and concentrated, trying to center himself in his memories from nearly a moon before. Finally, he realized where they were. "Over here, come on," he said wearily as he walked down the Narrow with Littlebell at his back. Not long later, he paused.

Digory glared at Ryd's back. "What now?"

"Hold on."

"Is it you who is lost?"

"Hold. On." Ryd said through clenched teeth. It was his turn to be irritated.

"Oh, look," Digory clapped Ryd on the back. "You've done it."

"What lie do you speak now?"

"Thanks," Digory said half-heartedly as he clapped Ryd's back again, hard, then walked off the path.

"Hey," Ryd said, then jogged after Digory, realizing instantly where he was.

Smoke rose from a chimney in a distant clearing.

Digory was far ahead and broke first into the manicured gardens inching up to the cottage. To his left the weeping willow bowed from a pile of snow atop it.

"Ahh!" he cried out suddenly, pawing at his own face in sheer shock and pain. "My eyes!"

"Digory!" Ryd ran forward, in concern and confusion all at once.

"Oh my Horned! Ryd?" Vera shouted from an open window of the green cottage. Ryd's heart dropped into his stomach from excitement. Her honey curls were pulled in a knot high on her head and a sole ringlet fell to her cheek, by her blue eye and danced as she spoke. "You came back for me!"

"Vera!" Ryd shouted as he sprinted towards her, thoughts exploding with happiness. She burst through the doors and tumbled into his arms.

"My eyes!" Digory cried out, still pawing at his face from where he lay in the snow-covered ground.

"I didn't recognize him!" she admitted to Ryd, lifting up a cask in her hand. "It will only take a moment," she said then added, "my dear," with a wide smile and an embarrassed giggle, then skipped over to where Digory lay moaning.

"I'm sorry!" she said as she splashed dark liquid from the cask at him. "I didn't recognize you without your beard."

Digory cried out in white-hot pain followed by cooling relief.

He collapsed into a ball in the snowy dirt while rubbing his face furiously. His vision started to return slightly, although it was still fuzzy. His eyes leaked as if he wept black tears. He coughed horribly.

Vera threw the cask down to the ground with an empty thud and ran back to Ryd's arms. They melted into a warm embrace despite the chilly weather. The snowfall picked up slightly and dotted Vera's dusky skin like white freckles until melting into tiny pools as clear as her eyes. He held her and stroked her hair.

"You came back," she said into his chest.

"I did," he replied with a knowing look in his eye. "I swore I would."

"What happened?" she asked, looking up at his injuries. "Are you alright?" She placed a hand to his cheek. The warmth of her palm was revitalizing. Ryd hardly noticed her eyes change color slightly, as his injuries quickly healed.

He nodded and held her close, "I am now." Digory groaned from where he sat, rubbing his eyes pitifully on the ground. "What'd you do to him?" Ryd glanced to Digory. "That's not permanent, is it?"

"No, no," she assured. "It's because of you."

"Me?"

"What you said," Vera told him. "I'm unprotected. Vulnerable. You were right. After you left, I decided something must be done. I must not allow myself to become prey." She paused to glance to the side at Digory again. "Mimi calls it pepper tar."

Ryd was impressed that Vera found way to protect herself and further, that she was willing to see it done. "What is it?"

"It's made from spices and sap," Vera said with a proud look in her eye. "If I strike the face, well, you saw the effects."

"And what you threw on him was antidote?"

She nodded. "It just takes a little while to wear off."

"What's a little while?!" Digory shouted.

"Not long," Vera told Digory without breaking her eyes away from Ryd. "A few hours."

Just my fortune, Digory thought to himself woefully, moaning, still rubbing his eyes.

As Ryd held Vera close aside the massive weeping willow in the building blizzard, he slightly craned his head down to look at her. He gently stroked her hair.

"I am so happy to finally see you," he said. "You have no idea." He felt like the harrowing journey he'd accompanied Digory on had finally been worth it, that he'd reached his prize. Now, all that was missing was Col.

"I'm glad you're here," she replied, looking up at him with wide blue eyes. He responded by kissing her on the forehead. "But," she paused, pulling back from him a bit. "Why? Why are you here? And why bring *him*?"

Ryd pulled her away from him. He held her at an arm's distance, gripping both of her smooth shoulders with square calloused hands.

"Vera," he said gently, meeting her eyes intensely, "you're in danger."

She chuckled lightly, smiling sweetly to reveal her deep dimple. "I already know that."

"No," he shook his head. "You've been discovered."

"Discovered?" Her expression clouded like a thunderstorm. "Who did you tell?" she added with mounting anger.

"No!" Ryd's eyes widened innocently. "Not me. Not us," he added, glancing to Digory. "I know not who."

"Then how do you know…" Vera started, but Ryd interrupted.

"Digory overheard," Ryd explained, glancing to where Digory lay. "He's…" Ryd started, then trailed off, trying to think of how to explain Digory's knowledge, "very close to the Vanguards." He added with a gulp, "He heard that Hector Graves knows about you."

"Hector Graves?" she said slowly. Mimi warned her about Gravesblood. How they would stop at nothing to kill her and experiment on her. How, in the present day, they were the bloodline to fear the most after Brochet. "Are you sure?" she asked in a breath above a whisper. Ryd felt her heartbeat shudder in her chest.

"Digory," Ryd said. Digory's condition seemed to have improved slightly. The black tar on his face has been mostly rubbed away. The skin beneath was bright red, particularly on his face where he had recently shaved. "Hector knows Vera lives, right? We come to rescue her?"

"Aye," Digory said, squinting at them with bloodshot, watery eyes. His whole face was splotched. "Hector ordered Brochet to do Graves's dirty work and retrieve you. Unlucky for you, Sybil didn't take kindly to being given orders. She commanded me to disobey him," Digory lied, with Ryd silently nodding to corroborate the story. "To bring you to shelter at Westerviolet."

"Why would she do that?" Vera hesitated. "I've heard Mimi's opinion of the Lady of Westerviolet. Prihim's too. He says she's a snake like all Brochets are, no matter how beautiful." She tilted her head to meet Ryd's loving gaze. "How can we trust her?"

"She holds blood in high regard," Digory explained, lying too easily, wincing as his eyes leaked painful, peppered tears. "She may disagree with your bloodline politically," he said, then snorted phlegm, "but Sybil respects that you're Vanguard." Vera frowned in contemplation. "She's no monster," he added, internally smirking at the irony.

He knew Sybil was as monstrous as they came.

Ryd squeezed his beloved's shoulders. "Vera," he breathed, studying her delicate features and ebony skin. "Forget Sybil," he said, "or him," he added in a seething glance to Digory. "You can trust me."

"So, what?" Vera asked hollowly. "Leave Littlebell? My home? I could never."

"But you must!" Ryd nearly shouted. "It's the only way to keep you safe," he added more gently, hands digging into her fleshy arms. He was fully overwhelmed to be in the presence of the woman he'd been pining for throughout his haphazard travels throughout the Kingdom, afraid if he let go of her, she'd dissipate into mist like a dream.

Vera studied Ryd's expression for what felt like a long time with only the silence of snow between them. Ryd watched white flakes catch on her pale eyelashes.

"First we must tell Mimi."

"No," Digory interjected in a loud boom.

"What did you say?"

"Can't do that," Digory answered curtly, finally able to sit up and open one eye with consistency. The white-hot burning had subsided to an irritating ache. Like he got soap in his eyes.

"Surely I must," Vera replied quickly, "I must," she repeated, voice tinny, bordering panic. "I must tell Mimi where I'm going lest she fall into sickness from worry. I can't *just leave*." She looked to Ryd with pleading eyes, but he deferred to Digory's judgement.

"Listen to him Vera," Ryd said gently, heart breaking for her because he knew how difficult what he was asking her to do would be.

"If you want her in danger too, then do as you please," Digory taunted, beginning to feel like himself again despite the pepper tar assault. He flexed his jaw to hide a smile. "Hector knows you live, girl. No one aware of your whereabouts is safe."

She frowned. "Then why Westerviolet? How am I safe there?"

"He would never think to look for you there," Digory retorted as he peeled his other eye open. He was finally able to get a good look at this girl Ryd was so taken by, and he instantly understood why. She was stunningly beautiful, shockingly so, almost too beautiful to be real. Arguably as beautiful as Sybil, in a different way. The stuff of legends. "Tomas is an old ally," he added, inwardly both pleased for Ryd to land such a beauty and gutted with guilt for what was to come next. "Trusted."

"You see?" Ryd pulled her in for a tight hug. He kissed her forehead again. "You must come with us," he breathed into her honey blonde curls. "I will keep you safe, my heart. At Westerviolet we can be together."

"This is all happening so fast," she said quietly into Ryd's chest. Without warning, she pushed away from his embrace totally.

Instantly Ryd's face clouded, burning with scorn. "Don't you want to be with me?"

"I do!" she turned, eyes pleading, caught off guard by the bite in his tone. She thought of her beloved city, full of laughter and life. She thought of her grandmother and how much her disappearance would wound the woman. She even considered who would care for Ruby. "Ryd, this is so much. Too much. I can't... I can't leave my home."

Ryd felt like he might explode from frustration. "There's nothing for you here!" he shouted.

Digory watched the lover's spat as if in the crowd of the Baneswood Games, with a slight smile, amused by the entertainment. He almost felt as if he should be cheering or heckling.

Vera took a step back. "How can you say that about my home?" she asked in a shocked breath.

Ryd lost it. "Home?! Home?! These people you call kin might as well keep you chained to a post and kick you for how you're treated. They lock you here, away from the Kingdom. Vera," Ryd said with pleading eyes, "you don't live!"

She stepped back, hurt and aghast.

Meanwhile, Digory was enjoying the interaction greatly. Ryd was doing a splendid job.

At her reaction, Ryd immediately faltered, realizing he'd been too cruel. "This is not your fault," he said, trying to regain her warmth, hoping she knew he was attempting to care for her. "You're a prisoner." He wondered how she couldn't see it herself. "They stifle you. Like an underfed foal," he explained, "you can't grow."

"Ryd... but..."

"Vera," he stepped forward. "I beg you," he pleaded her as he took another step, looming over her slight yet curved frame. "Let me protect you. Let me free you. Come with us. Please Vera."

She looked up at Ryd. "Are you sure this is right?" Ryd blinked slowly, then nodded solemnly. She took a deep breath.

"Okay."

"Okay?"

Vera nodded. Her face-framing ringlet bounced.

"When he's feeling better, we will take to the road then," Ryd said with a wide smile, full of renewed hope. He glanced at Digory.

"No," Digory barked. "I'm fine. We go now."

"You sure?"

With leaking eyes, Digory gave a shaky thumbs up.

"Alright," Ryd shrugged, knowing how stubborn Digory was. "To the road."

And to the road it was.

THE DEAD LINE, CREED POINT

About 100 years ago...

It was nearly time to call it a day and signal for the men on his patrol to come in. Now that Bin Norland had lost elderclaim to his brother Ruben, he spent most of his time at Creed Point, overseeing patrol of the Dead Line. It was a blustery day and nearly freezing with un-melted snow overtop of rocky mountainous covered mostly in evergreens. Bin pulled his cloak tight and watched the smoky breath in front of his face as he sighed, thinking about his beloved wife and child waiting for him at Ravenshroud.

He had lost nearly everything. He'd sacrificed his title, his honor and all his friends to save Lilli and he couldn't be more pleased with his choice. Standing there in the crisp air with Creed Point's massive ancient structure at his back, he felt an unexpected sort of calm. Although Bin no longer was who he was before, he'd evolved. What mattered to him before he met Lilli felt like a fuzzy dream now. Now all he cared about was her happiness. Lilli's happiness and their new babe Lasha's, of course.

Bin was enamoured with the baby girl maybe even more than her mother was. He smiled in reverie, wondering how much the girl will grow before he sees her again. Each trip to the Dead Line and back she seemed to nearly double in size. He was glad she was doing so well, and was such a happy baby, always laughing and smiling. He thought about how small her hands were, how it felt when she gripped one of his large fingers in her tiny palm. Bin itched to leave and head back to Lilli's side early yet knew he had to stay. He'd shirked away from all his other blood duties. The least he could do was his

215

currently appointed job.

As the men marched towards him, headed from Frost Cove, Bin noticed something was not right. He saw dark emerald cloaks behind the lines of hulking Warmen. Bin's stomach knotted instantly and his adrenaline spiked, for he knew what those cloaks meant.

A battalion of Westerviolet Foot Guards approached, led by none other than Lucien Brochet himself. Florian Busk was at his flank.

Bin had anticipated a confrontation by Brochet in the beginning, but after a year passed with no word, he'd dropped his guard. He'd thought that the brutal attack on Littlebell and the disgrace of his own name was enough to satisfy Lucien's need for revenge, but he had been wrong.

"Brochet," Bin said in a shaking, yet good natured tone, weakly smiling at his old companion. "It is good to greet you."

Lucien's snow-white cloak billowed out behind him, flapping in his wake with the crisp wind. The middle years man deeply frowned. "Save your pleasantries," he said cooly. "The time for diplomacy is over." He added with a sneer, "long over."

The inflection in his tone made all the hair on Bin's neck stand up, yet he was used to Lucien Brochet's ways. "I do not fear you, Brochet," Bin said, deep voice booming, dark eyes focused. "We were boys together. Friends." He paused and raised his eyebrows. "Brochet, you have to understand, I did what I must do." The man was married, Bin thought to himself, so surely, he knew what the love of a wife meant. Of a child. "Brochet, surely we can make some kind of arrangement. I will owe you…"

"Oh, you do owe me greatly, Norland," Lucien spat, transforming their typical way of interacting into an insult. Bin steeled further at his inflection. This man was nothing like his one-time companion. Or perhaps he was, this was just Lucien when you were not in his graces.

From Lucien Brochet's side, Florian Busk stood with his chest confidently out, despite a slight slouch.

"I know what you commanded him to do in my name,

Brochet," Bin accused, glaring meanly at Florian, who shirked at the attention. "What more is owed after so much damage? After so much blood?" He thought about Littlebell burning in his name, his beloved's home, and shuttered.

Lucien lowered his sharp eyebrows into a flat line. "More," he hissed. He took a step and behind him the Guardsmen followed suit, all together in a loud thump of a stomp. "I require our arrangement fulfilled." He paused. "To completion," Lucien added, narrowing his eyes.

Bin felt panicked bile rise in his throat. Before he could catch himself to lie, to claim anything other than the truth, he outburst from his heart. "You can't have her!" he cried like a mad man, seeing Lilli's face in his mind, lunging towards Lucien nonsensically without warning, pulling his broadsword from its resting place between his shoulder blades with a metallic twang, chucking it over his head with all his might.

Lucien chuckled as he quickly and easily stepped aside, yet he'd underestimated Bin. Bin expected Lucien to be unawares so, instantly after throwing his sword, Bin expertly tossed his own dagger, crafted of blue glass with a stone hilt. The markedly Norland blade tumbled unbelievably quickly, straight towards Lucien's heart.

It was only at the last moment Florian Busk threw himself in front of the blade. He wasn't sure why he flung himself in the weapon's path. By the time he had a moment to think, the dagger was lodged deeply in his shoulder. He collapsed in burning pain, sticky hot blood running down his arm, sizzling in melting drops on a dirty white snow bank.

Lucien deeply laughed, slightly at first then with growing bravado, until he was full belly chuckling. Bin clenched his hands into fists as his mind raced, hoping to his Ancestors that Lucien hadn't been to Ravenshroud yet. "You ask what more is owed as you aim to take my life," Lucien observed, nose raised into the air as he took a wide step over Florian, whimpering on the ground. "Your negotiation tactics are so poor." He paused and slightly smiled. "No wonder you need me."

"Lucien, please," Bin said, losing hope, dropping to his knees in the dirt. He was without a weapon and he'd already called the men in for the day. They'd long ago stomped up the mountain and gone inside to rest until morn, as conditioned to do. Bin knew he was alone amidst the evergreens, half a creed from Creed Point where his brother Ruben was, with the other advisors and high natives. No one could help him now. "Please, let me go home to Lilli. You can have anything else you want, just not her."

"I can have everything I want, including her," Lucien countered. Bin felt like he was punched in the jaw. "Haaris," Lucien shouted over his shoulder without taking his playful hazel eyes off of Bin. "Show Lord Norland what we've brought for him."

At that, the elite Guardsman Haaris stepped forward from the group clutching a dirty satchel, holding it at the top in a clump in his fist. He stood with impeccably straight back, eyes forward, unmoving aside Lucien, awaiting his blood elder's command. Haaris, as Guardsman Commander, always did exactly as he was told.

"I said," Lucien hissed with narrowed hazel eyes unmoving from Bin's worried gaze, "show Lord Norland what we've brought." He sneered as if he was enjoying himself. "What he was too cowardly to do himself."

On Lucien's command, Haaris tossed the dirty sack to Bin's feet. Out rolled his beloved Lilli's severed head.

Like a broken mirror, Bin's mind shattered into dozens of shards. He tasted bile. "Lilli, my love," he cried, already on his knees in the snowy dirt, scrambling across the ground to be near her. It couldn't be true. "Lilli!" his voice cracked and broke with his heart as he ran his clumsy fingers across her blood-matted braid. Bin collapsed into himself, holding her decapitated head in his arms like he'd held their child. "My Lilli," he repeated in a whisper as hot tears sprung from the corners of his eyes, stroking her cheeks, waiting to hear her laugh or tease him. She was his last chance for absolution. Brochet had taken everything from him, he thought, until he reminded himself of his daughter. "Where is she?" he growled, looking up from his wife's dead, no longer blue eyes.

"Oh, you mean the babe?" Lucien asked offhandedly, as if someone asked where he'd left his horse. He half smiled then meanly shrugged.

"BROCHET," Bin shouted with all the air in his lungs, vision pulsing with lust for the man's blood — anything to make him pay for what had been done. Still holding Lilli's head tight in his grip, fingers pressing deep into her clammy skin, he lunged for Lucien. He had no plan. He could only see red.

Instantly, as they'd been trained to do, the Guardsmen protected their Lord and elder. Several leapt from their resting positions around Bin to tightly secure him. It took four men to quiet the large Norland, until he finally slowed fighting. Eventually Bin's shoulders hung like wilted petals. He knew, instead of feeling this way, he would rather be dead. The Guardsmen holding Bin forced him to his knees again.

Chuckling, Lucien sauntered towards the defeated Bin's side. "Look at me," he commanded the once mighty man. Oh, how far Bin has fallen, Lucien thought, delighted. He was pleased whenever a situation came out favourably for Brochet in the end.

Bin reluctantly raised his head. All the light had gone out of his eyes.

"Kill me if you wish," Bin said in a sigh, realizing that was Brochet's intent, "but my brother will not stand for it."

At that Lucien widely smiled. Bin hated when Brochet smiled like that since they were boys, like he knew something you didn't. "You are a dolt, a far more stupid one that I initially gave you credit for," Lucien chided. "How do you think I was able to breach Ravenshroud's defense to overtake your fair dame? How do you think I knew where you were posted, why you were not assisted by Warmen forces when you didn't return back this eve after post?" He sniffed once, taking another step to where his thighs nearly pressed up against Bin's slumped shoulder. "Look at me," he hissed again, in a low rumble, like a snake about to strike.

Bin raised his gaze to settle on Lucien's hazel glare. "My brother truly betrays me?" he asked like the hallowed-out man he was.

Lucien nodded, smiling, having no reason to lie. "He does. For your betrayal of your father's commands." He warmly recounted the pleasant encounter with Ruben not a moon ago where he said that very statement, nearly word for word. Bin's prideful younger brother was sharper than he was, with a much keener knack for politics, Lucien thought, smiling, enjoying Bin's misery. This was the least he could provide, after all the trouble he had caused.

"I just wanted to change my life," Bin said sadly, to almost no one at all, enormity of his ruined world crashing down on his shoulders. The weight was unbearable. "I wanted to be a better man", he said, taking shallow breaths, rubbing the dead Lilli's blood-matted braid with his thick fingers, unable to let go of the last piece of her he had left. "How could you do this?" he asked, taking shallow breaths, neck craned to meet Lucien's eye. "We were friends."

Lucien Brochet took several steps backwards, frowning deeply. "How could *I*, do this, to *you*?" he asked, long and drawn out, raising a dark eyebrow with each inflection. He brought a hand to his chest. "Bin Norland, I knew you were stupid, but I never took you for a downright dolt." He then chuckled and shook his head and returned to hover directly in front of Bin. He lowered to his haunches, squatting to a seat on his feet.

The men locked eyes.

Lucien lowered his voice to a disconcerting whisper, face reddening, vein starting to pulse on his neck. "You nearly ruined me," he said evenly. "Your weakness and cowardice nearly toppled me from my birthright, from my legacy. You inbred First dweller," he added, face turning a deep burgundy, eyes starting to bulge, widely smiling, "barely worthy of cleaning my boots much less interfering with my plans!" At his outburst he spit, and his thick hair flung out of place, then he took a moment to take a breath and right himself. No need to lose composure. There was a way to make things right.

"Excuse my outburst," he said as he breathed and smoothed his hair, standing from his squat, white cape flapping out behind him. "I have decided we are done here," Lucien added as he raised his bare right hand, beginning to grip it into a fist. The guards on either side of Bin knowingly took several steps back, themselves not being sure how his powers worked, not wanting to catch the brunt of anything.

"My daughter..." Bin croaked as his face started to turn blue.

But Lucien simply gripped tighter and smiled.

"You have done a great service to Brochet, Lord Busk," Lucien said with a half-smile. He tilted a goblet of ale he held toward the bandaged young man.

From across the Westerviolet Lord's Study, Florian timidly smiled, warmed by Lucien's compliment, yet cautious, knowing how volatile the man truly was. He nodded his head. It was hard to take credit when he wasn't sure how he'd done what he did. He'd just leapt in front of that dagger because he felt he had to. "I appreciate your gratitude, Lord Brochet."

"Ah yes," Lucien said. "I'm sure you do," he added, swirling his goblet. "Not many receive my gratitude, as you call it. Very few indeed." He took a few paces. "What you did for me was a great service. Protecting me as you did." He spoke down his sharp nose, nearly unblinking, eyes unwavering from Florian's shaking gaze.

"I... I... barely did a thing," Florian Busk stuttered back, unnerved by Lucien's full attention.

Lucien fully smiled. The man was too stupid to understand the truth of the matter and Lucien was happy to allow him to play the hero. He was grateful the man was so happy to be used as a shield. It made concealment of the action that much easier. It wasn't that Lucien hid his powers, it was that he controlled who had access to the knowledge of them. Usually, only those about to die learned of their existence. Regardless, the Busk man had proven loyal, even in spite of his brother's untimely demise. Lucien found that to be worthy of reward.

"You saved my life," Lucien countered sincerely, "and as reward for such a noble gesture, for protecting the Westerviolet elderclaim and the glory of Brochet," he paused, eyes sparkling, letting Florian hang in the suspense for a moment, "the blue-eye bloodline," he finally said.

Florian's sunken brown eyes grew wide. "The... blue-eye bloodline?" Lucien couldn't possibly mean the child, could he?

"Yes, yes there you go, now you're understanding. I knew you were clever," Lucien added only slightly mockingly. "She will be yours, for you to do as you wish, marry to one of your sons, keep for yourself or dispose," he half smiled, "I care not."

"Why..." Florian paused, completely dismayed. This was an impossible dream come true for a disrespected bloodline like Busk. "Why, I don't know what to say."

"It will not be until she is eighteen years," Lucien added with a raised eyebrow. "After Brochet has finished with her."

"Certainly," Florian added with a wavering smile, then a gulp. "Of course."

ANIMUS ROCK VILLAS

Present Day

Sybil's swollen breasts were bursting from her low-cut sleep gown. She fussed with the ill-fit garments as she walked down the long hall from her chamber, unable to sleep, as always. Yet, this eve, a particular series of thoughts kept her awake. After a visit to the Apothecary to confirm her suspicions, she'd been grappling with the knowledge for days. A life growing inside of her. She was fully unsure how she felt about it and more concerned with how it could be put to Brochet's advantage. To her advantage.

She decided, before anything else was to be done, she must tell Montague.

Sybil pulled her black shawl tight around her angled shoulders. She set her jaw as she strolled confidently through the thorny carved door, into the master chamber.

"Montague," she said curtly. "We must talk."

"Talk?"

"I have something I must discuss with you."

"Ah," he looked up slowly, shifting his weight, placing the piece of parchment he held aside. He pushed himself upright in the pale armchair. "Good," his voice rumbled like thunder, "you're here."

"Oh?" She took delicate steps into the chamber, sleep gown parting to expose smooth pale thighs and scandalously bare feet.

"I have something to discuss with you too," Montague replied stoically, face mostly cast in shadow.

She took a seat a chair to match his, placing her svelte form gracefully.

"You first."

Monty nodded and silently offered Sybil the decanter of mad honey ale on a side table. Unlike their previous interactions, Sybil shook her head to decline. She'd been sick of late; hardly able to keep down water, much less ale. A fire roared between them in a black-brick fireplace along the far wall. Dozens of tall, rectangular vases rested on the onyx stone mantel above the flames, each with a different bouquet of fragrant blooms. Sybil had never seen such exotic plants before and wondered if those flowers were native to Graceview as she twirled one of her dark waves of hair between a finger and thumb. She knew very little of Graceview. Her pale cheeks were flushed and half illuminated from the roaring fire on her right, while fully engulfed in shadow on her left. She listened to Monty with wide dark pits for eyes.

"I heard a rumor," he said. His typical jesting tone was absent, but Sybil paid no heed.

She leaned forward with pleasant inflection, "Oh?"

He nodded once, steadying himself internally. "It is troubling."

Sybil entertained him with a glint in her eye. "Why is that?"

"Brochet is responsible for the fall of Busk," Monty said. Sybil chuckled, flashing her white teeth, turning her head at the absurdity. "It isn't a joke," he said flatly.

"Oh, Montague," she said, wondering what his angle was. "It is." She batted her eyes. "That's preposterous."

He frowned as he poured himself a heavy goblet then he took a contemplative sip. "It isn't, Sybil," he said, voice deepening. "Your men were there."

He'd done more research into Galla's claims. Indeed, there were countless reports of a man flashing the Brochet emblem and besting countless Busk Pawns within the Dark Arena itself.

She still smiled, picking at the edge of her shawl mindlessly. "I don't know what your play is Montague, but I'm intrigued."

"No play woman," he said curtly, lips pressed into a displeased line. He took another sip. "Brochet emblem spotted. Tomas's name thrown. Ralph's men cut down by swords instead of engulfed by the Dark Arena flames alone."

"Nonsense," Sybil dismissed.

He gestured with the goblet. "Are you sure you don't want any?"

She shook her head 'no' and pulled her shawl tighter as she crossed her legs the other way. Her tone chilled considerably, realizing this was no jest. If Montague was serious in his accusation, she could be in real trouble. Sybil wondered who schemed against her. "Who is your source?" she asked with narrowing eyes.

"I never thought it would come to this." He finished his goblet with a refreshed sigh, then set it down with a clank.

"Come to what?"

"I never expected this of you, Sybil." He sighed again and rubbed his forehead with a long finger. "I expected many things, but not this."

She chuckled, raising her hand dramatically to her chest. "Me? Whatever have I done?"

"Behind my back… and Tomas's…" Monty looked down briefly, then to meet her eyes; under-eyelids raising painfully, as if he was deeply stung by her supposed betrayal.

Sybil wondered what could turn the man's typically jovial inflection so grave. "What do you insinuate?"

"Galla had suspicions," Monty said carefully, "but to make her disappear for them, Sybil?" He shook his head woefully.

"What!" Sybil sat back and immediately lowered her voice to a whisper. "How dare you?"

"I liked her, Sybil."

"Montague!" She raised her voice again, shrill. How could he insinuate she had anything to do with Galla's disappearance? An accusation like that was grounds to send her to Magistrate for deliberation. "How could you?"

"Don't flatter yourself," Monty said curtly as he poured another goblet full. Leaning towards her added, "You are beautiful, but your veil is thin." He squinted green eyes at her and took another sip. "I see you, Sybil."

"No one sees me," Sybil said and shifted her weight in the

pale-green chair while glaring hate at him. "Explain yourself," she said cooly. "Now."

"I see this working one of two ways," he spoke with his hands. "Cooperate, or don't."

"Mont..."

He interrupted loudly, wanting the slap the stubborn woman. "I'm not squeamish, Sybil." He paused, then added, "I'll expose you."

Sybil broke into a brilliantly wide smile then laughed again, dark hair bouncing and glinting in the firelight, black eyes burning. Her reaction unnerved Monty and he shifted in his seat. "Expose what," Sybil asked sweetly, "exactly?"

"If it were simply Galla that would be one thing," Monty said, eyes unfocused, nearly speaking to himself under his breath.

Sybil studied Monty's morose expression. After a substantial pause, she finally questioned, "But?"

Monty leaned backwards, matching Sybil's crossed arms. "I saw your face," he said. "Sybil, I saw it," he repeated with a distressed crack in his tone, not wanting to believe where the thread he pulled led him.

"I don't follow," Sybil said dismissively, glancing down casually, picking more at the seaming of her shawl, just starting to unravel.

"Herman. Millie," Monty vilely spat. "You weren't surprised." A spike of adrenaline sent a shiver down Sybil's spine, yet outwardly she remained calm.

"Montague," she sighed, as if placating a child. "What nonsense do you speak of now?"

"In the commotion, no one else noticed, but I did," he said slowly. "I'm very observant, Sybil."

"Oh?" Sybil coyly raised an eyebrow. "What did you observe?"

"You were amused."

"How could you say that? It was horrible," she added in a hush, bringing hand to her chest, mimicking horror perfectly. At that Monty began to clap, slow and dramatic as if praising a performance. Glaring, Sybil let her hand drop into her lap.

"You are wrong," she said calmly, façade slipping away like a cloth from a polished table.

It was unnerving how quickly she could change right before one's eyes.

"You are evil," he said grimly. Sybil giggled like that was the funniest thing she ever heard. "Stop that," he commanded, frowning at her.

She wiped a laughing tear from her eye and ignored him fully. His attempt to thwart her plans for the Kingdom was laughable. He was nothing, a joke. She was a spider and he, an irritating fly.

Monty fumed and clenched one fist while he set his mad honey down with a loud clank, vision pulsing from the ale and wrath. He asked painfully slowly through gritted teeth, "What is so funny?"

In that instant Sybil realized what a fool this Thorne man was to address her in such a way. How had she been so taken with him before? How could she have stooped so low? How did she dare let him touch her? She felt the slight affection she once held for him steeling in her chest, as if her heart was molten metal and he'd doused it with ice water. "I should thank you, Montague," she said lightly.

He frowned. "For?"

She crossed her legs the other way, flashing an expanse of creamy thigh. "You have revealed your true character willingly," Sybil said. Her smile was warm, but her eyes were cold. In them was the absence of light. As if they were filled with shadow. "You make my decision easy."

"What decision?" Monty asked warily as he leaned forward where he sat. The fire to their side hungrily consumed the flaming logs, burning in orange embers.

"Such a shame," she said while looking him up and down, enjoying his confusion fully. "To think, until now I gave you the benefit of the doubt."

"About?" Monty asked cautiously. He poured more, then sank backwards in his seat. His drooping eyes were heavy from drink, highlighted by black bags.

"Don't be coy," Sybil smirked at him, thinking back to the night she'd eavesdropped on his interlude. "You and the Minney boy."

"Sybil," Monty sat up. "Don't," his tone warned.

"You should be more careful," she added, visibly amused now, fully pleased she was able to toy with him so easily. She was glad she'd saved mention of Montague's taboo predilections until now. "You should know better than to keep your chamber unlocked," she told him.

He glared at her, clenching the goblet in his left hand, digging fingers into the arm rest on his right. "What did you see?" he asked slowly. He cursed himself for not going directly to the Magistrate about Sybil. If she'd truly witnessed his affair with Juste, it would be more than enough to have him sent to the First, even if she never mentioned his connection to the mad honey trade. The laws in Animus Rock were old, particularly regarding relationships between Vanguards, and homosexuality was not looked upon with kind eyes.

"Enough," she said carelessly, unblinking, half-smiling as if challenging him to respond. It was clear why the man was still a bachelor. But, to engage oneself not only with a man, but one's own kin? Juste and Monty were close cousins, after all. The immorality was unspeakable.

Monty frowned, glowering, and didn't answer although he wanted to. He was running scenarios in his mind. Attempting to manipulate the situation. But he was heavily clouded by mad honey. And he was no match for Sybil. The fire crackled and popped loudly as it died to their side, in competition only with serenating crickets outside. Apart from that, it was morosely silent.

"If you were simply sordid, that would be one matter," Sybil said as she looked down to examine the unravelling shawl's thread between her fingers. She popped her head up. "But," she said, "legality is involved."

Monty narrowed his eyes. "What is your meaning?"

"Surely in light of what's happened, the Council frowns on Mad Honey possession," she gestured to Monty's goblet, "and use."

"Surely," Monty repeated with a bite, understanding her intent to expose the mad honey trade he and Juste were so intimately a part of, out of spite. "I see," he said.

"I was willing to ignore your flaws and sin," Sybil went on sensationally. "Your hypocrisy," she added. "But now," she lowered her voice, threatening him with her eyes, "you've become a nuisance."

"Me?" Monty sat back, confusion clear on his comely face despite the dim light, bolstered by ale. A log in the fireplace collapsed in an explosion of orange sparks, then faint sizzling, followed by a loud pop. Heat billowed outwards.

"Oh yes," Sybil nodded. "Very much so."

Monty finished his goblet in a gulp and hiccupped, then leaned menacingly towards her. "You're the nuisance, Sybil."

She tugged at the unravelling thread on her shawl, still staring intently at it. "What's your endgame Montague?" she asked without looking up. She was enjoying toying with him greatly, punishing him for how terribly he treated her. But he would be sorry, so sorry, once he knew she carried his babe. Then, she owned him.

"You've made a mess of this Kingdom."

"A mess you say?"

"Isn't it clear? I want you gone."

Sybil balked, surprised he'd go so far as to suggest it. "Gone?" she asked, realizing Montague was fully convinced of his theories indeed, to risk insulting Tomas and sparking a feud with Brochet. He must truly believe the accusations.

"To Westerviolet," he grunted, nearly slurring now.

"You cannot order me anywhere. I will not go."

Now it was Monty's turn to laugh and he chuckled as if he'd heard a bad joke. "It is happening, Sybil," he said.

She pulled her shall tighter. She narrowed her round eyes. "How?"

"I wrote Tomas."

"You wrote my father!?"

"You aren't ready," Monty spat back. "I told him you aren't

229

ready for Council. He should call you back to Westerviolet where you can be better trained to not risk sullying your good bloodline's name."

"You didn't."

"It's already done."

"You shouldn't have," Sybil said hollowly as she rose from the armchair. "Really."

Monty stood when she did. "Where are you going?"

"It's clear you've decided," Sybil told him.

Monty frowned and swayed as he stood, gripping the back of his armchair to steady himself. "Decided what?"

"To join Prihim," Sybil said with half a smile.

"VILE CURSED CUNT," Monty bellowed. He threw his weighty iron goblet full of mad honey at her and it crashed against the wall and splattered like dark blood. She giggled at him. "Stop laughing," he commanded, pointing his finger. She didn't. "Why are you laughing!?" he shouted indignantly, reminded sharply of Jessamine, as if he was a child. It felt like he was being taunted by his own sister all over again. She laughed at him the same way. This sent his blood boiling.

Sybil shook her head. "Montague," she said intimately with a withering smile. "You are a fool. A cursed fool."

Monty bounded to her in long-legged strides, then grasped her violently by the neck. The momentum of his action thrust her against the wall. It was too swift for her to grab her dagger. Monty clenched her thin throat hard. Shallow wheezing breaths escaped Sybil's lips while her throat exploded in pain and she silently gulped for air with eyes wide, half-terrified for her life and half-pleased she had enlivened him so. It reminded her of something her great grandfather Lucien had taught her long, long ago, when she was much younger than even Rose. *The first man to lose his temper, loses the war.* She kicked at Monty to free herself, but he was taller and stronger.

Finally, when her face turned a pale shade of blue and her eyes started to roll back in her head, Monty dropped Sybil to the floor. She gasped and crawled away on the marble as her robe pooled around her. She clutched her black shawl and her impossibly smooth white-pale thighs flashed in firelight.

"Go home Sybil," he said low and deep as she crawled away. Then, in tilted vertigo from too much ale, Monty shut his eyes. He sighed loudly. He was not typically one for violence, he told himself inwardly. It was the honey that made him volatile. He took a deep breath and steadied himself on the wall. If she would just leave, he could steady himself, he thought.

Sybil brought her hands to her neck and rubbed the already bruising skin delicately. She cleared her throat daintily, then smiled as she stood.

"What is it now woman?!" he bellowed at her, infuriated and unnerved by her smirk. Who smiles after nearly dying?

Sybil rose, rubbing her neck, shoulders squared to Monty, hair cascading down to cover her breasts like a goddess, black eyes focused fearlessly. "You have no idea what you have done," she said slowly, already envisioning his demise. "None."

Monty marched towards her in bounding, menacing steps and pinned her again, this time with his narrow, long forearm. Who does she think she is? He shoved his body up against hers. Sybil smelled rank ale from Monty's breath and spiced, exotic perfume from his robes. Her cheeks flushed and heart raced, yet her eyes stayed locked on his. He glared at her with a smile that reeked of triumph, feeling callously formidable for physically overpowering her so. *A trait only the weak possess*, Sybil thought.

She blinked once, allowing him an instant of victory. "I do not fear you," she said evenly, then smiled brilliantly, letting his illusion crash down on his head.

"Curse you," Monty spat. His cheeks burnt hot. With monumental force he slapped Sybil hard across the face. Anything to stop her psychological assault, the effects extrapolated by mad honey. Every laugh was like knives through his brain. Something about her disapproval was particularly painful. His slap spun her head around and she collapsed to the floor, still smiling. Her lip bled, painting her teeth red. The blood dripped down her neck, breasts, and silk gown, staining the light fabric. Sybil's shawl was strewn across the floor to her side and her exposed shoulders rose and fell violently as she fought to breathe, despite strong emotion. Her thoughts raced like a spider planning a web, working through her next moves. She was not sure what she would do next, but she was sure Montague would pay for what he had done.

For an instant, Monty softened, watching her shuddering frame from behind, imagining her crying, and his eyebrows raised in sympathy. Then, she turned her head. She wasn't crying at all.

Sybil was still laughing at him.

"Ahh!" Monty shrieked, insane with fury at her insulting amusement, flashing back so many years ago to Jessamine. His younger sister who bested him in everything. His younger sister who didn't know when to shut up. The one who got more Vanguard blood than he did, with pale skin. With blonde hair. The one who was father's favorite. The one he'd long ago tossed from Graceview's highest balcony and claimed it was an accident.

He grabbed Sybil by a thick bunch of hair from the back of her head and jerked her upright violently. In the same moment, without an instant of thought, seeing Jessamine's taunting smile in his mind's eye, Monty punched Sybil in the stomach with all of his might, just to get her to shut up. The blow landed with a fatal thud. Sybil painfully gasped, doubling, hands jumping to her womb. Her eyes glassed momentarily, then they focused and narrowed. Something snapped within her mind. She cracked a slow, nonsensical grin.

"WHAT DO YOU SMILE AT!?" Monty cried. He wondered if she'd fully gone mad. Veins bulged from forehead and neck.

Sybil shook her head and chuckled three times. "You..." she trailed off, righting herself to stand, ignoring the red, sticky liquid beginning to run down her thighs. Ignoring the crippling, cramping pain. Ignoring the empty, lifeless feeling instantly within her. "You really don't know," she said threateningly, smiling blood. She was a frightening sight to behold.

In response, Monty shoved her against the adjacent wall again, attempting to quiet her lunacy. He was overwhelmed, frustrated, drugged and drunk. She gasped and cried out in sheer agony, as she was in a great deal of pain, and slowly looked up. Sybil's wide black eyes met Montague's hooded green ones. "You'll wish you hadn't done this," she said genuinely through wheezing breaths, still nonsensically smiling. "Trust me."

"Curse you Sybil," Monty said, then spit at her face.

That final act was as if the King rescinded his last reprieve for Montague in her mind. He was condemned. She was done with him. And the babe he had forsaken, before he knew it existed at all. She laughed at him, flashing her impossibly warm grin despite being covered in gore. Monty couldn't take the condescending inflection and slapped her again across the face, then punched her in the stomach with his right, then left, having lost all sympathy for her. Internally he was grappling with the villain she truly was. And he was very, very drunk.

Sybil gasped for air and fell, clutching her midsection, then moved to stand. Monty pushed her down. He kicked her twice in the side with a hard boot.

"Go the curses home!" he shouted at her, voice cracking. "Leave me alone!" The horror of what he'd just done to a woman, much less another Vanguard, settled upon him like chilly evening fog. Jessamine's lifeless face flashed in his mind's eye, then he swallowed that guilt hard. He steeled himself the best he could, hating Tomas's daughter in his mind, telling himself she deserved it, although his eyes began to leak tears. It was like he knew on a deep level what he'd done was irreversible. He wept for himself.

After his final kick, Sybil doubled as a searing, serrated blade sliced through to her innards and jostled them about. She scooted to sit upright. Through heavy rattles and tears pooling in the corners of her eyes, insanely, Sybil still chuckled. "You are a fool," she scathed, still smiling pleasantly wide, revelling in the power she had over Montague despite the abuse. She knew a great deal of her power came from being what she wasn't expected to be. She took great pride in being underestimated or misunderstood. "A fool," she repeated, still holding her womb, then she threw back her head and laughed.

"SYBIL?!" he shouted ridiculously, eyes wild, hair unkept and breath rank from ale, "What is it?!"

She paused, tears in her eyes. Her façade lifted momentarily. "Can't you see?" she whispered.

"WHAT?!"

"I'm with child," Sybil replied. "Or," she paused, "I was." She glanced briefly to the dark stain between her legs, then back to Monty.

Monty backed up like he'd been stuck by an arrow. "What?" he choked, frowning, shocked. His gaze distant. He'd never imagined himself a father although he was quite fond of children and to have the possibility dangled in front of his face then instantly wrenched away was unbearable. "No…" he said, doing the math in his head before trailing off.

"Yes."

"It can't be."

"But," Sybil assured, "it is." She'd visited Animus Rock's Apothecary less than a fortnight ago to confirm what she'd already known before the Guildsman's tests. Her breasts had nearly doubled in size and she hadn't bled on the dark moon twice now. And, besides that, she had felt the life growing inside of her. Not physically, but the same way you can feel another person enter a room, even if your eyes are shut. Another soul was with her. And now it was gone. She paused, feeling hot blood suctioning her ruined gown to her inner thighs. "Was."

Monty took bounding steps across the chamber and stood to hover in front of the fireplace. He played with an ovate leaf protruding from one of the rectangular vases. "Whose?" he asked her vacantly over his shoulder.

The question toppled her calm. "Yours! It's yours! It's your bastard!" she screamed blood at him.

"Lies," Monty growled, turning to look at her, wincing at the sad battered sight. "A trick," he said as if he needed that to be true. He steadied himself on the wall. Sybil shook her head. Loose, dark hair stuck to her ashen, blood-specked brow. "Bare," he muttered, eyes wild, forehead beaded in sweat. She gasped to breathe, still clutching her stomach, shaking her head. "You lie," Monty said again, but it was undeniable that a dark red stain indeed pooled between Sybil's legs on the fine floor. He knew what that meant. He'd seen it happen to his kin before, as the Vanguard Curse was terribly common. "Go!" he shouted at her before she could refute his accusation. He pointed with a long finger at the door.

"Go?" Sybil asked, face pallid from blood loss. "Montague, go where?"

"I don't care the curses where!" he bellowed, shaking his head, ear-length hair dancing. "By morn, both you and the girl, be gone." He stormed out the chamber and slammed the carved thorn door behind him.

For an eternity afterwards, Sybil lay bruised and dazed in her own blood, frozen. She shook in shock from pain. Her eyes swelled tears as she fantasized about moments with a newborn that could now never come to pass. She had been excited despite the fact the child would have had mongrel blood. Despite the fact that her father would disapprove. Despite the fact that a bastard would cripple her plans for the Kingdom, and with Graves, and likely cost her the throne. She hadn't cared about any of that. She had been excited regardless. That excitement was gone now.

Finally, clutching her stomach with one hand, feeling warm blood slick between her legs with the other, Sybil threw back her head. She wildly laughed. Anyone who saw her would think she'd gone fully mad.

Possibly, she had.

WESTERVIOLET

Although he'd never admit it, Lord Tomas Brochet was unnerved.

"Progress?" Tomas asked, only half glancing up from his reading. Budic shook his head once, firmly, with a low-set brow. "Nothing?"

"No, my Lord."

"He couldn't have gotten far," Tomas muttered, long eyebrows fluttering. "Incompetent!" He smacked a pile from his desk, wondering how the son of a Stablemaster could have bested his top men. It had been nearly a moon. His capture should have long ago been secured, Tomas thought, as the parchments floated to the floor like feathers. Just one misfortune after another. Tomas crunched the latest note from the missive tight in his fist.

"My Lord," Budic said as he limped, armor clanking with his irregular gait. A roaring fire threatened his back as he approached the Lord at his front. Large horizontal windows to the side of the study chilled with frost.

Tomas Brochet stood behind the solid wooden elderdesk with red face and tousled hair, shaking the crumbled papers in his hand emphatically. "Do you hear these lies, that the… the… *earthblood* writes about my daughter?" he scathed, mood deeply fouled by what he'd just read, ready to murder every Thorneblood and burn Graceview down.

"Yes, my Lord," Budic lowered his head.

Tomas shook the papers again. "I will have Montague Thorne's head on a plate!"

Budic took a step. "My Lord."

"If his father had any idea."

"If Sybil is true…"

Tomas interrupted, red faced, "Of course Sybil is true!"

"Of course." Budic bowed his head low. He could only hope the Lord was right.

Tomas was tired of discussing the vile accusations against his daughter. He changed the subject quickly. "Basil's spawn should be here by now."

"You already sent for the Omen?"

"Days ago," Tomas said nonchalantly. Budic looked at him, stunned. "I tell you I trust my daughter."

"With respect," Budic took another bold, yet hobbled step. "What the Thorne writes is dire."

Tomas scoffed. "You can't trust a Thorne. It's a scheme. He lies. Sybil is true."

Budic wasn't so sure and the information the letter contained was unsettling. "Busk really did burn. And rumor is the Busk Browns were cut down. By swords, not flame," the shaken Commander added warily.

"Monty conspires with Lachlan's traitor," Tomas dismissed, "and Rupert," he added, tying it all back to the rabid dog his men had yet to run down. "Through Burkhart's boy. He must."

"My Lord," Budic started gently, "what if Sybil had a part in Herman or Millie's death?"

Tomas waved a hand. "Preposterous."

"But, what the letter Thorne..."

"Enough."

Budic smelled something and wouldn't let it go. He knew Tomas's vision was glided when it came to Sybil. "You say Thorne follows coin. Is there coin to be had in this?"

"Of course, there is always coin to be had," Tomas said quickly straightening. Renewed calm washed over the old man. He set the crumpled letters down and smoothed his wild hair. "We must find Burkhart's son. What... what is the boy's name?"

"Ryd."

"Where the curses is Ryd?!" Tomas outburst again, just as Second Gawen strode into the study.

"What is it?!" Tomas shouted at the Second.

"My Lord, they have arrived."

"Who?"

Gawen was still awestruck having just witnessed a legend. He still didn't believe it was true that she existed, despite seeing her himself. "You...you... just have to come outside," the Guardsman Second faltered. "Digory's back," he added, as if that would explain everything. He'd assumed the man had been out on the Lord's business and had just returned successful.

Tomas dropped his brows. "Why would I give a creed about that?"

"My... my Lord," Gawen replied, caught off guard by Tomas's reaction. "In his capture is the traitor."

"Traitor? Boy I have not time for..."

Gawen's adrenaline caused him to cry out and interrupt Tomas. "Burkart's son!"

"Burkart's boy has been found?" Budic said with piercing intensity. "Bring me to him! Justice must be served for Aslf!"

"Not all," Gawen said with half a smile. He took a step.

"What then?" Tomas barked, "Speak!" without giving the young man time to reply

Gawen shook his head in disbelief. "Just come outside. You must see her with your own eyes." Tomas and Budic exchanged sceptical glances as the young man gestured to the door. "The legend is real," Gawen added with excitement. "The blue-eye is here. Come!"

"I told you!" Tomas's face brightened. He pointed at Budic. "Sybil is true!"

"It can't be," Budic whispered under his breath. "She can't be real. She... she's just a dream." He was painfully stunned. "I must see for myself."

"Arrest the traitor," Tomas commanded Budic. "The Minney girl is my concern, then the Omen's."

Budic slightly bowed. "Yes, my Lord."

"Have Basil's men sent to me upon arrival, will you?"

"Of course, my Lord."

"Good." Tomas paused, then turned with new energy. "On with it, then," he shouted at Gawen hovering in the doorframe.

The young Second hurried out.

"After you, my Lord," Budic said and gestured towards the exit, bowing his head customarily.

Tomas nodded, then took athletic strides after Gawen. Budic hobbled behind them.

In the North Tower courtyard beneath the disapproving stares of looming Brochet statues, Ryd postured with his chest out, protective of Vera behind him, thoughts panicked and racing with fury, trying desperately to calculate a last move. Digory stood aside. He'd led them there intentionally to betray them. Now, he did little to stand between the pair and the humming horde of Guardsmen in dark emerald capes surrounding them.

Cador was apart from the bunch. "Move away. Step away. Men!" he commanded. "Back ta yer posts!"

The Guardsmen grumbled and mostly ignored Cador's shouts while clamouring to see. They muttered and mumbled to each other back and forth.

"Is it her?"

"Is she real?"

"I thought she was legend!" someone cried.

"Quiet! Yer a mess of dolts!" Cador shouted at them. "She's real and she's Vanguard. Back up." The crowd pulsed in protest beneath the grey misting sky. "It's orders!" Cador argued back. "Aye! Get back I say!" He gestured with an outstretched sword.

"Aside, you heathens!" Tomas barked at the crowd from behind. Instantly all fell silent, lowering their heads to stare at their boots. Tomas approached with Budic and Gawen closely in tow wearing a white woollen cloak with huge silver buttons. He was quite the contrasting sight next to his dark-cloaked guardsman and the grey weather outside. Tomas also had green gloves and darker green trousers tucked into simply designed, practical leather boots. Today, as always, his skin was pale, yet vibrant. The tip of his nose, and cheeks were bright red, irritated by the whipping winds.

The sky was dark, bitter cold, and misted unpleasant chilly

rain. It amplified the dreary mood.

"Just in time," Cador said offhandedly to Gawen. Gawen nodded. Both hovered aside each other off to the side of the exchange, now that the Lord had arrived.

"Good work," Tomas said to Digory. "You're without beard," he added with a hint of surprise and amusement, the most emotion Digory had ever heard directed towards himself from the Lord, apart from scorn. Tomas paused and studied him. "It suits you," he finally said. The words bounced around in Digory's head, painfully loud, like a gong.

He took a step back, wordless, not sure what to think or say. He simply crossed his arms and nodded.

Ryd glared daggers at the exchange with trembling Vera huddled behind him. He wondered why Digory hadn't defended him yet. In the back of his mind, he fought against himself, telling himself Digory couldn't have betrayed him, not after all they had been through. This was all part of the plan. It had to be.

"Good," Tomas said to Digory. "I appreciate few words," he added, then turned towards Ryd protecting Vera. "Now, you," Tomas glowered. "This is a *predicament.*"

The crowd of Guardsmen around them grumbled and whispered, wagering on what type of punishment would befall the man. There was good coin in wager at Westerviolet, particularly amongst the Guardsmen, especially if you knew how to bet.

"Your father would be so ashamed," Tomas added pointedly, matching the expression of the statues standing around them exactly. The ominous figures glared down sharp noses baring disapproving smirks and frowns.

"B... but... My Lord," Ryd said with extreme confusion as he bowed his head. "Sybil sent her here. For protection."

Tomas laughed, throwing his head back in a cackle. "Is that what he told you?" he finally asked as he straightened, looking at Digory. "Well done."

Ryd took a step back, fully stunned at this realization. He felt Vera's fingernails dig into the flesh of his shoulder.

"She's the lost blue-eye," Tomas said, then smiled wide as if a prayer had been answered. "Do you know how hard we searched for her? Your father too. No, you couldn't. You were a child. But, old enough remember the clamour to find the girl." Tomas paused dramatically. The entire crowd of both Guardsmen and various other natives hung on the speech. "And now," he finished after a dramatic pause, sweeping his gaze around the courtyard, "she is ours! Glory to Westerviolet!" he chanted.

Everyone cheered, "Glory to Westerviolet!"

"No," Ryd put his arms around Vera. "You can't have her."

"Oh, how sad," Tomas sauntered towards them, cloak billowing in his wake. "You think you have a choice."

"My Lord..." Ryd cried and his voice cracked. Digory winced and shifted his weight yet didn't look away.

"I tire of you," Tomas dismissed. "Guardsmen," he turned and barked. "Back to post. Immediately. All to linger volunteer themselves to the Lair." Then he added very slowly, "Am I being clear?"

Immediately the crowd dispersed, like cockroaches splashed with light.

Tomas turned back to Ryd. "I understand what happened with Clemmo," he started, "why you would usurp the man and even why you would conspire with the New to fell Busk. But," he paused, narrowing his eyes, almost more fascinated than offended, "why kill your own?"

"What are you talking about?" Ryd asked, low and deep. What did the Lord mean about Clemmo? Sweat beaded at his brow despite the cool weather. His heart raced in his chest.

"I should have known your blood was tainted. After your grandfather's betrayal," he added scathingly.

"Lord..."

"You cut down the Commander's nephew," Tomas ignored the traitor's interruption, as if he hasn't heard it and went on, "there is no denying. The question is, why?"

"What?!" Ryd exclaimed, not even sure who the Commander's nephew was. "My Lord, I could never, I would never. I do not even know the man!" He backed up.

Vera looked up at him with wide blue eyes. "What is he talking about, Ryd?"

"I…" Ryd's adrenaline was spiking. His mind darted back and forth. "I didn't do that!" he refuted again wildly. Digory silently looked down as Ryd continued to protest, bewildered. "I… I didn't do anything!"

"Why kill from Westerviolet? You wear the brand. You know that is nearly highest offense."

Ryd knew to be accused meant his fate was grim. "Vera," he turned back over his shoulder, "I swear! I don't know what he's talking about."

"Pity you couldn't save your brother from him," Tomas gestured at Digory. Digory inhaled deeply and bit his lip. He backed up slightly. He braced himself.

"WHAT?!?" Ryd shouted.

"My Guardsman here cut him down, naturally," Tomas said with a smile, "for kidnapping Lady Rose."

"Ryd, stop!" Vera clung to his shoulders, yet he tore away from her with bloodlust in Digory's direction.

"Aye!" Cador stepped in and grabbed Ryd from behind. Ryd wrestled to get free but was no match for the Guardsmen's strength. His thoughts pulsed with images of the last times he saw Col. Of how he promised his father he would protect the boy. Of how he'd trusted Digory this whole time, and it had been built on a lie. It was too much to bear. He felt his mind breaking.

"Oh yes," Tomas confirmed as he noted Ryd's distant reflective gaze, restrained by Cador, "the boy is dead."

Digory took a step back. His movement caught Ryd's eye.

"YOU!" Ryd turned gaze towards Digory and it ignited his fury all over again. "It was you!" he shouted and pointed. His bright eyes were wide and wild. Glassed. The feeling bubbling up in his throat was so painful, Ryd thought he would cry blood.

"Hey," Digory held his hands up, heart in his stomach. "Ryd, wait."

"He did as commanded," Tomas added carelessly.

"Digory, WHY!" Ryd shouted at him. "WHY," he croaked, kicking and bucking to be free from Cador's grip, to no avail. "After everything? How could you!?"

"Ryd... I... I can't..." It was the first time in Digory's life that he was at a loss for words.

"Take him to the Lair, Cador," Tomas gestured with a flip of his wrist.

"No!" Vera cried in agony as she leapt forward. She clung pitifully to Ryd's chest.

"Vera!" he shouted as big tears flowed down his flat cheeks. They entwined fingers and pulled together for a brief moment before being torn away. Ryd watched in horror as a grimy Guardsmen with hungry eyes grabbed her and dragged her from him. Her ruby fox cape fell from her shoulders and landed in mud. In that instant, it felt like all of the hope was sucked out of Ryd's life. He no longer had a brother, lover, or friend. Digory was back to being what he was before. An elite Guardsman. Terror in a dark green cloak. Sybil's hand, but no more.

"Ay!" Cador grunted. "Quit that," he commanded Ryd as he wrestled with him. "Come on now."

"Digory," Tomas barked casually and flitted a few fingers. "Hold the girl." Digory nodded and walked to where the men held Vera.

Watching, in shock, Ryd breathed pitifully, "Digory, how could you?"

Digory slightly turned his head. He blinked at Ryd with so little emotion it sent a chill down Ryd's spine. He knew he had no ally there. He didn't recognize the man. It was like Digory changed completely under Tomas's gaze. He was just as cold as him now.

"Vera," Ryd turned quickly. "Run! Go, anywhere, just away from here!! Run!"

Feral-eyed, Vera took off.

At the same time, Tomas shouted, "The blue-eye!"

Digory leapt with impossibly honed reflexes, far faster than any of the others, and grabbed her wrist. He pulled Vera close to him. She bucked and fought and cried and screamed, yet Digory held her tight.

"Vera!" Ryd shouted in agony, gutted with sorrow as Cador dragged him across the lawn, into the castle.

Finally, Ryd's cries faded in the distance and disappeared.

"Oh good," Tomas said lightly. "They're here. What serendipitous timing." He pointed at five men incoming, headed their direction, having just exited Westerviolet's bazaar.

Quentin Graves and Edwarde Norland walked in front of the pack, followed by three additional Brothers, all garbed in Brotherhood cloaks, armor, and emblems. Polished swords and storied daggers clung to their hips. One of the three Brothers in follow of the Vanguards carried a bow with a quiver of delicate arrows.

Digory observed the guests and their weapons with analytical eyes. He took steps back with his fingertips dug into Vera's arms, holding her firm, feeling her shuddering heartbeat beneath his grip.

Quentin approached Tomas yet couldn't take his eyes off of Vera. "My Lord," he bowed to the elder man in respect.

"And you, boy," Tomas said without warmth. He didn't bow. He had no respect for Basil's dead kin.

"I take it this is her?" Quentin asked, knowing Lord Brochet to be ornery, wanting the exchange to be over with.

"It's your father with the dead eye, not you," Tomas said. "You can see it so." Quentin gave him a look of disdain while Edwarde stifled a deep chuckle. "You, though, look exactly like your father," he told the square-jawed blond. Tomas nodded in approval, thinking of Hadrian's impressive visage. "True Norland."

Edwarde blinked pale green eyes in thanks.

Meanwhile, Vera still wept and fought against Digory. She bucked and kicked at his feet. As she was short and not very strong, Digory held her easily.

"You can't do this!" she said shrilly into his ear. "I am Vanguard! Once my family finds out, you will be sorry! Mimi will kill you!"

"It's alright, it's alright," he whispered to her. "Quiet, will you?" He nearly begged into her ear, trying his best to be gentle. He felt he owed Ryd that much.

"How could you?" She dripped venom. "You betrayed us. You betrayed him!" she spat at him. "Let me go!" She kicked and wiggled, yet Digory held strong. Her heart fluttered and honey curls bunched in his face. He tasted bile yet reminded himself of his true purpose. To steel himself, Digory imagined Sybil.

"I knew we shouldn't have trusted you," she scathed at him.

Quentin eyed the feral woman closely. "Give her some," he directed offhandedly to a Brother, "will you?"

The man removed a green vial from his cloak.

"What is that?" Digory asked with concern but was fully ignored.

In silence, the Brother held the vial under her nose. Instantly her body went calm, but her eyes stayed wide.

"What'd you do to her?" Digory asked, near indignant as he held her warm, limp form.

"It makes her more pliable," he said, "nothing more. She's perfectly fine." Quentin approached. His grey skin matched the churning clouds in the overcast sky. "In fact, she's all there. She just can't move." He snapped his fingers in front of Vera's face. Her eyes were glassed open. She didn't respond.

"She can hear us?" Digory asked.

Quentin nodded with a slight smile.

"You paralyzed her." Every instinct in Digory screamed at him to protect Vera from these deadbloods, but he pushed the feeling aside in his mind.

"It's not permanent," Quentin retorted offhandedly, as if that made it better.

"Enough questions." Tomas waved his hand. "Hand them the girl."

Edwarde approached with one of the other Brothers. As they brutishly took Vera's half-conscious body, Digory studied the tops of his boots. He couldn't look at her wide-pleading eyes as they dragged her away. Inwardly, he chided himself for his weakness, feeling a storm of guilt, unsure how to handle it. These emotions were fully foreign to him. He pressed them inside.

Tomas addressed Quentin. "Basil intends to honor this as fulfilment of the oath. On Graves honor, no longer Brochet debt owed." He was tired of owing anything to those dead men. Ready to be done with the pact his Ancestors made. Ready to ensure his daughter and granddaughter's safety.

Quentin nodded. "Truth. He does. Consider it fulfilled."

"For once me and the old dead bag agree," Tomas said with an uncharacteristic smile and sigh. "Tell your father I send regards."

"I will, Lord," Quentin bowed. "We appreciate this, you know."

"As do I," Tomas replied. "It is always refreshing when a compromise is struck sans blood."

"I admire you, my Lord, if I can say so."

"Why is that?"

"Even after freedom from oath," Quentin said in a friendly tone, "you still allow Sybil to Hector."

"I allow Sybil to *whom*?" Tomas clouded. "I would never!"

Quentin backed up. "It's what Hector wrote to father. I… I… only heard bits of it," he admitted nervously.

"The piles of lies are so high I'm lost in the maze of them," Tomas shouted at Basil's dead son, face getting redder and redder by the instant. "Go with your prize, before I change my mind!" He paced in the freezing courtyard. His stark-white cloak flapped. "Go!" Tomas barked.

"You heard the Lord," Edwarde said to the Brothers as they carried Vera off, towards a cart with horses nearby. Quentin was behind them, nearly running from Tomas's barks at his back.

"Never speak, nay, cursing THINK about my Sybil. DO YOU HEAR?!"

Quentin, Edwarde, and the other Omen Brothers hurried away with Vera.

Digory scratched rough stubble on his face. His world felt particularly dreary. It matched the weather outside. He frowned.

"You," Tomas turned to Digory. "Come to the Air Hall," he commanded as wind whipped his cloak.

"Me?" Digory said, fully surprised, wide-set fiery eyes opening wider. "But..." he hesitated. "The Air Hall is for Vanguard only." He'd never even been to that tower of Westerviolet's castle. No native-bloods had. He wasn't even sure how to reach it. "My Lord. Are you certain?"

"Always," Tomas said.

Digory, stunned, bowed his head to the Brochet elder.

Tomas chuckled at the boy's obedience then walked away at a hearty pace for a man of his years. "Sunset!" he shouted over his shoulder.

Digory stood bewildered in the frozen, drizzling rain.

THE AIR HALL

Digory's heart thumped in his chest. He was unflappable when faced with death, yet here, in these cool halls, he felt himself unravelling. He was accustomed to having inside knowledge; of knowing what to expect. The unknown was more than he was able to bear.

This eve, like the rest of the day, was dull, metallic, and grey. It matched Digory's mood as he walked with a steady gait through unfamiliar hallways in the high reaches of the Westerviolet Castle.

These halls were narrow with high ceilings and lined with countless portraits of past Brochets, similar, but not identical to outside Strategy. The grand, life-size paintings of frowning, strong-jawed men and women were framed in ornate gold and hung atop black wallpaper with tiny silver, green, and bronze diamonds. Black wooden planks underfoot were well polished. Expertly woven runners lined the floors. Dust and cobwebs lined every corner.

These halls were very quiet and they appeared to not have been used in a very long time.

There were no windows on this level, in this hall of the castle. Instead, sparsely placed sconces moulded from black metal like striking snakes, with candles dripping between their fangs dimly lit the halls.

Digory stopped outside impressive wooden double doors.

The doors were three times the height of a man and cut from one single trunk of Jasper Tree, just as the Lord's desk was. They were titanic semi-circles that parted as the doors' opening. A deep, spiral wood grain spun out from the center. The huge doors looked to Digory like half of a fallen tree was stuffed into the black diamond wall.

Upon close inspection, two narrow handholds were carved waist-height.

Digory adjusted his cloak and armor, scratched his face, and sighed as he pulled open the right of the pair of intimidating doors. It glided beautifully.

He'd never entered the mythical Air Hall before. Only Vanguards were permitted to. His heart thumped in his chest. Digory paused in awe upon entry. He felt every hair stand on end as if his whole body knew how taboo it was for him to be there.

Tomas stood at the far end of the hall, a speck in the massive space. The vaulted roof was five times the height of the hallway ceiling and covered in a mosaic of shiny green tiles. From it hung a substantial, ornate chandelier with candles that never melted, and were perpetually lit day and night.

The whole hall sparkled green like a forest of newly budded backlit leaves.

Massive square-paned windows segmented exposed stone at the far wall face. On the right and left sides were arched windows pointed at the top and flat on bottom, and paned clear. Harsh ice and rain beat down on the panes in a rhythmic hum. This allowed dark, low clouds to fill up every clear pane.

Although Digory had never been inside of a temple, he imagined this is what one should feel like.

Tomas, who had been gazing outside at Westerviolet's sad grey city, turned. He gestured and shouted with warm bravado, "Come forth. Much to discuss!"

Digory apprehensively scaled the long space to meet the Brochet elder, jaw stoic and set but thoughts racing for the entirety of his walk. Was the Air Hall enormous! Much larger than it seemed possible from the outside, despite the scale of Westerviolet's castle herself. It took an uncomfortable amount of time and with each step his thoughts compounded. Surely he was not going to be allowed to live long having seen this place, he thought.

What could Tomas want from him?

There was oddly no furniture, nor tapestries about, not like in the rest of the castle. The polished black floor was bare. All that adorned the hall were a series of standing mirrors dotting the floor every so often, each lined in a different type of mineral or crystal. The clear crystal one particularly caught the light and sparkled as if outlined in firebugs. Digory wondered what the purpose was for until he finally reached Tomas and stood aside him.

"My Lord," Digory said dutifully.

"Yes," Tomas turned with a charming smile. "Good," he said approvingly as he eyed Digory's refreshed Guardsmen attire, then immediately began to stroll through the hall. He gestured for Digory to follow. They paced each other.

"You have done well."

"Thank you, my Lord."

"Exceptionally well. Proven me wrong," Tomas said. "And I'm never wrong."

Digory looked at him. "My Lord?"

"Answer me, how was it done?"

"Was what done?"

"On occasion, honor is found in concealment but now is not one of them. The blue-eye,' Tomas urged with a smile. "Tell me."

The Lord's warmth unnerved him. "It was happenstance, my Lord," Digory said as they strolled, bootsteps clacking against the dark floors. "Travel through Littlebell cast me at her door and I noted her location. Later, I reported to Sybil and she sent me to retrieve her, then bring her to you." He added, "You owe the blue-eye to her."

"Good girl, Sybil," Tomas cooed under his breath. "Tell me," he changed his tone. "Where does the stable boy fit in?" Digory looked quickly at Tomas as a flash of Ryd's face stabbed him like an arrow to the throat. He swallowed hard.

"Don't hear me wrong, I am pleased!" Tomas added with a disarmingly warm smile. The affection made Digory uncomfortable. He felt like prey being lured into a trap, although he was not afraid. He wondered if he should be. "You felled two trees with one strike. Was this Sybil's doing too?"

Digory paused and looked to the side, pressing his brow as he watched a bolt of lightning crack outside and illuminate Pinewood in the distance. "No," he finally said. "It was mine."

"How?" Tomas asked. "You did say your journey happened you upon Littlebell." He stopped his gait and frowned deeply. His hazel eyes bore deep into Digory's red, but Digory didn't flinch. "Was he with the blue-eye?" Tomas grilled. Digory nodded. "Ah, ha!"

"What, my Lord?"

Tomas smiled wildly. Now he was sure his speculations were true, that the New had been conspiring with his own man gone rotten. "More proof of the conspiracy about to curse us."

"My Lord? What conspiracy?"

"Never mind that now," he waved this hand, mood shifting unpredictably like a churning river, starting his pacing again. The storm's lighting display outside pulsed all around them with each strike followed by deafening cracks of thunder. It was hard to tell what time of day or night it was. "There will be time for that shortly. Now, there are things more pressing."

"More pressing?" Digory was fully caught off guard. He'd never been addressed so informally by the Lord before and was unsure how to handle it. He'd never even spent this long in the man's presence.

"The old bastard Ralph. Do you know what happened to him?"

"I heard the Confines burned, my Lord," Digory said, remembering the surly bald man cackling as he fell to the flames.

"Yes, good, you heard," Tomas replied slowly as he side-eyed him, "So, you had no part in any of it? My daughter is exempt?"

"My Lord?"

"Oh, don't act as if everything you do isn't for my daughter."

"I know nothing of it," Digory replied simply. He looked straight ahead as screams from the burning Arena mixed with the smell of charred flesh flashed in his memory.

"Yes, yes," Tomas cooed, "I thought as much. Montague is a thieving liar," he added, muttering to himself as their footsteps echoed about the huge, empty hall.

The name was familiar. "Montague?"

"Monty Thorne," Tomas clarified. Instantly Digory felt the dolt. Who else but the man whose Villa Digory broke into not a fortnight before. "He wrote that Sybil has gone mad and is ruining Brochet," Tomas explained with a scathing undertone. "But then you brought me the blue-eye in her name. All is redeemed."

Digory smiled as he studied the old man's impossible glow. This was a side of Lord Tomas he had never seen.

"However," Tomas went on. "One dagger still pokes my side." Digory listened intently, flexing his stubbled jaw in anticipation. "Basil's scum. You heard him?"

"Aye." Disdain dripped from his word. The suggestion Quentin made seemed even more likely given Hector and Sybil's contact at Animus, but Digory didn't mention that to Tomas.

"Truth of it?"

Digory spat on the polished floor to convey his feeling. "I know nothing," he said as he took an intentional step towards Tomas. "My Lord," he added sincerely, "but I will gut Hector Graves before he touches her."

Tomas's lips curled into a smile. "Good boy. That was what I was hoping to hear."

"Just tell me when."

Tomas chuckled. "Wait to see how it unfolds."

"Your will," Digory bowed his head.

Tomas sighed. "Son," he said with unusually warm inflection.

Digory's head shot up. His adrenaline spiked so drastically he felt he might vomit. He nearly reached for his dagger on instinct yet resisted. "My... Lord?"

"It is time."

"Time for what?"

"Time for you to know the truth."

Digory stopped walking and stared at the slightly shorter Tomas gazing up at him with an expression that almost looked like guilt. What could he possibly need to say?

"I've always been unsure about you, but your mother insisted you had promise."

"Mother?" he paused as if punched in the stomach. "Lord Tomas..." Digory's voice deepened. "I have no mother."

Tomas frowned. Lightning cracked outside and lit up his face in a flash highlighting each deep wrinkle. The weight of the decision he made so many years ago, to keep the boy from his birthright until he'd proven himself to be of worthy stock, weighed heavily on him. "You should have known this long ago."

Digory took a step. "Lord? Known what?" He hung on Tomas's next words.

"Do you know what this is used for?" Tomas gestured about the hall. Digory didn't respond, thinking the question was rhetorical, until Tomas urged, "Do you?"

"Only the highest ceremonies. I've never been permitted inside."

"Do you know the most important ceremony that occurs here?"

Digory shook his head, 'no'.

"It is the designing of elderclaim."

"Why does that matter to me?"

Tomas cleared his throat. "Son," he said, then paused as he studied Digory's eyes. *So much of Farrah resides in him despite his mongrel blood*, the old man thought sombrely.

"My Lord?" Digory asked with intensity, snapping Tomas from his wistful memories of his sister. He nearly could predict the words about to fall from Tomas's lips, yet they were too unbelievable. Digory stared at the man with unblinking fury, wideset red eyes on fire.

"You are Vanguard," Tomas said.

Digory stepped back, aghast. "No..."

"Yes."

"But I am red-eyed."

"Yes, unfortunately," Tomas said with a sneer, "but of superior blood all the same."

"It... it... can't be..."

"And yet it is. The Ancestors seem to bless you despite my scorn. In your veins flows Brochet blood."

"How…?" Digory asked, feeling nauseous and like he might lose consciousness entirely. His world was spinning, "Are… are…" It was too detestable to suggest. "You're not my father, are you?"

Tomas belly-laughed at him. "No," he finally said. "I am not."

Digory exhaled a breath of relief. As he righted himself, he felt a newfound power. "Then," he asked in an inhale, "how?"

Tomas rubbed the bridge between his eyes. He sighed. "My poor, poor sister."

"Lady Farrah," Digory inhaled in a gulp, nearly choking on the already sacred name to him. "She was…"

"Your mother. That's right."

Digory instantly saw red. His life was a lie. "How could you do this to me?!" he shouted at Tomas, furious for all the years of a different life he'd been forced to live, sacrificed by the truth.

"Now!" Tomas shouted back in a tone to rival the thunder. "Don't think this realization changes our arrangement." He added slowly, each word booming, "I am still your elder!"

"Yes," Digory paused, never breaking eye contact with the Lord for the first time his whole life. He realized in that instant he was untouchable. "Uncle," he added with a smirk. To his amazement, Lord Tomas didn't rebuke him. It was too impossible to be true, and yet it was. Digory felt like laughing.

"Uncle…" Tomas started with a confused expression, then paused with a twinkle in his eye. "Ahh, yes I suppose that's right. Hm." He smiled, hazel eyes twinkling.

"Lady Farrah, my mother," Digory mumbled under his breath. "Mother," he repeated as he remembered the scent of her auburn hair and the slight wrinkles around her eyes were when she smiled.

"Truth," Tomas said in a nod.

"Why *did* you lie?" Digory asked more calmly, this time more hurt than wrathful. "We are… blood."

"That is right," Tomas said offhandedly, "but you are not pure," he added as if it was an obvious excuse to treat him poorly.

"Oh?"

"You've got mongrel blood."

"I figured, you know, my eyes and all."

"It is not time for games."

"Fine," Digory steeled. "My father is native, then?"

Tomas flexed his jaw and muttered, "Vanguard," as if he wasn't pleased about the fact one bit.

"What is it you say?" Digory asked, nearly laughing. "Repeat it again. I must have misheard you."

A flash of lightning followed by bellowing thunder crashed outside. "Oh, do not be smug about it, boy," Tomas chided. "You heard me. Your father is Vanguard."

Digory's mind raced. "I... I can't believe this." He ran a hand over his hair. He flexed his jaw. He was full-blood Vanguard. Newblood, but Vanguard all the same. How was this possible? "Really?"

"Oh, is it so unbelievable?" Tomas retorted. "You have no brand."

"Lady Farrah..." he trailed off and caught himself, "I mean, my mother," he said, throat tightening, "told me they skipped me. I was but an orphan at the time of the Branding with no kin to bring me for the ceremony."

"Skipped you?" Tomas repeated with an incredulous glare, then softened. "Oh, she was such a sweet soul to protect you."

Digory grappled with the newly revealed history of his blood. It was too impossible to believe, and yet, here he stood in the Air Hall, face to face with the Lord. "But..." he began to protest as countless reasons why the claims Tomas made were false bubbled in his mind.

Tomas chuckled to himself as he studied Digory's strong features. "I will provide you with variant proof," he said as he turned to gaze outside at the quickening thunderstorm. He looked back to Digory pointedly. "Why do you take no tonic?"

Digory felt exposed. He wasn't aware Lord Tomas knew he'd

never taken it. "Doesn't sit well with me," he defended gruffly. "I refuse it."

"Ah, certainly," Tomas conceded, then fell into silence. Long moments passed between the two of them with only the reverberating thunder booming every so often. Digory hovered off of Tomas's side and began to study the closest mirror to him, surrounded in clear crystals. "Have you ever thought why it's not forced on you? If all earthborn must take it." Tomas asked without turning to look at Digory. With each flash his frame was backlit by the blinding white lightening.

Digory shook his head. "Not really," he said dismissively. He'd only taken the tonic once when he was of age just as all the other children are commanded to at the ceremony, yet after that, he found ways to avoid it. Although many years ago, he still remembered how it made him feel, like he was asleep. Or dead. He couldn't think when he drank it. He figured he was not made to take it because he was under Sybil's protection. "I just don't take it."

He approached the mirror and stood in front of it, expecting to see his own reflection, yet there was not one. Instead, he saw a snowy expanse dotted in evergreens. Around the evergreens were delicate, translucent white flowers with pointed petals, as if they were made of ice.

"You know why you do not take it, don't you?" Tomas asked Digory. Digory turned to face Tomas and the largest lightning bolt yet sliced through the black cloudy sky. "It's not made for you or your blood. Oblivion tonic is useless to Vanguards. It's not for us. It's for them."

"For them?" Digory asked as he flashed back to memories of his own Awakening Day. They'd told him Oblivion tonic was meant to wake him up to the will of the Vanguard ancestors. Is that what Tomas meant?

"Oh yes," Tomas said with a nod. "It's specially formulated by the Guild for Westerviolet earthblood, although nearly every other realm has a similar..." he paused, "remedy," he finally added. "It dulls the senses by making them kind and compliant. It makes the earthblood perfect citizens of a civilized realm, but it does not function properly on Vanguard blood."

"Oh…" Digory trailed off as the enormity of the conspiracy against the Westerviolet natives settled upon him. He was partially impressed that such a monumental lie had gone undetected, yet he felt vindicated that he'd recognized the people's complacency long before he knew it was drug induced. A fearsome flash of lightning that snaked the whole sky followed by a low-rumbling boom illuminated the windowpanes behind him as he lowered his brow, seeming to mirror his internal turmoil. "What about my father?"

Tomas sighed. These long-ago memories were quite painful for him. "Farrah was," he paused, "rambunctious, just as Michele was before her," he added begrudgingly, thinking back to his beloved aunt who had long-ago betrayed Brochet for Morfit. "My mother died in birth of Farrah and father not long after during the Uprising, so, alas, she was mine to raise." He lowered his eyes. "My rules were too much for her," Tomas said, "and when barely in her twenty-years she ran off. Moons later, she sulked back to my doorstep, swollen with child."

Digory frowned. "Who is my father?"

"She claimed she was sullied by Minney."

"Minney?!" Digory shouted. The realization hit him like a bucket of ice water to the face. "WHO?!" he demanded wildly as he took two bounding steps towards Tomas. He stood nose to nose with him.

Tomas didn't balk. "Why, Giacomo himself."

Digory took several steps back, stunned. He felt sick. "That makes Vera my…" he was unable to say the words himself, "and Prihim my…"

"Half-sister, and half-brother," Tomas interrupted with a cruel smile. "Why, yes, I believe it does."

Tomas chucked to himself about the irony as Digory nearly collapsed, gulping for air in panic, as if underwater unable to breathe. He placed his hands on his knees to steady himself. He'd betrayed his own blood unknowingly. The knowledge made him physically sick.

"It also gives you Littlebell elderclaim after Prihim," Tomas added, "before the boy Leon," walking to place a hand on Digory's shoulder. "Now that Prihim Minney is incarcerated, your blood is very fortuitous."

Digory inhaled deeply and rose to stand, then turned his head to meet Tomas's eyes. He stared at the ancient man in uncomprehending shock. It was too much to process.

"It is why I bring you here," Tomas added as Digory looked at him in a daze. "You are the rightful Brochet heir, older than Sybil, and male," he explained with a widening smile. "Imagine," he muttered mostly to himself, lightening flashing bright outside, one man to rule both Westerviolet *and* Littlebell."

"What are you talking about?" Digory asked with a flat brow. "What about Sybil?"

"Oh Sybil," Tomas said flippantly. "She's sharp but wild and I have no means of taming her," he said. "She is too unpredictable to be elderclaim. Besides, you are older. You are male. You are the rightful heir."

"But..." Digory started, hesitant to betray Sybil. Tomas interrupted him.

"You are Giacomo's second born too," Tomas told him, seemingly losing patience with Digory's reluctance to accept the truth. "Older than Leon, the next in line for Littlebell's throne. That places you as elderclaim ahead of the boy, if you so demand it, and it is particularly fortunate timing since Prihim Minney is locked away in the First. Laila's an old woman, Giacomo might as well be dead and the youngest boy Leon is disgraceful, I've heard. The Magistrate will certainly vote for you," he said with a scheming smile, knowing he would ensure it to be so. "One last thing," he added, heading towards the Air Hall's exit.

"What more is there?" Digory asked hollowly, feeling like his world had been dropped from the highest reaches of the North Tower and shattered to pieces.

"Digory is not your name."

"Course it's not," Digory muttered to himself as he followed behind Tomas and his loud pontificating voice. Each word filled up the expansive reaches of the strange hall. Digory now walked right by the rest of the mirrors without wonderment, despite the varying scenes displayed within them instead of reflections.

"A mere nickname given to you by Sybil. Without Farrah, it stuck."

Digory slowly narrowed his eyes to glare at Tomas's white cape from behind. "What *is* my name?"

Tomas looked back over his shoulder without pausing his lively gait. "Without the beard, apart from your earthblood skin and eyes, you look exactly like your great grandfather Lucien."

"Is that my name?"

Tomas stopped and turned. Digory paused too and met his gaze. He smiled with deep winkles aside both and shook his head, no. "Your given name is Robert," Tomas told Digory amidst the flashing lighting and roaring thunder all around them. "Robert Minney Brochet."

Digory, rather–Robert, looked at Tomas with wide, disbelieving eyes.

"One last thing," Tomas said low and slow. "I deign you, Robert, Brochet elderclaim. May you now and forever more lead and honor this bloodline," he said, then cleared his throat. "Repeat after me." He removed his own dagger from sheath.

Digory nodded, feeling as if the lightening outside was running right up and down his spine.

"I pledge my life to the furtherment of Brochet," Tomas said as he brought the dagger to his hand and cut a gash in his right palm. Digory repeated, hearing himself say the words, as if he was watching himself from a distance. It was too unbelievable to be real, and yet here he was.

"The old ways are alive," Tomas went on and gestured for Digory to outstretch his hand. Digory repeated again and held out his hand. "Through my guidance I protect this birth right," Tomas recited with blood trickling from his hand as he cut an identical gash in Digory's palm. Digory repeated, feeling the lightening run throughout his body, as if he was on fire. "I swear to honor the hallowed blood that runs in my veins, as it did through the veins of the hallowed Ancestors before me," he gripped Digory's hand in his own.

Digory took a deep breath, blinked his burning eyes and repeated Tomas's final words, finishing the blood oath.

Digory, newly deigned Robert, Brochet elderclaim, with a stake to Minney elderclaim as well, bowed his head as he repeated the sacred vow. Hot crimson Vanguard blood seeped down his arm. Every vein in his body tingled.

His life would never be the same.

ANIMUS ROCK VILLAS

H ector studied Sybil. "Do you wear mourning garb for Herman, still?" He always observed the world around himself as if examining a specimen in the Anstout Laboratory. To him, it was no different.

"No," Sybil replied curtly. Her dark eyes were sunken and sallow. She was a mere shadow of her typical self. She pulled her black shawl tight.

Although a curious response, Hector didn't press. He didn't bother taking the time to learn patterns and react accordingly, as most preferred. Instead, he was blunt. It was far simpler. "Your contusions are extensive." He pointed to her woman's horrendously bruised neck. Sybil's hand leapt to the injury, face aghast. "I can pontificate at you if you wish," Hector added, noting her falsified expression. Why most feigned useless emotions, Hector understood naught.

At his accusation, indignation lifted from her face like a raised mourning veil. "Why don't you?" she asked lightly, with a curious smile.

"I respect you."

"Oh?"

"I will be true until that changes."

"Hm," Sybil said, thinking Hector to be the strangest man she'd ever met. She did admit to herself that his strangeness, albeit unusual, was refreshing. "To being true," she saluted and her lifted glass. Without emotion, Hector raised his in cheers.

They sat in the lifeless Graves Villa parlour with blackout curtains pulled tight. The black orb lanterns glowed overhead like dark rounded light-filled hives.

"Speaking of true," he said. "The information you provided last moon was rather fruitful indeed."

Sybil bowed her head. "I am sorry for your loss."

"Sybil," Hector said flatly. He stared at her knowingly across the parlour. "It is you and I."

"True, is it?" she asked flippantly. Hector nodded once. "To being true," she said as she adjusted the folds of her gown, remembering Millie's body flailing on the Fourth Tower hall's floors. "One question is on my mind."

"What is your question, Sybil?" He was admittedly amused by the woman's unpredictable thought process. She was nothing like others he knew. The novelty alone was stimulating.

"Must I go home?" she asked. She was ambitious and Hector was her quickest way to the Tourmaline Throne. Besides, now, after Montague's layers of betrayal, there were other, more pressing matters to rectify.

Hector stroked his sharp beard. "Thorne no longer hospitable?"

"Unless I prefer more of the same." Sybil caressed her neck.

Hector frowned. "Not acceptable," he said low and deep. It irritated him that she was harmed, the same as if a mare he planned to purchase had been unfairly mauled.

"So glad you think so," she said lightly, flattered by his reaction. "I agree."

Hector narrowed his soulless, deep-set eyes and watched Sybil for several long moments before speaking. "You and the child will stay with me," he commanded. "After melt, we depart to Anstout."

"Excuse me?"

Hector frowned. *Women are impossible*, he thought. "Is that not what you aim for?"

Sybil matched his frown. "You do not command me," she said in a pout. "No one commands me."

"I do," Hector said, "as we will wed." Overhead, his circling hawk made a loud screeching caw, as if to protest, but the woman didn't flinch. When met with Sybil's angry scowl he added, "That is your wish," with a slightly confused inflection. He leaned forward.

Sybil's expression instantly flipped from disappointment to joy without warning. Her face illuminated like a clear-sky full moon. "It is!" she cooed and gracefully placed her goblet down, then approached Hector where he sat. "But it must be done properly."

It was Hector's turn for rebuke. He sat back. "I will not be told what is proper."

"Brochet blood flows in my veins," Sybil replied. "I will not be treated like your pet Busk."

"Is that so?" He crossed his arms. He easily met her challenging gaze.

"Do you oblige?" she asked with a smile and doe eyes.

Hector's unfeeling expression lifted briefly to reveal a sinister sneer. He imagined how long it would take this woman to break under his command. The idea of such a challenge thrilled him. His expression was terrifying despite his painfully handsome, skeletal features. "Do not push me, woman."

"Now here is something you must learn if you intend to wed me," Sybil said as she took a few steps, warmly smiling, eyes threatening like jostling spears, "you shouldn't push *me*."

Given the challenge, Hector instantly stood, as if about to pounce. His svelte frame loomed over her. He leaned in threateningly, yet to his surprise, Sybil already held a dagger from beneath her sleeve to his throat, so close it dripped hot blood.

Hector Graves grinned as if he'd witnessed his hawk preform an amusing trick. She was impressive indeed. Tomas had trained her well. He stepped backwards with a newfound respect for the woman. "As you wish, Lady." Hector looked at her with grey eyes under sharp eyebrows, like his bird of prey. "You will wed me."

Delighted inwardly, Sybil coyly smiled. "Is that a question?"

"Woman..." he warned.

Sybil huffed. She'd not expected the love she had with Rosen, but certainly some token of affection to seal the intention of marriage should have been shared, she thought. Hector was such a strange man. "You are really that unromantic, aren't you?"

"What are you talking about?" He spoke in monotone. This was a contract, nothing more.

"Impossible," she said in a flippant sigh. "And yet you will have to do."

"Is that a yes?" Hector's voice was deep, impatient. A trickle of blood flowed from tiny slit in his neck flesh onto his light grey collar.

"One condition," Sybil said, gazing up at his greying beard from below.

Hector took a deep breath in and out, internally quelling a storm, doing his best to interact pleasantly although it was nearly impossible. Most were so stupid, even the clever ones. "What?" he growled.

She clasped her neck. "The one who did this," Sybil said. "Montague," she added, sneering in disgust. "He's in line with others as we spoke of previously."

Hector's overly analytical brain instantly began running scenarios to manipulate this information to his advantage. "That is truth?" His intensity was palpable.

Sybil nodded. "Juste," she explained.

At that, Hector walked across the room. He glanced over a parchment with the Echo's Omen foreword written on it. "A stretch to Prihim," he said dismissively. "Minney in name alone."

She shook her head and smiled deviously. "No."

"No?" He turned.

Sybil was a vision dressed all in black to nearly match the dark greenish purple bruise on her neck. "It's not Prihim who deals honey," she explained and took a step towards Hector, following him like his own shadow, "just what was led to believe."

A slow smile crept upon Hector's thin lips. "Curious," he said, realizing he may have fully underestimated Sybil Brochet. He had anticipated her to be soft, as women are. And yet she was like iron. Iron that wore a smile. "Then who?"

"I just told you," Sybil replied with a hint of impatience then regained her honied grin. "Juste Minney," she said. "He's the mad honey Animus interface. The one managing the flow of honey to Animus Rock from Littlebell. Montague and he are," she paused, "involved."

"How did you come to learn of this?"

"You know I shelter at his Villa," Sybil said. "I was unfortunate enough to open the incorrect door and witness their," she paused, "operation firsthand. Had I alerted them at that moment of my presence, I would have caught them in the act, but I thought it better to wait until the information was most fruitful."

"Indeed," Hector grumbled, then added, "What is it you want?"

She rubbed her neck with one hand and widened her eyes.

"Speak true, Sybil."

"Alright." Sybil met Hector's unflinching glare. "We will wed."

"Good."

"I'm not finished."

"What, woman?"

"We will wed," she repeated, "if you kill Montague Thorne."

Hector smiled wide for the first time Sybil had ever witnessed him truly smile, then bowed his head low. "I underestimated you, Sybil Brochet."

She grinned warmly. "Everyone does."

"Mother."

"Not now Rose," Sybil flipped her wrist over her shoulder, jostling her robe, dark red lined with soft black fur at the collar. She couldn't stand to see her daughter right now and took another sip of an iron goblet filled with simple ale. Even hearing Rose's voice felt like punishment. A reminder of a child never to be born.

"But Mother..." Rose prodded. Her hair was wild and cowlicked. She didn't want to disturb her mother, but she thought she should say something about the strange man in her chambers.

"Rose." Sybil was shrill. She sat up on the plush fainting couch in the Graves villa guest quarters and angrily met the black-eyed girl's gaze. Hundreds of mirrors in every imaginable shape and size littered the walls of this chamber and her perturbed expression was reflected around exponentially.

"But, Mother," Rose said. "I need to talk to you." She took a confident step. This was important, she reminded herself internally. She hadn't protested when she was forced into a strange Villa with no explanation, nor when Ellie was not allowed inside this Villa and relegated to the natives' quarters. But the man in her room was a different matter. It was worth disturbing Mother over. "I have to tell you something."

Sybil frowned as she exhaled through flared nostrils. Now that Rose had fully entered the chamber, both of their faces were reflected back upon each other from the countless wall-hung mirrors. She studied her own unkept reflection briefly. Sybil's hair was pulled into a low, loose bun and wavy tendrils fell to her cheeks. Her black-pupil eyes were puffy and bloodshot. Aghast at her countenance, proud Sybil wiped her nose with her fur-lined sleeve and looked away.

Rose saw her mother's face and was taken aback. "Are..." she paused, "are you okay mother?"

Sybil ignored the question. "Do you want a sister," she spoke distantly, "or brother, Rose?"

Rose scrunched her face in confusion. She thought about how she'd always dreamed of a sister. Her small heart began to fill with hope. "I don't understand," she said in a small voice.

"Don't you?" Sybil spoke calmly but her eyes streamed tears. Rose frowned. "Without Father..." she started.

"I told you never to speak of him!" Sybil screeched. Rose's face scrunched and started to turn red at the chiding. She bit her lip not to cry. She didn't understand what she'd done wrong. "It will be you alone," Sybil continued, pulsing her jaw.

"No brothers or sisters for you Rose. If you ever wished it," she added coldly, "forget."

"Mother?" Rose asked quietly, hot tears streaming down her cheeks.

Sybil met her daughter's eyes intensely. "Do you understand?"

Rose stared with confusion at Sybil's solemn face. The mighty woman had never looked so small.

"I have to tell you," Rose began.

"Rose," Sybil interrupted again, wearily, with a hint of motherly warmth. "Do you not see this is not the time?"

"But..."

"It is late. Please," she said shrilly, then sighed. She loved her daughter yet couldn't bring herself to look at the girl, knowing what had been recently lost. "Can we speak in the morn my beautiful sweet girl?" Whatever it was could wait until morning, when she was more herself, she told herself. More composed. A better model for the young Rose.

"But Mother..."

"Rose!" Sybil barked; thin patience gone. Whatever it was would have to wait. She didn't have the strength. She loved Rose too dearly to subject her to this. She was doing her daughter a kindness. Her shoulders shuttered in a near wail and she turned away before Rose could see her sob. To Sybil, vulnerability was the ultimate weakness. And she wanted her daughter to be strong.

"Go my sweet," she said as her voice cracked. "I don't want you to see me like this," Sybil added softly. She meant it with all her heart.

Bewildered, Rose shifted her weight from foot to foot. Then, she reluctantly sighed. She would have to tell mother about the strange man later. "Yes, Mother," Rose said.

"I love you my sweet," Sybil told Rose, instantly feeling guilty she hadn't given the girl her time. "We will speak in the morn."

"I love you too Mother," Rose said softly; defeated. She sulked back to her appointed chamber in the Graves Villa without a clue what to do.

Her small footsteps shuffled down the concrete hall.

The next morning, Sybil woke with a gasp from her dream. It escaped her instantly, as dreams tend to do, yet she was left with a horrible feeling in the back of her mind. Like something had gone terribly wrong and it was all her fault. She sat upright in the dark canopy bed, then stared at the pale morning light filtering through thin doors at the far end of the chamber. Like all dreams, once she'd broken from it, she couldn't recall the details. Still, she was left with the reverberating memory of what transpired all the same, like a resounding echo.

All she felt was horror.

She ran her fingers through her hair and sighed, then rubbed sleep from each eye. *Dreams are just dreams*, she reminded herself firmly. She rose, dabbed violet oil on her neck and berry balm on her lips. Thinking of how she was going to apologize to Rose for her chilly reception the day before, Sybil expertly tied her hair into a braided, knotted high-head bun. She left a few wisps of hair down to frame her face in loose, translucent waves then changed from her night clothes to a thick day dress.

Sybil assessed herself in a polished glass before heading down the hall. She knocked on Rose's bed chamber.

"My sweet," she said softly. "About last night." Sybil pressed up against the heavy wooden door. She listened inside for a response, but none came. She hadn't intended to upset Rose and felt awful for her selfishness. "I know you're angry at me, Rose," she said and waited for a response. Nothing. "I'm not perfect, you know!" she shouted louder at the door to rouse the girl. "Even mothers cannot be perfect sometimes!"

She paused and ran her slight hand up and down the dark woodgrain of the door. Still no response.

"You mustn't punish me Rose," Sybil's tone angered a bit. "I am here now." She waited again, then added. "I was upset last night. I'm better now," she said, wondering what it was Rose had to tell her. "Well," she prodded, "what is it?"

Impatiently, Sybil knocked four times on the heavy wooden door. When that received no response, she pushed her way into Rose's bed chamber within the Graves Villa.

Her scream cut the morning.

The room was in shambles. Pillows stabbed and feathers strewn about. Every mirror, and dozens covered the walls, was smashed. Heavy, dark linens were ripped and lay everywhere. Black curtains were torn to thin shreds and bright light streamed in. The high-glass windowpane in this chamber had been cut. A perfect rectangle had been taken from the pane, as if expertly carved away with some kind of magical knife.

And all about the destroyed chamber were spatters of blood.

ABOUT THE AUTHOR

E.M. Willett was born to be a writer. It's her calling, apart from motherhood. She also enjoys baking, gardening and reading. She lives on a small farm surrounded by an old oak forest with her husband, young children and dogs where she writes late into the night.